MW01172410

KNOT FOR A MOMENT

DEVYN SINCLAIR

INFINITE ENDINGS, LLC

Copyright © 2023 by Devyn Sinclair

All rights reserved.

No part of this book may be reproduced in any form or by any electronic or
mechanical means, including information storage and retrieval systems, without
written permission from the author, except for the use of brief quotations in a
book review. No part of this book may be used to create, feed, or refine artificial
intelligence models, for any purpose, without written permission from the
author.

Cover by Devyn Sinclair

For all the girls who love bad boys on motorcycles, getting your hair pulled, sleepy morning fucks, warm cookies, being worshipped— even when that means getting put face down and ass up—by men who adore you, and rocking a sassy attitude to match all your kinks...

This book is for you.

AUTHOR'S NOTE

Dear Readers,

Knot For a Moment is not a book that's meant to be dark. However, as with most of my books, there are some sensitive themes and situations. If you feel like this could be a problem for you, please protect yourself. No work of fiction is worth your mental health.

The full list of content warnings is available on my website, or through the QR code below.

Devyn Sinclair

CHAPTER ONE

SLOANE

Craig muttered a curse as the light turned red again. I checked my phone. "We have plenty of time before it starts."

"We need to be there before it starts. We need to be there *now*."

His voice tipped into a growl, and I frowned. "Why?"

The silence persisted through the light going green, and us turning onto the boulevard where the concert hall was. "There's something happening beforehand we need to be there for. That's all I'll say."

I'd checked the concert listing, and there wasn't anything on the schedule before it, so I wasn't sure what he was talking about. But maybe he was one of those guys who needed to be in the movie theater before all the previews started.

The concert, I was excited about. Sitting through it next to Craig? Less so.

It was our third date since I'd called him. Mostly because he was familiar, decent in bed, and watching Petra and her pack brought on a loneliness I couldn't bear, even though I was happy for her.

I glanced over at him, noting the tension in his hands on the wheel. The reason I'd let our first situation—friends with benefits and nothing more—fizzle into nothing, was this. He'd become a little too much.

Frankly, I was already over it this time. He'd insisted on dates instead of just falling into bed. Which was fine, but this was the end result. He got frustrated with little things and it was exhausting. Even when we were meant to do something fun.

Still, there were worse guys. I could deal with frustration for a few decent orgasms, and a concert by my favorite composer.

The light finally changed to green, and Craig pressed on the gas hard enough to shove me back into the seat.

A text from Petra came through.

BEE 🐝

> I'm still fucking jealous, for the record.

SLOANE

> I'll think of you the whole time.

BEE 🐝
😑

I jerked against the seatbelt painfully as he slid into a parking spot. "Come on, Sloane. We're going to be late."

We weren't. There was still half an hour until the show started. The restaurant had been busy and running behind, so we were later than he wanted. We weren't *late*.

Craig shoved the car door open and got out. I barely had time to get out on my side before he locked it, the beep echoing down the city street.

Good luck that there had been parking. If he was this agitated right now, I didn't want to see him circling the block waiting for an open space.

"Wait, please, these shoes are a nightmare."

They were hot as fuck, which was why they were on my feet, but they were a 'sit and let people come to you' type of shoe.

Craig waited, hands jiggling in the pockets of his suit pants, until I got myself untangled from my purse and onto the sidewalk. Then he turned and started walking toward the concert hall, barely slowing at all.

"Craig."

"We're already late, Sloane. I don't want to hear it."

What the fuck was his deal? I rolled my eyes and started to follow him.

Even if he hadn't been a foot taller and already hard to keep up with, he was walking so fast I'd never be able to catch up. The distance between us grew, and I stopped in the middle of the sidewalk.

How long would it take for him to notice I wasn't behind him? Something deep needed to see when he'd notice, and what

2

he'd do when he did. The concert hall was on the next city block, and he didn't even pause when he crossed the street.

Sadness hit me in the chest. I swallowed, fingers tightening on the thin strap of my purse. The concert was supposed to be amazing, and one of my favorites. Alexander Serrat's music...

One day I wanted to dance to it. More than just my own private sessions. It moved me, and in my head, I imagined a sweeping, modern ballet set to my favorites of his pieces.

I couldn't go.

No matter how much I wanted to sit there and be washed away by sound and emotion, I couldn't walk in there and see Craig waiting, angry I was taking so long, and then sit next to him the entire concert feeling him seethe.

If he wasn't angry about it, I would be distracted the entire time, thinking about what he might say to me after. And after that... I would never be able to enjoy sex knowing he'd been annoyed with me half the night.

I thought I could overlook the little things that had bothered me last time, but I couldn't. When I broke down and called him, craving the comfort of a body I knew and the feeling of just being with someone, it had felt like enough. But it wasn't.

I wasn't.

Somehow, I was never enough.

Not even to wait for while fucking walking.

Craig still hadn't noticed I wasn't with him. It seemed so small, but I wanted him to see me. I wanted to be the priority, concert be damned. Did he think I wanted to miss the beginning or whatever the hell he had planned? He hadn't even looked. Like it didn't matter to him whether I was there or not.

An ache I couldn't describe filled my chest, and I turned to the street, raising my hand in the air. It only took a minute for a cab to pull over to the curb and for me to get inside. "Pavilion, please."

The driver pulled into traffic, and I pulled my phone out of my purse. Craig would probably text me once he figured out I was gone. He'd probably call me petty, or a bitch, but my soul was too tired to care.

It didn't seem like too much to ask for someone to value me for who I was and not just... as a body.

Pavilion wasn't far, and the cab dropped me off outside, the line to get in already forming. The circus-themed club was one of the most popular in Slate City, and for good reason. The atmosphere and music were incredible, and it was a great place to lose yourself, if that's what you were aiming for.

Tonight? I was.

Technically, I wasn't supposed to dance here. There weren't any official rules against it, but Slate City Ballet made it clear they didn't approve of their dancers dancing at clubs. The horror. So I kept it quiet, but I needed the outlet. As much as I loved ballet, I loved more than just the classics. My body needed more than pirouettes. Sometimes you just needed to shake your ass.

Instead of joining the line, I turned and walked around the block and down the alley to the back, nodding to Bob as he saw me approach. He grinned. "Didn't know you were dancing tonight, Lo."

"I wasn't supposed to, but I'm going to see if they have room for me."

His eyes narrowed. "You okay?"

This wasn't the first time I'd come to the club in order to distract myself from something happening in my life. But I didn't feel like breaking it down. Movement was my safe space, and it was what I needed. "Fine. Just... need to move."

The expression on his face told me he didn't believe me, even for a second. But he nodded. "Have fun."

"I'll try." I flashed him my best smile—the one I learned no one questioned except those who knew me best. Petra, and—

I shook my head and pushed through the back door and into the locker room. Adina sat at the mirror, painting neon and shimmering paint on her dark skin. One of the aerialists, when she danced, the lights in the club picked up all the sparkle and shine. She looked ethereal and was always one of the favorites.

Adina glanced up when I walked in, and her eyebrows rose. "I didn't see you on the schedule."

"I'm not." I sighed. "I'm just hoping there's an empty space for me to dance."

Adina's eyes took in my outfit and the high heels. "That bad?"

"I don't know what you're talking about."

She rolled her eyes. "Yeah, okay."

"I'm okay. Promise. The night just didn't go how I expected it to, and it got to me a little."

Nodding, she stood and stretched. "Well, you know we have your back if you need us."

"I do know that." I shot her a grateful smile.

Adina touched my shoulder on the way past. "Sarah didn't come in, so one of the veils is empty."

"Thank you."

I grabbed the sparkly black catsuit I kept here in case of nights like this. It clung to me like a second skin and made me feel powerful and in control. Like I could command anyone's attention. Exactly what I needed.

Pulling my hair back into a high ponytail, I tossed my heels and purse into the locker and clocked in. A couple hours of dancing and I could go home and forget that no one ever seemed to choose me.

It wasn't true. I had amazing friends, and they loved me. But seeing them so in love and bonded with their packs made me feel like I was on the outside of it. I wanted it desperately, and it wasn't going to happen.

The traitorous voice in my mind whispered, *it could have.*

I shoved open the door to the club, drowning my thoughts with pounding bass and sinuous melodies. Even early in the evening, the club was already packed, and I wove my way through dancing bodies, everything in me feeling lighter.

Whenever I came here the chaotic atmosphere and mix of scents that made it past the cancellers had me loosening up and moving to the rhythm before I ever made it to my assigned station.

A flicker of warmth in the air had me turning and looking. Sweetness. It was so familiar. My heart pounded in my ears. The breath of scent was gone before I'd really registered it, but I'd know it anywhere.

Don't be ridiculous, Sloane. More than one person can have a scent. He's not the only person who smells like that.

My mind wasn't convinced, adrenaline coursing through my veins. Standing entirely still on the dance floor, I looked. Everywhere the lights shone they played tricks on me, showing me flashes of dark hair and steely blue eyes I'd tried and failed to forget.

Get the hell out of here, I ordered myself, pushing through the rest of the dancers and up to the higher level of Pavilion's space.

On the second floor, Adina was right. One of the veils was empty. A platform surrounded by layers of sheer fabric that partially hid you from view. The lights and the movement gave way to shapes on the outside. Sexy outlines of the dance.

I leaned down, flipping the hidden button which turned on the machine that controlled the fabric and was connected to the music. If you wanted to dance with them yourself, you could leave it off.

Tonight I craved the flashes and glimpses that made people look without really seeing. The music changed to something slower, angelic vocals floating over a bass rhythm that spoke about darker spaces and breathless gasps.

All around the club, the air changed and charged with that energy. Hips tilted into hips, and more than one kiss was shared in the writhing crowd.

This.

This was what I needed.

Closing my eyes, I raised my hands over my head and let myself dance.

I danced until I couldn't remember anything else. Just me and the music. The music was the only thing always there.

It always would be.

CHAPTER TWO

SLOANE

*M*y phone's alarm screeched through my consciousness like a bear had decided to maul my brain. Even with the terrible noise, I wasn't completely sure I wanted to move. But eventually the torture device that was my phone needed to be silenced.

There was a reason I chose that sound as the alarm. Because it was terrible enough to always wake me up and get me out of the delicious cocoon of my bed. Unfortunately, today was a day I actually *needed* to get up. I'd been dreading it and looking forward to it in equal measure.

First day of the new season. Not much dancing today, just a normal class before a company meeting and going over roles. The next couple of weeks would be intense while we brushed up on our repertoire to put up a show fast while we rehearsed the next ones. It wasn't the way we usually did things, but it was now.

My first day as a principal dancer.

Exciting.

Terrifying.

I needed to not throw up.

And definitely not fall on my face in front of the new bosses and new dancers. There were some, but we didn't know who they were yet.

I consciously loosened my jaw and tried not to grit my teeth. My meeting with the new creative director hadn't exactly gone well, which could make things awkward at best, hell at worst. It wasn't his choice to make me a principal, and it was already clear he resented it. I was the last promotion of the old executive and creative director.

It was my dream come true.

Arching my back until it cracked, I finally got my ass out of bed and into the shower. After last night at Pavilion, I'd barely had enough energy to crawl into bed, let alone clean myself up.

But it was good, and exactly what I needed. Both my head and heart felt lighter.

My phone chimed, and I grabbed it off the bed.

A text from Petra, my best friend. The picture was of her smiling in the foreground, and in the background was Stormy, her rescued clouded leopard. The cat was sprawled upside down in the hammock of her gigantic cat tree, and for all the world, it looked like the cat was smiling.

> **BEE 🐝**
> Stormy and I say good luck today!

> **SLOANE**
> Thank you! Maybe a late lunch or dinner after? I'm sure I'll need to bitch about something.

> **BEE 🐝**
> Absolutely. Is it okay if we eat here? I can have Blake send something over.

Petra was still recovering. She'd been kidnapped and nearly murdered thanks to her wicked witch of a stepmother, who was now in jail, and a billionaire media mogul who *had* been in jail.

I liked to think of myself as a good person, but I didn't think I was the only one who breathed a sigh of relief when the news broke that he'd died in prison. It meant Petra was safer, and that was all that mattered to me.

But the attempt on her life still haunted her, and she was still working on being comfortable away from home.

> **SLOANE**
> Absolutely. I need to cuddle with Stormy anyway.

> **BEE 🐝**
> Want some Saffron Market?

One of Petra's bonded Alphas happened to own our favorite restaurant, and my stomach growled even though it was barely eight in the morning and nothing on their menu was good for breakfast.

YES. Please. You're a goddess.

I flipped back to my other texts, my anxiety spiking when I saw all the ones from Craig.

CRAIG

Sloane? Where did you go?

You were right behind me, but I don't see you.

Where the hell are you!? If I go inside, you can't get your ticket. Or anything else.

I swear to god, Sloane, if this is a joke, it's not funny.

Fine. I tried to do something nice for you, and this is how you treat it? Serves me right for even trying.

There was a break for a couple of hours.

CRAIG

So you decided to just bail? After you're the one who made us late?

That's a really dick move.

Those tickets were expensive on top of the thing you decided wasn't worth your time. I thought you wanted to go. Guess I was wrong.

Sloane?

Where the HELL are you??

Fuck this. I don't need this.

You know, when you said you wanted to go out again, I almost said no. Cause you left the first time. But I gave you a chance and made myself clear that this time it was more. You came back to me, so don't pretend you don't want me.

Turns out you're another Omega bitch looking for a free meal. Next time, I'm not taking you back.

I rolled my eyes. There wasn't going to be a next time. Learned my lesson there.

CRAIG

> Or is this your way of telling me you need me to chase you? That you want more from me, even if I'm already trying?

> Fair enough, I can do that, Sloane. But if I give you more, you're mine. I'll give you one more chance.

> Fuck you for leaving me there and embarrassing me. But don't worry. Either way, I'll fuck the lesson into you.

My stomach twisted. He wasn't wrong. It was a dick move, leaving him there. But it was also a dick move not even to pay attention to the person who was with you.

The rest of it? I didn't even know what to do with that. But it made me even more glad I left. I knew he'd be pissed, but that was extreme. And definitely not me telling him to try harder. You had to stretch really far to get to that conclusion.

What if it had been a real emergency and someone had died? Maybe he'd be a little more sympathetic.

Whatever. We were done.

Still, I swallowed. Responding to things like this made me nervous. The only reason I'd reached out at all was because my loneliness got the best of me after I went over to Petra's and saw the way her Alphas looked at her. The tenderness they showed when a loud sound in the kitchen gave her a flashback to the day she'd been taken.

I wanted that.

SLOANE

> I'll reimburse you for the ticket.

Quickly, I shut my phone off and tossed it in my bag. The last thing I needed was to be distracted by *Craig* today, or worse, have my phone go off during company class or the meeting. As it was, Petra would probably give me hell for going out with him again, and she was absolutely right.

I grabbed my keys and jogged out the door. If I wanted to stop for coffee, I needed to hurry. Luckily for me, my favorite coffee shop near the theater wasn't busy, and I walked up to find most of the company still outside, milling around in the beautiful plaza.

A few dancers smoked away from the others, and one of them spotted me with a grin. "Hey, principal."

"Hello to you too."

Claire scooped me into a hug, careful not to get any ash on my clothes. "It's about time, honestly."

I winced. "I just hope it doesn't come back to bite me."

"If the new guy can't see how fucking talented you are, that's his problem." She kept her arm around my shoulder, and I inhaled a breath of her scent. Rich like incense and something a little darker. Mysterious. It was nice. Thankfully. There were some people in the company whose scent I couldn't stand, though you'd never get me to admit it out loud.

"I agree," Dion chimed in. "Fuck 'em. Metaphorically. Unless he's hot, then maybe actually fuck him. They sent me the bonus rehearsal contract without a meeting, so I haven't met him."

I wrinkled my nose. "Not hot. I mean, he's fine, but I have no plans on... that front."

They laughed. Dion was one of the few other Omegas in the company, also a principal. Dark skin with chocolatey brown eyes that made you feel warm and welcome no matter what was going on or who was around you. We started at the same time and were fast friends by the end of the first company class.

He also smelled like candy. The kind of sweetness you encountered when walking into a store just *filled* with chocolate and sugar.

"He doesn't like me," I said. "I was late to that meeting."

Unlike last night with Craig, that had actually been my fault. I left lunch with Petra too late to get there in time. In my defense, I hadn't known the meeting was with new management. I didn't even know we *had* new management. Mark wouldn't have cared about the five minutes, but Ian, the new creative director, had been pissed.

Brette, a beta standing next to Dion, snorted. "If he's that

11

upset about being late to a meeting that didn't matter, he's going to have a hell of a time here."

Most of the dancers in the company had a loose sense of time. Between stretching and getting our shoes on, company class rarely started on time. But we did what we had to, and we always got the work done.

"Noted," Dion said. "Watch out for the new guy. But circling back, we do need to get you some plans on *that front*," he emphasized the words while rolling his eyes, "this season."

I raised one eyebrow. "And why is that?"

"Girl." He looked me up and down. "Because you're hot as shit, and I don't want my friend to end up a dried-out husk. You deserve some good dick."

I winced before I could stop it. Craig's words still hung around in my brain. "I think I'm good."

Dion looked at me, sensing the tone. "Want to talk about it?"

"Nope." The 'p' popped. "I very much do not."

"Well, I'm still determined to get you some dick as good as what I got."

We laughed together. Dion had three bonded Alphas, and the guys were absolutely head over heels for him. It was cute the way they showed up with flowers, and they were present for more performances than they weren't.

"Yeah, that would be nice. But I'm not thinking about it right now. The next couple of weeks are already going to be a nightmare."

"Fucking right," Claire muttered.

I needed to remind myself to get some bags of ice. My feet were definitely going to need it during the compressed rehearsal period.

Behind us, the roar of an engine sounded. We turned to look and saw someone ride up to the curb on a motorcycle and stop, parking the bike there. The bike was sleek, looking both fast and sexy in ways only motorcycles could.

The ground fell out from underneath me. I knew that bike. And its rider.

No.

Was I still breathing? Probably not. I no longer had the

control over my body to inhale. Every part of me was frozen, watching him as he shrugged out of his leather jacket, exposing broad shoulders, perfect abs, and a few tattoos. He had more now than when I saw him last.

"Who's that?" Dion asked.

The man took off his helmet, and now I couldn't breathe. Too much. I was struggling not to hyperventilate. This was the last thing I expected today. Was there any way for me to get out of it? Could I fake being sick?

That wouldn't help with the rest of the season, but maybe I could go hide for a million years.

"Must be one of the new dancers. Or staff." Claire said.

"Dancer," I said. My voice sounded like it had been dragged over glass.

I felt Dion step closer to me. "You know him?"

All I could do was nod.

The man still straddling the motorcycle pulled on a black t-shirt before finally dismounting and heading in our direction. He hadn't seen me yet. There was still time to run. But I couldn't seem to control my feet. The pavement must have melted over them with how thoroughly I was rooted to the spot.

He smiled at everyone as he approached, giving a small wave. "Still locked?"

"Yeah," Claire said. "Honestly, one of us should have copied the keys at this point."

Laughter fluttered through the crowd, and he looked toward us, to where Claire spoke beside me. His scent reached me. The smell of freshly baked chocolate chip cookies. The gooey kind you bit into and moaned like you were having the best orgasm of your life.

I closed my eyes, savoring the scent like the first time I'd experienced it. My memory paled in comparison to the real thing. Overwhelming. Life-changing. The scent that made nothing else matter.

He saw me, and his face went slack. "Sloane?"

All my friends looked at me, now curious about how he and I knew each other.

I saw the moment my scent hit him. Saw his body go rigid

and his eyes go wide. The air between us tightened. It felt like the ground evaporated even though he hadn't moved any closer.

This wasn't real. It couldn't be.

Asher West was here. Staring at me. Nothing but fury in his eyes.

CHAPTER THREE

SLOANE

Claire stepped in front of me. The look in Asher's eyes was everything I'd feared. A hundred versions of this moment had played out in my mind, and I knew it would have to happen someday. Dancers as good as Asher didn't come along every day, and Slate City Ballet was the best. It was inevitable.

Behind us, the loud clanking of the door unlocking released the tension in the air. I turned and moved, pushing through the company to make it inside before Asher could.

I barely nodded to Jerry, the older man who took care of the facilities. Later, I'd drop by his office and bring him a raspberry scone. They were his favorite, and his weakness. Those scones were the reason I could get extra studio time when I needed it, even if no one should be in the building.

The lights were on, so I booked it to the studio, quickly taking a place on the barre in the corner. Claire was right after me, dropping her bag by mine and sitting in front of me, shielding me as I sank to the floor and started lacing on my practice shoes.

"What the hell just happened?" She asked quietly. The rest of the company was filtering into the large room and taking their places, cheerful conversation filling the space. The interaction between Ash and I was only noticed by a few people, thankfully.

Dion came over and flopped down on the other side, boxing me in the corner. "Yes. Please tell me what I just witnessed. Because first, I want to make sure you're okay, and second, it looked juicy as hell."

I swallowed. "It's a long story."

"He looked like he wanted to kill you," Claire said.

"He might," I managed a smile I didn't feel. "We haven't seen each other in five years. And—"

The air changed. I knew without looking over he'd entered the room. They looked over their shoulders, confirming it.

"Forget whatever I said about the new creative director," Dion whispered. "If you guys can fix whatever the hell that little display was, you should bang him."

My entire face flushed red. It was a good thing Ash wasn't closer. Just the scent of him would have me perfuming, and that...

My memory flashed backward five years.

I was so relieved to get back to the studio. Heats were bullshit, especially when you were alone. It was too late by the time mine hit to make any kind of arrangements. I was ready to get back to dancing.

Peering in the window to the studio, I smiled before I stepped into the room. The scent slammed into me like a brick wall.

Slipping my toe into my shoe, I laced the ribbons around my ankle and tucked them in before doing the same with the other. "It's complicated."

"I love complicated."

Claire saved me. "Let it be, Dion."

I stood and switched on and off my toes a couple of times. "Let's just do class," I said. "I'll tell you when I can. It's too long a story for now, and I'm not ready."

As many times as I'd imagined Ash and I meeting again, I didn't think about what it would do to the people around me. How could I explain what I did when I wasn't sure I understood it myself?

"Fair enough, buttercup." Dion stood up and leaned in to kiss my cheek before sneakily looking across the room. He laughed. "Thought so."

I glanced up and found Asher's eyes on me. And Dion. He glared at my friend beside me. I turned and put my hand on Dion's arm. "Please don't. He has a right to be angry with me."

"I just wanted to see his reaction," Dion whispered with a smirk. "And no matter how angry he is, that man wants you."

One more look, and I was trapped in his gaze. I'd never seen Ash look at me like that. Like he wanted to come over here and either kiss me or wring my neck. It wasn't clear if he'd decided which.

A sharp two claps had everyone standing at attention.

Madame Hubert swept in, along with the accompanist. She smiled at us and curtsied. We curtsied back.

"Welcome back, my dears." Her light European accent was comforting. Many of us had seen her for classes over our break, but now we would see her every day. As ballet mistress for the company, she made sure we were where we needed to be technically. Every day. "Let's get started, shall we?"

Everyone put their hand on the barre, and we began.

Immediately, my mind eased into familiarity. Even with Ash in the room and my stomach in knots, we'd still done class together hundreds of times. Class was one of my comfort places. I lost myself in the freeing repetitions of *plies* and *ronde de jambe*, letting muscle memory take over.

Asher's gaze didn't leave me. The only time he wasn't looking at me was when we turned in the opposite direction on the barre. It was a physical thing. Hot and heavy and rich, like being dropped into a balmy sea where everything was golden and shining. But I couldn't look at him. I couldn't risk starting to perfume in class.

Madame Hubert walked slowly around the room and checked our form before barre was over. The men quickly lifted and moved the portable barres from the center of the room so we could proceed with the rest of class. I resolved to ignore Ash until later, because there was nothing either of us could do here and now.

And still, I was aware of his every breath and movement in the room, even when I wasn't looking. I could see him in the mirror when I moved through the combinations, and I caught little threads and pockets of his scent through the room, and no matter how small, it still hit me like a battering ram.

Warmth and butter and chocolate. The feeling of breaking apart a still-hot cookie and watching the gooey strings of chocolate cling to each other. The decadence of something so simple yet so delicious.

We were moving into *reverence* before I realized it. I was moving so fully on instinct.

Finishing the slow, diagonal movement across the studio, I

curtsied deeply to Madame Hubert before retreating to the corner where my bag was.

Applause broke out at the end, and we thanked the accompanist. The applause continued, but only from the few people now walking into the studio. Mark Thurman, our retiring executive and artistic director, along with two others.

Ian Chambers, our new artistic director, was supposed to be incredible. I'd seen videos of his work, and it was undeniably beautiful. I wasn't sure about him though, given our not-so-great meeting a few weeks ago. Still, I hoped he did right by the company.

Glancing over at Dion, I shrugged. He wasn't bad looking. Young and clearly fit, he had the body of a dancer and wouldn't have any problem illustrating choreography. But on the scale of my attraction to him? It was an absolute zero.

"Welcome back," Mark said, smiling at all of us. Older, with salt and pepper hair, Mark was both a friend and a father to all of us. No one wanted to see him retire, but he claimed he was ready. "This is a hello and a goodbye. I wanted to stop by and see all of you one more time, along with introducing your new fearless leaders."

Laughter broke out.

Mark gestured, and Ian stepped forward. "Many of you know Ian Chambers already, if not from having meetings with him, then by reputation. I couldn't be more thrilled to see what kind of life he brings to SCB."

Ian nodded to all of us.

"In a second, Ian's going to talk to you about *Giselle* and the chaos we agreed to by bringing forward a repertory piece. But first," he motioned the second man forward. "This is Gabriel Black. He's the new executive director."

I hadn't really looked at him before, and I did a double take. A dress shirt with the sleeves rolled up and built arms with his hands tucked into the pocket of his slacks. Sandy brown hair just long enough to put your fingers through it and *grip* if you needed to, and a smile that could make it possible. I wasn't close enough to see the color of his eyes, but the way he scanned his gaze over each of us was warm and kind.

Like stepping forward had pushed his scent through the room, it hit me. I didn't need anything to tell me it was his scent. It *was*. The sharp yet deep sweetness of tobacco and the subtler warmth of vanilla. The combination was intoxicating. Like the best drink you'd ever tasted, and you'd happily drink it until you were blackout drunk and not give a shit about the hangover.

Fuck.

"It's nice to meet all of you. It's an honor to be here, and I hope we can continue the incredible success of this company. You might not see me day to day, but my door is open if you need anything. Quickly, I want to address something. Along with me, two members of my pack are also employees of SCB. Asher West," he nodded to where Asher sat on the other side of the room, his gaze still firmly fixed on me like it was impossible for him to look at anything else. "And Jace McKenna, who will be working as one of your physios. I just wanted to be clear that having pack members in the company will not mean they have special treatment, and I don't intend for our pack bonds to affect SCB business."

I stared at him. He was Asher's packmate. And another scent match. Oh god, I was *so* fucked.

As I watched, Gabriel's body stiffened. If you weren't looking for it, you wouldn't notice. But I did. His eyes snapped directly to mine. Both Claire and Dion noticed. But Gabriel didn't say anything. He just smiled and looked at the rest of the company. "I look forward to an excellent season."

"I just have one more thing to say." Mark stepped forward again. "Working with this company has been the greatest honor of my life. You'll see me around, because I could never stay away from seeing you perform, but each of you has a place in my heart. Thank you."

Applause erupted, and Ian took center stage. "We're going to get to know each other quickly during the next few weeks," he said. "The design staff have been working diligently, and so the sets and costumes are coming along well. You'll receive emails about when your costume fittings will be.

"Tomorrow we'll start with choreography. Thank you in

19

advance for the work you've agreed to, and the training you've been doing."

When we found out we were doing a fast production of *Giselle*, everyone in the company began to brush up. We'd put on Giselle two seasons ago, and bringing it up again was lovely. Still, it would be difficult. I'd learned the role as an understudy, but I hadn't danced it before.

Ian kept talking about role assignments, but Dion placed his hand over mine where it rested on my leg. He kept his voice low enough only I could hear. "You're scent-sympathetic with Asher?"

Pressing my lips together, I nodded once.

"And Gabriel?"

Another nod.

He curled his fingers around mine. "Isn't that a good thing?"

God, I wanted it to be. But I had no idea if Asher would ever forgive me, and I didn't know what his other packmates thought of me. There was too much up in the air.

"There's been a bit of a change in the schedule. The performance of *Giselle* needs to be moved up. It will be intense, but I believe we can do it. We'll be putting up the show with the first cohort a week from tomorrow."

What? I looked over at Claire and Dion, who had equal looks of shock on their faces. We knew the rehearsal period would be shorter. It was the new temporary contract we'd signed. But a week? That was insane, even with us brushing up and us being familiar with the show.

Ian didn't seem phased. "Once the show is up and running, we'll begin work on *Swan Lake*." Ian smiled. "For the first bit of my tenure, I want to work on familiar classics while we all learn a new style of working. Roles will be posted. I look forward to working with you. I know it won't be easy, but you are the best. You'll rise to the occasion."

It was short and to the point. People murmured to themselves, and they had every right. It wasn't what anyone expected. But I had bigger problems. Now that people were moving, I needed to get the hell out of here.

"You have plans, Lo?" Claire asked.

"Yeah." I cleared my throat. "I'm going to have lunch with Petra and then given tomorrow," I thought about our new reality. "I'm going to brush up on some stuff. I need to go downstairs and grab some shoes so I have some prepped."

Across the room, Asher and Madame Hubert were conversing. Gabriel was speaking with Mark and Ian.

"I'm going to meet Addison and do the same," she said. "Need some interference getting out?"

"You don't think I'm crazy?"

The corners of Claire's eyes crinkled in a smile. "I might not be a scent match with Addie, but I've seen plenty. If it's meant to work out, it will. But you're my friend, and you're my first priority."

I blew out a breath in relief. "Then, yes. That would be great."

"Done."

Hugging Dion briefly, I hefted my bag over my shoulder and waited for Claire to make her move. She stepped into the conversation with Asher and Madam Hubert, and as soon as she held out her hand to him, I bolted. Out the door and around the corner to the stairs and down to the shoe room.

I loved the shoe room. There was something comforting about the rows of shelves crammed with every kind of shoe imaginable—pointe, ballet, character, jazz—and the gentle silence of a room filled with so many soft things.

My heart rate eased, and I breathed in the familiar dusty smell before going down one of the aisles and finding my cubby.

Fresh pairs of shoes waited, and I grinned, grabbing three pairs to stick in my bag. I'd rather prep them and sew my ribbons at home than be late to rehearsal because I needed to do it at the beginning. Ian already didn't have a great impression of me. I wasn't going to make it worse.

I turned and froze.

Asher stood at the end of the aisle, staring at me with the same anger and passion as the first time he'd seen me. I pressed a hand to my stomach to quell the anxiety and the butterflies.

He prowled toward me with intent, and I shivered. If there was one thing I was sure of, it was that Asher West would never hurt me, even if he were furious with me. But I still had no idea what to say.

Stopping in front of me, his scent wrapped around me like a warm blanket. Comforting and so much *fucking more*. The perfume I'd been desperately trying to avoid swirled around the two of us. I had to look up to meet his gaze. So familiar, and so strange after so long.

"Sloane." His voice broke on my name, and then I was in his arms.

Ash pressed me up against the shelves, my body entirely cushioned in pointe shoes. One hand in my hair, the other curling around my waist to keep me close, and his face pressed into my neck while he inhaled me like I was oxygen.

A purr roared to life in his chest, so strong and pure it made my body melt against his. Pangs of regret washed over me at the thought of missing so much of this feeling. Of running when I should have stayed and fought.

I shuddered and closed my eyes, breathing him in, savoring the warmth of his body and scent.

"This is why you left?" His words brushed over my skin, bringing back a hundred memories that felt so different now that he was here and now that he *knew*.

Ash pulled back and looked at me. "Why?"

What could I possibly say to make it better? That I saw how happy he was and after everything, I couldn't be the one to take it away from him? That even though it was everything I wanted, I was a fucking coward? That I worried as soon as he knew we were scent-sympathetic, he'd look at me in disappointment?

His fingers tightened in my hair. "Why, Sloane?"

I shook my head, unable to speak. Tears filled my eyes, and I wasn't sure if they were embarrassment or relief.

"Blue," he whispered, pulling me against his chest. "Talk to me. Please."

My old nickname just made the tears come faster, and they soaked into his shirt. I smelled like blueberries and pancakes. Ash had started calling me blue not long after we met. "I can't," I whispered.

"Please," he begged, lips brushing my temple. "I need to understand. I'm so fucking pissed at you, I don't know whether I want to fight with you or kiss you."

A sob caught in my throat, and the door to the room opened. A few members of the corps entered, chattering about the new productions. One of the guys came down our aisle and stopped when he saw us.

I pushed against Ash and he let me go.

"Sorry," the guy, Jacob, said.

"It's fine." I swiped my tears away and moved, pushing past Jacob and heading to the door.

"Sloane," Asher called.

I couldn't not look. His gaze burned into mine, eyes on fire. A look that told me we weren't done, and he was going to find out every secret I'd ever kept from him.

The door opened again, and I forced myself to walk through it and sprint up the stairs before I went back and spilled them myself. He felt so good, smelled so good, and I was cracking in two with shame and fear.

I had no doubt Asher would make me tell him everything, but today? I wasn't ready.

CHAPTER FOUR

ASHER

*F*uck.

The door closed behind Sloane, and it took every ounce of strength in my body not to go after her. I was here, standing in the middle of her perfume and still unsure whether I wanted to throttle her or pin her to the wall and fuck her into oblivion.

Blueberry pancakes. But not like I'd ever smelled them before. Not the pleasant sweetness of my best friend who didn't know how special she was. This scent burned me. It set my lungs on *fire*.

Her scent hung so strongly in the air I swore I tasted syrup on my tongue. The depth and the warmth made my mouth water. All I wanted to do was hold her against my body and *inhale*. One moment hadn't been enough. I needed so much more than that. I needed everything.

I pressed the heels of my hands into my eyes, trying to drag my mind back to itself. When I'd encountered people with scent matches, I didn't understand it. I'd convinced myself scent-sympathy was nice, but wasn't a big deal if I didn't find it. I'd never understood why Sloane wanted it so badly.

Now I knew.

The very foundations of the world had been ripped up from underneath me when I saw her, and a second later got punched in the face with her gorgeous, exquisite scent. She was all that mattered, and she couldn't even look at me.

Five years...

"You okay?" The corps member who'd stepped into our aisle in the shoe room stood a few feet away.

Was I okay?

No. I was very much not okay.

"I—"

He held out a hand. "I'm Jacob."

25

I shook it. "Asher. Ash."

"Nice to meet you." Glancing back at the door, he looked at me again. "We all really love Sloane, so—"

A growl raced up my throat just hearing her name in another man's mouth, and I shoved the instinct down. He was a Beta, and though he had to read the feral vibes coming off me, he still stood up for Sloane. "We haven't seen each other in a while," I managed. "We're still figuring it out. But I would never intentionally hurt her."

He nodded, still eyeing me warily.

This wasn't what I had planned for my first day at a new company. I knew Sloane would be here, and I had traced a thousand different ways of asking *what the fuck* and *why* she'd disappeared. Not once had I imagined it would be this.

"I look forward to working with you," I said. "Thank you for having her back."

Jacob smiled. "No problem."

"See you tomorrow."

It was an effort to walk slowly toward the door and not follow the path of Sloane's scent the way I had on the way down here. She was already gone. I knew that.

My chest ached. Five years. She'd known for five years and never told me. I didn't understand *why*. Now that I knew what it was like, walking away from this would be torture. Had she been in agony this whole time?

A memory hit me out of nowhere and froze me on the stairs.

I tucked my chin over Sloane's shoulder where she was doodling in her notebook. Pictures were taped here and there. Purple curtains and other fiery and vibrant colors. Like a blazing sunset. Pinks and golds and violets turning to blue. Lights and pillows. "What are you doing?"

This close, I felt her smile. "Nothing."

"Doesn't look like nothing."

"It's just a daydream. What I'd like a nest of mine to look like."

I stared down at the page, taking in the little details she was noting. "It doesn't make you sad?"

Sloane laughed, and I loved the sound of it. "Why would it make me sad?"

"Because you're not there yet." Sloane was open about her desire for a scent-sympathetic pack. She wouldn't settle for less. "And as much as I want it for you, it might not happen."

"Yeah." Her little sigh betrayed that I was right. "I can still hope, though, and that hope helps with the pain."

She doodled the little symbol she drew on everything in the corner of the paper before grabbing my hand and drawing it on the top of my thumb. It didn't mean anything, it was just a little symbol she liked.

"I hope you get it," I said.

"Me too."

And then she had. She'd found out we were scent-sympathetic and had walked away.

Grief struck me in the chest. What had I done? What could have made her walk away from the one thing in the world she truly wanted?

I grabbed my bag from the now empty studio and headed straight to Gabriel's office. He tried to stop me when I went after her and failed. The whole pack knew about Sloane, and they'd been interested in seeing what would happen. Safe to say they didn't think of this.

Pushing the door open without knocking, Gabriel turned from where he was looking out the window. His office was in the admin portion of the building, much higher than the theater itself.

"Did you—"

"Yes." He didn't even let me finish the question. "Yes, I did."

We hadn't had a chance to talk, and every piece of me was relieved it wasn't the rare situation where only one of us was scent-sympathetic. If both Gabriel and I were, Jace and Roman were almost guaranteed.

I didn't even make it to a chair. I fell back against the wall of his office, nearly sliding down it. "Gabe, what the fuck." Not a question, just a statement.

He chuckled, but his eyes were just as haunted as I knew mine were. "Did you find her?"

"Yes."

"And?"

My whole body shuddered. "And up close it's so much better. I can't even breathe. The fact that I'm here right now and not tracking her down across the city is a miracle."

He looked at me. "Did she say anything?"

"No."

Gabriel raised his eyebrows.

"I asked her why, and she started crying." Placing a hand to my chest, I tried to add pressure to ease the ache there. She was sad. She was *broken,* and it had to do with me. The Alpha instinct to take care of an Omega—*my* Omega—hated that her tears were my fault. "She said she can't."

"She can't?"

I shook my head. "I don't know. I—" He sat down and I let myself sink the rest of the way down to the floor and buried my face in my hands. "What do we do?"

"First, let me tell you that just because I'm keeping myself calm doesn't mean I don't feel it. If I hadn't been talking in front of the entire fucking company, I don't know what I would have done."

"I need to find her."

"No," Gabe said, though it sounded like the word was dragged out of him by force. "Something is wrong, Ash. We both know that if tears are her reaction, chasing her down just to get to the bottom of it isn't going to fix that. Sloane's not going anywhere, and she's going to have to talk to you very soon anyway."

I asked the question with my eyes, and he put a clipboard down on the desk in my direction. A copy of the roles for *Giselle* that had been posted.

Pushing myself off the floor, I grabbed it and scanned down the list of names. They were arranged by cohort, so everyone knew who they'd be rehearsing with. I found my name and the group.

COHORT 3:
GISELLE: SLOANE GLASS
ALBRECHT: ASHER WEST
HILARION: DION REYNOLDS
MYRTHA: CLAIRE HART

I looked up at my packmate. "Did you do this?"

"No. I don't have anything to do with casting. Ian put together the groupings he wanted based on watching back the archives of the last few seasons and the interviews he's been doing with Mark the last few months."

Relief surged through my chest. Sloane and I dancing together was...

The last thing I wanted was for her to think I'd tried to force her close to me by having an exception made. But these roles were perfect. Sloane was an incredible dancer, with both the passion and the ethereal quality needed for the role. And most of the second act was her and me.

"The others need to know. We need to talk to her. She needs to meet you and them." My hands tightened around the clipboard, and I put it down before I broke it. Every instinct was *screaming* at me to go and find her. Take her in my arms again and bathe in her scent before making her *mine*.

Gabe laughed softly. "You think I don't want to go find her right now? I wish I'd caught her on the way out the door and had her pressed up against these windows right now."

"I hate that I can *hear* the 'but' in your voice."

"But," he said, "she needs to lead this. I don't mean we'll let her avoid us, but even if it's something we won't care about, there's a reason she ran from this."

I appreciate that he said *this* and not *you*. That's what it felt like. She ran from *me*. I needed to know why, or I was going to go insane.

"I think I might need you to knock me out when we get home," I said.

He laughed once, turning and picking up his phone and his coat, not realizing I was completely serious. "You might have to do the same to me," his statement was clearly a joke. "I planned on staying here the rest of the day and getting started on things."

"But?"

He smiled grimly and pulled open his office door. "But if I do, I'll be using that computer to look up her address, phone number, email, and I won't be able to control myself with that information. Let's go tell Roman and Jace."

Gabriel grabbed me by the arm before I could turn and *lunge* for the computer. "Stop."

I can't. I can't.

The way her words sounded while she was pressed into my chest. *I can't.*

All the fight went out of me. One day. We hadn't seen each other for five years. I could make it one day. Even if I had to ask Roman to punch me in the face to do it.

CHAPTER FIVE

SLOANE

I swiped away my tears and made sure no one else saw me crying. The beginnings of new seasons were already hard enough without people thinking there was drama.

"Lo." Dion's voice caught my attention.

"Yeah?"

He looked me up and down, noticing everything, and thankfully, he chose to say nothing. "I won't slow you down, but the lists are up." Dion nodded toward the bulletin board.

"Oh. Right. Am I going to be happy?"

Smirking, he hooked an arm around my shoulder as we walked over. "Better be, bitch."

I traced my finger down the paper until I found my name.

COHORT 3:
GISELLE: SLOANE GLASS
ALBRECHT: ASHER WEST
HILARION: DION REYNOLDS
MYRTHA: CLAIRE HART

My heart stilled in my chest. Did he do this? Did he push us together? Logic immediately stepped in and told me no. Ian would have been working on this for months now. The only way to put things in place for a rapid fire season like the one we were doing was for everything to be prepared in advance. Though I didn't think anyone in the company appreciated how long they waited to tell us about the changes.

Dion, Claire, and I were often paired together. It was why we were so close. Our heights and our styles worked well together. And once upon a time... Asher's and mine had too.

"Are you going to be okay?" Dion asked quietly.

Taking a shaky breath in, I nodded. "It's not like I'd be able to avoid him the whole season."

"Why would you want to?"

The question wasn't sarcastic. Dion understood. He was scent-

31

sympathetic with his Alphas and knew what it felt like. And besides that, he was right. I didn't want to avoid Ash, or the rest of his pack.

But that didn't erase my shame or fear.

"Have you ever done something you knew was right at the time, and even though you wished you could take it back, it's been too long, and you just have to live with it?"

"Lo, whatever the hell it is, that man does not care. The way he practically broke his neck trying to get out of the studio and follow you? I've never seen anyone so desperate."

I shook my head. "I didn't know he was coming. I'm not ready for it. It's been five years, Dion. If I'm scent-sympathetic with the two of them, chances are I am with the rest of the pack too, and I'm not fucking ready. I'm terrified."

Dion's eyes grew firm, and he took my face in his hands. "Do you know why you're a principal?"

"What?"

"A principal dancer. Do you know why?"

Raising an eyebrow, I let my sarcasm drip. "Because I've been here a while and that's the way ballet companies work?"

He laughed, but didn't let me go. "There are people still in the corps who have been here longer than you, Lo. It's not *only* because of talent. It's because you're relentless."

"*Relentless?*" My jaw dropped.

"That's right. You don't back away from anything until you get it, no matter if that means putting in extra hours at home or bribing Jerry to let you in here so you can dance. You don't back down from a challenge, and you *never* fucking give up."

I swallowed. "Thank you. But I don't get why it's relevant."

"Because this is the first time I've seen you remotely scared of anything, and I would know that of *all* the things we have to deal with, especially in our line of work, this is nothing to be scared of. And if any one of them thinks about doing anything to hurt you, I have three very devoted Alphas who will kick their asses and make sure the two of us get some hits in too."

A laugh bubbled up out of me, though my tears started to reappear. "I appreciate that."

He pulled me into a hug. "It's going to be fine."

"I hope so."

"I know so." Releasing me, he tapped me lightly on the nose. "See you tomorrow. And *don't* wallow."

Rolling my eyes, I backed away toward the door. "No promises."

Finally turning my phone back on, I ignored the texts flowing in from Craig and opened my thread with Petra.

SLOANE

I'm on my way.

BEE 🐝

See you soon!

The early fall weather was lovely, in that strange space between seasons when it could still tip one way or the other. On days like this, though Petra and her Alphas didn't live close, I would usually walk anyway and enjoy the fresh air and exercise. Today I needed to get there fast.

Lifting my hand in the air, I stepped off the curb right next to Asher's bike and hailed a cab. I climbed into one and was off to Starling Tower before he came out of the building and found me standing there.

I waited in the lobby for someone to come get me. Since the incident, Petra's pack was keeping security tight for their own peace of mind. Harrison smiled at me when the elevator opened. "Sorry about this."

"I'd rather you guys feel safe in your home."

"Me too," he said softly.

The elevator lifted us all the way to the top, where the Atwood Pack's four-story penthouse was. "Where's Petra?"

"Upstairs," he said. "You can go up."

"Thanks."

I slipped into the second elevator and went up to the top floor. The whole thing belonged to Petra, with the biggest bedroom in existence, her nest, and plenty of room for a kingdom's worth of giant cat toys.

"*No*," I heard Petra's voice as I stepped out. "You can play with literally anything else right now, but you have to let the leggings go."

A soft, playful growl followed.

Petra was on her knees in front of Stormy, the two playing tug of war with a pair of black leggings, and Stormy very much didn't want to give them up.

"You should really buy her a pair."

Glancing over, Petra smiled. "I know. It's my own fault. I let her play with my leggings right after we got her, and now it's her favorite thing."

I wandered over to one of Petra's giant beanbag chairs and fell into it, curling up in my best friend's scent. She smelled like honey and cinnamon, which was one of the reasons I called her Bee.

"Stormy—"

The cat landed with a *poof* next to me in the giant bag, nuzzling my arm before curling against my side like she was still a kitten and not a cat nearly the same size as me. "Hey, pretty girl," I scratched her behind the ears. "Thank you for snuggling. I need it."

She chuffed and pressed her head into my shoulder. Stormy always seemed to know when you needed a cuddle, and I loved that about her.

"What's going on?" Petra asked. "This isn't the vibe I was expecting. You're always excited after the first day of a season."

"It was fine. When's the food getting here?" I dodged the question. "I'm starving."

"Blake said it'll be here in half an hour. Why are you changing the subject?"

Instead of answering her, I curled into Stormy, burying my face in her fur.

"And the question doesn't disappear in Stormy's fur."

"Sure it does."

Petra sighed, exasperated. "*Lo.*"

"Fine." I sat up, careful not to jostle Stormy too much before sliding to the floor in front of the beanbag so I could lean on it. "First, I need to apologize."

34

She frowned, sitting down against the other beanbag. "Why?"

"Because..." I picked at my nails. "There's some stuff I haven't told you. I should have. I just barely knew how to deal with it myself, let alone tell anyone else."

"Okay, you're scaring me a little," she admitted. "What's going on?"

I cleared my throat. "Okay, remember the meeting I had to go to that day after you and I went to lunch? You were with Cole?"

"Yeah." She smiled. It was right after she met her Alphas and had been overwhelmed with the newness and *rightness* of being scent matched. "Why?"

"You were right." I leaned my head back into the beanbag. "I was late. But I didn't think anything of it. The meeting was with Mark, and he'd never be mad at me for being a couple minutes late."

Stormy slid off the beanbag, flopping down on the floor between the two of us, and Petra waited for me to continue.

"It wasn't just with Mark. Ian Chambers was there, and no one knew, but he's going to be the new artistic director. Mark is retiring. He's been talking about it for years, but we all thought it was a joke. And Ian is a big deal in the ballet world. He was... less than pleased about me being late."

Petra frowned. "But you didn't know he would be there."

"Doesn't matter. 'If you're a professional, you're on time regardless of who's present, and I expect this never to happen again.'" I curved my fingers into quotation marks.

"Seriously?"

"Yeah."

"So... was he like a massive dick to you today?"

I shook my head. "No, we didn't even speak. But when we were getting ready for the Gala, and while we were there, you'd asked me what was wrong. That's what was wrong. I'm Mark's last promotion to principal, and I couldn't get it out of my head that I would start out being the black sheep right away. Never a good thing."

"No." Petra looked at me, and everything told me she was

thinking. Because so far, what I'd told her, while it sucked, didn't account for my mood today.

"Anyway, I'm just setting the stage. I've been anxious about the first day for a few weeks. Now, for the other thing."

She laughed as the elevator chimed. "Why do I feel like you're going to tell me someone died?"

"Not that."

Blake entered the room, bags of takeout draped over his arms and a smile on his face. The magnetism between the two of them was electric. My best friend lit up before running over to him and jumping into his arms despite the takeout bags.

He laughed, somehow managing to set the bags on the floor before he could support her legs around his waist. "I thought you were going to just send someone over with the food," she said.

"But then I wouldn't have the excuse to come home and kiss you." He did just that, and I had to look away. The way they looked at each other was the way I wanted to be looked at.

The way Asher had looked at me today.

I couldn't reasonably explain the fear that lodged in my chest. When I'd walked into that studio and scented him while he was kissing Vivian, smiling like the world was perfect, I left because I couldn't bear a look of disappointment when he just found happiness. Happiness I helped him find. Now I was afraid that I'd ruined it because it had been too long.

"This was a nice surprise," Petra murmured.

"Good. I'll be back later. Nice to see you, Sloane," Blake said before he kissed Petra on the nose and left.

She grinned as she brought the bags of food over and set them around. Stormy nudged a bag with her nose, but didn't seem overly invested in stealing our food away from us.

"Sorry about that. What were you saying?"

I opened a styrofoam container of saffron rice and took a bite. Petra raised an eyebrow, and I covered my mouth with my hand. "Fine. You win." Shoving another bite of food in my mouth, I got comfortable.

"Five years ago."

"Oh, we're going *way* back."

"Yeah, to when I came back from the conservatory." Petra

36

and I had both spent time at conservatories, but hers was for music and mine was for dance and the visual arts. Neither of us graduated.

Petra watched me carefully. She always suspected something different from what I told her, which was that Slate City Ballet offered me a spot early and I chose to take it. In a way, it was true, but it wasn't the reason I left. "You remember Asher?"

"Yeah. Alpha. You and he were good friends. I thought I was going to have to murder him for a little while 'cause he was stealing my best friend status."

"Never. Well, I got my first heat. Kind of unexpected. I missed three days of class. At the same time, I'd been helping Asher get together with Vivian, another Alpha dancer from our class. They went out that weekend during my heat."

"Here." Petra passed me some chicken. I had no idea what it was called, but it was fucking addicting. "Okay, so they went out. I thought you and Asher were just friends."

I nodded. "We were. Anyway, my heat finished, and I went back to class. I walked in and saw Asher and Vivian in the studio. They were smiling, looking at each other like there was no one else in the world. I don't think I'd *ever* seen him that happy. He kissed her, and I remember feeling so happy for them."

Petra froze with her fork halfway to her lips, like she knew what was coming.

"Then I walked through the door, and his scent hit me."

"No."

Pressing my lips together, I closed my eyes. "Yeah. I'd never felt anything like that. It was instantaneous. Like a battering ram."

"Sounds familiar." Petra had met her first Alpha at a political fundraiser for her father, and what she'd felt and looked like, I understood immediately. It was nothing, and then it was *everything*.

"I... Asher's been through a lot," I said. "And we'd already established we didn't have feelings for each other. He was so *happy*, Bee. I couldn't go in there and rip it away. If he'd looked at me like he was disappointed, I—" Even the thought hurt to admit. "It would have broken me. So I turned around and walked

37

out of the studio and never went back. I came home, and got an audition, nailed it, and was part of SCB before anyone could try to get me back to school."

My best friend stared at me, mouth hanging open. "Lo."

"I know."

"You've been scent matched for *five years*?"

I could only manage a whisper. "Yeah."

"Wow. Okay. Not what I thought you were going to tell me, but how does that—" She went entirely still like she'd been turned into stone. "Oh my god."

"If you're thinking that Ash is the newest member of the Slate City Ballet Company as of today? You're thinking right. If you're thinking he came up, saw me, and got a face full of my scent? You're also right. Not to mention his packmate is the new executive director, and he smells fucking incredible too."

Her eyes lit up. "Isn't this a good thing? He knows. He's here. You can meet them." Her smile betrayed how happy she and her Alphas were. "I'm so happy for you, Lo. Really."

"Thanks."

"You don't seem overjoyed by this."

"I'm scared," I admitted. "He caught me in the shoe room, said he was so fucking pissed at me he didn't know whether to fight me or kiss me. You should have seen it, Bee. When he scented me... he was so angry."

She snorted. "If I knew Cole had scented me five years ago, known he was scent-sympathetic, and decided not to tell me? I'd be pretty pissed too."

Guilt twisted in my chest. "I was trying to make him happy."

"For five years?" Petra spoke with her mouth full, which was more comical than anything. "You can't think he's still with her."

A giggle slipped out, some of the weight off my shoulders. "What was that? Wanna try again?"

She tossed a piece of bread at me, and I caught it. "You can't think he's still with her."

"I honestly don't know. I didn't let myself keep track of him. If I had, I never would have been able to stay away. Though, I guess if I had checked up on him I would have known he was joining SCB."

I dug around in the bags and found a bottle of water, setting aside the chicken and rice to stroke my hand down Stormy's side. It was a good thing she couldn't really purr, or else she'd kill everyone with her cuteness.

"So, let me get this straight," Petra clapped her hands together. "You're scent-sympathetic with a man who used to be one of your best friends. *And* with his packmate, which probably means everyone else too, depending on how many there are. Did it seem like he was *actually* angry?"

"No," I admitted. Nothing about Asher holding me—enveloping me and showing me how perfectly we fit—said he was angry. "But it didn't mean he wasn't."

"What are you afraid of?"

This was Petra, and only because it was her I could say the truth out loud. "I'm afraid it's too late. That he—*they*—won't forgive me."

"Can't find that out unless you actually talk to them," she pointed out.

"Weren't you scared at all?" It hadn't been long since Petra met her guys. Frankly, it was a bit of a whirlwind. Every member of her pack was incredible and perfect for her. They would do anything for her, and had, including save her life from a homicidal maniac.

Petra laughed and rolled her eyes. "That's a stupid question and you know it. Of course I was scared. In my head, a scent-sympathetic pack meant something bad was going to happen, like the way I lost my mom. I was terrified of that, and they answered every one of my fears.

"So, let me guess. You think Asher said something about you to the rest of his pack and they think you're a terrible person?"

"Something like that," I muttered.

"Is that something he would do? Really?"

I sighed. "No."

Her face said *I told you so*.

"I just don't know what to do."

Petra pulled her knees up and clasped her arms around them. "I waited one night—*one*—to fall into bed with my pack just to make sure we had our heads on straight, and you were furious I 'went to bed with cookies instead of cock.' You need to build a time machine and go back in time to *that* Sloane, because I'm not going to let you bury your head in the sand because you're scared of the best thing that ever happened to you."

"How do I do this?" I said. "I can't just pretend the five years didn't happen."

"I don't imagine they will either," she said with a shrug. "But that's between you and Asher. You still have to get to know the rest of his pack, and *putting* those five years between them and you helps no one."

I melted over onto the floor. "Fuck."

She laughed. "That about sums it up."

Sighing, I stared at the ceiling. "Is it crazy to take it slow?"

"If it helps you, it's not crazy. Not what I thought you'd want, but no, absolutely not."

I covered my face with my hands. Not only were we crashing a performance, I now had to deal with what were potentially the most important relationships in my life. I was so absolutely, entirely fucked.

"Take it the speed you need, Lo. And no matter what happens, I'm here for you."

"Thank you."

Stormy chuffed, rolling over onto her back like she agreed to have mine. The two of us laughed, and I tried to put aside the thoughts whirling in my mind and simply enjoy some food.

CHAPTER SIX

ROMAN

The formal room by the front door had the best light early in the day, so I'd taken to sitting here for a few hours before I went to my studio in the back.

It was easy to slip into the place of simple silence. No thoughts, just me and the piece of paper in my sketchbook, as I figured out how to whittle away at a chunk of stone until it did exactly what I wanted it to. The piece for this commission still eluded me. I had a vague theme, but so far it wasn't clicking.

The front door opened, and Gabriel's voice reached me. "Ash, I'm going to chain you in the backyard if you don't stop."

Asher saw me and came striding across the room, motorcycle helmet in hand. "I need you to punch me in the face."

I stared at him. "What?"

"Punch me. In the face. Make it good. Knock me out."

Glancing at Gabriel, he had a hand over his mouth and was dying with silent laughter.

Clearing my throat, I went back to my sketchbook. "While I can't say I've never thought about punching you in the face, why would I do that?"

It had taken years for me to be so comfortable speaking with them. With anyone, honestly. Every time words came easily, it was still a relief.

"Sloane." Ash's tone was somewhere between awe and fury.

I didn't look up. "You knew you were going to see her. I'm sorry it didn't go as well as you planned."

"Oh, I wouldn't say that," Gabe said.

Jace walked in from the kitchen, leaning in the doorway. "Did we all decide we're actually going to use this room now?"

Ash turned to him. "Okay, I should have asked you first. You probably know some shit where you can pinch a nerve and put me to sleep."

"You're right," Jace said sarcastically. "I do. It would be a

41

really bad idea though, cause I'd have to punch you somewhere vital. Can't guarantee that outcome."

"For fuck's sake." Asher pushed through Gabriel and Jace, taking his backpack and helmet with him. His steps told me he was going to the kitchen.

Gabriel cleared his throat. "It turns out Sloane is scent-sympathetic with Ash. And me. I caught her scent in the middle of my introduction speech to the company, and..." He was clearly at a loss for words. "Yeah. It's real. And if it's the two of us?"

The chances of a one-off scent match were rare, but not unheard of. A scent match with two members of a pack but not the others? Nearly impossible.

My breath grew shallow. As both an Alpha and a man, I wanted the closeness and comfort that came with a relationship. I craved being able to love and care for someone—if she were an Omega, even better.

And still, even having heard Ash talk about Sloane, knowing she was sweet and kind, the fear of new people lurked in my mind. New people were often uncomfortable with my general silence, and more often than not, they decided it wasn't worth waiting out the time it took for me to get comfortable. Or worse.

Swallowing, I looked at Gabriel. "Why does he want to be knocked out?"

He grinned. "Got a pretty good taste of her scent, and his instincts are telling him to go find her. Doesn't think he'll be able to stop himself."

Jace's face was slack with shock. "What does she smell like?"

"Blueberry pancakes." That was Ash, back from the kitchen with a drink. It wasn't alcohol, though I wouldn't have judged him for it. His leather riding gear was gone. "It's why I used to call her blue. Only it's not just fucking blueberry pancakes, it's the blueberries, the pancakes, the syrup, the butter. So many layers to her scent I could *only* breathe that for the rest of my life and be fine."

He wasn't kidding.

"And she's not here meeting the rest of us... why?" Jace asked.

"Because Ash made her cry."

Ash's head whipped around to Gabe, eyes wild. "I didn't *make* her cry."

Setting his hand on Ash's shoulder, Gabe smiled. "I'm messing with you." Then he looked over at Jace and me. "Believe me, if I thought it was an option, I would have made it happen. Whatever made her disappear on Ash five years ago needs to be resolved. But if she doesn't hate the sight of us thanks to this asshole, I fully intend to court her."

I made a face they knew too well. *Without asking us?*

Gabe rolled his eyes and stuck his hands in his pockets. "Believe me, you're going to like her."

That, I didn't doubt. But would she like us? Would like *me*?

"What did I do?" Ash mumbled, sitting on the floor. "I don't get it. How could she walk away? Why did she think she needed to?"

In the four years we'd been a pack, I'd never seen Asher like this. He seemed devastated as much as enthralled, and I hoped as soon as I met her I would feel the same.

"You'll find out," Gabriel said. "Hopefully tomorrow, so the rest of us can meet her. Officially."

"How are you so calm?" Jace asked.

The easy mask dropped off his face. He wasn't calm at all. If anything, his instincts were just as out of control, and he was hanging on by a thread. "Sheer force of will."

"But you want to...?" I asked.

"Yes." No hesitation. "If there hadn't been people in the studio I probably would have fucked her against the mirrors."

Jace looked down at Ash with sympathy. "None of us are going to hit you. Even if we wanted to, we wouldn't with a show this close. Gotta keep your face pretty. I'll lock you in your room if you think it will help."

"Probably not. I'd be out the window before any of you knew I was gone."

"Come on," Jace hauled him up by the arm. "Gym. We'll spar."

"I thought you said you wouldn't hit me."

They disappeared down the hall, and Jace laughed. "I'm not

going to clock you barehanded while you're defenseless and just standing there. But with a glove and you fighting back? Sure. And maybe you'll burn off some of that excess energy."

Gabriel looked at me once they were gone. "You okay?"

"Yeah."

"Whatever you're thinking, it's not true. She's going to love you just as much as the rest of us."

The words got tangled up in my brain, just like they always did. It was less often now, but conscious words were always harder. And no matter how much work I did to make them easier, I'd always struggle. Anxiety rattled through my limbs and made my hands shake. I put down my sketchbook.

Slowly, I focused my mind and looked at Gabriel. "Are... *you* okay?" The words were slow.

He let out a strangled laugh. "Not even close."

"Really?"

Gabriel sank into a chair across the room. "I was just talking, and it's exactly what Asher said. Like the best thing you've ever scented in the world. And I looked up and saw her. I just *knew*. She's mine. And I might laugh at Ash to help him keep sane, but I'm about five minutes away from where he is."

I smiled, my fingers tightening on my sketchbook. "Do you need a punch too?"

Smirking, he stood. "I'll let you know. For now, I'm going to punish myself on the treadmill for a while."

He left, and I sat in the sun. The peace I normally felt sitting here was gone. Time to go. I made sure I had all my drawing supplies before passing through the kitchen to the back door. Our townhome on the west side of the city had a long and narrow backyard, and what used to be a carriage house and garage was now my studio. Both floors. We had a new garage.

Since I was the only one of us that didn't work outside the home, it made sense. The bottom floor contained all my supplies. Giant hunks of rock and tools. A pulley system to get the stone up to the second floor where the glass ceiling gave me better light to sculpt by.

I already had a piece of marble on the second floor, which is what I'd been sketching before they dropped the news we might have found our Omega. The beginnings of a new commission. Nerves twisted low in my stomach, along with hope. Just a tiny seed of it, like a spark of light that refused to be ignored now that it had appeared.

But I couldn't start sculpting. The design wasn't ready and I felt too unsettled. Still, I couldn't simply sit in the house like it was a normal day. It was very much not a normal day. Everything could change, and it could be amazing, or it could...

I leaned against my workbench and pulled out my phone. Asher had spoken to us about Sloane when we decided to move to Slate City. How they'd been friends, how she'd disappeared, and how she danced here. I remembered her a little from conservatory. We hadn't been friends. I knew her in that way you vaguely knew people in school without *knowing* them. But I hadn't looked into her more than that.

Now I did.

SLOANE GLASS

I typed her name into the search bar.

Immediately, her face popped up in the results, and the image hit me in the gut. The photo displayed most prominently didn't feature her looking at the camera. She was mid-movement, head thrown back and hair flying, arms crossed delicately in front of her, neck arched, legs showing her bending *back* into the movement. She was breathtaking.

Another image showed what must have been her picture for Slate City Ballet. A small mysterious smile and looking at the camera playfully. Her eyes were so blue. So *fucking* blue. Nearly violet. And this was only an image.

The anxiety in my body eased.

I knew there was no way to tell a scent match from an image alone. In spite of that, I felt something when I looked at her.

Blowing out a breath, I put my phone away. As tempted as I was to go down the trail of learning everything about this beautiful Omega, I wanted to know *her* and not what other people said about her.

Too many people made decisions about me before they knew me. I wouldn't do the same.

Opening my sketchbook up again, I spread it out on the workbench. Something clicked in my head, a problem I hadn't quite been able to solve about the sculpture I was designing. Not a full idea, but getting there. Suddenly, my sketching felt easy, and that little pinprick of hope grew brighter.

CHAPTER SEVEN

SLOANE

The hot tea in my hand wasn't nearly enough to help the sleep clinging to my eyes. But I would suffer through it. I knew firsthand what getting addicted to coffee this early in the season would do to me. And given that this week was already going to be painful, I wasn't going to sign up for caffeine withdrawals voluntarily.

Not to mention coffee sometimes made me jittery, and I was already plenty jittery because of what I knew was about to happen.

After I left Petra, I picked up some ice bags, went back to my apartment, and prepped my shoes for today before refreshing myself on my notes for *Giselle* and going through some of the more difficult sequences at a lower intensity.

This show was going to be a delicate balance between pushing my body to do everything it possibly could and making sure I could still walk.

I shook my head. Realistically, this was a mistake. During a normal season we rehearsed a show for at least a month before opening. I didn't really appreciate being pressed into something so... challenging. No one had said anything yet, but my guess was others felt the same.

Ian knew what he was doing, and it would be fine once we got the hang of it. But it felt like getting shoved from a horse-drawn carriage onto a high-speed train. The *only* reason this would work was because we'd staged it before, and most of the company was the same.

I glanced around the plaza. No sign of Asher's motorcycle. Yet, at least. I hitched my bag higher on my shoulder and reached the door a few seconds after some girls from the corps.

The rehearsal breakdown was already on the bulletin board, people walking by and finding which studio they would go to.

The corps would work with the staff *répétiteurrés* and the principals would be working with Ian.

But first, class.

Class happened every day. It was our way to center and warm ourselves up. Review technique and prepare for whatever was ahead of us during the rehearsal day. And though it wasn't a rule, people usually stayed in the spot they picked the first day of the season.

I made my way to the corner, sipping my tea before stretching a bit and getting my shoes on. Dion dropped his bag dramatically and bent over to touch his toes. "Feeling better?"

"Yes and no," I mumbled. "Guess we'll see what happens today."

One thing I knew for sure. Asher West wouldn't let this simmer between us. He'd never been one to beat around the bush, and I doubted our time apart had changed that. Once it was settled—whichever way it went—we could figure the rest out.

I blew out a breath in relief. Strange that it made me feel better, but it did. The inevitability of us crashing together was so much simpler than feeling like everything was up in the air. Because it was a sure thing.

Dion smirked. "I don't know what that thought was, but keep thinking *that*."

A laugh burst out of me. "Why?"

"Because that's the first time you've actually fucking relaxed since yesterday?"

I glared at him. He only grinned. "Stop knowing me so well."

"Can't, Lo. Too late for that."

Across the room, Asher entered the studio, our eyes snapping together like someone turned a spotlight on the two of us. A switch flipped, and we were just... aware.

He smiled, but even from here, I saw it didn't reach his eyes. It wasn't anger this time. Something else entirely. My heart stuttered. What did he think? Could I ever fix it?

That was the height of my fear. That I'd waited too long, and I couldn't fix what I'd broken, no matter if I'd done it for the right reason.

Claire came rushing in at the last second, dropping her bag and getting her shoes on seconds before Madame Hubert came in. "You okay?" I whispered.

"Yeah. Addison has a cold and I lost track of time. Plus, traffic."

Madame Hubert tapped her cane on the floor, and the entire company came to attention. Class was familiar. Class was a safe place. Even with the chaos swirling around outside of it, there was value in having this be the same. It never changed.

We changed. What we could do on a given day. Our mood. The struggles of a piece or in rehearsal. But every day we all started in the same place. You could have the worst day ever, and it was made better because you knew you could start over in the morning.

It went by too quickly, and before I knew it we were bowing, chatter rising and everyone grabbing their gear to move to smaller studios.

The principal studio was one floor up. Asher left first. I followed the trail of his scent, stomach growling because I wanted the cookies he smelled like. I'd been so nervous I hadn't eaten breakfast. Later though? Later, I needed some fucking sugar.

He stood by the back barre, looking down at his phone before I approached him. Dion had been behind me, and though he was in our group, he kept his distance. The traitor. Claire was in a different studio today.

I set my bag down gently.

"Sloane." Asher's voice was quiet.

"Hi."

He reached out to touch me and stopped. I had to stifle the whine that rose, because not touching him felt just as wrong as touching him did. Nothing about this was *right* yet, and I hated it.

"I didn't ask for us to be paired," he whispered. "If you don't want to dance with me—"

"*No.*"

The hope in his eyes was painful. "God, I missed you."

Tears pricked my eyes, and I wrapped my arms around myself. The others were entering the room. "I missed you too."

Asher stepped into my space. His scent filled every crevice around me. Sweet and warm. Nothing had ever felt like this. He lowered his voice so no one could hear him but me. "I am never going to be able to make it through this day if I can't touch you," he breathed. "Please."

One nod was all it took.

He pulled me into his arms again. Gentler than yesterday, but his hands betrayed him, the way his fingers tightened and released like he had to remind himself we weren't alone. He let out a shuddering breath as we both relaxed and my body melted into his.

"When rehearsal is over, you and I are going to talk about this." No room for argument. "Understood?"

"Yes."

So slowly it nearly felt like slow motion, Ash turned his head and brushed his lips across my cheek. "No running away."

The only reason I wasn't perfuming right now was the suppressant I took this morning. It wasn't that I was embarrassed for perfuming, but when you were in rehearsal with twenty other people, perfuming was distracting. Plus, it was no one else's business.

"Like old times until then?" He pulled back and smiled, more light in his eyes now.

"Like old times."

Ian strode in followed by a woman in dance gear. His choreography assistant. "Stagger your groups," he called, pointing to spaces on the floor. "I know this is going to be tough. Anyone here who has *no* knowledge of the choreography?"

Thankfully no one raised their hand. I wasn't the only one who'd been frantically reviewing notes and videos the past couple of weeks.

"Good. It's going to be a long day, and we need to get through act one. We'll review the choreo, see where everyone is so we can refine and dictate the rest of the week as we see fit." His eyes fell on me. "Good of you to be on time, Miss Glass."

I flushed, but said nothing. Beside me, I felt Asher look over. Now wasn't the time to explain that particular dig.

That was about as much warning as he gave us. We began at the beginning, moving through the principal choreography.

Muscle memory was a hell of a thing. When you danced as much as we did, it was almost better than your *actual* memory. All of us were a little off, but for going from zero to sixty, we weren't half bad.

The first time Ash put his hands on my waist to help me turn. The first lift. The first time he looked at me as Albrecht the love struck prince, I thought I would pass out. The passion in his gaze and body was entirely real.

It terrified me as much as it made me bloom. I trusted Asher with my body. He would never let me fall, even if it meant falling himself.

Dion kept making faces at me when Ian wasn't looking, nearly making me laugh. I had to glare at him to tell him to knock it off. The last thing I needed was Ian pissed at me for *two* things. Especially if he was still annoyed at me being late.

But mostly, I floated through the day, time marked only by the time Asher was touching me and the time he wasn't. I couldn't keep my head straight because he had his *hands on me* and it was what I wanted.

My body ached, and my toes were *definitely* bleeding, but I found it hard to care when I spent the whole day wrapped in warmth and the scent of baking chocolate.

Still, by the time we finished, the sun had set and every part of me hurt.

Ian looked at all of us, sweating just as much as we were, considering he'd displayed most of the choreo. "Well done. I know this isn't easy, and I promise this will be the hardest rehearsal period of the year. But if we can make it through this, it will be a whole new way of working for SCB. More shows means more income, and the more we can do with it.

"I know this isn't ideal, and I know no one here was happy with the speed. But I've seen your work, and I wouldn't have chosen this path if I didn't think we could be successful. I plan on being here with you all for a long time. Good work. I'll see you tomorrow."

He was fired up and passionate. Despite not being his biggest fan, even I was impressed by his work ethic and the belief we could actually do something which seemed impossible.

Dion grabbed my hand. "You were on fucking fire, you know that?"

"What do you mean?"

He snorted, which made me laugh. "I mean that you made that look effortless. If everyone in this company didn't love the shit out of you, I'd tell you to watch your back."

My eyebrows rose into my hairline. Before I could say anything, an arm snaked around my waist. "He's right. I would have said you performed this yesterday."

"I just reviewed the choreo notes from a couple seasons ago. I was the understudy for Giselle and Myrtha."

A low laugh vibrated through my entire body. "You were still incredible."

Dion looked back and forth between the two of us, his eyes landing on mine in question. I nodded, and he smiled. "I'll see you guys tomorrow?"

"Sure thing," Ash said, arm still around my waist. "Now—"

"Not here," I said quietly and pulled away.

He followed me when I grabbed my bag and left, weaving through the building to where I knew no one would be. Down a couple levels, in the dim, black-painted halls behind the theater's main stage. The light was low, spilling out from a couple of the rooms down here, and somehow it made it easier than standing in full brightness.

I dropped my bag on the ground and kept going a bit before I wilted against the wall. Asher's bag hit the ground next to mine. His eyes told me there was no way to avoid this any longer. As much as I wanted it over with, I wanted to hide from him and that gaze.

Bracing one hand on the wall, he slipped the other behind my neck, gently tilting my face up so I could see him. "It's just you and me, blue. Help me understand."

Nowhere to run now.

CHAPTER EIGHT

SLOANE

I didn't say anything at first, overwhelmed by the closeness of his body and mouth. After a whole day of dancing and being teased, it was almost too much.

Fingers squeezed the back of my neck once. "Talk to me."

"I don't know what to say."

"Want to start with why you disappeared? Why I'm just finding out about *this*?" He released me to gesture between us.

The memory was so fucking clear, even now. Looking through the studio window and seeing Asher with Vivian. A true, genuine smile on his face before he pulled her in and kissed her. The warmth that filled me, knowing he was finally happy.

And then everything else.

"I'm scared," I whispered.

His terror mirrored my own. "What did I do?" The agony in his eyes made my chest ache. "If you're afraid of me, Sloane, I won't know what to do. Please tell me what I did to make you walk away from this. Because the thought of you being in pain this long is destroying me."

"No," I shook my head. "It wasn't you. Not like that. I'm just..."

Asher hauled me against him. His arms wrapped around my shoulders, and every instinct in me relaxed. *Safe.* The whine I'd been suppressing all day came out of me, and his answering purr had me burying my face in his neck. "I don't care how long it takes, blue. I don't care if what you have to say makes me hate myself. I will stand here and hold you as long as you need to tell me. But first, I want to know why you're scared."

One breath. Two. Not having to look at him helped. "I'm scared you'll think I was silly. But I'm more scared you won't forgive me."

"That's not going to happen."

Another whine. "How do you know?"

"Did you murder someone?"

I choked out a laugh. "No."

"Did you cause irreparable damage to anyone's life?"

"Besides ours?"

"Fuck," he murmured the word into my hair. "Yes, besides ours."

There wasn't a way to shake my head with him holding me so close, but I tried. "Then no."

"Then I can't think of a single thing which would make me *not* forgive you."

Tears flooded my eyes even as I tried to hold them back. "I left because you were happy."

He stiffened, but just as quickly I felt him check the instinct and relax his body. Another purr, this time softer, to keep us both easy. "What do you mean?"

I curled my fingers into the back of his shirt, inhaling the sweet scent of chocolate and butter. The softer scent of batter. Every breath was a confirmation that this was good. Right. Okay.

"It was my first heat. I thought I was sick when I missed those classes, but it was really my heat. Didn't have enough time to make real arrangements, so I rode it out." Wasn't exactly fun, but it was what it was.

Ash ran one hand up and down my spine, the motion soothing. "That makes sense now."

I nodded. "I came back. I was there at the studio, and I saw you through the window with Vivian." Ash stiffened again, and this time he didn't relax. "You were so fucking happy, Ash. The smile on your face? It was beautiful. And I was happy for you. You kissed her, and it was like the sun had come out."

The man holding me hadn't had a good childhood. There was more pain in his past than I wanted to think about, and it was a miracle he'd turned out this way. As a caring, loving person instead of the monster he could have grown into.

"Then I stepped through the door, and your scent—" A hiccuped breath. "I knew. And I had to decide right then. Before you'd seen me and before my scent had a chance to make it into the space. I couldn't do it. After everything you'd been through, you'd finally found someone who made you happy, and I'd *helped*

54

you find her. I didn't want to rip everything out from under you when you'd just found them. Or worse... for you to see me and be disappointed I was your match."

He still held me and still purred, his cheek lowered to press against mine. But his hold tightened. Like by keeping me in his arms we could somehow go back and fix it.

"And after. Later. When I thought about whether I'd made the right choice, all I could think about was the look on your face. Would it be anger? That same disappointment? Something else worse? And the more time went by, the harder it was to overcome. I didn't look for you, because if I had, I would have—" Then, more quietly. "I know I'm a coward for it. And even if you do forgive me, I'm not sure I forgive myself."

"Sloane." His lips brushed my temple. "Of course I forgive you. Am I pissed at you for leaving? Yes. Am I pissed you would think I would be *disappointed* you're my match? A little. But I am not and never will be angry with you for trying to protect yourself. Especially when you thought you were doing it to help me."

He pulled back to look at me, and there wasn't disappointment there. I saw the emotions flickering there. The hurt and the frustration, but no regret and no disappointment.

"Do you believe me?" He asked.

"Yes."

Ash nodded once. "Good. Now it's my turn to talk." In one movement, he spun me so I faced the wall. One hand in my hair, pulling my neck back so he could reach it and speak into my ear. Every part of me was pressed against every part of him, and there was nowhere to go.

This was Asher the Alpha, and my Omega *loved* it.

His voice was near a growl. "You don't think if I'd known we were scent-sympathetic I would have never looked at anyone else? One breath from you and I would have been yours."

I shook my head, or tried. I couldn't move with his hand in my hair, his lips at my ear, and he had no idea what it was doing to me. "You didn't want me. We were just friends."

"*I* never said we were just friends. When you told people that, I kept my mouth shut, because I wasn't going to risk scaring you off or changing our friendship," he growled, the sound vibrating through me down to my toes. "There was never a time I didn't want you. I wanted you more than anything."

"Ash."

"*Anything*."

"If that's true—"

"It is."

"Why didn't you say anything?"

"You wanted scent sympathy. Desperately. No matter what I thought, I didn't believe you'd be with me because we weren't a match. So I tried to make myself move on, telling myself you were better off. But if we'd both made it to graduation and hadn't found it, I would have said something."

"What about Vivian?"

A slow kiss just below my ear. The suppressant was wearing off, and perfume filled the air around us. "Me trying to move on. My own desperation because I was so close to snapping and telling you everything. I didn't want to lose you, Sloane. Whatever way I could be near you. Every instinct I had told me you'd run if I admitted I wanted you. And after you left," he paused. "After you disappeared... it felt like Vivian was all I had. But in the end we were better friends, and she agreed. Didn't even last a year. We didn't have enough in common, and if I'm telling the truth, I was still in love with you."

I closed my eyes against the truth. "So I ruined everything for the last five years."

"No." Ash turned me back around, arms braced on either side of my head so there was still nowhere to look but him. "If you're a coward then so am I. If I'd told you I was interested at all, or had been less afraid of taking a risk, you never would have thought I'd be disappointed with you."

His eyes dropped to my lips, and I didn't even think about stopping him. Ash kissed me and held nothing back. Every moment in the last five years I'd wondered what it would be like... nothing even came close.

I lifted my arms to wrap them around his neck, and he let me, taking the opportunity to draw me in once more. He tilted my face and deepened the kiss so I couldn't even *think*, put me exactly where he wanted me, purr loud in the silence of mouths meeting.

Kissing Asher was like dancing a tango. Slow and smooth, filled with passion you knew was leading somewhere inevitable. Following the lead and not caring where it went because it was all pleasure.

Something snapped between us.

Suddenly I couldn't take slow anymore. My hands sank into his hair and pulled him closer. This Alpha was *mine,* and I needed him to show me. It felt like we'd been kissing forever. No awkwardness or hesitation. Just pure desire.

Asher lifted me, hands coming under my ass to press me against the wall. I clung to him, our mouths never stopping or slowing. There were five years of kisses to make up for, and I didn't care if I gave up oxygen to do it.

This was what we could have had. "I'm sorry," I whispered between kisses. "I'm sorry."

He groaned, breaking away from me and pressing his mouth into my neck. Pulled the strap of my leotard off my shoulder and dragged his lips over my skin. I wanted his mouth everywhere.

Everywhere.

"Are you going to run again?" Words and breath burned hot against my skin.

"No."

That was the truth. I was done running. From him, his pack, and everything else. I'd already fucked up enough. Like hell was I going to destroy this. I was still scared, but I didn't care.

Ash kissed back up my neck and beneath my jaw, every press of his lips at once reverent and wild. "Tell me you're mine."

"I'm yours," I breathed. It was true.

A low rumble, somewhere between a growl and a purr. *"Mine."*

If I hadn't been perfuming already, that would have done it.

Ash kissed me again, hard. His mouth was punishing and pleasuring, marking himself on me and taking what was already his. He kissed me until we were both gasping.

"Come home with me. Meet my pack."

He still had me pressed up against the wall, my legs wrapped around his hips. Carefully, I dragged my hands over his shoulders. "I can't. It's not that I don't want to," I said quickly. "I do. You don't even know how much."

"Then..."

I curled forward enough to lean my forehead on his shoulder. "If I go home with you, I don't know what will happen. I'm exhausted. I can't spend half the night having sex and then wake up and have this kind of rehearsal again."

Where his mouth touched my neck, I felt him smirk. "You're so sure it would be sex."

"You're so sure it wouldn't?"

He laughed softly. "Fair enough."

"I need to ice my feet and sleep. Speaking of, I should probably get out of my pointe shoes."

Ash put me down, but not before he let me slide down every inch of his body. "Then I'll come home with you."

"You don't have to." I sat down on the floor and gingerly began to take off my shoes. My feet hurt, and I wasn't surprised to see some blood. "You don't have to say you're tired too, I know."

"Sloane." Asher's tone had me looking up at him, and he crouched down beside me, dropping another kiss on my lips. I leaned into it, not quite believing it was real. "No matter what caused it, I haven't seen you in five years. If you don't *want* me to come home with you, tell me that. Otherwise, like hell is my Alpha going to let you walk away from me. I need you in my arms, even if that doesn't mean finally learning what you sound like when you come."

Heat dropped through my body, a flush rising to my skin, and his smile told me he knew exactly what his words would do. That's why he said them. "Are you sure you don't have to go home?"

One side of his mouth tipped up. "I've got an extra set of clothes in my bag."

"Are those normally there, or just since yesterday?"

"I should probably tell you I put them there for you, but I usually have extras in case."

Most dancers did. And he didn't know, but it actually made

me feel better that it wasn't just for me. I hissed as I took off the other shoe. I got soft socks on and my normal shoes. But it wasn't comfortable.

"You okay?"

"I will be."

"I can carry you." My side-eye made him laugh. "Come on."

He wove our fingers together as we grabbed our bags and headed for the stairs. That simple movement, like it was a given. I had a vision of us walking to our conservatory classes hand in hand, and it stole my breath away.

"I—"

Asher squeezed my hand once. "I know. We'll talk about it."

Being with him, Gabriel, and the others was complicated because of the company. I didn't want to hide them, but I also didn't want it to seem like I was getting benefits. Especially if Ian's crosshairs were on me.

"Will they like me?" I didn't have to clarify who I meant.

A laugh burst out of Ash, echoing in the stairwell. "That's not a question."

"Sure it is."

"I went home yesterday and asked Roman to punch me in the face so I didn't try to find you. Gabriel was calmer, but only because he had to be. All of them, even the two of them who haven't met you yet, are going to be jealous I'm with you tonight."

Out in the plaza, we headed toward his bike. I'd ridden it before, but now I was up close, I wasn't sure it was the same. He shifted his bag around, grabbing his leather jacket and putting the bag in a compartment beneath the seat. "I didn't bring extra clothes specifically for this reason. But I did bring an extra helmet just in case."

I blushed, and he smiled, brushing a piece of hair out of my face and behind my ear.

"What's your address? Before I turn you into a backpack."

I gave him the address. "A backpack?"

He winked. "Pressed up against my back and holding on for dear life."

Ash helped me with my helmet before putting on his jacket

and helmet. I took the opportunity through the dark visor to just look at him. It was good he was coming with me. I didn't want to be alone either.

"Okay, backpack." His voice was louder than I expected in my ear as he climbed on. "Let's go."

I climbed on behind him. Ash didn't hesitate to reach back and pull my hands around his waist. "Don't let go."

There wasn't any chance of that now.

Asher revved the engine before speeding away, and my shriek was mixed with his laughter.

CHAPTER NINE

SLOANE

*H*aving Asher in my apartment was... weird. Walking in with him behind me made me look at it with different eyes. I'd decorated the place for me, and it was comfortable. But I wondered what he thought of it. If it looked like a place worth spending five years away from him.

"Where's the ice?"

"Can I get you a drink or something?"

He raised one eyebrow and pointed at the couch. "Sit your ass down on the couch and tell me where your foot tub is."

I stared at him, testing whether or not he was serious. He was. Faster than I thought possible, he closed the distance between us and lifted me off my feet, carrying me over to the couch and setting me down. "Where is it?"

"Under the kitchen sink."

"Okay." He leaned in and kissed my forehead. "Stay here."

I was too tired to even think about disobeying. My feet needed this sooner rather than later. I could only soak them in the ice for fifteen minutes or things got a little rough.

Ash kneeling in front of me and gently peeling my battered feet out of my shoes and socks did things to me. I winced, and he slowed down. "Kit?"

"My bathroom. Down the hall, through the bedroom."

He came back and began to clean my feet. After the ice bath, I would bandage them. The mixture of ice and epsom salt would help, but regardless, this week would be painful. "I'm not sure this is a good idea," I said softly. "A week to do this? I don't understand why he's pushing it so hard. Why not bring us back sooner and do a proper rehearsal run?"

That first meeting with Ian and Mark where Ian had gotten angry was not only a meeting with him. It was to sign a waiver for extra rehearsal time and the run of *Giselle*. But what he'd said and what we were doing were opposites.

61

Our normal schedule was company class and two three-hour blocks of rehearsal split with a lunch break. Today we'd... I glanced at the kitchen clock. Holy fuck, we'd done almost twelve hours today. No wonder I was in pain.

Not only the length of time, but in a normal rehearsal run we were bouncing between different shows. Switching it up meant different choreography so we didn't work the exact same spots on our feet. And different roles made it so we had more rest. The same show over and over for double the length of time each day? Brutal.

Asher glanced up before guiding one foot into the cold water. "He couldn't because of the current contracts."

I frowned. "What do you mean?"

"He couldn't call you in earlier because of the contracts at SCB, and he didn't have the power to change them. Next year I imagine he will, but that's why we all signed the waiver for extended rehearsal time. Ian wants to make a splash. If this isn't the best season Slate City Ballet has ever done, he'll consider it a failure. I didn't even think about it when I signed it. Now I'm questioning everything."

"Perfect." My sarcasm dripped off the word. "You've worked with him before?"

"I have. Not in a couple of years, and he wasn't my favorite, but he is good at what he does."

With my feet in the bath, he grabbed his phone and stared down at it for a minute. "They okay?"

He grinned. "They're jealous, but fine. And I'm starting a timer."

When he sat down and pulled my body close so I could lean on him, I had a flashback. Us, just like this, watching a movie. It wasn't the first time we'd been this close, but it was different now. I wanted so much more, but I hadn't lied to him. Exhaustion weighed down everything, including my eyelids. So I rested against him, focusing on the warmth of his skin and not the pain of my feet being frozen off.

I drifted, Ash's hand brushing up and down my arm until he shifted me. "Times up, sweetheart."

A soft whine left my throat. Him calling me sweetheart made my stomach tumble. "Okay."

I lifted my feet out of the ice, skin red, and reached for the kit. He took it out of my hand before I could even open it, drying my feet off.

Asher lifted me off the couch and carried me into the bedroom before setting me on the bed. "Take a quick shower, and we'll work on your feet. I'm ordering us both food. Is Indian still your favorite?"

I nodded.

"Good." He kissed me like he couldn't stop himself from doing it. "Quickly. So you're not on your feet long."

That was an order I followed. The longer I could keep off my feet, the better in the long run. I exited the bathroom in my towel to find Asher standing by the bed. "Hi."

The way his eyes consumed me made it very difficult to cling to the idea of not having sex tonight. I *wanted* to have sex tonight. But I also wanted to survive to actually spend time with Asher and his pack.

"Come here." He guided me to the bed and sank down in front of me with the bandage kit.

My face flushed. I wasn't sure if I was more vulnerable because I was tired, but him touching my feet and caring for me felt... overwhelming. "I can do it."

Ash only glanced up once. "I still know how to take care of feet, blue."

"But—"

Reaching out, he caught my hand and held it. "It's going to be strange," he said quietly. "Even though we want to act like no time has passed, we both know it has. Trust that I won't do anything I don't want to do, and I won't force you into something that makes you uncomfortable. But also trust that my Alpha needs to take care of you right now. Please."

He held my gaze, and I got lost in the blue of his eyes, the richness of his scent. "Okay."

It didn't take him long to bandage my feet, and better than I could. "The food will be here soon. If you don't mind, I'll take a shower too."

"Of course." It gave me a chance to pull on some underwear and a silky, purple nightgown that was too short to be decent. Would I be torturing him a little? Yeah. But I would be torturing myself too.

I rubbed some lotion in and took a look at myself in the mirror. Everything was different, but I still felt the same. Surely there should be a mark on me somewhere representing how much had shifted...

The bathroom door opened behind me. Ash stepped out with a towel around his waist and the remnants of the shower still dripping down his chest. So we were both torturing each other.

"Fuck me," he groaned. "I can't sleep in your bed."

"We've slept in the same bed before," I pointed out.

"You weren't wearing *that*." He pointed, and I froze.

The motion had revealed one of his tattoos. He had a few. Some on his shoulders, arms, and over his heart. One on his wrist. And now, apparently, one on his ribs.

I would know that symbol anywhere. Could find it about a hundred different places in my house right now. A nothing symbol. At once curvy and sharp, a little like a backwards five, it was something I'd always doodled. It didn't mean anything.

Asher had my doodle tattooed on his ribs. I reached out to touch it, having crossed the distance without even realizing it. "When did you get this?"

"Three years ago," he whispered. "I wanted a piece of you, and it was the only thing that felt right. It's from the last note you left me."

"Ash, this is..."

One finger lifted my chin. The depth of emotion in his eyes was terrifying. Mind blowing. It completely stole my breath.

The doorbell rang before our lips could meet. "That's our food," he said with a grin. "Now get off your feet before I have to pick you up again."

I rolled my eyes, but did as he asked. As soon as my body hit the bed, I felt it. Exhaustion pulling me down once more.

Ash's chuckle rolled through my sleep-darkened mind, and his arm slid under me, lifting me to sitting. He was now in only a pair of boxer briefs, and I didn't remember him changing. "Any other time I'd let you sleep. But you need to eat something. I know you haven't."

"And how do you know that?"

He didn't bother to take things out of the takeout containers, instead handing me a plastic dish of chicken curry. "Because every time we ever walked to class together you would never eat because you said you didn't like how it made you feel during class. Or are you going to lie to me and say you had something other than that tea this morning?"

I glared at him. It wasn't like I could lie about it, considering we'd been together since then. He knew I hadn't.

The first bite reminded my body *exactly* how long it had been since I'd eaten. I groaned, digging into the curry like a starving woman. "Fuck me, this is good."

Ash didn't say anything. He was eating his just as quickly. I wanted to consume so much more food than the one container. But I also didn't want to make myself sick. "Will you judge me if I eat the leftovers for breakfast?"

"Saves me from having to make sure we get food on the way to class."

I made a face. He wasn't wrong. I didn't like eating first thing in the morning before class. It made me feel heavy in my steps. "Maybe I'll bring it for lunch instead." Suddenly I blinked. "Ian literally didn't let us break for lunch today, did he?"

"He did not." Ash didn't sound happy about it. "But it won't happen again. No matter how hard we're working, we need to eat."

"What's going to stop him?"

A smirk. "Gabriel."

My eyes went wide. "Will that get you in trouble with Ian?"

"I don't care if it does. He wants to push us, he can. But he's not going to harm people while we're around. Especially now that you're here with us." He gathered up the dishes and took the leftovers out to the refrigerator. "My Omega will not go hungry because Ian has a chip on his shoulder about the contracts and company transfer."

My Omega.

I loved hearing that. My whole body tingled with it. I was somebody's. Someone *chose* me.

Asher pulled back the blankets on my bed and got me underneath them before turning off the lights and joining me. He pulled me against his body, tangling our limbs together. My head fit under his chin, and he was *hard*.

Stroking my fingers along his spine, I smiled into his skin. "Struggling?"

"You have no fucking idea." His tone was teasing.

My whole body relaxed, realizing I was safe with Asher and I could sleep. Anxiety that had been living under my skin for years was gone now. We could have been doing this the whole time.

"I'm sorry, Ash," I whispered. "You have no idea how sorry I am."

He rolled me underneath him, whole body pinning me to the bed. "I'm sorry too."

"But—"

A kiss silenced me, and we let it happen, deepening until we had to pull back or it would go further. "Listen." Our breath was loud in the darkness, both of us catching it. "There is still more to talk about. A lot happened to both of us in the last five years. Maybe there was a reason for it. But what we *can't* do? Is keep dwelling on the fact that it happened. It did. No matter the reason, and no matter whose actions got us here."

"I know. I'm just not sure I can move on so quickly when I feel so guilty."

His lips met my skin, and I gasped. "You're here with me, blue. Nowhere else. What happened before doesn't matter as long as we're together moving forward. We'll talk about it when we need to, but I don't want you to think you need to keep apologizing to me. I forgave you and I meant it." Then, after a moment. "I'm sorry I didn't tell you how I felt. Maybe things would have gone differently if I had. If you look at it that way, I drove you away."

I tensed, and he kissed me softly. "See? You don't agree. And there's about a hundred ways both of us can spin it to make it our fault. So let's agree to give each other and ourselves some grace while we figure this out. Because I am not letting you go, Sloane."

"Please don't."

He rolled us back to the side, keeping me close. I let myself sink down into sleep, but I still heard him. Like a vow or a prayer. "Not a chance in hell."

CHAPTER TEN

ASHER

I opened my eyes and had to hold back my purr. The dim light told me it was morning, though our alarm hadn't gone off yet. Good. I didn't want to move with Sloane tucked against my body, a tempting blend of curves and silk, and that scent I couldn't get enough of.

At first I thought a sound had woken me, but I didn't hear anything now. Fine with me. I tightened my arms around *my* Omega.

Pounding broke through the quiet. Insistent and intense. That must be what woke me. It sounded like someone was banging on the door to her apartment.

Looking down at Sloane, she hadn't moved. I couldn't stop myself from pressing a kiss to her forehead. She was so tired, and though there was nothing I wanted more than to take her home and fuck her into my mattress and have the others join, I would happily hold her until we got through these rehearsals.

I slowly extricated myself from her and made sure the blankets were around her before I left the bedroom.

The pounding started again as I neared the front door. An angry voice came with it. "*Sloane.*"

He stopped banging when I undid the chain and deadbolt. I opened the door without bothering to put on more clothes. The Alpha in me wanted this man to know I'd been in bed with my Omega. Her scent was all over me, and it was going to stay that way.

"Who the fuck are you?" He asked.

About my height, sandy hair, and a beard, I couldn't deny he was good looking, but I didn't feel even a shred of jealousy toward the man showing up at Sloane's door this early. That was how inevitable we were. She was mine. *Ours.* End of story.

I tilted my head. "I could ask you the same thing."

"I'm her boyfriend."

"Funny," I said. "Considering I'm one of her scent-sympathetic Alphas, I doubt that's true."

Rage entered his eyes. "I don't care who you are. *SLOANE,* get the hell out here." He raised his voice and took a step forward.

I matched that step. "If you think I'm letting you in here right now, you're mistaken."

"What's going on?" Sloane appeared in the hallway, still in that purple nightgown which made her look fucking edible. Her voice was soft with sleep, but as soon as she saw who was standing at the door, she paled.

Anger that rivaled this man's burned low in my gut. She was afraid of him. And if he hurt her, past, present, or future, he would have to deal with me.

"Craig? What are you doing here?"

He sneered. "You haven't answered any of my calls or messages. Now I know why." It was aimed at me, and I didn't care. "Thought I'd come get the money you owe me and find out why the fuck you're avoiding me."

Sloane crossed her arms and came to stand next to me. For the moment I refrained from touching her. She needed to stand on her own for this. "Not everything is about you, Craig. First, I just entered rehearsal season, and you would know that if you listened to anything I told you on our *final* date. Second, we're done. Why the hell would I answer you? And third, I don't want to talk to you. Thought my silence would make that clear. I'll send you the money for the ticket today."

"Are you fucking serious?" Craig tried again to take a step forward, and I angled my body in front of Sloane. I didn't like the energy he had. "I don't even know what I did to make you walk away."

Just yesterday I asked myself the same thing. But I didn't think Sloane's answer would be the same.

"That's easy," she said. "You failed to show me the least bit of respect, Craig. You didn't even *notice* I wasn't walking behind you. I didn't move from where I almost tripped on the sidewalk. Thanks for not helping me, by the way, and you got all the way to the theater before you even looked. I'm not perfect, but I'm worth more than that."

Damn right.

His lip curled. "So you act like a bitch because *you* made us late and *you* chose to wear impractical shoes and I was trying to hurry because of a surprise I arranged *for you*? Really?"

The way Sloane's shoulders sagged made me itch to pull her into my arms. "I wanted to see the concert, Craig. You know I did. But I want to be worth more than a show." She shrugged. "I'm sorry."

It was clear he didn't accept her answer, but he didn't say it. His eyes did. I didn't like that look. "Fine. I want the money."

"I told you I'd send it later."

"I came all the way over here to show you that I'm trying, and hopefully figure out what was going on between us. The least you can do is actually keep up with your part of the bargain."

"I don't—"

I held out a hand to stop her speaking. "Go get my wallet," I told her quietly. "It's in my bag."

Like hell was I going to get it myself and leave her here with him, and I didn't think he'd take kindly to me shoving the door closed in his face. Craig was the worst kind of Alpha. He was a ticking time bomb ready to go off when it hurt someone the most. I wasn't willing for that person to be Sloane.

"You don't have to pay him for me."

I stared at her, telling her with my eyes I wasn't moving from this door, and I wasn't going to take no for an answer. She pressed her lips together, a blush staining her cheeks. As much as I loved seeing that pink there, I wasn't going to let her be embarrassed about this. The only person who should be embarrassed was the asshole at the door.

When she came back, she had a robe on over her nightgown, and my wallet was in her hand. I took it from her gently and opened it. I counted two-hundred dollars and held it out to him. I knew how much concert tickets were, and I doubted Craig had sprung for the good seats. "We done here?" I asked him.

For a second I thought he might hit me. The anger simmering in his gaze told me this went deeper than what was happening here. Instead, he went to open his mouth, looking at Sloane, and I put my body in front of hers again. "If the next words out of your mouth aren't 'Goodbye, Sloane,' you'll regret it."

He narrowed his eyes at me, jaw flexing before he turned his gaze back to my Omega. "Goodbye, Sloane. For now."

"We're done, Craig."

He didn't respond, stalking down the hallway. I didn't like that he was even in the building. But I shut the door and locked it, turning to lean against it and hold out my arms.

She came to me, and I tucked her against my chest, purr springing to life. As long as I lived, I'd never get tired of the way her body softened and eased against mine. "You okay?"

"Yeah. I can pay you back. I just didn't have cash."

"You'll do no such thing," I said. Keeping cash on me at all times was a habit I couldn't break. When you had a childhood like mine, you learned to make sure you always had a way out whenever you needed one. Often, a way out meant money.

In the bedroom, my phone's alarm went off, and I groaned. "I guess we can't go back to bed."

"No."

But I didn't release her. "You want to tell me about him?"

Sloane shrugged. "There's nothing to tell. I saw him on and off for a bit last season. Strictly friends with benefits, and we just kind of fizzled. I called him up recently. Mostly because he was familiar, and I was lonely. You heard the rest. I was just done. And the next morning you showed up."

Despite the pang in my heart from hearing her say she was lonely, I smiled into her hair. "I did."

"Sorry. I've barely looked at my phone. He said some stuff after I bailed on the concert, but I didn't think he was serious, just pissed off. I definitely didn't think he'd just show up."

"Can I see it?"

"Yeah, it's in my bag. I'm going to brush my teeth. I'll grab an extra for you."

Glancing at her, I made sure my tone was teasing. "You keep extra toothbrushes?"

"Everyone keeps extra toothbrushes."

"Not everyone, sweetheart."

Sloane narrowed her eyes. "I'll tell you one thing that hasn't changed in the last five years. I'm still not a morning person."

"Don't worry. We'll get you caffeine." My fingers twitched with the urge to reach out and touch her again, but I let her retreat, opting for her phone instead.

The battery was low, but it was still on. Her password hadn't changed. There were a couple of messages from her best friend, and I didn't read those. I only clicked on the messages from the asshole who woke us so rudely.

The more I scrolled, the more I saw red.

CRAIG

> I'm trying, Sloane. I really am. But I can't try if you won't fucking talk to me.

> I don't know what game you're playing with this silence, but once this little speed bump is worked out, I expect you to respond.

> Remember, there's a reason you came crawling back to me. No one else wants you.

> You think anyone's going to take a chance on you when all you do is ghost? You're fucking lucky I'm taking another chance on you. Now answer me.

The anger pouring through the messages was unreal. A few of them had me shaking so badly I had to consciously tell myself to relax or I would break her phone.

I took screenshots of the messages and opened a message to myself. My number had changed, but our old text thread opened. Nothing for longer than we'd been separated. But there was still an unsent message.

SLOANE

> I miss you.

Fuck. I'd already been determined to shower Sloane with love and every possible proof I wanted her. Seeing that message just made the need stronger.

I put in my new number and sent the pictures to myself.

Sloane handed me a toothbrush when I stepped into the bathroom, and I saw her toss back a purple pill. Stepping up behind her, I lifted the hair off her neck so I could taste her skin. I wanted to worship this woman. "You're taking suppressants?"

"This week? Yes. Would you rather me be perfuming in the studio all day?"

"Selfishly, yes. I want to bathe in your scent."

She smiled and met my eyes in the mirror. "Ian already doesn't love me. Let's not make it worse." And before I could ask, she shook her head. "I'll tell you later."

We got ready quickly, and it was familiar. But more than that, it was natural. There was no frustration of stepping over each other or annoyance about sharing a space, it simply *was*. And I couldn't wipe the smile off my face.

"Don't forget your lunch," I said, handing her a plastic bag with some of the leftover Indian containers.

"Right."

I tugged her under my arm. "Let's get out of here. I'll drop you off and go get us something caffeinated."

"Delivery service?"

"Perks of an Alpha with a motorcycle."

She laughed, locking the door behind her. "I think a car would work too."

"Yeah, but that's not as cool."

"You men and your *cool* toys."

"You better believe it." I smirked as I fitted her helmet on. "But the toys always work with you and never against you. Team players and all that."

Even through the gap in the helmet I could see her blush. This was going to be fun. I winked and made sure my new—and only—backpack was comfortable.

CHAPTER ELEVEN

SLOANE

True to his word, Asher dropped me off in front of the plaza and left, promising me something to inject caffeine into my veins and wake me up. It was probably a lost cause, but I didn't tell him that.

And I wasn't going to turn down the offer. My determination not to get addicted to caffeine wilted in the face of twelve hour rehearsals. Not even coffee was going to make up for that.

I glanced at the bulletin board to make note of the rehearsal spaces in case they changed, and they had. Along with a very particular note that there would be forty-five minutes for lunch.

A smile tugged at my lips. I guess it worked.

Sweet tobacco and vanilla wrapped around me, so much stronger than it had two days ago, and an arm reached around me to pin a new piece of paper to the bulletin board. I had absolutely no idea what it said.

Gabriel stood behind me, pulling back from the board and looking down at me. "Hello, Sloane," he said quietly.

"Hi."

He smiled, and now, this close to him, I saw his eyes were a warm green that erased whatever was left of my morning chill. "I promise I wasn't trying to corner you or waiting to catch you here."

"I... I didn't think that."

Once again he glanced in either direction. There wasn't anything wrong with being scent-sympathetic. But I was very aware of the appearance of it. Gabriel knew it too. Suddenly having the newest principal as a scent match could look strange.

"Could I speak to you for a moment?" The words were soft, but his eyes were heated. His hands flexed like he was resisting reaching for me.

I looked at my phone. There was still time, and now that Ash and I were okay, I was desperate to know the others. Part of me wasn't sure it could be as seamless as last night and this morning had been with Ash, but I wanted to find out. "Yeah."

All that heat shifted into warmth I wanted to drown in as he smiled. Then, lower. "Only if you want to, Sloane. There's no pressure here."

Anxiety fizzed in the tips of my fingers. More anticipation than nerves. "It's okay," I breathed. "I do."

Gabriel inclined his head, and I followed him away from the studio wing and into the administrative one. I almost never came over into this wing unless I needed to fix something with payroll or my contract. It was mostly empty this early.

We didn't run into anyone, thankfully. There would no doubt already be rumors about myself and Asher in the shoe room. And maybe us leaving the studio together yesterday. The ballet world was a vicious place for gossip, and no matter my fear-lessness when it came to dance, I preferred my private life to stay private.

He gestured to an open door. "My office is upstairs, but I don't want to keep you from rehearsal."

I shut the door behind us gently. "I'm not sure what Asher has told you about me—" My voice died in my throat when I turned. This wasn't Gabriel the Executive Director, this was Gabriel the *Alpha*.

"Ash has never said anything remotely bad about you. Even when he was in the dark and wanting to know why you'd disap-peared. But it seems like things are better now?" There was a teasing sparkle in his eye that I liked.

"They are."

He was older than Asher by a few years, and if I saw him on the street, I never would have said this was his job. Black henley with sleeves pushed up to the elbows and dark jeans that seemed too casual for SCB but worked for him. If everyone was a little more casual around here, I wouldn't care. Everyone could afford to loosen up a bit.

That included me.

We stared at each other, and I had no idea what to do. This small, warm room filled with his scent. I wanted to drink it in. I wanted to feel him against me the way I felt Ash.

I swallowed. "I am... not great at this. I have no idea what to do or say, but I want to know you. All of you."

Gabriel's eyes darkened with heat. "May I touch you?"

My heart skipped a beat. "Yes."

Reaching out one hand, he trailed his fingers down over my arm, heat sinking through my thin sweater. "I'm sorry we had to meet the way we did." A quick smile. "Or rather, that we scented each other the way we did. I would have preferred less of an audience."

"Are you going to show me why?" It was both a dare and an invitation. Everything about Gabriel told me the cool and calm Executive Director was a mask and fire burned underneath it.

Fuck me, I wanted to burn.

Gabriel tugged on my sweater just hard enough to get me to step closer. That was all he needed. One arm swept around my waist, the other guiding my face up to his.

No hesitation and no questions. He kissed me slowly and deliberately, hands holding me against his body exactly where he wanted me. Unhurried. He didn't have to say the word *mine* for me to feel it. I was his, and he would take the time kissing me any way he liked. The realization made me want to move—to press closer—and the way he held me prevented that.

The sharp sweetness of his scent swirled, tongue tracing my lips in an unspoken request to dance with mine.

And *fuck* what a dance.

Everyone in the company needed to retire. Gabriel's tongue was the star of the show now, and if he was this good at kissing my mouth...

I moaned. The sound was completely involuntary. I couldn't make myself do anything right now. Gabriel owned my body and soul for however long he wanted to have them. And still, a small voice told me *he's holding back*.

He smiled when we broke apart, whispering words against my lips. "Nice to meet you, little one."

My fingers curled into his shoulders. A fresh wave of heat dropped through me, along with desire I couldn't control. It was good I took the suppressants. I was already going to be hiding a wet spot in my tights.

"Nice to meet you."

Gabriel carefully stroked a hand over my hair, not messing up the bun it was in. "I know this seems like a lot to navigate, but I hope you know how happy we are."

"I want to meet everyone. The timing's not ideal."

"It's not. But we'll make it work." He leaned in, giving me plenty of time to stop him. I didn't. This kiss wasn't as deliberate. It was barely contained. Gabriel gathered me up, my feet lifting off the floor. So much fire rested on the other side of this carefully constructed facade. I felt it. Wanted it. Rehearsal be damned.

A low chuckle vibrated through me, followed by a rich purr. "I need to let you go, or this will be far more complicated."

"We can do complicated."

He set me down on my feet once more. "Yes, we can. And I promise we will."

I whined, my still-sleepy Omega brain craving warmth and darkness and cuddles far more than going to class. Gabriel's purr rose in volume. "I'll see you very soon."

"Promise?"

"Yes."

It was the only thing that allowed me to take a step back. I didn't look back in case I wasn't fully in control, and sprinted to the break room to shove the Indian food in the refrigerator.

Some members of the corps entered the studio at the same time I did, and if they noticed Gabriel's scent on me, they didn't say anything. Then again, his scent was far more obvious to me than everyone else.

Ash stood in my corner, and two iced coffee cups rested on the floor. Dion was on the other side by Claire. I smirked at him. "You know you're breaking a cardinal studio rule by changing spots."

"I know, but it's still early enough in the season that I hope people will forgive me. Besides, they said it was okay."

I looked over at Claire and Dion, who grinned at me and pretended ignorance. "I should have known you would be on his side immediately."

"Oh no," Claire said, lowering her voice. "We're on *your* side.

But he brought you coffee. And considering his scent is all over you, I think we made the right choice."

"I'm not the only one whose scent is on you," Ash said quietly, pressing the cold coffee into my hand. "Good."

Searching his eyes, I didn't know what I was looking for. Whether there would be some kind of resistance from him about Gabriel and I. Of course there wasn't. "Thank you for the coffee."

He reached down and squeezed my hand. "I hope you like it."

I didn't take a sip until I was already on the floor, packing my shoes with extra padding. Gel toe pads *and* wool. Just shy of the padding being too much for my foot and the shoe together.

Blueberry and coffee exploded across my tongue together. My head whipped up to find Ash smothering his laughter. It wasn't my normal order. I didn't even know you could *get* blueberry coffee. It was delicious, even if the whole reason was because he wanted to tease me about my scent. "Did you get the same thing?"

"I needed to taste you somehow," he murmured.

"Oh my god." A snicker came from behind me. "Dion, don't even think about it."

"No idea what you're talking about, Lo."

Claire grabbed my hand before the music started. "You seem better. Really. Are you?"

"Yeah." I couldn't keep the smile off my face. "I am."

She smirked. "Then I don't have to play watchdog?"

"No," I laughed before stepping back.

Class next to Asher was distracting. Waves of his scent kept hitting me, and I wanted to step closer to him. But in the end, it didn't matter. His eyes were on me and mine on him the entire time, no matter what. At least if we were next to each other, we wouldn't be eye-fucking each other from across the room.

Today was act two. Which, arguably, was worse than act one. At least for the principals. I loved *Giselle*, but it wasn't an easy ballet.

The bright spot was the break for lunch, when we walked into the break room and found a huge catered spread waiting for us. I still ate my Indian, but the gesture brought everyone's energy up. It wasn't as big a struggle to get to the end of the day.

But when Ian finally declared us finished, I sank to the floor immediately, thankful I'd had the presence of mind to throw some extra fluffy socks in my bag.

Ash knelt beside me. "You're coming home with me tonight."

"Ash—"

He gripped my wrist gently. "We're not savage animals, blue. They know what's happening here. We're not going to pounce on you. But Jace is a physio. He's already gone home for the day, and I want you to see him."

Gabriel had mentioned it, and in the haze of everything, I'd forgotten. I stared at him, feeling struck dumb by too many hours of dancing. "I don't have clothes."

"I can go get your clothes. Please, blue."

I nodded and looked around. It was a shitty thing to be grateful for, but I wasn't the only one who was struggling. Claire's head leaned back against the wall, everything about her claiming exhaustion. Skylar, Isabelle, and Chloe, the other Giselles were exhausted too. And we were supposed to have a dress rehearsal in four days? This was impossible.

"I don't think I can do this," I whispered. "I don't think any of us can."

Asher's mouth was a grim line. "Let me get you out of here, okay? We'll talk about it."

He went to lift me into his arms, and I stopped him, instead letting him help me to my feet. "I don't want him to see."

The glare he shot Ian made me wonder if he could set things on fire at will. "What the hell happened?"

"I was late to my meeting with him. Even though I had no idea he was going to be there, he was pissed. Went off on me for being disrespectful. Along with the comment about me being on time yesterday, I don't think he has the best impression of me, and I'm not wanting to add to that by being carried out of the studio." I touched Asher's arm. "Even if I would like that."

"Let's go," he said, clearly holding himself back from saying anything else.

I followed him out, not fighting him when he lifted me into his arms as soon as we left the theater. He took care of everything. The helmet, our bags, and putting me on the bike. I leaned against him and closed my eyes, holding on.

We'd been through rough rehearsal periods before. When you were doing three different shows and dancing pieces in all of them. Why was I so tired *this* time? I'd always been able to hold myself together.

The engine revved, and we sped away from the plaza. A little piece of me whispered the truth. For the first time in forever, I had someone to help take care of me. This was more than just exhaustion from rehearsal. It was exhaustion from *years* of being alone. From going home and having to bandage my own feet, make sure I ate, make sure I woke up.

I wasn't going to roll over and suddenly let someone else do all the work and make all my decisions, but it was nice to know someone had my back. For a while, I could relax and let someone hold me while I breathed.

My hands tightened around Ash's waist.

CHAPTER TWELVE

SLOANE

"*Y*ou live here?" I asked when Ash lifted off my helmet and I could see more clearly.

The street was lined with big, shady trees that scattered the streetlights into fractured shimmers that washed over everything. Townhomes stretched in front of us, down each block. But not what people thought of when you said a town-house. These were essentially tall mansions.

All the way on the north side of the city, we weren't too far from where my grandmother lived. And very far away from where I did.

"Hopefully soon you'll live here too."

I stared up at the house in front of us, words failing me. My mind hadn't made it that far. Ash chuckled and kissed my temple. "You want to come inside?"

"Yeah."

He didn't try to carry me this time, but he laced our fingers together on the way up the stairs. "I shouldn't be nervous, right?"

"No," he said. "You should absolutely not be nervous."

The code lock on the door beeped, and he pulled me into a small entryway where there was another door and another lock. "You trying to keep people in or out?"

"We just feel better having more than one lock between us and everyone else. It helps in case you have angry men show up at your door."

"He got his money. He won't be back."

"I'm not so sure about that," Ash muttered, pushing the door open. "Hello?"

Oh my *god* that smelled incredible. Someone was cooking Italian, and I was too hungry to know what the smell was. Just that it was incredible and my stomach wanted it *now*.

"Hey," a voice called from straight down the main hallway. "In the kitchen."

In front of us, stairs rose and curled back on themselves. A formal sitting room to the right, dining room to the left. But they seemed like the display rooms where people didn't spend much time.

Ash tugged me down the dim hallway toward the warm brightness spilling out of the kitchen. Someone stood facing the stove in front of a steaming pot, and a low curse echoed over the boiling water.

I got my first look at him. Well-built shoulders and a shirt that stretched over them. Medium brown skin, and hair shaved close. I wasn't tall, and I guessed he had a few inches on Ash, which meant he was probably a full foot taller than me. Through the food cooking, I found his scent.

My mouth watered. *Butterscotch.* Smooth and delicious, full of memories. I hadn't had a butterscotch in forever, and now it was all I wanted. Were butterscotch and chocolate chip cookies a thing?

They should be a thing.

Asher cleared his throat.

The man turned around, eyes skipping over Ash entirely. They locked on me. His chest expanded once. Twice. "Holy shit."

He abandoned the food entirely to stand in front of me. He was *gorgeous.* Hazel eyes that picked up the brown in his skin and added a mixture of green I wanted to get lost in. "When Asher said you were beautiful, he way, *way* undersold it."

Heat rose to my cheeks. "Thank you." I didn't bother mentioning that after twelve hours of rehearsal, I doubted I looked my best.

"This is Jace," Asher said.

"Hi." I couldn't take my eyes off him. Pretty sure I was in heaven between their two scents. "Whatever you're cooking smells incredible, but not as good as you do."

Ash took my bag and set it on a nearby chair, moving to rescue the pot which was now almost boiling over. Jace and I remained entranced by the other. "Sorry. This has all been kind of strange."

He smiled, taking my breath away all over again. "I don't

mind strange. Let's be real, this is all strange. Scent-sympathy is strange."

I nodded when he reached for me, letting him pull me into his arms. A low, rumbling purr started in his chest, and I was tired enough that it would put me to sleep. I turned my head and leaned it on his chest, enjoying the sound and being held.

"Jace, she needs your professional skills," Asher said, the sound of steam and pouring water covering his voice.

"What's wrong?"

"Nothing a month's worth of sleep won't fix," I mumbled into his shirt.

I hadn't moved, but I heard the clinking of dishes and glassware. "Ian Chambers is more of an asshole than I remember, and he's pushing too hard."

Jace's arms curled more protectively around me. "Need me to rough someone up for you, baby girl?"

Heady, dizzy arousal dropped through me. "Oh, fuck." I locked my hands behind the small of his back, making sure he couldn't go anywhere but stand right here.

Fingers carefully undid my bun and slid through my hair, soothing my aching scalp. "You're surprised?"

"No one's ever called me that before."

"I've never called anyone that." The words were low. "Always wanted to, but it never felt right. With you it does."

My stomach flipped. It did feel right. I wouldn't pretend to understand it. If someone had asked me three days ago if I was someone who liked pet names, the answer would have been no. Between Jace and Gabriel, I'd already learned that wasn't the case.

"Let's eat," Ash said. "So we can help you."

"But this is comfortable."

Jace ran his fingers through my hair again. "You can sit on my lap if you want."

My whole body flushed pink, and I was too tired to think about that. Not tonight, anyway. "That's okay. I'm already going to have a hard time resisting all of you."

Slowly, he pulled away and helped me up onto a barstool. The high bar separated the kitchen from what looked like a breakfast nook peeking out into the backyard.

"Where's Roman?" Ash asked, putting a plate of spaghetti in front of me.

"Still in his studio. I'm sure he'll come in soon. Don't want to bother him if he's in the zone."

I looked up. "What does he do?"

"He's a sculptor. He was actually at the conservatory with us. Just in a different program."

"Oh."

Jace sat next to me, his hand straying to my knee or my shoulder. He couldn't keep his hands or eyes off me, and I'd never been so happy for someone to watch me eat. "Are you going to eat too?"

"I'm more concerned about you at the moment."

"I'm fine."

"Hmm," was the only sound he made, accompanied by a stroke of his hand down my ribs.

The front door opened and closed, and suddenly there was a third Alpha in the room, and my whole body *tingled* with the possibilities. Gabriel smiled when he saw me, coming around the bar to hug me from behind.

"It's not fair," I groaned. "I hate that you have to be off limits."

Gabriel chuckled. "We don't *have* to be."

I hung my head. "No, Ash is right. If I'm going to make it through this week, I can't. Even if I want to."

"We need to talk about that," Asher said, staring at Gabriel. "We're going to end up with injured dancers. I don't know why Mark agreed to this. Or the board. This is a really fucking bad idea."

"Mark's not a bad guy," I said.

Asher's eyes softened when he looked at me. "I didn't say he was, sweetheart. And because he's *not* a bad guy, I don't know why he would agree to something this intense."

Gabriel's arm remained around my shoulders. "I can give you all the reasons Ian gave why it would work if you like."

I shook my head. "We never have performances this fast. And I understand about the contracts. What I don't understand is why we didn't make the show later instead of earlier. I mean..." Looking down, I pushed what little was left of the spaghetti around. "I can do it. But if we'd known, I would have stepped up my training."

Even when we found out about the shorter run and I *had* beefed up my training the last couple of weeks, it didn't prepare me for this. The silence in the kitchen was deafening.

Ash leaned on the kitchen island, his whole body rigid, fingers white where he gripped the counter.

"You done, baby girl?"

"Yeah."

Jace picked my hand up off the bar. "Let's go get you fixed up then."

He helped me down off the stool with strong hands on my waist. I was tempted to just cling to him like a cat and let him carry me. "Where are we going?"

"Our gym," he tugged me back down the hallway out of the kitchen. "It's on the second floor, and I have a workspace there as well."

Behind me, I heard voices. Ash letting go. "This is *bullshit* and you know it, Gabe. Just because I'm in better shape than Sloane is doesn't mean I don't feel it. The show needs to be pushed back."

A softer answer I couldn't hear as we climbed the stairs. The walls here were a rich forest green which complemented the dark wood of the floor and banisters. Art lined the walls, an eclectic mixture that somehow fit the blend of modern and classic I'd seen so far.

"Do you guys have an elevator?"

"We do. It's actually in the back corner of the kitchen. I wanted to see how well you're walking." He squeezed my hand.

"Oh."

The gym looked like every commercial gym I'd ever seen. Based on the three Alphas I'd met so far, I guessed it got plenty of use. I blinked at all the equipment. If I lived here, I would be able to get rid of my gym membership.

The thought froze me and warmed me at the same time. Half an hour and my mind was already moving in. "There's a sauna over there." Jace pointed to a dark doorway. "And my physio room is over here."

The room we entered was much warmer than the physio room at the ballet. Red walls that seemed to wrap around you like a blanket. A massage table in the center and all the other tools of the trade lined against the walls. The lights were low and cozy when he turned them on.

"Hop on up." He said it, but lifted me onto the table himself before moving to take off my shoes.

"I promise I'm usually more energized. Don't want you to think I'm a limp noodle."

Jace glanced up, amusement in his eyes. "It sounds like you've had a rough couple of days, baby girl. Don't apologize for it. As much as I'd like to fuck you on this table instead of work on you and give you a massage, there's plenty of time for that. I'm not going anywhere."

"How do you know?" The shoe coming off made me close my eyes.

Standing, he shifted my legs apart to stand between them. "When Asher and Gabriel came home from the company meeting? I've never seen either of them like that. Ash and I sparred for two hours before he could even think about stopping because every instinct told him he needed to get to you. Gabe was quieter about it, but he still ran on the treadmill for longer than we sparred. Scenting you for the first time?" Jace sighed and lifted a hand to my cheek. "It's a before and an after. You weren't there, and now you are. Nothing else matters."

I felt it too, but it was still scary. After so long being alone, having... a pack. It didn't seem real. "When my best friend found her pack, they were all in right away. And it was a whirlwind. I want that. I wish we could get carried away and not have to care about anything else. And the fact that we can't is my fault."

"How do you figure?"

He laughed at the look I gave him. If I hadn't left conservatory, maybe we'd all already be together. And maybe we wouldn't. Asher was right. We couldn't dwell on the past forever.

The Alpha from my thoughts poked his head into the room.

"I'm going to go to your apartment," he said, holding up my keys. "I'll get everything you need. Anything specific?"

I shook my head. "No, just dance clothes. Toothbrush. The suppressants. I've got nothing to hide."

Jace stepped aside so Ash could kiss me. "I'll go rifling then."

"Don't take too long. You're tired too."

"I'm okay, sweetheart."

Gripping his shirt, I didn't let him step away. "I heard you. You're exhausted."

He pressed his lips to my ear. "I'm never too exhausted for you." Then he was gone.

Jace knelt in front of me, picking up my left foot. "I'm going to feel, okay?"

"Yeah."

I wasn't injured. But making sure I *stayed* uninjured was just as important as any recovery. I flinched as he gently flexed my foot back and forth. "Tell me where it hurts."

"It's just sore. Achy. Nothing sharp. Promise. I'd tell you if there was something wrong."

He nodded, moving to my other foot and repeating the process. "I'm going to help you while these rehearsals are happening like this," he said. "After as well, but I'm not taking risks with your feet. Or any of the other dancers. I'll talk to Gabriel about pulling people out of rehearsal for some evaluations."

"Thank you."

The smile he gave me turned my stomach into a gooey mess. Along with the sweet scent of butterscotch, I would be a puddle by the time this was all finished. "I'm going to go downstairs and get some ice packs for your feet while you get undressed. Then I'll make sure everything's loose." He winked.

It felt as strange for him to leave the room while I stripped as it would be for him to stay here and watch me. God, I wanted to let loose the way Petra had.

He saw it and stepped closer once more. "No one ever knows when or if they'll meet their match. Yes, it's a bit of a letdown for us to be in the midst of something so intense when we want to fall into bed with you. But I hope you know that being scent-sympathetic is more than just sex for us, baby girl. It's so much more than that."

A gentle kiss had me melting and falling into him with a soft whine. "I know," I sighed. "Doesn't mean I like it."

His laugh reached deep down within and stirred both lust and longing. "I don't either. Get comfy okay?"

"Okay."

I was colder when he pulled away, quickly stripping my clothes off without even stepping off the table. Pulling the sheet over me, I breathed out some of the tension. This was nice. I could live with this kind of pampering even after this performance mess was over.

"You ready, baby girl?"

"Yeah."

At least I knew I wouldn't be the only one both enjoying and suffering when he touched my skin.

CHAPTER THIRTEEN

GABRIEL

I watched Jace lead our weary Omega out of the kitchen. Her whole frame drooped, and I didn't think she could see it.

"This is *bullshit* and you know it, Gabe. Just because I'm in better shape than Sloane is doesn't mean I don't feel it. The show needs to be pushed back." Ash had fire in his eyes.

"I know," I said. "But as much as I wish there was something I could do, there isn't."

"Why the fuck not?"

I took the stool Sloane had vacated and ran a hand through my hair. "Because Ian is very convincing. And I can do a lot of things. I *can't* fight an entire board of trustees who are fully behind Ian's new vision for SCB."

He shook his head, moving to serve us both some food. "What the hell did he say to them?"

"A longer version of what he told you in the company meeting. He spun a version of the company that not only performed more often and brought in more income, but made ballet more accessible to people by performing beloved classics.

"The company still has a good portion of the sets and the costumes from the last production of *Giselle*, so he's foregoing part of his artistic vision in favor of getting the show up quickly. Because the contracts are different, the scene and costume shops have already been working. We just couldn't do the same for the dancers."

Ash shoved a plate of spaghetti in front of me and didn't bother to sit down before eating his. "Still." His mouth was full, and I fought off a grin, knowing it wouldn't help right now. "You've been doing this for a while. You didn't think it was a bad idea?"

"No," I hung my head. "If I'm honest, I didn't. And if you'd been in that room I don't think you would have either. Ian is passionate and knowledgeable. He's also got complete confidence in himself and his vision. The way he laid it out seemed sensible and easy."

"Right," Ash muttered. "Not actually how it's working out."

"I know. I'm man enough and Alpha enough to own when I've made a mistake. This was one. I'm going to do what I can for the rest of the season. The rehearsal schedules are on my desk and I started going through them today. I don't care about a gap in the performance schedule. This will not happen again. But tickets have been sold and more than half the trustees will be there on opening night."

"Gabriel..."

"I *know*." I shoved myself off the stool, unable to keep still. The familiar anger rising up from where I'd been keeping it leashed. "I know. I hate the fact that I even have to say this. Pushing back this production will be a PR nightmare the company can't afford. We've pushed money into advertising this, and moving it will make us look unprofessional, unprepared, and shake the confidence of the donors and trustees who are already skeptical of the change in leadership, myself included. Not to mention you all agreed to the overtime rehearsals in writing."

He opened his mouth to protest, and I stopped him. "You don't have to say it. What you were told and what he meant were two very different things. You think I like watching Sloane like this? Or you? Or any of the other dancers who are going through it? No. It makes me want to tear something limb from limb, but I can't do that. The rest of the season I can take care of, but my hands are tied and I am fucking *furious* about it."

The steam of my rant ran out, and I leaned on the back of one of the chairs in the breakfast nook. I felt the wood creaking under my hands. Good. The faint feeling of fragility in the chair was the only thing keeping me from putting my fist through the wall.

If I could go back in time and change my mind, or give myself some kind of hint about how far Ian would take it, I would. It certainly wasn't making me feel good about the beginning of our working relationship. If we didn't have half the company quit in protest, we would be lucky.

I was going to do something, I just wasn't sure what. Being bound so tightly had me ready to snap.

"I'm sorry," I told him. "I'll do whatever I have to in order to get you guys through this. The group schedule came through. You're on opening night."

"Fuck." Ash swore under his breath and closed his eyes. "I need you to know if she gets injured I'm not going to be able to hold myself back."

"You'll have to get in line."

He finally looked at me. "I'm sorry for implying you hadn't tried, or that you weren't. It's just—"

"I get it. If roles were reversed, I'd think the same. But I don't want you to think I'm any less pissed about it. The only reason I'm not showing it is because I can't get anywhere if I go in there and start setting things on fire."

Ash finished his food and put the dishes in the sink. "She's staying here," he said. "Or if she insists on going home, Jace is with her. I want her protected any way we can."

"You have no arguments from me."

"Good." He leaned down and grabbed something off Sloane's bag. "I have to go to her apartment so she has clothes for the next few days. She was too tired to go there first."

I sat back down with my own food. "Make sure you're resting too. You're not invincible either."

"Thanks, mom," he smirked, but there wasn't real humor behind it. "I know. I'll be fast."

The spaghetti was good. We didn't cook that much, but the few things each of us had adopted and learned we were good at. The front door opened and closed when Asher left, and barely five minutes later, Jace came in and went straight to the fridge. "She okay?"

"She is. There's definitely strain, but she's not in the danger zone. She can't keep this up for long, but for now, she's all right."

That was a relief.

"Tomorrow I want your clearance to pull principals so myself or the other physios can check them."

"Done."

"Thanks."

A bit of Sloane's scent clung to him. It hung in the air around my seat. I wanted the house filled with it. Every crevice, so there was never any doubt she belonged here forever.

Behind me, the door to the backyard opened, admitting Roman. He stopped as soon as he entered. "She's here?"

"She is."

I heard the depth of his inhale. The first hit of blueberries and sweetness set your lungs on fire, binding you to the precious little Omega so deeply you never wanted anything or anyone else. Even considering it felt like you were tearing your own soul out of your chest, and it all happened in a second.

I fucking loved it.

"Where?"

"There's food." I nodded to the stove. "Jace is helping her right now, making sure her body is okay from rehearsal. But she wants to meet you." She told me as much this morning.

He hesitated, moving toward the stairs like he couldn't stop the pull of going to her. "She's not going anywhere. I promise." I would do everything in my power to make sure it was true.

"You were right," Roman finally said, finding the few words he needed. "She smells incredible."

I smiled. "She's yours?"

A single nod.

"Then she's all of ours."

Our Omega.

I couldn't speak for the others, but it was something I had wanted more than anything. And now that she was here, I was going to love her. Cherish her. And absolutely never let her go.

CHAPTER FOURTEEN

***

SLOANE

*J*ace wrapped my feet in ice packs covered in softness as I relaxed on the table. And then his hands were on my skin, massaging, loosening at the same time he made sure my body was in performance shape.

It felt so good I didn't care.

"Is there anywhere I can't touch you, baby girl?"

"No," I murmured.

He lifted the sheet to the side, continuing his massage down my side and onto my ass. Arms, elbows, and hands, he reached muscles I forgot existed. It was all I needed to know he was very, *very* good at his job, even if this kind of massage wasn't always part of it.

I think I fell asleep, waking up when he tugged the sheet back up to my shoulders and removed the ice from my feet. "I need to have you do this when I can stay awake."

He hummed softly. "I'm not done yet."

Gently, he moved my arms so they fell off the table before he lifted one and slipped beneath it to sit next to my head. "You trust me?"

"Is this where you murder me?" My sleepy voice contained a giggle that wasn't fully formed.

"No," he chuckled. One of his hands held mine where it was over his legs, weaving our fingers together and flexing them. It felt good. But it was nothing compared to his other hand. Long fingers dug into my hair, burying themselves near the scalp and *pulling*.

Long and slow. Delicious and only bordering on pain. It released tension in my neck and shoulders. It also felt sexy as hell. He shouldn't do this to me while I was so relaxed. I would give in and fuck him in a heartbeat.

"Oh, fuck," I moaned. "I want to know why every physio doesn't do this, but I also don't want anyone to do it but you."

Jace moved his hand to a different part of my head and pulled before massaging the back of my neck. There was oil on his hand, and I didn't care if it was in my hair. It felt too good.

"I'm glad no one else has." Was his voice deeper? Was I imagining it? He began to purr. "As good as it is for you, I don't want anyone else touching you like this. Except the rest of the pack."

The rest of the pack.

My pack.

A sigh fell out of me, along with any lingering tension I'd been clinging to.

"Good girl," he whispered. "You can relax. You're safe with us."

"I know."

Slowly, he got up and switched sides so he could reach new parts of my scalp. "Minds and bodies are different," he said as he flexed my fingers in his hand. "It takes time for your body to know something, even if your mind believes it. Your body, baby girl, is learning it can trust me."

It definitely trusted him. I was a puddle on the table, and I didn't only mean my current state of relaxation. Him pulling my hair, the purring, the gentle but firm touches were all getting to me, and between my legs, my body wanted to *trust* him.

Perfume swirled in the air around us now that the suppressor had worn off for the day. "I could let you do this forever."

"And I would, but I think you need something else."

I sighed. "We can't."

The smile in his voice was clear. "You're right. I can't fuck you without all of us getting carried away." He stood, still holding my hand, and crouched down by my ear. I turned my head to face him, memorizing his beautiful eyes.

"But not being able to fuck you doesn't mean I can't make you feel good, baby girl." He smirked. "It might even help you sleep better."

Arousal shuddered through me, followed by heat. Heat in his eyes, heat in my body, heat everywhere. I *wanted* them so badly, and even if it only took the edge off for the night... I wasn't strong enough to say no. "I think I'd like that."

Jace winked. "Turn over for me."

He helped me, curving his hand under my neck to hold it steady. I expected him to take off the sheet covering me, but he didn't. That same hand smoothed the hair back from my forehead as he leaned in to kiss me.

The sheet pulled up from my feet, still leaving me mostly covered and warmer than without it. This felt... soft and intimate. No pressure. That intangible tension disappeared once more.

"There you go," he whispered. "Fuck, baby girl, I'm going to love making you this relaxed all the time."

"Promise?"

His answer was his palm sliding along my thigh and another kiss. The first touch of him between my legs made me moan. I'd been turned on for days now, my body telling me that my Alphas were here and I needed them. My hips arched off the table, and Jace pushed them back down.

I was so wet his fingers slid over my clit when he reached it. He smiled into our kiss, purring. "Glad I'm not the only one."

"Are you surprised? All of you are sex on a stick."

"And you haven't even met Roman yet."

Before I could answer, one long finger slipped inside me. Fingers normally weren't my favorite way to do this, but as soon as he added a second one, I realized I might have to rethink my preferences. That, and everyone else who'd tried had no fucking clue how to finger someone.

Jace pulled his fingers out of me. I opened my mouth to beg him to put them back and stopped. He never took his eyes from mine as he lifted his fingers to his mouth and groaned. "Fuck me, you taste so good."

"Jace..."

"Once we can, I'm going to spend some quality time between your legs, baby girl. I want my face soaked with blueberries by the time we're done."

His fingers slipping back into me blanked out my thoughts. Jace's thumb rested on my clit almost lazily. Long, slow movements. He wasn't in a hurry, no matter if my body was.

The way his eyes took me in, it felt like I was laid bare. Entirely exposed. Yet I was safe. With all of them. I wanted them to see everything and I wanted to learn everything about them in the same way.

"What do you like, hmm?" He rocked his fingers into me, curving them and moving them, feeling where I tensed and listening to my breath catch. "What does this needy pussy need to feel good?"

My whole body shuddered. "You could probably just blow on me right now and I'll fall apart."

"Oh, I'm going to do more than that."

Twisting his hand to move my legs further apart, he pushed deeper and harder, thumb dragging over my clit. Little sparkles of pleasure popped like firecrackers through me. He could keep up this slow pace, and I would get there. It would take a long time, and the end would be explosive. Jace seemed like the kind of Alpha who wouldn't mind spending all that time, and for the first time, I thought I might enjoy it.

I usually didn't have the patience. My sexual encounters were hard and fast and dirty. Whether it was someone I fucked at a club or a couple of dates where I let them take me home. A quick orgasm or two and I'd been able to walk away satisfied. And I'd been happy with it, or so I thought.

A few movements of Jace's magic fingers and I realized how different it could be. I'd had plenty of sex, and I didn't think any of the fucks had even come close to this. The depth and the knowledge there could be so much more.

Jace grinned suddenly, like he saw the realization in my eyes. "This is going to be fun, Sloane."

He stood without warning, leaning over me to get a better angle. It wasn't slow now. The movements of his hand were driven and purposeful.

One hand landed lightly on my chest, warning me not to move. Jace wasn't holding me down, but it had the same effect. I was frozen under his attention as his fingers melted any coherent thoughts I had left. And still, his eyes never left mine, alight with lust and pleasure.

The way he moved, testing and shifting until he saw my reaction, every little shift of his hand sent new sparkles of pleasure through me. "Close your eyes, baby girl."

I hesitated, worried about losing the connection we had. But the next wave of pleasure had them closing anyway, hips arching into his hand. Jace focused his efforts on my clit, using my own wetness and teasing me. His thumb circled and his palm ground onto me, and I stopped resisting.

Something in my head was still holding back, worried about going too far with one of them and not all of them. That I couldn't let go without making sure they felt good too. Jace's palm on my chest and the calm certainty of his movements brought me back and let me breathe.

He wanted this for me, and something about that made emotions and nerves and pleasure all come rushing to the surface. Pleasure washed up over me in a smooth wave.

It was like sinking into a hot bath made of nothing but honey and sugar. Butterscotch. A perfect peak that rose and fell, sweeping up and through, my body shaking in the aftermath.

Jace leaned down and kissed me slowly, pulling his hand back from me. "I want to do so much more than that."

"Me too."

With equal gentleness and slowness, he helped me sit up. "There's a shower in here. You feel okay taking one?"

I leaned on him, purposely giving him my weight with a smile. "Are you joining me?"

He groaned. "I would, but I'm only so strong, baby." A laugh and a kiss met my pout. "But I'll happily hold you after. You're going to sleep so well. Promise."

"Fine," I sighed heavily, intentionally laying it on thick. "Where am I going?"

"Right through there." He pointed through the gym into another darkened room. "Towels and everything else you'll need are in there. And before you can even question, if I were going to join you, I'd take you to *my* shower."

"Next time."

"Soon," he promised.

"Where am I going to sleep?"

He smiled. "I'm not sure yet, but I'll talk to the others while you're getting clean."

"Okay."

Jace made sure I was steady on my feet before he released me, fingers lingering over the sheet that still clung to my body. "Thank you," I said quietly. "For... all of that."

A low purr answered me. "My pleasure, baby girl."

I forced myself away from him or the restrictions I needed to keep myself healthy were going to crumble like the old moth-eaten costumes in the theater's basement.

Like last night, I rushed through the shower, barely staying in long to get everything done. But it wasn't until I stepped out I realized... Ash hadn't come back yet. Or I didn't know if he had. And I had nothing to put on except for the towel.

"Jace?" The gym was empty and the physio room dark. He could still be downstairs. I crept through the gym and looked out into the hall. "Hello?"

Movement caught my eye. Someone coming down the stairs from the next floor. He stopped when he saw me, and I couldn't stop *staring*.

The man was tall. Taller than all of them. Clearing well over six feet, he was a giant. A giant who currently wasn't wearing a shirt, with only low-slung sweatpants on his hips. My eyes traveled over the muscles on display. The hair on his chest and the tattoos I couldn't make out.

Dark hair fell to his shoulders, damp from his own shower. And his scent...

Pine and mist curled around me. The darkness of cool woods and the fresh sweetness of wilderness air. He was like breathing in through a fucking forest postcard, and it hit me just as hard as the other scents.

I searched his face. Asher mentioned he went to school with us.

Yes.

Vague memories of seeing him across campus or in the dining hall came into focus. I didn't think we'd ever spoken, but we wouldn't have had a reason to.

His chest rose and fell in a deep inhale, but he didn't move.

"You're Roman?"

A nod.

I took a step toward him that seemed to release him. He

dissolved the distance between us. Dark brown eyes searched mine, and I still hadn't heard him speak. My head tilted all the way back to meet his eyes. "I remember you. Not much, but I do."

His eyes lit with relief and interest. Roman still didn't speak, but it didn't feel strange. His eyes and face were expressive, and this was all weird to begin with. "Asher went to my apartment to get me some clothes, but I don't know if he's back yet."

With one hand he reached out, pinching a strand of my damp hair between his fingers. It made me feel delicate and precious. Like I was a piece of glass he didn't want to break.

"It's nice to meet you," I said. "I'm sorry it couldn't be earlier. Things have been... rough." Though that word was a fucking understatement to describe our rehearsals.

"I—" he cleared his throat. That single syllable showed me the depth of his voice. "Can I?"

The way his hand hovered, I didn't need more than that. "Yes."

Roman moved faster than I thought possible for someone so large, scooping me up and lifting me into his arms. We climbed to the next floor and stepped through the door into a large bedroom. The walls were dark, but it wasn't oppressive. The darkness made it cozy. There was a desk with scraps of paper and scale models of sculptures. That was the only thing I saw before the bed.

Huge, dominating the center of the space. God, I wanted to sleep.

Setting me down on the bed, Roman turned to the dresser and fished around in the drawers, pulling out a t-shirt. On him, it would fit. On me, it would be a dress. "Here." The single word was soft, and he looked away before I dropped the towel.

We didn't need to be so modest with each other, but it was sweet. I slipped the shirt over my head, wrapped up in the cool wildness of his scent. The only thing that would make it better was if it were warm from his skin.

"Where should I put the towel?"

He took it from me and tossed it into a hamper in the closet before lifting me up again, spreading us out on his bed and curling around me. Everything about him dwarfed me. With my head against his shoulder my toes barely passed his knees. I liked it more than I thought I would.

Maybe there would be a time when I looked back on this time and not marvel at how natural it all felt. But right now? This was a miracle. The comfort I felt with Roman wrapping me up, a rough purr in his chest, and nothing separating us but the thin fabric of his shirt brought tears to my eyes.

Roman relaxed with me in his arms, and I did too.

"Talking isn't... easy for me," he said quietly. "It will take time."

"That's okay." I touched him where I could, dragging my fingers down his back and across his ribs. "I'm so tired I can barely think."

"Would've come up earlier. Didn't want to interrupt."

"You're not an interruption," I said quietly, curling further into his arms. My mind was already softening and fading. "Sorry I'm going to fall asleep so fast."

His purr strengthened and his arms tightened. He moved briefly, and it got warmer. A blanket. My eyes were closed, but I still searched for him, pressing my face into his neck, where his scent was so strong.

My big Alpha.

Somewhere I registered him lifting my hand and kissing the inside of my wrist. "Still mine. Even asleep."

I fell asleep smiling.

CHAPTER FIFTEEN

ASHER

*W*alking into Sloane's apartment building without her when I knew she was at home was all the incentive I needed to not stay long. The fact that she was at our home at all had me settled and happy. Primal knowledge that our Omega was safe under our care, and we were doing everything we could to keep her that way.

I paused as I approached her door. A note was taped to it. Pulling it off, I grit my teeth.

Call me when the pretty boy isn't holding you hostage.

Only one person that could be from.

I didn't take any pleasure in being right about Craig coming back here. Twice now he'd been able to get into the building despite not having a key to the outer door. Which meant he waited and followed someone inside, he somehow had a key, or he was buzzing randomly until someone let him up.

The key thing seemed less likely. From what Sloane said, they'd barely had any real time together, and if he'd been able to copy her external key, there was no chance he *wouldn't* have copied her apartment key as well.

I shoved down a rising growl. This morning would have gone very differently if Craig had suddenly been standing over the two of us in bed.

Something about the Alpha made my skin crawl. I didn't trust him, and it wasn't only because Sloane was *mine*. She knew that as well as I did, and I'd already seen how little she wanted him around. It was his treatment of her and this behavior that set my teeth on edge.

Tucking the note into my own bag, I set it aside for later. Sloane didn't need to worry about an asshole like Craig when she was already in the middle of this nightmare rehearsal scenario. As far as I

103

was concerned she was staying at our house until *Giselle* was over, so she wouldn't have to worry about running into him, and when she could have more than a few hours sleep, we'd talk about him.

Her apartment was quiet.

In spite of my joke about rifling through her things, I wasn't going to. I didn't have any desire to snoop through Sloane's possessions. What would I be looking for? Proof she had a life while we were apart?

Nothing either of us could do about that.

I found a bag in her closet a bit bigger than her dance bag, but still soft enough that I could take it on my bike. I grabbed what I thought she'd need. Rehearsal clothes and some comfortable lounge clothes for after. When she was relaxing with us.

At home.

She would laugh at me if she saw my smile.

Toothbrush, toothpaste, and suppressants all went into the bag. Her dance bag was already with us. I took careful stock of the bedroom, thinking about anything else I could grab. In the end, I took some soft and fluffy socks from her drawer.

What was that?

I spied a toy hidden next to the socks. The kind that latched onto the clit and sucked like its life depended on it. It looked like some other toys were hidden further back, but I didn't explore.

So my Omega liked toys. I could work with that. And it made my comment about teamwork this morning even funnier.

Sloane's bedroom—her whole apartment, really—was lovely. The pale purple walls in here reminded me of the sketches she'd used to make. But everything was *her*. Softness and femininity with the quirky touch that made her who she was.

I wanted that special touch all over our home and her space there. It still felt too good to be true. She was my Omega. I never imagined I'd get so lucky.

That was all I needed from here. If she needed anything else I'd come back or we would buy it.

Locking the door behind me, I heard a voice behind me. "You know Sloane?" An older woman looked out from the door across the hall.

"I do," I said, holding out my hand to her. "I'm Asher, one of Sloane's Alphas."

A gasp. "She bonded?" She shook my hand. "Noreen."

"Not yet. We found out we were scent-sympathetic a few days ago." The complexity of that discovery wasn't a casual hallway discussion. "She's at my pack's home. I'm just grabbing a few things for her."

"Oh. That's good. I thought you might be the other man."

I frowned. "Did he leave a note?"

"Yes. Pounded on the door for a while. Second time today."

"I witnessed the first time," I forced a smile. "If he comes here again, would you mind telling me or Sloane?"

Noreen nodded. "Of course. He hasn't exactly made a good impression."

"I appreciate it. Sloane won't be home for a few days because of rehearsals. Do you have Sloane's number?"

"I do."

"Thank you, Noreen. Have a good night."

"You too." She smiled. "Say hello to her for me."

I lifted a hand in a wave. "I will."

Craig hadn't made a good impression, huh? I wondered if he'd been shouting more stuff through the door. Later, we could ask Noreen. But the selfish part of me didn't want to hear information I couldn't act on right now.

Outside, I glanced around, my instincts high. What was his angle? Would he be the kind of man who waited and watched? I saw nothing.

The miles evaporated under my wheels, and all my instincts relaxed once I was through the front door and back home.

Gabriel and Jace were in the kitchen. "Where's Sloane?"

Jace laughed. "She's with Roman. Asleep. I'm just about to go up and bandage her feet. He ran into her while she was getting out of the shower and bundled her into bed."

"Why do you look pissed?" Gabriel asked me.

I told them what I hadn't been able to before about this morning and the note on the door. Neither of them were happy either.

"You're right," Gabriel agreed. "Something to be dealt with next week."

I sighed. "Yeah. Now I have to see this snugglefest upstairs."

Jace chuckled. "It's pretty fucking adorable."

He had a kit in his hand, and all three of us took the elevator up to Roman and Jace's floor. The lights in Roman's room were still bright. And it didn't matter to Sloane. She was out, cradled in Roman's arms. She was so small compared to him she looked like a doll.

And the look on his face...

Roman looked down at Sloane like she was a wonder. A miracle come to life. I recognized the way he held her, because it was the way *I* held her. Like he wanted to pull her so tight to his body she merged with him, but also not, so he didn't hurt her.

"Having fun?" I kept my voice low.

Roman flicked his eyes up to mine for half a second. "I... don't dare move."

Jace crouched by the bed and lifted the covers to expose Sloane's battered feet. She didn't even stir. "I think you're okay. She's completely passed out."

"She's..." his fingers flexed against her body. "I can't explain it."

"You don't need to," Gabriel whispered from the door. "We get it."

All five of us in the space felt like pure harmony. Something you didn't know was missing until you felt the resonance humming between all of us.

I didn't want to walk away, but both Sloane and Gabriel were right. My own body was fading. "I'll be back to wake her in the morning," I told Roman, setting her bag on the floor by the bed.

All I wanted to do was curl up with her, but she was here with us and safe. And it was everything.

Creeping into Roman's room in the dim light of morning, Sloane still slept peacefully, and he did too. His hand was underneath her shirt so he could feel her skin where he held her, and it also exposed how very naked she was beneath.

One hand outstretched on the bed, I touched it gently. "Time to wake up, blue."

Sloane stirred. "Nooo. Five more minutes."

Exactly what she used to say to me when I woke her up for our actual classes. Our professor would roll her eyes and playfully throw a shoe, but we always made up our work, so it was fine.

"Can't give you that today, sweetheart."

Her gorgeous eyes opened and locked on mine. It took her mind a second to catch up to where she was. Then she smiled, pressing back into Roman. "Hi."

I lifted her bags where they were. "Your things are here, and Jace is making you a smoothie for breakfast."

"I'm okay."

"Little one, you are going to eat breakfast." Gabriel stood at the door, dressed to go. "Ash told us you don't like to, and I understand why. But if I can't stop Ian from forcing you to rehearse for twelve hours, I'm going to make sure you're eating enough to survive it."

Sloane was small, like most dancers. She still had to eat.

She sighed. "Okay."

"Good girl."

A tiny whimper she tried to hide came out of her, and she curled closer to Roman. I raised an eyebrow at Gabriel. He smirked.

Toys and she liked being called a good girl. God, the things I was going to do to this woman when we finally went to bed.

Roman finally opened his eyes and buried his face in her neck. "Good morning."

Sloane sighed. "This is nice. Let's do more of this."

"Waking up?"

"I was thinking about sleeping in and cuddling, but sure."

I nodded. "That's on the docket for 'as soon as humanly possible.' But we have to go soon. I let you sleep as long as I could."

"Okay."

Instead of staying to watch her dress—I should receive a

fucking medal for resisting that kind of temptation—I grabbed her smoothie from Jace and waited by the front door.

She came down a few minutes later, dressed and bleary. I gave her the to-go cup. "Don't worry, Jace makes good smoothies. And this cup is tight enough for the bike."

Sloane nodded, staring through my chest. I saw a shimmer of tears and hauled her into my arms. "I've never dreaded dancing," she whispered. "Am I really that weak that two twelve hour rehearsals broke me?"

I growled. "It's not just two, sweetheart. We both know that. And fuck me, you're not weak. We're going to get you through this. And then we're going to spend as much time as you want in bed. Promise."

"Okay."

Kissing her temple, I took her hand and led her outside, sending up a silent prayer that I could stop myself from killing Ian for the rest of this process.

CHAPTER SIXTEEN

SLOANE

*T*he next few days were a blur I barely remembered.

If the pack hadn't devoted absolutely everything to taking care of me and Asher, I wasn't sure I would have been able to do it.

I wasn't the only one. All three of Dion's Alphas started dropping him off and picking him up, the look in their eyes the same as the ones my pack gave me.

My pack.

The thought made me smile whenever it popped into my head.

Addison was there for Claire too, now that she'd recovered from her cold. Hell, outside the theater door in the evenings there was a crowd of people waiting to take their dancers home. I'd never seen anything like it except on show days.

In the rehearsal room there was growing frustration and resentment. None of us could say anything because we'd agreed. Sat down with Ian and signed the waiver.

Never again.

Frankly, it was going to be hard for me to be in rehearsal with him at all after this. He was relentless, picking on everything. Not only with me, but *especially* with me. The digs about my lateness kept on, even when I had to break in new shoes in the middle of rehearsal because he was making us dance them to death.

I swore Asher was seconds away from decking the man. It was only me touching him that held him back.

The dress rehearsals were as rough as we expected, but we made it through. Of all the cohorts, we were the least lucky in performing first. We had the least time. But I was going to look that smug bastard in the face after curtain call and smile, showing him he didn't fucking break me.

Shrill shrieking entered my consciousness. I sat up, whirling around for the noise only for Gabriel's arms to come around me. "Woah, little one. You're okay."

My heart pounded in my chest, and I fell back onto the bed with him holding me. The alarm on my phone. That's all it was. I smacked the screen to turn it off. "Fuck."

He kissed softly under my jaw. "Breathe for me."

"I'm breathing," I promised. "I'm breathing."

It was opening day. I needed to get to the theater for class and last-minute brush ups before the show. Makeup and costumes. Three performances and I could have a breather for a few days.

I closed my eyes and allowed myself to inhale Gabriel's scent, turning into his chest. His *bare* chest. I didn't even remember getting to his bed last night. "How did I get here?"

He chuckled softly. "You fell asleep on the bar."

"Sorry about that."

Pulling me hard against his body—letting me know that waking up with me was affecting him just as much as it was me—his face went stern. "Don't apologize for something that's not your fault."

His shirt was gone, putting us nearly skin on skin. He was overwhelming, chest and upper arms covered in tattoos you couldn't see when he wore clothes, giving a glimpse of the Alpha underneath. There hadn't been time for me to explore, but I wanted to touch every inch of him. His eyes, locked on mine, burned with the words he'd said.

For the first time I saw the truth of it. The agony and the fury. Gabriel cared about more than just me. Every day there'd been catering, extra massage therapists staying late for anyone who needed them, and the company was covering cabs to and from home if anyone needed them.

He was always smiling at the theater. I'd barely seen him enough to realize how angry he was about all of it. I already knew there was no chance he would let it pass unanswered. "What are you going to do?"

"I don't know yet," he admitted. "Figured I should wait until I think I can be in the same room as him without punching him in the face."

"But watching that would be fun."

He brushed his lips over mine. "Don't tempt me, little one."

I reached over for my phone and saw the time. "*Shit*."

It was later than I thought. We were going to have to book it to get to the theater on time. Rolling out of Gabriel's arms, I nearly fell off the bed and winced. Where were my bags?

There.

Wherever I ended up sleeping, they made sure I had what I needed. "I'm sorry," I said.

"Sloane, I'm going to take you over my knee and turn your ass red if you keep apologizing."

My face flushed even as I frantically pulled on fresh tights and a leotard. I never thought I was the spanking type, but these Alphas hadn't even fucked me yet and they proved I wanted all kinds of things I hadn't realized.

Gabriel's laugh told me he saw me blush.

"See you later?"

"Yes you will." A promise.

Jace stood at the bottom of the stairs with Ash, smoothie in hand. They were good, and didn't fuck me up in class like I'd expected.

Catching me around the waist, Jace kissed me. "Break a leg, baby girl."

"You'll be there?"

"Bet your ass. Roman too."

"Okay."

"Come on, blue." Ash grabbed my hand, and we were gone.

Class was normally full of chatter before the music started. Not today. It was almost entirely silent other than the blocky sound of pointe shoes on the floor.

Claire pulled me into a hug we both needed. "Ready to do this?"

"Is *fuck no* an acceptable answer?"

"It's the only one I have, so yes."

Nausea swam in my gut. A combination of nerves and whatever the hell else. If I collapsed into a cold after this weekend, I would be zero percent shocked.

I spend half of lunch in Asher's arms, just breathing each

other in. I didn't feel better physically, but being held by him was enough. For now.

"Sloane, costume department is ready for you." Alice, a corps member, called out to me.

"Fuck," I muttered.

"You've got this, sweetheart." He squeezed me tighter for a minute.

Turning, I smiled. "Thank you, Alice."

Last-minute costume fittings morphed into last-minute pickup rehearsals.

Ian was in rare form. "If you don't keep your leg higher in that arabesque, Glass, I'm going to come over there and hold it up for you."

I glared at him and lifted my leg higher. Why would it make sense for me to mark my rehearsal instead of going all out in a studio just before I was about to perform? I barely managed to keep my sarcasm in my own mind.

"And don't forget the arms in act two. They're still weak."

"Wonder why that is?" I asked under my breath and Claire choked on her laugh.

He whipped around and looked at me. "Have something to say?"

"No." I straightened. "I would like to rest my feet before the performance now."

"Fine." Before he released me, I saw him roll his eyes.

How in the hell did this man have the reputation he did? Everything I'd ever heard about him said he was a genius. The dancers who worked for them were bettered by his teaching, and it was an honor to be in a production he touched.

All we'd experienced was a bully who thought Slate City Ballet was his own personal toy box. Who cared if he broke the toys?

The nausea pulsed in my gut again, dragging through me. Fuck. That was more than nerves. Whatever the hell my body thought it could do to quit on me tonight? Too fucking bad. I was going to do this.

By the time I sat down in the dressing room, it had passed a bit but still lurked under the surface. I pulled my hair back into a tight bun so it was out of the way and started doing my makeup. It would be down and curly for act one.

Claire knocked and came in. We were sharing the room this run. "Woah there."

I looked at her in the mirror. "What?"

"Uhh," she laughed. "You're perfuming quite a bit. Which is fine, considering how sweet your scent is. But you're usually careful about it. You and Ash get carried away?"

My entire body went still.

Fuck.

Fuck.

I'd been in such a rush this morning, I hadn't taken the suppressant. And I'd spent the last week sleeping in my Alpha's beds. Scent-sympathetic Alphas, which made Omega's instincts go crazy.

And in the dressing room alone, with no one else's scent to push against mine, I hadn't even noticed.

This wasn't nerves, and it wasn't me getting sick.

I was going into heat.

"Are you fucking kidding me?" My face dropped into my hands.

Claire's face went slack with shock. "Oh, no. We need to call Skylar." The next cohort.

"No."

"*No?*" She looked at me like I was crazy. "What are you going to do? Dance until you're presenting on the stage?"

Straightening my spine, I continued my makeup. "There are scent cancellers in the shoe room. I'll borrow a spray and keep it going whenever I go on stage and come off."

"Sloane."

"Don't, Claire."

She watched me as I continued my makeup, staring at me in the mirror. "Are you sure?"

"I am."

When my first heat hit I thought I was sick too. I should have fucking known. Luckily my heats since hadn't felt like this, but it didn't surprise me with the intensity of the connection between my Alphas and me.

"Okay," she said. "I'll go get that canceller for you then."

"Thank you."

I finished my makeup for act one. It would be different for act two. Paler and more like the ghost creature I was supposed to be.

Claire came back with a bottle of the scent canceller the costume shop used and didn't even ask before she started spraying down my costume with it.

"You probably think I'm crazy," I said.

"No, I think that the entire company got swindled into working with a jealous and petty man who, for whatever reason, has it out for all of us. You specifically."

"It's that noticeable?"

She snorted inelegantly. "Sloane."

"Other than being late to that first meeting, I don't know what I've done wrong."

"Sometimes you don't know," she said. "Sometimes you never know. I worked with a professor who hated my guts at the ballet school I went to. I never did anything to her, but she still treated me the way Ian treats you. Gabriel needs to do something about it."

"And that won't make it worse?" I asked. "I'm already walking a tightrope with three of my pack working here. I don't think anyone in the company cares, and we haven't exactly hidden it." If these rehearsals hadn't been twelve hours a day and turning my Alphas feral, we might have had a shot at keeping it quiet.

Considering Ash had barely been able to keep his hands off me any time we weren't dancing, that ship had sailed. No one had said anything or even mentioned it so far.

"I don't know if it will make it worse," she said. "But I know that this company won't be here next year if he's completely unchecked."

Claire finished with the spray and set it down beside me and quickly began to work on her own hair and makeup. She didn't perform until act two, so she had time. But her role was difficult as well.

I sprayed myself down before Claire helped me lace into the

costume. Pain pulsed in my gut, and I was already beginning to go hot. "Sloane," she said.

"I know. It's my own fault. I forgot my suppressant this morning."

She gasped. "You've been taking suppressants?"

"I didn't want to be filling the studio with perfume while dancing with Ash."

Meeting my eyes in the mirror, she didn't have to tell me how bad this might be. Being scent-sympathetic already made everything in Omegas go haywire. Pushing it down made our body snap back with intensity. The show was a little over two hours. I could make it that long.

"If you need something you tell me," she said. "Got it?"

"I will." I didn't have the energy to tease her or protest. Just enough to get my shoes on and head backstage, because it was time. Then I paused. "Can you tell Dion?"

"Absolutely."

He needed to know so he wasn't blindsided the second we began to dance.

I went stage right and placed my hands against the wing wall, flexing my feet and stepping in and out of the rosin box. Behind me, the comforting warmth of chocolate chip cookies wrapped around me. Was it better? How the fuck was it *better*?

Oh, because you're an Omega in heat and one of the Alphas you want to fuck the living daylight out of you is wrapping his arms around your waist.

Heat and pain spiked through me. "Shit." I placed my hands over Asher's where he held me, unable to stop my body from bending forward to fight the pain.

"Sloane?" He sounded panicked. "Are you okay?"

"I'll be okay," I said quietly. "I have to be okay."

Like my body was determined to betray me, a whole new wave of perfume decided to ignore the metric ton of scent-canceller on my body and clothes. No shit, since Ash held me, the source of exactly what it wanted so close.

He turned me in his arms, examining me for where the pain was. I breathed through it and it faded. This was doable. It was.

It *was*.

Asher's eyes went wide as he inhaled, scenting the stronger scent of my heat. He backed me against the wall. "You're going into heat? Sweetheart, we have to get you out of here."

I grit my teeth. "I'm not going anywhere."

"You want to dance through your heat?"

I dug my fingers into the brocade of his costume. "Like hell am I going to throw away all of this fucking *torture* because I forgot to take a pill, Ash. I am going out on that stage and I am going to fucking dance this part. I have to." My voice broke, and I blinked back tears. If I started crying I might not stop, and I couldn't cry as Giselle until the end of act one.

It was my debut as a principal. You only had one, and I wasn't going to bail on it. On an opening weekend of a show? This was important, and he knew it, no matter how much pain I was in or had been in for the last week.

Asher's jaw was tight. I saw it work, like he was grinding his teeth. "Okay. But the other two performances? You can't white knuckle your way through those."

"I know. I know."

He nodded. "Then we'll get you through tonight. And when it's over, we're taking you home and giving you the heat you deserve, Sloane. I fucking swear it."

Out in the house, the cacophony of a crowd was growing. The orchestra was warming up. No one paid attention to us in the corner.

"Three more days," I said. "If I hadn't forgotten, I could have made it through our cohort. Now Skylar and the rest of them will have to scramble."

"Skylar is an Omega too," Ash whispered. "She'll understand."

I looked up at him, sinking into his eyes. "Don't hold back, Ash. Please. Dance like it's the end of the world."

He kissed me, soft and chaste, not messing up my lipstick. "I'll leave everything on stage, blue. Promise."

The stage manager called places. Ash, as Albrecht, was the first person to enter. He needed to go. But he lingered another moment, taking my face in his hands. "I don't know if this is the right time to say it, but I love you, Sloane Glass. I've loved you for

116

a long time, and you're one of the strongest people I've ever met. You are incredible, and everyone in the audience is fucking lucky to watch you dance."

"Ash." He blurred behind the tears I fought and kissed me, harder this time. We held on as long as we could, consuming the other until the overture was almost over and he needed to go. I wiped the lipstick from his mouth, pain and longing filling me in equal measure. I needed him.

I needed all of them.

"Break a leg, sweetheart. Two hours until I can finally make you mine."

He ran off just in time to make his entrance to a theater full of applause.

My hand on my chest, I caught my breath. Warmth swam through my veins, dragging through me with sick claws, trying to break through and unleash full heat.

Asher West loved me.

He loved me.

It was exactly what I needed to hold on to when my body rebelled. Because it was going to.

"Sloane." Claire appeared with the canceller, spraying me down again and fixing my lipstick before I stepped behind the door to Giselle's house, and opened the stage door to bright lights and thundering applause.

CHAPTER SEVENTEEN

JACE

I watched from backstage as Sloane came on stage to applause that *shattered* the air. Her promotion to principal hadn't gone unnoticed in the ballet world, no matter the shit show behind the scenes had been. People were excited to see her and her debut.

She was graceful and delicate, dancing with intent and wild abandon at the same time. I couldn't take my eyes off her.

Gabriel offered me a seat in the box with him and Roman, but I wanted to be backstage in case she needed me. Or any of the other dancers.

Asher, too, was in rare form with his dancing. A sensual edge I didn't usually see, and had no doubt it was because he was dancing with our Omega. They fit together, folding together and twirling apart, the chemistry between them entirely real.

Their dance with Dion, too, was great. This would undoubtedly be a success, and Ian would take the credit. But everyone in the company would know it had nothing to do with him and everything to do with the tenacity and hard work of the dancers on stage. *All* of them, corps included.

The act proceeded through the group dances, and finally there was a change. A moment where both Sloane and Asher were offstage. He ran off through the wing and straight at me, chest heaving, eyes wild. He looked like he was on the edge of rut.

"You're doing great," I said. "Really. This is awesome."

Asher's hands landed on my shoulders. "Sloane's going into heat."

"Excuse me?"

He shook his head. "After everything she's gone through for this, she wouldn't leave, and frankly, I don't blame her. But she knows she can't do anything about it after tonight. We need to get ready for this. The nest."

"What can we do in this amount of time?" I wanted Sloane to

119

have the perfect nest, but in two hours? Maybe three if you took into account after the show and getting home.

No wonder Asher was out of mind. He was all over her while her heat perfume slowly drove him crazy.

"Here," a new voice said, handing me a piece of paper. Claire. One of the other Principals, and Sloane's friend. "Call Addison. My partner. She's a designer, and she can get it done. Plus, she's just recovering from a cold and needs a project or she's going go stir crazy. Couldn't be here tonight. She's had to do short notice installations before."

"This short?"

She laughed. "This short. Do you know what she would want?"

I looked at Ash, and he closed his eyes, briefly covering his face with his hands. "Fuck. Yes. She used to doodle and scrapbook about a nest. I have no idea if it's what she would still want, but it's all I've got."

"Tell me. We can redo it later if she wants."

"It was like a sunset. But the kind with purples, pinks, violets, and golds. Maybe some super dark blue. Lights and a shit ton of pillows. Soft things like velvet."

Claire nodded. "Addie can work with that."

"Okay." Ash kept catching his breath. "The others have to know."

"I'll take care of it, Asher. You take care of yourself and her. As much as you can."

He glanced back toward the stage. "I'll check in at intermission."

Then he was gone, back into another wing for his next entrance. I looked at Claire. "Thank you."

"It's no trouble. Addison loves Sloane. She'll be salivating over this."

I sent a text to the pack group text.

JACE

> Mayday. I need you guys down here. Sloane will understand.

GABRIEL

What's going on?

JACE

Get down here and I'll tell you.

I dialed the number Claire gave me.

"Hello?"

"Addison?"

"Yup!" Her voice was cheery. "Who's this?"

"My name is Jace McKenna. Claire gave me your number. I'm one of Sloane Glass's Alphas."

A short silence. "Oh. Hi. What can I do for you?"

"Sloane's on stage, but she's also going into heat. Claire said—"

"Got it. Tell me what she likes and give me the address. How much time do we have?"

Relief washed through me in a wave. "A couple hours. Three at most." I gave her our address and repeated what Ash said about what she wanted.

"I'll need someone at the house in an hour to let me and the team in and show us where we're going."

"Someone will be there."

"Then consider it done."

"You're a lifesaver, thank you."

Addison laughed. "I know."

The line went dead just as Gabe and Roman came backstage. "What's going on?" Gabriel asked, fully in protection mode.

"Sloane's going into heat."

"You're fucking kidding me."

"Considering Ash practically collapsed getting offstage to tell me? No. Not kidding. Claire's partner is a designer and is going to fix the nest. Someone has to be there to meet her in an hour."

Gabriel turned to Roman. "I can't leave. After the show I have to present the bouquets."

"I'll go. Someone with an artistic brain should be there to help." He smirked.

I shook my head with a laugh. "Okay, asshole."

He was instantly serious again. "Is she okay?"

121

"I haven't seen her. I can't imagine dancing while going through pre-heat is comfortable."

Gabe sighed, looking past me to where our Omega danced once more. "I understand why she stayed, even if I want to spank her for it. Debuting on a season opener..."

We all understood it. Didn't mean we agreed with it. I handed Roman the piece of paper with Addison's number.

"I do wish I could see the rest of it," Roman said.

"We're recording this one." Gabe set his hand on Roman's shoulder. "You'll be able to see it anytime."

"Good."

"She's going to appreciate this, Roman," I said. "She's going to love it."

"Stay for the rest of the act at least, and then head over to meet her."

The three of us turned back to face the stage, where Sloane was front and center. Her dancing looked effortless. And it was so much more impressive now that we knew she was dancing through more than the normal amount of pain.

She was beautiful and strong as hell.

I couldn't wait to spend the next few days making her believe it just as much as we did.

CHAPTER EIGHTEEN

SLOANE

I lost myself in the dance, playing the part of a love struck girl with a weak heart. Asher's hands on me burned, but not as hot as I did.

Performing under stage lights was already hot. With my heat rising, I was on *fire*. A being made entirely from it. There wasn't room for anything other than the steps and my character.

I took the pain raking through my gut and turned it into the pain Giselle felt when she overextended herself, and further, when she had her heart broken. Ash locked eyes with me, and in his eyes I saw the words *I love you* even as I fell, allowing him to catch me as I died in his arms.

It wasn't scripted, but Ash kissed my limp form, gathering me up with what felt like genuine agony before the curtain fell.

He didn't wait, scooping me up off the floor and carrying me offstage to my dressing room. "Talk to me, blue."

What could I say? Pain and nausea gripped me like a hand squeezing around my stomach and ribs. I burned from the inside like a fuse, ready to explode at a moment's notice.

Claire pushed her way into the dressing room with us. "Give us a second, Asher. I'll help get her into the act two costume and makeup."

"I can help."

I heard the gentleness in her tone. "I know you can. But her being near you isn't going to make any of this easier."

He cursed, but set me down on the chair. "You're doing so well, sweetheart. Fucking stunning. I'll be right outside, okay?"

"Okay." I didn't want to let him go.

When the door opened I glimpsed Gabriel and Jace standing there waiting. A waft of their combined scents had me whining. A whole new wave of pain and need crashed down on me. "I need them."

"I know you do," Claire said. "You're going to have them soon."

She helped me dress, and it felt more like someone dressing a doll than having any participation. "I'm sorry, Claire."

"You'd do the same for me in a heartbeat. When your heat is over, buy me a coffee and we'll call it even."

"It's never felt like this," I admitted. "Like everything's warm and shiny. I think I might be a phoenix."

She chuckled. "You're certainly dancing like one. And I mean that as a good thing."

The makeup for act two was pale and ghostly. I wore a long, graceful white dress which made me feel feminine and beautiful and at the same time able to dance deserving men to death.

"We've got five minutes," she said. "Ready?"

I shook my head, then nodded. "Yes? I don't know."

"Stay here for just one second." She slipped out the door with the spray bottle of scent canceller, another waft of my Alphas hitting me in the chest. Fire roared through me, and desire so strong it *hurt*.

"Get the fuck out of here," she said. Answering growls. "Scenting you together is hurting her. You want her to make it through act two? Walk away right now."

Incredible sadness weighed me down. I didn't want them gone. I wanted them *closer*. My rational mind agreed with Claire, but my rational mind wasn't in charge right now.

"Okay, Giselle," she said. "Let's go murder some men."

"I don't want to murder them. I want to fuck them."

Claire laughed. The hallway outside the dressing room was blissfully free of scent. "Fine. Murder *then* fuck."

"I can do that."

We entered backstage just as Dion went on stage to grieve my death. And I let myself fall into it again. The dead girl who still loved the man who'd betrayed her. Some people liked to think Albrecht was an asshole, taking advantage of the weak village girl, and only performing his grief so people wouldn't think him a monster.

My preferred interpretation of the ballet was that Albrecht

was forced into a royal engagement he didn't want, and that he never wanted to hurt Giselle.

I rose from my grave and forgave Ash's broken character. There were real tears in his eyes. Together, we danced, and I protected him from the angry spirits of heartbroken brides.

My body was a candle in the darkness of the stage. I was the light. I was the breath and life of the forest even though Giselle was merely spirit. And when the sun rose, I looked over into the glowing light with the hope I felt.

It wasn't merely hope for Giselle and Albrecht's salvation. It was *my* salvation. The show was nearly complete, and I was still alive. I was still dancing. The heat hadn't broken me.

The curtain fell.

For three heartbeats, nothing but silence filled the theater. Then the audience roared. Ash wrapped me in his arms, holding me close as we waited for curtain call. "You were incredible," he whispered, voice raw. "I've never seen you dance like that."

"Can I be done?" I asked quietly. "I need you to take me home."

"You're almost done, sweetheart. I promise."

He brought me to the curtain, and every muscle memory I had kicked in. The perfect curtsey under the lights.

Out in the audience, the crowd was standing.

Tears filled my eyes. They were standing for me. For *me*.

Gabriel was on stage with us, handing me the biggest bouquet of roses ever. For my principal debut and opening night. I'd never been given one before. Despite my body aching and the fire trying to erupt within my veins, I would remember this moment for the rest of my life.

I looked past Gabriel to where Ian stood, and I smiled at him, just like I said I would. He'd tried to break me and failed.

Your move, fucker.

Three more encores, and the curtain closed for good.

Claire appeared. "I'll get her changed. Whatever you guys need to do to get ready to leave, do it. Now."

"On it," Asher said. Not before he kissed me, long and slow. A teasing preview of what was about to happen when I walked into their house. If I could still manage to stand by the time we got there.

"Do I have to change?" I begged. "As long as you guys don't tear it off me..."

"Fuck it," Gabriel's voice came from beside me. "We'll be careful, little one." He looked at Ash. "Get your stuff and hers. You don't want to leave your bike here the whole heat."

The look on Asher's face was thunder and lightning. But he went, with a searing look at me.

"Go," Claire said. "Get her out of here."

Gabriel's sharp sweetness wrapped around me. That intense fresh tobacco and warm vanilla. "We've got you now, little one."

Now that I wasn't on stage and didn't have to be strong, I melted. "It hurts."

A hand stroked down my back as we strode through the hallways. "I know it does, baby girl. We're going to make you feel better."

The back door to the theater opened into an alley none of us visited. A car waited for us there, Jace opening the back seat and Gabe pulling me down onto his lap. The frothy tulle of my skirt poofed around us, almost reminding me of the pictures of women in white bonding or wedding dresses that filled up cars.

I pressed myself into Gabriel, kissing below his ear, trying to get the sweater he wore off, off, *off*.

"Hold on, little one," he whispered.

"I've already been holding on. No more."

Gabe's hands deftly undid my bun so I was a tangle of blonde hair and tulle. Hell, I looked like the dead and broken spirit I was supposed to play. She'd probably look more like this. A mess, lipstick smeared, thighs damp because slick was soaking through my tights, wrecked and we hadn't even started.

He sank his fingers into my hair and pulled me back so he could see me. "Just a little longer. Once you let go you don't want to stop, and none of us want to spend your heat in the back of a car."

My whine made him pull my lips to his. "Please," I begged. My hands shook, fire building under my skin. The mixture of their two scents in the car lit me up like a firework with need. I felt him find the ribbons on my shoes and pull them off. They hurt, but not as much as the burning in my gut. It wasn't nausea anymore, not while I was with them. It was pure arousal and desire cutting through me until I was nothing left but pieces.

"Close your eyes," he whispered.

I obeyed.

Gabriel tilted my head to the side, exposing my neck. One single finger from his free hand traced down the column of my throat and along my collarbone. Every inch of movement was deliberate. Under his hands, I froze. I still burned, but while he held me safe and solid I could bear the burning. "Tell me your favorite ballet."

"Now?"

A soft laugh. "Right now."

There were too many. The classics and the modern ones. So many I wanted to dance... "It's a tie."

"Between?" Lips on my skin. I gasped into the burst of heat that exploded between my legs.

"Classics? *Swan Lake* and *Onegin*. New ones, *The Winter's Tale*."

Gabriel hummed, the vibrations teasing my throat. "Good choices."

"Why?"

I felt his smile. "I need that beautiful mind distracted so we can get you home."

"I promise I won't want to stay in the car." Moving my hips, I rocked down onto him, the hardness in his pants clear. "Just fuck me."

A growl from both of them melted me. I knew they meant it as a deterrent. It wasn't one. I *wanted* that sound against my skin. Between my legs. Why did the image of my Alpha's growling make me want to see if they could get me off from that alone?

"He told you no, baby girl. We're almost there."

Gabe pulled my head to his shoulder, wrapping me up so I couldn't move or resist the purr rolling through him. But it didn't relax me. All it did was make me blind with arousal.

"See?" Gabriel whispered. "We're here."

My head snapped to the window. We were outside their home. My home?

At least for the next few days.

They got me out of the car and into the foyer. Roman stood at the foot of the stairs. I threw myself into his arms and nearly climbed him in order to kiss him. *Roman* hadn't told me no. Roman who I wanted desperately even though we barely knew each other. He was *mine*.

He smirked, kissing me back. "Hello."

"Whose bedroom are we going to?" I asked.

Roman let me drag down his body, and those dark eyes reflected everything I felt back at me. "No bedrooms."

"What?" Agony and sadness crashed down on me. Had they brought me back here not to help me? "But—"

"Sloane." Gabriel turned me to him, his lips pressed to my forehead. "Take a breath for me, Omega."

It hurt to breathe. It hurt to exist. It would hurt and burn until I had a knot inside me. The only thing that mattered. "Alpha." The tears spilled over.

"We're not going to a bedroom because we're going to the nest. Ash will be here in minutes, and we're going straight there, okay? We need you to tell us if you have any limits."

Limits weren't a conversation I wanted to have right now. Who needed limits when I had four Alphas I wanted to lick like popsicles? Hell, I'd let them fuck me even if they *were* popsicles. A little temperature play never hurt anyone.

What would a Roman popsicle taste like? He smelled so good, and I wanted to taste that fresh mountain air even in a condensed form.

Snippets of a conversation with Petra, Eva, and Esme popped into my mind. Petra, beet red and embarrassed, asking the question.

Is it normal for them to taste so good? I literally crave the taste of their... you know.

Laughter and joy. *Yes, it's normal, and yes, it doesn't get less weird. You just have to go with it, because let me tell you, the craving doesn't get weaker.*

My whole body flushed redder than the red pointe shoes sometimes used in Stravinsky's *Firebird*.

Jace stepped up behind me and lifted my hair off my neck. "What are you thinking about that made you perfume that hard, Sloane?"

"Nothing. Nope. It's fine. I'm good." I almost choked on air. "I'm good. No limits I can think of other than bonding and anything that will permanently injure me. Not that I think you would do that. And not that I don't want to bond with you I just don't want to have heat brain when we do. But I don't have any thoughts. No thoughts. Zero things in my—"

Gabriel kissed me, the other two laughing. Jace's hands rested on my hips even as Gabriel held me against his body. "Not very convincing, baby girl."

I had a brief flash of what it would be like to be trapped between them and nearly fainted. "I don't know if I can wait much longer," I spoke into Gabriel's mouth.

"You don't have to," Roman said.

The sound of Asher's bike tore through the air outside. The dark smudge of him moving through the windows made my hair stand on end and every inch of me tingle. My last Alpha was here.

The door opened and Asher strode in, bags over one shoulder, helmet dangling from his fingers, never taking his eyes off me. He dropped everything on the floor, hauled me into his arms and kissed me.

Yes.

Ash was close to rut. The whole performance he was worried about me, touching me, scenting me. I'd pushed him almost as far as the heat had pushed me.

Somehow my legs were around his hips and we were moving. My back hit the wall of the elevator. Outside myself I realized we weren't alone. The others were here with us.

Good.

I didn't have to wait.

My hands shoved the leather jacket off his shoulders. He hadn't even put a shirt on beneath it, miles of bare skin and muscle along with the scent of chocolate and dough and batter. God, I was going to come from his scent alone.

The doors to the elevator slid open on a floor I'd never been to before. The top one.

Ash carried me through the hall and pushed a door open. Then he stopped and put me down. I stared at him, confused about why he wasn't touching me anymore. A whine and a cry came out of me to be met with a smile. Wait...

Gabriel had said a nest. They had a *nest*? My heat brain had skipped right over that like it was nothing.

Like Ash saw my realization, he smiled wider and turned me around into a wonderland.

The small round room in front of me was a dream. Delicate golden lights lined the edges, almost like we were caught in a storm of fireflies. The cushions in the nest looked like a sunset. The darkest navy blue of full night to the nearly neon pinks, purples, and oranges I loved. They looked *so soft*. A pile of blankets in similar colors was at the edge of the nest. I caught a glimpse of some metallic gold here and there.

My mouth dropped open in shock. For a moment my mind was clear. "What... how did you know?"

"You thought I didn't remember?"

"It's perfect," I whispered. Emotion rose in my chest. "But *how*?"

"The whole story is best for later, baby girl. But Roman came home and helped get it ready for you."

"You did?" I turned to him. His eyes were turned away, like he was embarrassed. "For me?"

"For you." Those same eyes filled with want consumed me. One corner of his mouth tipped up. "But you owe me a dance. Because I missed act two."

"You can have as many as you want." I twisted myself up to kiss him, and I wasn't nearly tall enough. He had to meet me halfway. I was ivy climbing on his stone wall.

Pain and fire ripped through me, taking away my moments of clarity. Hands found my shoulders and unlaced the back of the costume. "Out of the dress, baby girl. It's far too white for what's about to happen to you."

Safe. I was safe, and my Alphas were here. What Jace said came back. It took brains and bodies different lengths of time.

That night it had taken my body longer. This time it was my mind.

I stepped out of the costume and shivered out of my tights, entirely naked with them for the first time. These were my Alphas. This was my heat. It all clicked together in my head, and I became a nova.

Gabriel closed the door behind him, and I finally fell into true heat.

CHAPTER NINETEEN

SLOANE

I tumbled into the cushions with need and instinct driving me. Pillows shifted and blankets spread themselves like I wasn't the one moving them. I just knew they had to be where I put them because otherwise it wasn't right and I needed it to be *right*.

At the same time, I shuddered, pain wracking my stomach. I'd been like this too long. I'd never resisted a heat like this. How did I fix it?

Asher looped an arm around my waist and flipped me, tossing me onto my back on soft velvet pillows. "Time to stop thinking, sweetheart." Then, softer. "Time to have the heat we should have had a long time ago."

I wanted every single one of them more than I wanted my next breath, but it was right that Asher was first. After everything, it had to be him.

His lips met mine a second before he thrust inside me, both of us groaning.

Finally.

The tension that had simmered between us sang. Like the delicate humming strings of a symphony in an empty theater. Nothing but him and me and the way it was meant to be.

"Fuck." His voice cracked. "Fuck, Sloane."

I grabbed his face. "I know."

Were there flames coming off my skin right now? Every shiver of burning pleasure sizzled across my vision. Ash hadn't even started to move, both of us caught in this perfection of a moment.

"Ash," I breathed. "I need you. Please."

One hand curled beneath my thigh, lifting so he could drive into me that much deeper.

And Asher West fucked me.

Pleasure crashed through me in a wave, carrying me so far

away I might not come back. The only sensation was the movement of Asher's hips and the length of him driving home. He was mine.

He was *mine*.

My nails scraped down his back as I pulled him closer, drawing both a hiss and a curse. "I shouldn't admit this," he whispered in my ear, thrusting with ruthless, brutal intent. "And instead tell you I was a gentleman in my thoughts about you during those years in school. But I wasn't. Every fucking day I made myself come to thoughts of you. Of keeping you in the studio until everyone was gone and fucking you breathless. Or watching a wet spot grow on your tights in the mirror as you knelt in your pretty pointe shoes and sucked my cock. Or knotting deep in your ass so I could use your clit to make you *beg* for more, only to deny you until you couldn't take it."

Every night I'd let myself imagine what it might be like to have his mouth on mine, his filthy words in my ear, was nothing compared to this.

"To deny you purely for the sake of showing you what it was like to be without you."

I arched beneath him, orgasm flaring. It was as much pleasure as it was *relief*. And there was a finality to this I craved. No more going back and no more questions. I belonged to him.

To them.

"How long should I deny you my knot?" He asked, teeth scraping over my neck.

I whined. "Ash."

"Another time." He drove into me, our mouths clashing, tongues battling, his hips grinding where I needed them. Flickers and flares of light and ecstasy and *bliss*. He tasted like cookies. I needed to *taste* those cookies. "Another time for teasing, and another time coming for me."

The hand on my thigh slid up my body to my throat, gently but firmly pinning me in place while he fucked me. His other hand slipped between us and found my clit, adding more to the rocking of his hips. He never looked away, pinning me with his gaze as he finally made me his.

Heat curled inside of me, gathering the cloud of an orgasm together before it shattered apart and took me with it.

Everything tightened. I had no more control of my body, writhing on Asher's cock, arching against the hand at my throat, unable to contain the orgasm he fucked out of me. I watched his eyes fall closed and felt his hand tighten as he buried himself deep, knot locking into place *exactly* where I needed it.

Ash collapsed on top of me, kissing me hard, even as he thrust his knot deeper, giving both of us aftershocks. "I love you, Sloane," he whispered. "I love you so fucking much."

"I love you," I whispered. It felt right and perfect to say it. A long time coming.

Gently, he pressed his forehead to mine. We breathed each other in, along with the gravity of this moment. No matter how it happened, we were always meant to be here. Together. Entangled. Belonging to one another.

He grinned, kissing along my jaw. "I'm also going to thoroughly enjoy watching you get fucked by your other Alphas."

The knot in me released too quickly, Asher's own instincts knowing I would need another one sooner than later. He kissed me one more time before pulling back, leaving me spread across the nest, wanton, wrecked, and fully on display.

My other Alphas were naked, and after a week of pretending I didn't notice their bodies beneath their clothes, I *looked* at them. Roman's chest I'd seen and felt, but everything else made my mouth water. Including the *piercing* I saw peeking out above the head of his cock.

Jace stroked himself casually, and Gabriel watched me quietly. Intently. Still holding back, even now. They were all at the edge of the nest. "You're so far away."

"We can change that," Jace said, coming to me and lifting me up. "And you still didn't tell me what made you turn red."

"I did. I said it was nothing."

Jace placed me on my knees and held me against his chest. One clever move and he slipped into me, the angle and his curve hitting me in all the right places. "Oh, fuck." My head lolled back on his shoulder. Hands stroked up my ribs, teasing my nipples, weighing my breasts in his hands like they were only his to play with. I loved his hands on me. They brought shimmering arousal to the surface like a mirage.

He wasn't moving fast enough.

"You said it was nothing, but I don't believe you. You're in heat. You're in your nest. Nothing is off limits and there's no shame." He drove up into me and stole my breath. "Tell me."

"I wondered what a Roman popsicle would taste like. What he would taste like."

"A popsicle, huh?" Ash said. "There are different kinds of popsicles."

One arm around my waist, Jace held me against him and fucked me, the slap of our skin together loud, rhythmic, and erotic. He groaned in my ear. "You feel so fucking good, baby girl."

I couldn't speak or think or breathe.

"But I think you need more. I think you want to taste Roman while I fuck you. I think you want my hand in your hair, holding you still so he can push inside your gorgeous throat, and I'll fuck you harder just to push you deeper."

An orgasm flashed behind my eyes, dragging fiercely sharp claws of ecstasy through me. It didn't stop because he didn't. Jace tilted my head to the side. "What do you think about that?"

"Yes, yes, yes," I chanted in time with the way he fucked me.

I fell against the cushions, bracing myself. Jace's hands on my hips dragged me back onto his cock, and he didn't stop, driving himself deeper, grunting with every thrust.

One large hand cupped my chin, making me look up. And up. And up. All the way up Roman's body to where he stared down at me. Keeping our gazes locked, he knelt. He was so tall it was the only way to put me face to face with his cock.

Roman was bigger than the rest of them.

Every one of my Alphas had gorgeous bodies and gorgeous cocks. They were good. *Great*. The one fucking me right now was perfection, curving into me in ways that shot off fireworks behind my vision. And they were all a perfectly reasonable size.

But Roman? I didn't even know if I could fit him in my body let alone my throat.

The bit of hair on his chest trailed down his stomach all the way past the cut V of his hips to where it was neatly trimmed, close to the skin. Something about that made me shudder. The hair was sexy on its own. But the sight of it trimmed down had always been something I loved.

I couldn't explain it and didn't try to. But more than once I'd seen pictures of models with the barest hint of trimmed hair visible above low-slung pants and *melted*.

The cool and pure scent of him wrapped around me. Jace didn't have to grip my hair. Roman did that, gently and firmly, guiding my lips to the tip of him.

Holy *fuck*.

My eyes closed, and I surged forward, tasting his skin, the ball of his piercing knocking against the roof of my mouth. He tasted so good. Fuck popsicles. We weren't keeping popsicles in the house when I could get on my knees and taste them.

No fucking popsicles.

I moaned, my mouth as full of him as I could take. Jace had slowed down, slowly teasing me with shallow thrusts while I adjusted to Roman. Now he pulled away entirely. I whined around the cock in my mouth, and it turned into another moan.

Jace's hands came down on my ass, gripping hard, and his tongue dragged over me, fucking me deep, not caring that Asher had already been there before him. He tasted all of me, teasing me just enough that I wasn't sure if I wanted him to just keep his mouth on me or fuck me again.

Pulling back, I heaved in breath. "I don't think I can take more of you," I told Roman.

"Yes, you can." Gabriel's voice startled me, and I looked over at him where he still knelt at the edge of the nest. He smirked. "Don't look at me, little one."

Roman's hand pulled me back, and I closed my eyes, savoring the smoothness of his cock over my tongue. Jace licked me long and slow. "I'm going to need more time than I can spend right now tasting your cunt," he said, fitting himself against me and driving deep. Exactly like he said, the movement pushed me deeper onto Roman. To the limit. He was at the back of my throat. There was no way.

But the way Jace fucked me... I was already taking more than I thought.

New sensation on my clit threw me into a spiral of dizzy pleasure. Asher's mouth and tongue, sealing over my clit from underneath. So fucking close to where Jace fucked me. All three of them together—I broke.

Pleasure rippled from everywhere and nowhere. It was all I could do not to collapse and let their cocks be the thing keeping me up. Jace hadn't knotted me, so every dragging thrust felt like throwing gasoline on the flame. Asher's greedy tongue and Roman's gentle insistence, fucking my mouth not nearly as hard as I needed him to.

"You can take so much more," Gabriel said, suddenly closer. I shook my head, and Gabe's hand replaced Roman's in my hair. "Yes, you can, little one. You're our Omega. You can take whatever we give you. Maybe not at first." I heard the sultry implications. "Maybe we'll need to work at it together, but you can and will."

No questions or alternatives.

Everything snapped into place, like a lock that had been stuck for years before finally releasing. Another wave almost took me over, but not quite.

All at once, Ash released me and Roman pulled back, allowing Jace to pull me back up and *fuck* me. "You want to come again, baby girl?"

"Yes." A choked whisper.

"Say please."

"Please."

Gabriel sat at the edge of the nest again, posture lazy and indulgent. Arms flexing, emphasized by those fucking lickable tattoos, he stroked his cock slowly with his eyes on us. There was infinite time in that gaze. He was going to fuck me. He was going to *ruin* me. But he would do it when he was ready.

"Ash," Jace said, slipping his hand down my hips and holding me open.

Ash was already there, once again sealing his mouth over my clit, licking me in time with Jace's cock. No one could resist them together. Even if I wanted to make it last, I couldn't. I came silently, trembling, pussy squeezing down on Jace's cock so hard I didn't think he'd ever be able to pull back.

Good.

"Goddamn," he came, one more thrust locking us together. His breath hot on my skin, hands roaming, his cum filling me with warmth. I wanted it forever and I needed more. The drive to have them fuck me and knot me hadn't disappeared. It had grown.

Jace's teeth came down on my shoulder, not breaking the skin. "Your fucking pussy was made for my knot," he laughed low, goosebumps running over my skin. "Which is good, because my knot will be spending a lot of time there."

A desperate whimper I didn't recognize came out of me. "Please," I managed the word again, though I didn't know what I was asking for.

Jace's knot eased enough for him to release me and lay me down. But he didn't leave, reaching and pulling my legs up toward my head and spreading me open. "What—"

Roman's big hands covered the underside of my thighs, holding me, bending me nearly in half. He dropped his face close to mine, nearly brushing my lips with a teasing smile. "Ready?"

I bit my lip, fighting to keep still. "Yes."

He did kiss me then, teasing my lips open with his before he pushed in. And in, and in, stretching me open and filling me up until his hips were flush with mine and I couldn't *breathe* because I was so fucking full.

My air and voice came in breathy gasps that made Roman smile. Male satisfaction rolled off him, and I needed more of it. This quiet Alpha who I wanted to know *everything* about. I reached for him and couldn't reach him. Not with my legs pinned against my shoulders and thrown over his.

"You didn't," I gasped for air. "You didn't come in my mouth."

"No."

I whined, arching, and he didn't move, forcing my body to adjust.

It did, white-hot need fusing with my bones and turning me into the phoenix I'd felt like onstage. I was the firebird right now.

I'd dance them all into oblivion and make them worship me. *Let* them worship me while I did the same right back.

"Why?" My voice shook. "I want to taste you. I *need* it."

He kissed me, rocking his hips slowly, getting me used to him. Getting me ready. "And waste a perfectly good knot?" His whisper teased. "Don't worry, Sloane. You'll feed from my cock soon enough."

I swore my eyes rolled back in my head, the words sinking deep into my consciousness and reaching the most primal part of me. The Omega that needed to be claimed and owned. Taken in every way imaginable. Pinned down and fucked.

He didn't hold back.

Roman gripped the back of my thighs once more, pulled back, and drove home.

I came right then. The size of him pushed me over the limit. Nothing but brilliant light in my eyes and roaring in my ears. I was the sun that lit up the nest, happy to burn up and explode.

Could you die from orgasms? Because this felt like I could. It didn't stop. Every thrust was a new wave sending me into ecstasy and blazing through my heat. I didn't know how long it took or where I was. All I knew was that Roman was kissing me and I felt *good*. Better than I'd ever felt.

The swell of his knot grew inside me, the sharp dagger of pleasured perfection popping the bubble of need. Satisfaction settled over me like a blanket. Yes.

Roman rolled, pulling my boneless body with him, readjusting me so I was draped over his body. No energy left to move or speak. His purr rumbled beneath my ear, and I closed my eyes, for the moment, satisfied.

I managed a smile before exhaustion pulled me under.

CHAPTER TWENTY

GABRIEL

Sloane passed out with a smile on her face. She was so fucking cute I couldn't stand it. Though cute was the last word I would use to describe what I just witnessed.

Incandescent?

So fucking hot I nearly came just watching her take their cocks like she was born to be fucked. My own cock was so hard it ached. When I had my chance to sink inside her, I knew it would change everything.

I couldn't fucking wait.

But our little Omega needed the rest she'd so viciously been denied for the last week. Having her heat now? I loved it. *Craved* it. At the same time, all I wanted to do was bundle her up and let her rest. Take as much time as she needed to recover.

Roman gently curled his hand around the back of her neck, holding her to his chest like she was made of the glass she was named for. I took a blanket from the stack she hadn't touched yet. Metallic gold. It felt right to cover her in something that made her look as valuable and precious as we knew she was.

"Well then," Asher chuckled softly. "Okay."

Jace scrubbed a hand over his face, but he didn't take his eyes off Sloane. None of us did.

"The last thing I want to do is leave her," I said. "But I need to make some calls to make sure everyone knows what's happening. For the shows tomorrow and make sure I'm covered."

Ash nodded. "Don't take too long."

"I'll just be outside." I grabbed my phone from the pocket of my pants where I'd dropped them and closed the door behind me. The air in the hallway was colder and not drowning in the scent of blueberry pancakes.

My growl split the air, and I smothered it. I needed to be back with my Omega as quickly as possible.

First things first, I dialed Mark Thurman. The previous exec-

141

utive director of Slate City Ballet was supposedly enjoying his retirement, but given what I knew of the man, he was probably having difficulty adjusting to life at a slower pace.

"Oh god," he answered the phone. "Gabriel, please don't tell me you burned the place down already."

In the background of the call, I heard the buzz of conversation. That's right, he was probably still at the theater. Where there was a reception for the donors, and our absence was no doubt *painfully* obvious. Once we found out Sloane was in heat, nothing else mattered but her.

"Not yet, though I suspect you knew that, considering where you are."

"Fair point. But where are *you*?"

I took an even breath. "Sloane Glass?"

"She danced beautifully. I'd love the chance to tell her."

"She's my Omega," I said.

Silence on the other end of the line.

"Or rather, she's my Omega, along with Asher West, Jace McKenna, and the final member of our pack, Roman Hughes."

Mark laughed finally. "I'll be damned. Congratulations."

"Thank you."

"Still doesn't explain why none of you are here. I'll be honest, Gabe, it's a little awkward."

I didn't doubt it. "It's why I'm calling you, and I'm calling Ian next. Sloane went into heat just before she went on stage. Because it was her debut, and the rehearsals were... let's call them 'intense,' she forced herself through it."

Mark swore. "She danced like that while in *heat*?"

A smile broke over my face. "Yes."

"Honestly, that makes it more impressive."

"You see why I'm calling now."

"Yes," he laughed. "How can I help?"

"Can I bounce the exec calls to you for a few days? Everything should go smoothly, but I don't feel comfortable leaving my office absent, especially with Ian."

Mark's voice grew darker. "Something I should know?"

"Yes, but it's a conversation I don't have time for right now. After? I'll tell you everything."

"I'll hold you to that. Need me to pull up the next cohort?"

I blew out a relieved breath. "Yes, please. Apologize to them too. The four of us are over the moon, but for everyone else..."

"They'll understand," he said. "Heats happen. It's not the first substitution because of one, and it definitely won't be the last."

"Thank you. Truly."

"Don't thank me," he scolded. "Take the time to care for your Omega and don't worry about anything else. I'll make the announcement after you speak to Ian."

"Sounds good. I'll call him now."

"Let me know when you guys come up for air." He hung up laughing.

Typing out a brief text to my secretary, I told her what happened, and that Mark agreed to be the point person until Sloane's heat was over. She'd take care of making sure any calls went to him. Then I dialed Ian.

"Where the *fuck* are you?" If you could whisper a scream, he was doing it. "And where are the principals? People are waiting on them, Gabriel."

"Sloane Glass went into heat before the performance. For obvious reasons, the cohorts will be rearranged. Mark agreed to take point for me for a few days until it's over."

Stunned silence. "What? Until it's over— *you're* seeing her through her heat?"

My jaw tightened at the implication that I wasn't good enough to do that, or that Sloane didn't deserve it. "Considering she's my Omega, yes, I will be doing that. Asher West as well. And the rest of my pack. I'm aware it's not convenient, but it is what it is."

Ian didn't have to say anything for me to feel him seething on the other end of the line. I knew he wouldn't be happy, but this was life. Heats came and went. You dealt with them. It was no one's fault.

"Do you know how this looks?" he hissed. "Her disappearing after the show like she's actually a fucking ghost? We promised the donors and board a show. You think they're going to donate when the star is off on vacation getting fucked?"

The nest door opened and Jace came out, letting me get a hit of her perfect perfume. He mimed *food*, and I nodded.

"Ian, I would think carefully about the next thing to come out of your mouth. Because if it's insulting Sloane's professionalism or suggesting she triggered her heat to get out of performing, you will not like my response." I let my growl seep into the words.

"Should I prepare to give her all the leading roles now?" The poison in the words shocked me. "The executive's Omega gets all the best roles."

Rage cracked through me, and my phone creaked in my hand. "Say that again. I dare you."

That seemed to have the effect I wanted, but my anger didn't lessen. "Mark will make an announcement about what happened. If I hear you said anything about myself, Sloane, Asher, or anyone else at the reception, you will deal with me. And if you want to stay at SCB, get your head out of your *fucking ass*."

I hung up without waiting for a response and texted Mark it was done, with an added request that he tell the donors we would arrange another event for them to meet Sloane and Asher if they wanted to.

Silencing the device, I went back into the nest.

"What the fuck is that?" Ash asked.

"What do you mean?"

"I mean you walked in here with Alpha rage pouring off you, and you need to get it *out* of the nest before Sloane feels it and wakes up."

I looked at her and breathed. Just the sight of her calmed me enough to let the anger go. Or rather, let it slip beneath the surface to where I could deal with it later. Asher wasn't wrong.

"Ian," I said. "I'll deal with him after the heat."

"Do I want to know?"

"No," I said through gritted teeth. "You really fucking don't."

Roman glanced at me. "Are you calm enough to hold her?"

Holding Sloane. The tension melted from me. I needed to hold my Omega so my instincts knew exactly how she was. Safe, breathing, and under our care. "Yes."

I crossed the nest and lifted her from Roman's chest, keeping her enveloped in the blanket. Sinking down into the cushions, I let her slight weight anchor me, purr rising without a thought.

She snuggled closer in her sleep, and I just stared at her. This woman—this Omega...

With everything in me, I hoped we could show her exactly what she already meant to us. I wanted her in our home and in our beds. No more separation or questioning. After the heat, she was moving in. The need to hear her say yes was the only thing keeping me from calling a moving company to take care of it while we were locked in here.

Jace came back with bottles of water and a smoothie for Sloane when she woke. "I didn't know what you guys wanted."

"Not hungry yet."

I didn't think there was anything that would make me move from this spot or release her. Not until her eyes opened. Lifting her upward, I kissed her forehead, just enjoying the feeling of her in my arms.

"It doesn't feel real," Ash said softly. "After all this time. I just... I don't know if I'll ever get used to her being mine."

"You will," I whispered. "Because any world where she's not ours isn't one I want to live in."

Soft murmurs of agreement, and a soft sigh from my very sleepy Omega.

Cuddling her closer, I tucked her head beneath my chin, closed my eyes, and savored the feeling of existing exactly where we were all meant to be.

CHAPTER TWENTY-ONE

SLOANE

This purr was nice. Warm and steady. The heady combination of tobacco and vanilla cradled me along with a strong set of arms. My eyes fluttered open, and the first thing I saw was the ceiling of the nest. The lightest portion of the color scheme, with oranges that flickered briefly into yellows in between the twinkly little lights.

"Welcome back, little one."

I smiled and snuggled deeper into Gabriel and the blanket. The heat wasn't driving my brain for the moment, so I was choosing to not be quite awake yet.

"Here." He pressed a cup with a straw into my hands before continuing his slow path of stroking down my body over the blanket I was wrapped in.

Strawberry and banana exploded across my tongue. Icy cold that made me shiver when I was a being currently made of fire.

"Is it good?"

I nodded, leaning my head on his chest and not removing the straw from my lips. It was good. Jace made it, because he made the best smoothies. I needed to thank him later. Preferably by making him give me *his* butterscotch smoothie.

My secret smile at the thought didn't go unnoticed. The Alpha in question appeared in my line of vision. "Am I going to have to fuck the thoughts out of you again, baby girl?"

I shook my head.

His eyes crinkled with his smile. "Good."

The smoothie slowly disappeared. When was the last time I ate? Maybe this morning? Was it still the same day?

My eyes closed, and I continued to rest on Gabriel. I was so tired. I'd been tired before the heat and this wasn't going to make it better. I wanted them, and I knew before long I'd be begging. But at the same time...

"Gabriel?"

"Yes, little one?" His purr strengthened.

"When my heat is over can I have a few days off? I just— I need to sleep."

I caught the barely there hitch in his purr and the way his fingers tightened where they held me. "Of course, Sloane. Everyone in the company is going to take some time. I'm making sure of it."

"Thank you," I sighed the words.

"I'm going to fucking kill him," Gabriel muttered.

We all knew who he was talking about, but I didn't want to think about him now. "I don't want him in the nest with us."

"You got it, sweetheart." Asher's voice came from across the nest. I didn't turn to see him. This was so comfortable.

"What time is it?"

Gabriel chuckled. "I'm honestly not sure. You've been out for a couple of hours."

I gave the empty cup to Jace, where he waited with an outstretched hand. "That was good."

"Gotta keep your strength up," he said with a wink.

Another sigh fell out of me, and I reached up to trace the lines of one of Gabe's tattoos near my eyes. A *fleur-de-lis* rendered in dark blue ink that seemed to pop up from his skin. "I'm happy I'm here with you," I whispered. "I just wish we'd had more time, so it doesn't feel like I'm forcing you into something when you barely know me."

"Is that what you think?" Gabriel asked quietly.

"I don't know," I admitted. "It just happened at the wrong time because I forgot the suppressant. We could have been ready. Not inconvenienced you and everyone else."

It was the exhaustion talking, I knew that. But I still didn't want them to feel forced, no matter what.

Gabriel peeled the blanket away from me. His face was hard. Not from anger—this was something else entirely. What I'd seen flashes of in his office and the unguarded moment in his bedroom this morning.

The second—the *second*—he touched my bare skin, everything flared to life again. Pure fire raced through my veins and lit me up like a neon sign. Wetness crept down my thighs from being

148

so fucking close to this Alpha who hadn't fucked me yet. I needed him to fuck me.

I whined, gasping for air because somehow all of it had disappeared. "Alpha."

Gabriel hauled me up higher, putting his mouth to my ear. "Let's see if we can clear up a few things, shall we?"

"Wh—"

"*Present*," he commanded, and I scrambled to obey. I practically fell off his lap, putting myself on my knees and stretching my arms in front of me with my ass in the air. Everything exposed, the small breeze of his movement on my wet pussy making me shiver.

One hand stroked down my spine to my ass like he was admiring everything available to him. My Omega preened. I smiled into the cushions, loving the attention and craving so much more. No more worry and no more concern. I was in heat and I needed a knot. My Alphas would give me one.

Why had I thought anything else?

Gabriel fit the head of his cock against me, and grabbed my hips, sinking into me with a groan that matched mine. He didn't stop there, spreading his body over me until we were lined up limb for limb, his fingers gripping mine and holding my arms down. Nearly pressed flat on the floor of the nest, everything was *him*.

"Alpha—"

"Quiet, Omega." One hand released me to grab my hair and turn my head so my cheek pressed against the velvet. His lips now at my ear, he rocked his hips and held me where he wanted me.

The command made me shudder and whimper, unsure if I should beg, fight, or submit.

"You're going to stay right here," he said. "And take everything I give you like the good girl you are. If you understand, you may say 'Yes, Alpha.'"

"Yes, Alpha," barely the whisper of a breath. A brand new burst of slick and arousal gushed around his cock.

His hand came down on mine again, and he pulled back, only to slam deep. Not once or twice. All the way out and all the way in. Over and over again.

Gabriel was unleashed. A snarl rolled along the skin of my back, and my Omega answered it. I arched my ass into him, taking him deeper. He needed to fuck me harder. Deeper. I needed to feel him so far in me I'd never get him out.

He knew.

And my Alpha fucked me harder than I'd ever been fucked in my life. All I could do was take it. Raw, ruthless, brutal pleasure coiling through every limb and every cell. Every stroke made me moan, and he didn't quiet me again.

"The next time you say something like that, I *will* spank you," he said. My muffled moan made him laugh. "Maybe I'll do it anyway."

"Yes, please," I begged. Never in my life had I wanted to be spanked, but Gabriel made me want it. To let him give me pain just so he could take it away and give me pleasure. For this Alpha to give me the structure I desperately craved and needed.

Energy snapped between us a second before I came. Primal understanding of who I was and who he was. I could and would push him, and he would push me right back, and win. I always wanted him to win if it meant he fucked me like this.

I screamed, shaking harder because he held me down with no sign of stopping or slowing.

Teeth scraped over my neck and shoulder. "You belong to Ash, little one. You belong to Roman. You belong to Jace. You belong to *me*." His hips drove me into the nest floor, not letting the orgasm fade.

"Your heat could have happened the day we walked into that studio and it still would have been perfect, and you still would belong to us. You are not a *fucking* inconvenience. Do you understand?"

"Yes, Alpha."

Gabriel lost control of his rhythm for a second, moaning in my ear. It was the hottest sound I'd ever heard. "Fuck, I'm going to come too fast because your pussy is perfect."

A smile broke over my face. Even in the midst of mindless fucking, I wanted to tease him. To lean into the push and pull. I wiggled my ass back against his hips, and he knocked my legs wider with one knee, spreading me open. It let him all the way in, until I felt him everywhere.

"And after I'm finished turning your ass cherry red, you're going to say sorry to all of us on your knees with a cock in your throat. Understood?"

"Is that meant to be a punishment?"

It wasn't just his laughter that answered me. "Just the way it is, little one. I won't let you doubt this or doubt us. We are your pack. It doesn't matter how long it takes. We're going to know everything about you."

Gabriel pulled out of me and rolled me onto my back, sliding in again to the hilt. Every part of me was still pinned, my wrists under his hands. He barely missed a beat. "All your favorites. The taste of your cunt at every time of day. How to get those little whimpers out of you that make my cock *ache*. And you'll know everything about us too."

He shuddered above me, head dropping to his chest as he came, slamming his cock so deep I saw stars before his knot drove me into the golden bliss of coming all over him. "*Gabriel.*" I needed to move. All this pleasure had to go somewhere or it was going to kill me.

If it did, it'd be a good way to go.

My Alpha's lips took mine in a savage kiss. Claiming. Leaving his mark on me without his bite, but in its own way just as permanent.

He still rocked his knot into me, dragging out all the pleasure with shimmering gold sparkles like the ones above our heads. *Woah.*

"There you go," he whispered, thrusting hard one more time. My vision disappeared. Everything tightened. Goosebumps and tingles everywhere. My nipples hardened and my heart stopped. I couldn't even breathe.

I hauled in air, gasping like I'd been drowning.

I had. In Gabriel.

Lifting his hands off my wrists, my Alpha cradled my face. "What are you not going to do?"

"Doubt you," I said. "You're my pack."

It felt like the words resonated in the space between the five of us.

Gabriel smiled. "Good girl." I whined, and it only made his smile deeper. "I'll be here if you ever need a reminder."

Huffing a laugh, I threw an arm over my face. "So you're telling me all I have to do is pretend to doubt you and you'll fuck me like this?"

A low sound, somewhere between a growl and a purr. "Careful, little one."

"What if I don't want to be?"

"Hmm," he hummed into my neck. "Then you better get used to sleeping on your stomach."

I flushed, need washing over me again. He meant that my ass would stay red from his hand, and the thought of feeling him even when he wasn't there was so hot I wanted him to start now.

"But you'll be careful," he smirked. "You're a good girl."

I squeezed down on him and was rewarded with a low curse. "I'm not *only* a good girl. Sometimes I'm bad."

"Is that so?" Jace sprawled next to me, his face coming over mine. He kissed me, swallowing my moan at the loss of Gabriel's knot. "Well, good girls taste even better, so I think I should check."

"How?"

Jace pulled me over to him, twisting us so my knees landed on either side of his head. "Drown me, baby girl. Make me taste blueberries and syrup for the next hundred years."

"Oh, god."

He kissed my clit so softly I barely felt it, and yet I felt it *everywhere*.

Jace's hands dug into the softness of my hips and ass, pulling me down onto his mouth. Just like when he touched me on the massage table, Jace took his time. There was no part of me his tongue didn't touch, and every time my pussy flooded his mouth, he smiled.

His tongue curled under my clit, teasing and swirling like it was the flavor he needed to live. The climax was slow. A tide sweeping in with every stroke of his tongue. Until I braced on my hands, fucking his mouth as hard as his tongue fucked me.

"That's one, baby girl."

"One?" I sounded ragged. "One what?"

"Orgasm. I warned you I was going to spend some quality time between these pretty thighs. It starts now."

Jace consumed me again, and I could barely keep myself upright. In front of me, Gabriel appeared, now standing, a feral light in his eyes. He bent to kiss me. A deep, drugging kiss that had my eyes struggling to open when he pulled away. They were drenching me in pleasure and I wanted every fucking second. It wasn't enough. It wasn't *enough*.

He kissed my temple. "Ass or mouth, little one. You choose."

Beneath me, Jace laughed. The words made me soak him, and he took his time drinking me in.

"Mouth," I moaned. "Need to taste you."

"Taste *yourself*," Gabriel growled, sliding his cock between my lips. "Taste yourself while he tastes you."

Gabriel wasn't small, but he wasn't the monster Roman was. So when he curled his hand behind my neck and pulled, his cock slipped deeper than I thought possible. He moved my head, allowing himself to slip into my throat.

His cock tasted like both of us, and it wasn't remotely strange that I loved the flavor of us together. My eyes fluttered closed. Between Jace's tongue and Gabriel's cock, I was a hostage to their will. A very willing hostage.

"Help me out, Jace." I didn't fully register what Ash was asking for until Jace gripped my hips and shifted me, tilting me to consume my ass with just as much fervor as my pussy. I groaned around Gabriel's cock.

Ash dragged his mouth down my spine. "Since you chose mouth, your ass is free."

"Shit," Jace spoke between strokes of his tongue. "If those kinds of words are all it takes to make you gush, there's more where that came from, baby girl." He moved me back, sealing his mouth over my clit and sucking so hard I saw stars.

Gabe pulled me back long enough to let me breathe, thumb dragging over my lower lip. The warm approval in his gaze felt like stepping into warm sunlight. I wanted to curl up and live in that glow. His smirk sent arousal tumbling downward.

153

I was on the edge of exploding, Jace's clever tongue driving me to the edge but not taking me over. My hips rocked, grinding down into his mouth. He didn't pull away—he pulled me closer, letting me fuck his face the way I needed while I watched Gabe.

The Alpha in front of me bent down, sweeping his tongue into my mouth, that tongue mimicking everything Jace did. I moaned, unable to do anything but hold on and let the pleasure come. Heat burned beneath my skin and in my gut.

I still needed more.

"I love tasting you on your own tongue," Gabriel whispered. "And I was right about you taking more."

"More," I gasped. "Not all." Even with him deep, he hadn't been all the way in.

"You sure about that?"

He slid into my mouth again and didn't stop, guiding my mouth down the length of him until my lips met skin. All of him. Every inch.

I came.

A firework made of starlight that kept me grinding into Jace's mouth and savoring the sensation of taking *everything*. My pussy clenched, craving a knot, desperate to have one.

Ash chose that moment to fit himself against me and push into my ass slowly. Any other time I might have needed more time—not now. Heats changed everything, and Asher pushed himself into me until I was entirely impaled on two different cocks. All that was missing was the third.

Oh *fuck*.

Gabriel pulled back and gripped the hair on the top of my head. The tip of him rested on my bottom lip as he stroked himself. "Keep your mouth open, Sloane."

I missed the fullness of him, and yet I was already so full. Ash's hands rested on my ribs, holding me still. Jace's hands still held my hips on his face where he licked my clit like it was his own personal lollipop. Gabriel's hands worked his shaft, arms flexing in the worlds best arm porn. Roman was at the corner of my eye, watching the four of us like he could memorize every detail. And me?

I was *theirs*.

154

Everything faded into a hazy radiance, and I surrendered. They moved in sync, pushing me towards another, bigger orgasm. Ash stopped holding back, fucking me onto Jace's mouth hard and fast. I was going to come from him fucking my ass, and I never had before.

So many things that had never been possible before them. They made everything feel new and effortless. Emotion swelled in my chest, adding to everything.

Gabriel came hot across my tongue, pure vanilla and the extra spice of his scent. "Swallow, Sloane." His hand shifted from my hair to cover my mouth, sealing it closed so I had no choice. As if I would have chosen differently. I drank him, the submission just pushing me further into this place of mindless *feeling* I craved.

"Good girl," he whispered, leaning close. "Going to come with a cock in your ass and a tongue in your cunt, aren't you?"

I nodded where he still covered my mouth.

Joy and something more lit him from within. "Will you come when I tell you to, pretty girl?"

Could I? I was barreling toward the end at the speed of light. The only thing I could do was try.

Ash wrapped his arms around my chest, holding me closer while he took me without the mercy I didn't want. Under Jace's attention, my clit was so swollen and sensitive I was pretty sure he could choose to make me come any time he wanted.

My eyes closed. I fell into that place before the orgasm where everything felt bright and electric. Sometimes *better* than the orgasm itself because you could submerge yourself in it. Every part of you tightened held its breath waiting for the final peak, and every moment you held on was delicious.

So close. So fucking close. I'd never held on so hard, fighting the urge to give in so I could see the approval in all their eyes.

"Come." Gabriel whispered the word against my lips, and I fractured. My voice echoed off the walls of the nest. Everything was fucking pleasure. Sizzling and swirling, taking me down so deep it felt like I hovered, my body deciding whether to stay conscious or fade into soft oblivion.

Ash growled in my ear, knot swelling in my ass just before he filled me with blazing waves I could feel. We collapsed off Jace,

Ash holding me to his chest. Jace followed, guiding my eyes to his. "Good job, baby girl."

I watched him lick his lips, not remotely cleaning himself of *me*.

"You did so good," he whispered.

"I could get used to this." Asher's smile colored his tone. "A soft, satisfied Omega in my arms with my cock knotted in her ass."

"Just one thing," Jace said. "You're not satisfied, are you, baby." Not a question.

Words weren't an option right now. They'd fucked the voice right out of me. I was satisfied, and I wasn't. All of it was barely a breath on the growing bonfire of my heat, and every touch fanned the flames higher.

I shook my head.

"Guess we'll just have to try harder," Ash said. Knot releasing, he pulled me to my back underneath him. His gaze roved over my body, taking in every wrecked piece. "You ready for more?"

"Yes," my voice was nothing but air.

Asher leaned close and took my lips. "You know I love you?"

What little strength I had I used to loop my arms around his neck. "I do know that."

"Good. Because I'm going to fuck you so hard you're going to doubt it." He rolled me over again, palms spreading my ass, tongue getting me ready for him to start all over again.

"Tell us if you need to stop."

"No," I gasped, his tongue spearing into me. "No, don't stop."

They didn't.

CHAPTER TWENTY-TWO

SLOANE

*H*ot breath against my skin woke me, the slow and sensual feeling of lips on my skin. More than that —warmth and wet, a tongue dragging through the center of me, stopping to trace the entrance to my pussy before circling my clit with unhurried indulgence.

The movements weren't for me. They were for him. Mouth between my legs because he wanted to be there even when I slept.

I reached without opening my eyes, a hand meeting mine and pulling it down to my side. A gentle reprimand. When I gathered enough energy to open my eyes, warm brown ones met mine. Roman looked up from between my legs, nothing visible but his eyes. He slid his tongue all the way into me while I watched him slowly fuck me.

This was *luxury*.

He pulled back briefly, his skin soaked with my slick, and smiled, self-conscious. "Sorry. Couldn't wait to taste you again."

"I don't mind."

Mind? That made it sound like he'd taken my chair. He climbed up my body, dropping his mouth to my nipple, pulling it into his mouth and more, consuming me. Again, slow. Sultry. Leisurely.

"And by mind," I gasped when he switched to my other breast. "I mean this is the best way to wake up."

Roman dragged his mouth upward, tracing the lines of my collarbones with his tongue before kissing below my ear. "I would have done more," he whispered roughly. "But I wanted to ask."

The thought of waking up with him already inside me had perfume swirling around the two of us, body melting and pussy soaking. He inhaled, slow and deep against my neck. "You like that idea?"

"Yes."

"Good to know. Now I'll have to decide whether to wake you up with my tongue or my cock when you're in my bed."

"No reason it can't be both."

He chuckled, the sound soft and dark. "True. Now can you be quiet enough for me to fuck you?"

I looked to my left. Ash slept a few feet away, and beyond him I saw Jace's darker shoulder. Gabriel was probably somewhere sleeping too, since he spoke quietly. "I can try. No promises."

Roman kissed me, taking his time to adjust us. If I'd been tired before the heat, I was exhausted now. It had been days—no idea how many. All I knew was I'd been fucked every way I could imagine, plus a few. And they still had more ideas about what to do *to* and *with* me.

A couple of times they took me to the shower and cleaned themselves off me. Which ended up with us spending hours there, my fingers and toes pruned from being fucked under the water.

So despite Roman's soft kisses and touches bringing the heat to life once more, a slow fuck sounded incredible.

Easing himself between my thighs, he curled my legs around his waist before taking me slowly. That sweet soreness made me shudder. The heat took away the sting of pain, mostly. But nothing could *truly* erase the feeling of being ravished for days. I wouldn't trade it for a fucking second, but I pressed my face into Roman's shoulder and moaned.

"I need something to call you."

I pulled back at that and raised an eyebrow. "My name not good enough?"

The way he rolled his eyes brought a smile to my lips, and I was kissing him before I even realized it. Roman rocked, creating a smooth rhythm that wasn't going to drive me to madness... yet.

He was silent for a while, our faces so close we shared breath. When we met he told me talking wasn't easy. I didn't know why yet, but I wasn't going to crowd him if he needed time to find the words.

"Your name is beautiful."

"But?"

"But they have names for you, and you like it."

Pink tinged my cheeks. He wasn't wrong. I did like it. "And you want one too?"

Roman nodded.

"Like what?"

"Not sure yet." Pushing himself up on his arms, he thrust harder. Still slow and steady, but growing. "Have to try some."

With him above me, it showed me how much bigger than me he was. More than a foot separated our heights, and he had to arch his shoulders to keep our eyes locked. But I liked how small he made me feel, and the way he looked at me right now told me he liked being able to overwhelm me.

I squeezed down on his cock and he purred. "Careful."

"Of what?"

His mouth opened and closed. Finally, "I only have so much control while I'm buried in your cunt."

"That's the thing," I said, reaching for his shoulders. "I never asked you to stay in control."

"Sometimes you need a sleepy fuck."

"Yes." Arching up to him, I stole a kiss and managed to pull his weight back down onto me. "Yes. And I want those. I want to wake up with you inside me and for both of us to barely move. Just enough until we're shaking. I want to wake up with you fucking me like you want to break me." I shivered at the thought, every vision unraveling my commitment to being soft and quiet. "But right now I just need you to fuck me."

He did.

I wrapped my arms around his head and buried my fingers in his hair, holding on for dear life. Roman wasn't fucking to break me, but he wasn't holding himself back. Every time he drove his hips into me his cock nearly bottomed out, and everything shuddered.

Every internal button my body had, he pushed. Over and over again. And that fucking piercing? He knew what to do with it, shifting his angle until it hit the spot that made my moan turn throaty and rough, my hips rising to meet his effortlessly.

"Kitten?" He whispered it against my ear.

The sound of his voice so low stole my breath and made me ache, but I shook my head, finding his lips with my own. "I have too many claws." Like I could prove it, I gently dragged my fingernails along his ribs.

"Fuck." His body jerked, and his mouth crashed down on mine. No more gentleness. We came together like we would die if we didn't, giving in. I locked my ankles behind his back and didn't let him pull away. The two of us locked together, fucking each other as much as he was taking me.

"I wonder..."

Roman scooped a hand under my ass, tilting me so he could thrust exactly where he wanted. Shallow and upward, not even half of his cock entering me. But it put that goddamned piercing right where I needed it.

The world went *white*.

A scream of pleasure tore out of me, legs flying out straight, arms reaching for anchors that weren't there as my body tried to run from the pleasure raging through us. Roman didn't stop, simply lifted me so I straddled his lap, impaled by him. And he wasn't moving anymore.

I caught my breath and braced myself on his chest. "Why did you stop?" I begged. "Please don't stop."

Roman used his hands to move me in a rolling motion on his cock. "In a second."

"He's waiting for us." Gabriel wasted no time, sinking to his knees behind me and fitting his cock to my ass. We hadn't done this yet. And with Roman already in me?

"I don't— I don't think..."

"Do you trust me, little one? That I'm not going to hurt you?"

I almost laughed. Gabriel hurting me wasn't something within the realm of imagination. Spank me, discipline me, make me his. Command me, play with me, fuck me. But hurt me? Never. "Yes."

He entered me slowly. An inch at a time. I couldn't see anymore. Everything was taken up by being so fucking full. Fingers traced up the back of my neck to grip my hair. He loved doing it and I loved it too. Just like Jace pulling on it, Gabriel's hand holding my hair tight did things to me I couldn't explain.

"Open your mouth."

I did, and he moved my head. Butterscotch coated my tongue as he pushed me onto Jace's cock at the same time he kept pushing deeper. One pull brought me back, and another push had chocolate chip cookies making my mouth water.

No strength to open my eyes for more than a second, I glimpsed my Alphas side by side, stroking their cocks. All four of them at the same time.

Could I?

In the darkness of my bedroom, hot and horny with desperation, I'd seen videos of Omegas taking four cocks at once in various positions. If I could take more than I thought? I wanted that.

Gabriel's hips were flush against my ass. They were both in me, stretching me to the limit. "Ready, Omega?"

Fire surged beneath my skin. I didn't even have time to tell him yes. They moved together, fucking in sync and apart and holy *shit* I didn't know which was better. I loved all of it.

Jace's cock was hard to swallow, curved as it was, but I still did it. Ash's was thicker but straighter. It didn't matter. With Gabriel's hand guiding me, I didn't decide who fucked my mouth. I didn't want to decide.

I wanted to be *worshipped*.

Roman's thumb brushed over my clit, unlocking everything. I was an Omega reborn. Made of light and pleasure, burning alive with it. I heard my own voice begging them for more, but I wasn't present enough to know what I said. All my conscious mind did was enjoy the ride.

Stretched to the limit, three cocks in me at once, I didn't stop coming. Their hands on my skin, their scents, their breath brushing past me, it all drove it higher.

Was it one long orgasm? One after another? It didn't make a difference and I didn't care. Butterscotch candy flooded my mouth. I sucked it down and wanted more. Jace's cum was candy I would never have enough of. Until Ash came down my throat and the mixture of the two of them had my eyes rolling back in my head, coming purely from my Alpha's sugar high.

"Please," I reached for something. Anything. This was different. It was too much and never enough. I really burned this time.

A real life flame that would take down the building along with me. "I can't breathe."

"You can, baby girl." Hazel eyes floated in front of me. "Breathe."

I shook my head. "I can't."

He smiled, but I couldn't focus, eyes wheeling. Beneath me, Roman roared, ramming upward, knot swelling larger than I'd felt before. He didn't stop coming, wave after wave filling me and spilling out in spite of his knot. White hot heat gathered in my core, incandescent and waiting to set the world ablaze.

Gabriel came, his knot pushing against Roman's.

It was what I needed.

The orgasm obliterated what was left of me, cresting in a wave that couldn't be escaped. It fell, crushing me, bringing me to collapse on Roman's chest, spent, exhausted, and... cold.

A shiver wracked me. Coming that hard hadn't destroyed *me*. It had broken my heat.

Fuck, that had been incredible. And still, relief and comfort washed through me. I made it through it, and so did they.

Roman stroked a hand over my hair and whispered. "Firefly?"

I wasn't sure if he was asking me if I was okay or if I liked the nickname. Either way, the answer was *yes*. "I love that."

"Yeah?"

"Yeah. And... my heat broke."

Ash knelt beside me where I was still knotted between them. "You okay?"

Emotion I couldn't fight swamped me, and my eyes filled with tears. "I think so."

He brushed away one of the tears with his thumb. "If I didn't know better I'd be panicked about the tears." I tried to shake my head, but he kissed me first. "You're okay, sweetheart. We know. Whatever you need, we'll make it happen."

"I don't know what I need," I admitted.

There had never been a heat like this, and the couple of times I'd actually spent one with someone, they weren't around after to take care of me.

Gabriel's knot loosened, and he gently pulled away. Roman's knot eased moments later. A blanket draped over my shoulders. I shuddered coming off Roman's cock and curling into softness.

"What happens now?" The words were absent, almost to myself.

Jace pulled my feet into his lap and slowly massaged them. "I think that depends on you, baby girl."

Snuggling deeper into the pillows so I could look at them, I took a deep breath. "What do you mean?"

"Well," Gabriel cleared his throat. "I hope it doesn't come as a shock that we want you here with us."

"Live here?"

He turned me slowly on my back so I could see him. The smile on his face was so big I couldn't help but smile back. "I almost ordered a moving company to go get your things while we fucked you. But I wanted to ask properly."

I blinked. "Don't you guys have to rearrange things before you move a whole new person into your house?"

Gabriel looked around pointedly. "I think we have a pretty good start. And since the rest of this floor is empty..."

Pulling the blanket over my head, I curled in on myself until I was a ball. It was all too much to feel and think about. The thought of going back to my apartment alone made my chest ache with sadness. It had been a good home, but I'd been so lonely there, I didn't want it back.

And still, in a contradiction, letting go of it after so long made me panic. Losing the armor you'd had forever would do that.

Chocolate chip cookies warm from the oven seeped through the blanket as Asher wrapped his body around mine. "Did we lose you, blue?"

"No."

"Then why are you hiding?"

I allowed him to uncover my face. "Because I want it so much and that's terrifying?"

In his eyes I saw the understanding I needed. It was scary because I'd been fighting on my own for so long, I still wasn't used to having anyone to rely on. I had my friends and I had my grandmother, but it was different.

Especially after five years of knowing what could have been and wasn't.

"Remember what Gabriel said. We're not going to let you doubt us or this. None of us are going to change our minds, Sloane."

Sitting up slowly, I leaned against his shoulder and looked at each of my other Alphas in turn. The same conviction lived in each of them.

"It's okay to be scared," Ash whispered. "Especially of something so big. But as long as you're not scared of *us*? There's nothing we can't handle."

I wasn't.

"Move in with us, baby girl."

Closing my eyes, I took a deep breath and blew it out. "Okay."

Laughter bubbled out of me. Suddenly I was in a tangle of limbs, blankets, and purrs. From now on I always would be.

CHAPTER TWENTY-THREE

SLOANE

Showers were underrated. Especially long, hot showers you could stand in forever. This shower in particular had my heart. It was *so cool*. Big, with a bunch of different shower heads. One of the sexy straight-down rainfall ones, but also normal ones for when you didn't want to deal with so much water in your face.

There was a bench, too. Which was great for sitting and savoring the hot water, since I was still exhausted. But given my... activities the last few days, I imagined there were also other ways to use it.

I looked around. This was *my* shower. On the same floor as the nest, in the bedroom that would also be mine. There was another empty room on this floor, still filled with some boxes.

The Lys Pack hadn't been here long. A couple of months while they all transitioned from living in the capital city, Concordia.

Rather, Gabriel and Roman had been here getting everything settled while Ash and Jace stayed behind to finish some obligations. That's what they told me while guiding me—still wrapped in the soft blanket—through the floor where I would live.

It made me feel better. If Ash had been here in the city for months and not tried to find me, it would have hurt even though I was the one avoiding him. The townhouse looked so good, I would never have thought they hadn't been here long. When I said as much Gabriel smirked and told me he made sure they'd had help to do it quickly.

I didn't have any clothes, unless you counted my *Giselle* costume, and I wasn't putting that back on. Or any of the dirty dance clothes from the week of rehearsals. Roman promised he'd take care of it, and though every single one of them still looked at me like they wanted to take me back into the nest for a few more days, they let me shower alone.

Bringing them into this amazing shower with me meant I wouldn't actually get clean. We would all get very *very* dirty.

The smile on my face didn't fade as I washed my hair and body with borrowed products. It didn't bother me. If I was going to move in here anyway, I would have all my things soon enough.

True to his word, a hoodie waited for me when I got out of the shower in a familiar blue. *Lakewood Conservatory* was embroidered across the front of it. Where the three of us had gone to school. Roman's hoodie was even larger than his t-shirt had been. The neck slid off my shoulder a bit, but I liked being surrounded by his scent.

This was the top floor. Well, there was the roof, but I hadn't been up there yet. Jace and Roman were on the floor below mine. The nest was empty, and I took a minute to look at it now that I had a clear head. It was beautiful. Like someone had plucked my vision for a nest right out of my head and made it appear.

It could use a few more pillows and blankets, but *fuck*, they'd done a good job.

I padded down the stairs, quietly taking in the house in a way I hadn't yet. *Our* house. My stomach did a little *flip* in excitement.

Roman's door was open. Just like the first time I'd seen him, and just like me, he was fresh from the shower in a hoodie and sweats of his own. His hair pulled back in a knot behind his head, he stood near the table I'd spotted that night, covered in sketches and models.

"Knock, knock." I tapped my knuckles on the doorframe.

He turned to me and smiled, eyes doing a slow perusal of my bare legs, the rest of me in his sweatshirt, and where my shoulder was exposed.

"Can I come in?"

"You never have to ask."

A blush rose to my cheeks. Now out of the heat, it still felt strange for it to be so fast. I appreciated the wild nature of Petra's courting so much more. I slowly came into his room, toes curling into the thick rug.

All I'd noticed last time was the worktable and bed. Now I saw it all, with rich green-black walls and dark furniture that seemed very much like him. A walk-in closet, and a comfortable chair in the corner near the windows.

And, of course, the bed.

"It feels a little silly to want to sleep after all of that. I *did* sleep."

Roman came over to me and lifted me off my feet with ease. My knees rested on his hips, and his hands slipped beneath his hoodie to hold me. He laid me down on his bed gently, stretching out above me without crushing me. Though I wouldn't have minded being crushed by him. "Passing out because we fucked you into exhaustion isn't the same as rest."

I laughed. "I guess that's true." Reaching out, I traced the lines of his face. "Can I take a nap in here since I don't have a bed yet?"

His purr rumbled between us. "Even when you have a bed, I think we'll all prefer you in one of ours, firefly."

Sinking my fingers into his damp hair, I pulled it out of the knot it was in and let it fall around his face. Then I smiled. "You know I don't even know your last name?"

"Hughes."

Roman turned us, pulling me to his chest, so like that first night. And I was tired, but I wasn't slipping under right this second. There were things I wanted to know.

"And you're a sculptor?"

"I am."

Laughing softly, I turned and hitched my leg over his hip like I was climbing him even though we were horizontal. "You'll have to show me."

He nodded slowly, and I pressed myself closer to him, breathing in the softness of misty trees and the sweetness of summer air. "Can I ask you something?"

"You weren't already?"

I smacked his arm, but I felt his smile. "You said talking isn't easy for you. Is it okay for me to know why?"

Like he needed the contact, Roman shifted his hand underneath the hoodie I wore once more, sliding his hand up my thigh, over my ass and up my spine. "It's—" The words cut off, and he took a deep breath.

"I don't ask to judge you," I whispered. "Just want to know more about you, and if I can help." It didn't seem like he even noticed the subtle relaxation at my words.

"I know."

"Good."

He traced his fingers up and down my back, touching the places he could feel my spine and shoulder blades. Roman's hands were big enough they nearly spanned the entirety of my back as it was. When he finally spoke, the words were deliberate and slow. "I'm dyslexic. Severe. I can read, but... it takes me a long time, and it's easier not to. I also—" he swallowed and I felt it. "For a long time it was hard to talk. My brain mixes words, letters, sounds, and even likes to rearrange the sentences. So in school I didn't sound smart. Was scared to talk. Got made fun of a lot, so silence was easier."

I held him closer, squeezing him tighter than I probably should have. People were cruel about anything they could be. Between myself and Petra, I knew more than a little about being mocked and the way stories took on a life of their own for people to spin into stories that hurt you. "I'm sorry."

"I worked on the speaking part for a long time. It's still hard sometimes. The anxiety and overwhelm are always with me. Easier with people I'm close to."

"And me?"

"Comes and goes. Still nervous you're not real."

Pressing my ear to his chest, I snuggled down into him. "I'm very real."

"I know, firefly." Slowly, his hand slid down to my hip, where his thumb rubbed tender circles on my skin. "Does it bother you?"

I pulled back to look at him and found his eyes guarded. "Why would it?" When his gaze slid away, I pulled it right back. "Of course not, Roman. You could never speak, and you'd still be mine."

The flash of pain in his expression made me want to hunt down anyone who had made him feel less than and do things that would probably get me arrested.

Then I smiled. "Besides. Even when you're not talking, you're *very* good with your mouth."

Finally, he cracked a smile along with me. I managed to kiss him, though I had to move up the bed to do it. "All of you make me feel safe," I said quietly. "I want that for you too. If you can't talk, that's okay. We'll find other ways to communicate. I'll learn sign language if I have to."

He tucked me deeper against his side and held me close so I was entirely surrounded. Warm and safe. Roman was almost a whole nest by himself. "I don't think we'll need to sign," he said. "But thank you."

Being surrounded by so much warmth, his purr relaxing me, I was fading once more. "You're going to think I can't stay awake around you if I keep this up."

"We have time, firefly," he whispered. "I'll still be here when you wake up."

When I opened my eyes, I wasn't in Roman's arms. Our legs were still tangled together, but he was propped up on an elbow, a sketchbook balanced on a pillow between us and earbuds in his ears.

He caught my eye and smiled. "Don't move yet."

"Okay." I closed my eyes again, enjoying the *heavy* sensation of waking up after a really good sleep when there was no pressure for you to wake up. "What are you listening to?"

The quiet voices I heard through headphones quieted. "A book."

"Oh?"

Roman sketched for another moment before he reached for his phone and set it down right in front of me. A book with a fiery purple cover and a beautiful woman. *Conquered.* "Fantasy," he said. "Interesting magic, romance. All of it."

"That sounds fun."

"It is."

Him listening to the book made sense. I was glad he found a way to make it easier. "Can I see?"

Roman didn't fight me when I tugged on the sketchbook. It was me. The way I was lying right now, swathed in his hoodie. My hair fanned out over the bed, eyes closed, lips slightly parted. I looked ethereal and magical, though I was only sleeping. "This is beautiful."

He reached out and grabbed my hand.

Whatever he said, Roman didn't need words to communicate. His eyes spoke everything he needed to say. And right now they said *you're beautiful*.

We got caught in each other's gaze, only interrupted by a knock on the door. Ash pushed it open, and a loud trill broke the moment. "Sorry," he said, holding up my phone. "For you."

He gave me the phone, and I winced. My grandmother's name. Shit. She was probably worried sick. I answered the call and put it on speaker. "Hi, Grandma."

"Well, it's about time you answered," she said with a laugh. "I know you've been in a haze of hormones and dick, but I'm still your grandmother."

"Oh my god." I took it off speaker. "You can't just *say* things like that."

Ash and Roman were silently dying of laughter, and I was going to combust. This time from embarrassment and not from sex.

"Because I'm not supposed to know how heats work? How do you think you got here?"

My grandmother was an Omega, but she'd never bonded. My mom was the result of close friends sharing a heat. No animosity, no drama. Sometimes I saw my grandfather, but not often. He traveled, same as my parents.

"I know," I said. "But you still have to make sure I don't have a heart attack."

"Which one of us is the old woman?" I was about to comment, but she didn't let me. "Thankfully, I was at the reception. I would have panicked if you didn't show up for lunch on Monday."

"Sorry."

I practically saw her wave a hand. "That's not what I meant. But I do want you to come over, and I want you to bring that pack of yours."

"How do you know they're my pack and not some guys I just took home?"

She snorted. My grandmother snorted. "Sure. That's what they are. Are you free tomorrow?"

"Tomorrow?" I glanced at Asher. He nodded. "Yeah, I can do tomorrow."

"Perfect. I mean it, Sloane. Bring them with you."

"Okay." I rubbed my forehead. "Just promise me you're not going to scare them."

"I make no such promise." She cackled before she hung up.

I flopped back on the bed, and my two Alphas finally laughed. Ash laid on my legs, resting his head on my stomach. "So we're meeting your grandmother?"

"You've already met her," I mumbled.

"Yeah, but not as *your* Alpha."

"If I don't bring you she'll keep poking me until I do."

Sliding his hands under me, he pulled up the hoodie so he could kiss my skin. "Any grandmother that talks about dick is okay in my book."

Lifting my phone again, I started to sort through the mess of notifications that had built up during the heat. There were texts upon texts upon texts.

PETRA

Hey, I was at the reception and I heard what happened. When you're done getting railed, call me.

I want to hear *everything.*

EVA

I'm on set for two weeks and you get a pack? BITCH you have some shit to tell me.

Petra told me about the heat. Let us know when you're alive again. We need girl time.

Look at me, manifesting! I told you we would get you some good dick and you went into heat. Just call me a magician. Gonna start manifesting for Ian to disappear now.

Oh, and tell me when you're back. I need details. We can compare dick stories.

There were a few more as well. Congratulations from Esme, and a check-in from Claire. There were new texts from Craig too, but I didn't bother to look at them. If they were anything like what he'd been sending me before, it would be more delusional, possessive bullshit.

"Ugh. Leave me alone."

"Hmm?" Ash seemed very comfortable with my stomach as a pillow. We'd laid like this before, but not with me practically naked. I was very aware how close he was to the apex of my thighs where he could use his mouth for all kinds of fun.

I sighed and tossed the phone aside. "Your favorite person."

A low growl that didn't have the effect he thought it did. "That reminds me. When I went to get your clothes? There was a note from him on the door. '*Call me when the pretty boy isn't holding you hostage.*' Your neighbor, Noreen, came out and talked to me about it."

I blinked up at the ceiling. "He went back?"

"Yes."

"Why?" It wasn't a question for Ash. He had no way of knowing any more than I did. "It doesn't make sense. I don't know where he got the idea that I want any of this."

Ash kissed my belly button. "When he showed up that morning he told me he was your boyfriend."

"What?" I laughed. "Yeah, no. We never made it that far."

"He clearly thinks differently."

Shoving my hands into Asher's hair, I drew his gaze to mine. "Well, he can fuck off."

I loved the sight of his mischievous smile. "Is it okay if I look at the messages he sent?"

"Sure." Better than me looking at them.

Craig and I had fizzled because I *wasn't* really interested in

172

him for more than sex. He was passably handsome, and when we met, he had been charming. That charm wore off the more I got to know him. His hints of temper and occasional put-downs. Calling him back out of sheer loneliness was easily one of the dumbest things I'd ever done, but I couldn't take it back now.

Not that it mattered. Even if I hadn't found my pack, it wouldn't have changed anything. He and I had been finished the minute he hadn't turned around and realized I wasn't with him.

Ash picked up my phone and started scrolling through. "Fucking hell," he muttered.

"What?"

"I'd rather you didn't know, if I'm honest."

That made me prop myself up on my elbows. "Okay, now I have to see it."

"Hold that thought." Ash pushed up off the bed and moved behind me, framing my body with his legs so I could rest against his chest. The fact that he needed to hold me while I looked wasn't a great sign. "It's that bad?"

All he did was put the phone in my hand, and I felt the blood drain out of my face.

CHAPTER TWENTY-FOUR

ROMAN

Sloane went pale so quickly my gut twisted. Her already light skin turned *white* with whatever she saw on the screen. Asher's arms were around her, legs too, holding her as close as he could, allowing his instincts to take care of her and relieve him.

"I don't understand," she said. "We weren't... It wasn't that serious. It was only a few dates. I haven't even texted him since the first day of class."

I held my hand out wordlessly for the phone, and she gave it to me.

"I won't pretend to know why," Ash said into her hair. "But it's okay. You're here with us, and that's not going to change."

Sloane's phone was open to her texts. And it was clear this man was unhinged, and I hadn't even started reading. There were no responses on Sloane's side. Just message after message after message.

I scrolled up a little, to a couple of days ago, while we were all still consumed with her heat.

CRAIG

Where the fuck are you, Sloane?

We need to talk.

I've been to your apartment every day. Why aren't you there?

Are you shacking up with that prick? The one who ordered you around while I was standing right there?

Do you have any idea what I tried to do for you at that concert?

I was going to take you backstage to meet Alexander Serrat. That's right, I got you a pass to meet him, and they were waiting for us at the door, and then YOU WEREN'T FUCKING THERE and I looked like some kind of idiot.

Tried to do something nice for you, and you humiliated me to go fuck a weak little playboy? When you could have me?

You have no idea what I did to get you that introduction. I put my ass on the line for you, and you threw it in my face.

That's not going to fly, Sloane.

I turned down people for you. I passed up pussy a lot better than yours because I felt bad for you, and this is how you treat me?

That's not how this works. I gave you a lot, and you're going to make it up to me. Whatever that cock's name is doesn't have more claim to you than I do. Fuck scent-sympathy. That shit isn't real. If you don't talk to me you'll regret it.

You're mine, remember?

I told you that if I tried, you were mine, and I'm trying so fucking hard, Sloane.

You are going to call me. You are going to come to me and present. I'm going to make sure you're good and satisfied. Hell, we'll even make you go into heat so you can feel what it's like to have a real Alpha.

You know what? Screw you. You're falling off as a dancer, gaining weight with all that bullshit Indian food and candy you eat. No one could ever want you.

But maybe I'll make an exception. Because I'm a good guy. I'll still fuck you.

The texts stopped until earlier today.

CRAIG

I'm not a patient man, Sloane. I'm not going to wait on you forever.

Fine. You want to be a bitch? I'll treat you like a bitch. You signed up for this. Never forget that.

I'm sorry. You know how I get. Sometimes I see red and say things I don't mean. And I know you. You respond better when I'm soft, so I'll try to be soft for you.

Just don't keep making me mad, darling. I'll treat you so right.

It's okay. Everything's going to be fine. I promise.

Already thinking of all the ways you're going to make it up to me.

I'll see you soon.

Sloane's silence had driven him to a place that was dangerous, and for these last few days, it wasn't even intentional silence.

It was a good thing she'd agreed to move in with us, because her apartment wasn't safe anymore. "You're not going back there alone," I said.

She shook her head, turning just enough to lean on Asher's shoulder and cling to his arm. I hated the way she looked right now. Even smaller than her slight frame, skin white as a sheet, gaze unfocused and distant.

"You're going to be okay," Ash said. "We're not going to let anything happen to you."

My firefly shook her head. "Everything he's saying? I never said I was his. He said that, not me. I don't know what he's talking about. I just... I don't understand. He wasn't like this when we were doing whatever the hell it was we were doing. Like, I drew away because the charm wore off, and I knew he wouldn't be happy. But I didn't expect *this*. How did I get it so wrong?"

Ash cradled her. "You didn't get it wrong, sweetheart. Someone hiding who they are and showing their true colors later isn't your fault. He feels wronged and entitled when he has no right. This has nothing to do with you."

177

"Feels like it has to do with me."

I put the phone down before I hurled it against the wall so she never had to look at those messages ever again.

"You know what I mean," Ash whispered. "There's nothing you did to cause this, and there's nothing you could have done differently. He's a dick, and that's that."

"Okay."

Sloane's voice was so small, I wanted to pin her underneath me again and pleasure her until she screamed the way she had at the end of her heat. Like she was an exploding star. So strong, so beautiful, and so free.

"I asked Noreen to call you if she saw Craig again."

She reached for her phone. "I don't have any calls or texts from her. Let's see."

Once more the phone was on speaker, but I didn't think we'd be laughing this time.

"Hello?"

"Hi, Noreen," Sloane said, her voice a little shaky. "It's Sloane from across the hall."

"Oh!" The woman's voice picked right up. "Hi, honey. You okay?"

"Yeah." It was a lie. "I know Ash mentioned someone left me a note. Have you seen or heard him again?"

Noreen made a disgusted sound. "Yes. I'm sorry I didn't call you. It slipped my mind. He was here again the day after your handsome Alpha came by. Pounded on the door. I told him to keep it down and to get out. Haven't seen him since."

"Okay, thank you, Noreen."

"You've been gone for a while. You sure you're okay?"

Sloane allowed herself a small smile. "I am. I went into heat, so I've been lying low. But I'll make sure to say hello when I stop by."

"Make sure you do."

"Bye."

The call ended, and Sloane looked at the phone. "Those texts said he'd been over to my apartment every day. If she hasn't seen him? What does that mean?"

Ash and I looked at each other. It meant the asshole was outside, watching to see when she came home so he could corner her and force her to let him into her apartment. So Noreen wouldn't be able to say anything to him.

The poison in his messages and the threats…

Rage tinted my vision, a growl growing in my chest. I didn't have any words. Not real ones. My tongue was tied with anger and fear for my Omega. I would tear the man limb from limb if he touched her. If she went back there—

"Roman?"

I couldn't stop the growling in my chest, focused on the asshole who thought he owned the woman in front of me.

Sloane crawled across the bed to me, straddling my legs and taking my face in her hands. "Hey, I'm right here, okay? I'm right here. I promise I won't go alone. At least one of you guys is going to be with me if I have to go back there."

My arms came around her waist, holding her to my body. The growl lessened, but it didn't disappear. She was here. Safe. Would be as long as she stayed right here with me.

She clung to me just as hard, telling me without words that she was scared, and that wasn't acceptable.

"I'd rather you not go back at all, sweetheart," Ash said. "We can get your things while you stay here."

"Is it weird that I want to say goodbye? Not just to Noreen, but to the apartment?"

"Not at all. We'll just be careful."

"I'm sorry," Sloane whispered in my ear. "I'm not going anywhere."

Shaking my head, I manage to find a single word. "No." I meant it in the way that she didn't need to be sorry. But I also didn't want to let her go.

A knock at the open door. Jace, now showered and dressed. "Thought I'd find you all somewhere. You hungry, baby girl?"

"I could eat something." Her face was still buried in my neck.

Jace picked up on the vibe. "What's wrong?"

Ash put his hand on her ankle. "You want to tell them?"

My little firefly shook her head into my neck.

"Okay," Ash said. "Why don't you grab some shorts from Roman before you come down, okay?"

At that I felt her smile, and my whole body perked up remembering she was naked beneath my sweatshirt. It would be so easy...

"I will," she said.

Jace's face was troubled as Ash put a hand on his shoulder and guided him out of the room. I needed another minute holding Sloane.

"Are you all right?"

I was good enough to let my purr rise instead of a growl. "I will be."

"Good."

"But if he touches you—"

"He won't. It was over before I even ran into Ash again. Completely over. Even if you all weren't here, his ass would be on the sidewalk."

I slid us to the edge of the bed, managing to avoid my sketchbook and her phone. "If I don't give you some shorts I'm going to fuck you again."

Sloane raised an eyebrow. "And that's a problem... because?"

My smirk reflected hers. "Because my Alpha needs to make sure you're taken care of in every way. Especially because of this." I slipped her phone into the front pocket of the hoodie. "And even with the nap, you're tired."

Her pout was so fucking cute. "Fine."

I dug around in my drawers to find something of mine small enough to fit her. In the end the pair of boxers I handed her had to be rolled several times, but it would work. She laughed. "I think we'll need to make some kind of arrangement. We're not going to my grandmother's house with me in your boxers."

"It sounded like she might appreciate that."

Sloane rolled her eyes, but she smiled. "She probably would. But I want my own clothes."

I stared at her, instincts rising, but I hesitated. This was all new, and I didn't want to smother her. She met my eyes. "What?"

"Can I carry you?"

Her cheeks turned a shade of pink I loved—more because it

meant she was recovering from earlier—and she nodded. "Yeah, I'd like that."

Sweeping her legs from under her, I lifted her up, kissing her as we walked to the elevator to go downstairs. Now that I knew what it was like to hold her in my arms, I didn't know if I would be happy with her anywhere else.

CHAPTER TWENTY-FIVE

SLOANE

*J*ace had given a giant middle finger to cooking, and I didn't blame him. Most of the time I did the same thing. And coming into the kitchen to find a giant spread of tacos and other food was amazing.

Roman watched me after he put me down, his gaze like a physical touch. I didn't mind it. After... however many days of them doing nothing *but* touching me, it was a little like going through withdrawal.

"What are you making, baby girl?" Jace asked, looking at the plate I was piling food on. A base of crunched up taco shell, meat, cheese, cucumbers, and tomatoes. Sometimes I went for guacamole but I wasn't feeling it tonight.

"Taco salad."

Ash coughed. "Taco *what*?"

I looked at him and lifted an eyebrow. "Did the heat damage your hearing?"

His eyes filled with heat that contrasted with his amusement. "Just because Gabriel is the only one who's said it doesn't mean he's the only one who would enjoy spanking you, sweetheart."

Turning so I looked over my shoulder at him, I stuck out my tongue and caught Roman smothering a laugh. "I said taco salad."

"And what, exactly, is taco salad?"

"It's tacos," I told him. "But not in a shell. You just mix it up and put it on a plate. Or a bowl. You guys have never done this?"

Ash lifted his taco. "Can't say that I have."

"Missing out." I turned to the fridge and opened it before I felt warmth against my back.

"What are you looking for?" Jace asked.

"You can't judge me if I tell you."

He laughed softly. "I'm not going to judge you."

"Ranch dressing?"

"Right here." He tapped the door. "I've never tried that with tacos."

I put probably too much on my plate so I could mix it up. "Don't knock it till you try it."

He picked the bottle right up after me and put it on the tacos he made, and the groan that came out of my Alpha sent a burst of perfume swirling through the room. "Damn, baby girl. You're right."

"See?" I smirked before carrying my plate over to the bar and sitting beside Ash. "I have good taste."

He snorted. "You forget that I've seen you mainline almost an entire box of Twinkies at three in the morning."

That had been a *night*. Punch drunk from exhausting rehearsals and classes. The two of us and our other friends had completely let loose. "And you love me anyway."

His eyes warmed, and he nearly pulled me off my stool to kiss my cheek. "Yes, I do."

It was a good thing too, because there was nothing graceful about the way I demolished the plate in front of me.

"I think I would enjoy seeing someone your size consuming that many Twinkies," Roman said from the table in the breakfast nook.

"I won't pretend it was a *good* idea. But you know... memories and all that."

Normally I was careful about what I ate, simply because, as a dancer, I needed food as fuel more than comfort. What Craig said about me only eating Indian food and candy wasn't true, and he could go fuck himself for that.

I'd just had my heat. No way was I going to restrict myself right now, and I didn't need to.

But when the plate was empty I was pleasantly and contentedly full. "Where's Gabriel?"

"In his office," Jace said. "It's across from the gym."

"Why?"

"Because he's a workaholic," Roman muttered.

"No," Jace laughed. "I think he's working on untangling the rehearsal mess."

184

"Oh." I looked at the rest of the taco buffet. "Does he know there's food?"

"I told him, but he probably forgot."

I slipped off the stool and Jace intercepted me to take my plate before I went to go find him. Roman caught me before I left the kitchen, pressing me to the wall. The way he looked down at me, I saw the rawness in his gaze. The *protection* there... I loved every bit. "You okay?" I asked him.

He brushed a stray hair out of my face and tucked it behind my ear. "Maybe."

I smiled. "Do you need to carry me up to Gabe's office?"

Roman's face cracked into a smile. "No, firefly. I'll be fine."

"I don't mind if you do."

"That's why I'll be fine." He leaned down and kissed me, both of us having to work for it. So tall and so short, it made me smile.

"If that changes, you know where I am." I left him with a wink and climbed up to the second floor. Gabriel's office was open, and it felt like him. Light, sandy walls and sparse furniture. Yet he sat in front of a set of monitors that took up a big part of the desk in front of him. A white t-shirt and sweats made him look adorably casual, along with the glasses he had on.

He was so absorbed by what was in front of him, he didn't notice as I came up behind his chair and pulled it back away from the desk.

"What—"

I climbed into his lap, draping my legs over the arms of the chair before I kissed him. He smiled. "You turning into a koala, little one?"

"If I have to. There's dinner downstairs."

"Right." One of his hands ran through his hair, leaving it sticking up in funny ways. "I forgot."

I hugged him further, just holding him. He typed a few things around my body, not remotely bothered by the fact I was pinning him to the chair. I liked it. "I didn't know you had reading glasses."

Gabriel chuckled. "I don't. Just normal glasses."

"Then why haven't I seen them before?"

"Contacts."

"Did you... have them in the whole heat? That can't be good for your eyes."

His hand came down on what he could reach of my ass in a gentle smack. "No. I need them for things that are more than a few feet away. Considering you were very close to me the whole heat, I was fine."

"Oh."

He smelled so good, and now full and happy, snuggling was probably going to lead to sleeping. So I asked another question. "You have a lot of monitors. Not exactly what I think of when I picture a stern, executive director."

"Well, I don't *only* work in here."

"You don't?"

He typed for a few seconds. "I might play some video games from time to time."

"Is my Alpha a secret nerd?" Pulling back to look at him, I smiled.

"A little bit. Though I don't know how often I'll play them now that I have *you* to play with."

I messed his hair up further by playing with it. "No. You're not going to stop doing things you enjoy just because I'm here."

"But I *thoroughly* enjoy doing *you*."

"I walked right into that one."

"Yes, you did."

Going back to leaning on him, he started typing again.

"My grandmother wants to see all of us tomorrow. Can you go?"

"Of course. I'd love to meet her."

"What about the company?"

Gabriel hummed and wrapped an arm around me briefly. "Don't worry about that, little one."

"I do worry about it." My words were muffled by his t-shirt.

He sighed, and the sound was heavy. "It's a bit of a mess, and unfortunately I have to play politics in order to get it all fixed. But we should be okay. The performances of *Giselle* will continue, but other than necessary rehearsals for whoever's up, I'm pushing all other rehearsals a full two weeks. And after, the rehearsal schedule will be *normal*. No more twelve hour days."

His tone betrayed everything he really felt about it.

"I know we signed those extra contracts," I said. "But the show being moved up? That's the part that made everything worse."

"Yeah." Lifting his hands from the keyboard, he held me tight against him. "There was a scheduling issue. Or so we were told. The stage floor is being refinished, and there was a miscommunication. This coming weekend, when the accelerated run was *supposed* to open, someone scheduled the re-finish because it was earlier than SCB's normal season."

So instead of pushing everything back, Ian had pulled it forward. Bastard.

"Mark agreed to cover me for the heat. When I finally got back to everything today, the contractor canceled the re-fit."

My body wilted without me even meaning to. So all of it had been for nothing, essentially.

"I know, little one. I'm sorry. Things happen when organizations transition like this, but there's no excuse for it. I found someone to come in and do the construction, since it did need to be done. The only reason it turned out this way was a vacuum in leadership. It's my fault."

"I don't agree with that," I whispered. "Ian should know better. When he gave us that speech the day you scented me, it felt doable. He made it believable. But it wouldn't have been so bad if he'd just pulled it back."

A thought occurred to me, and I let my brain sort through it to the end before I put it into the air. "How long has that floor thing been scheduled?"

"A while, I guess. Since before I came on board."

"So... he had to know. Ian knew the rehearsal run would be that short. They advertised it. Sold tickets. He knew, didn't tell us, and did it anyway." Gabriel said nothing, but I felt his breathing go slow and even like he was controlling himself. "Is he just that much of a dick? Or am I supposed to think he believed in us that much?"

Gabriel shook his head. "I don't know. I wish I did. Either

way, I'm putting things in place. Ian is the creative director, and that's what he will be. Everything else he's going to need fucking approval on."

That made me feel better. "Thank you."

"I wish I could go back and make it better."

Drawing tiny circles on his arm with the tip of my finger, I closed my eyes. "I know. But just like Ash and I can't go back and fix what happened back then, there's no going back. We don't need to. I'm here, and that's the end of it." Then, quieter. "I'm not going to let you beat yourself up about it forever."

"How about just a little longer?" He chuckled.

"A little." I sat up again so I could see his face. "We might have to go shopping or something before we see my grand-mother. Still no clothes, and I don't think going to my apartment is a good idea."

His Alpha appeared. "Why?"

"I'll let them tell you," I said. "I don't have the energy."

"In that case," he lifted me and turned me around so I faced the screens with him, nestled between his legs.

Gabe was hard against my ass, and I wiggled. "Still?"

"Sloane, don't count on my cock being soft around you. Ever."

I blushed. He didn't know how much those simple words meant to me. Completely aside from the sexual aspect, it was the *completeness* of it. He wanted me and would always want me.

"Claire's partner Addison was the one who helped with your nest, by the way. A lifesaver."

"Addie did that? I need to send her some flowers."

"Mhmm. She pulled everything, then Roman met her and her team here and helped them put everything together."

I watched as he navigated away from spreadsheets and things that looked like contracts and emails and to a web browser. "I like it so much," I said.

"We're going to make sure you like everything about your space here. But I noticed when I looked at Nest, Inc. on my phone that night, they also have some clothes."

They did. I'd seen them. Because I'd spent more time on the website Gabe was logging into than I wanted to admit. They were known for creating Omega nests, but they had everything under the sun to pamper an Omega. Including comfy clothes that happened to be stylish and adorable.

He set my hand on the mouse and eased himself out from behind me. "Order whatever you want to be delivered in the morning. We already have an account." I was about to ask if he was sure, and he leaned down to capture my mouth with his. "Whatever you want. It doesn't even have to be clothes. I'll be right back. Going to grab some food and find out what you won't tell me."

I pressed my lips together, worried about what he would think when he saw everything from Craig. Pulling my phone out, I handed it to him and unlocked it. "You're going to need that."

Gabriel looked at me for a few seconds before he took it. "All right. Now go shopping. I want at least five things in your cart before I get back."

I smirked. That wouldn't be a problem. Did he have any idea how long my wishlist from this store was? I wasn't going to order everything on it, but I would definitely get some.

Pulling up my legs into the chair, I went shopping. Leggings and sweaters since it was getting colder in the city, a scarf I'd wanted since the first time I saw it—a gorgeous deep violet in fabric that wasn't necessarily practical. It was just pretty.

A dress in that same pretty shade, and some more practical clothes. I didn't go crazy—I had plenty of clothes at my apartment. Moving didn't mean I needed a whole new wardrobe, and I didn't want to spend all their money. But I got enough things for a few days, including some pajamas and some shower things, basic makeup, and a pair of boots that nearly had me salivating.

I glanced at the clock. It wasn't late, but still late enough everything needed to come in the morning. My nap in Roman's room must have taken a few hours. Double checking the address and the delivery time, I finished the order.

"You could have gotten more." Gabriel stood at the door, midway through eating a taco.

"I have plenty of clothes at home so I didn't want to go crazy."

Finishing the taco in a couple bites, he put the plate on the desk and came behind me, placing his hands on my shoulders. "You're allowed to go crazy, little one. We want you to go crazy."

"Once I move all my things I'll feel better. See what I have and what I need."

Gabriel rested his chin on the top of my head. "Why do I get the feeling that's not the whole story?"

"I don't know what you're talking about."

He laughed before he slipped my phone back into the hoodie pocket. "They told me you want to go back to the apartment one last time."

"I do."

"Does that require your things being there when you do?"

Taking a second to think about it, I spun the chair around to face him. "I guess not." Going back was more about closure than anything else. Walking through that space and letting it breathe. Having it empty might be a nice full circle moment. "Why?"

Gabriel knelt down in front of the chair, stroking his hands up the top of my thighs, teasing the hem of Roman's boxers. "Because I'd rather get movers in there to clear it out while you're not there. We can go and monitor the process, but if Craig is watching for you, I'd like to minimize the time you spend there."

I felt my shoulders wilting before I could stop them. That same inexplicable shame rose in my chest. If I hadn't let my loneliness get the better of me, maybe I wouldn't be dealing with this. If I hadn't been such a coward. Or blinded by charm and a few decent orgasms.

Fuck, if I hadn't run away from Ash—

"Where did you go, little one?"

It felt too vulnerable to meet his eyes. Rationally I *knew* Craig's actions weren't my fault. But it didn't feel that way. I'd said yes to him, and then I'd made him angry. These were the consequences. There were so many different decisions I could have made and Craig wouldn't be in my life—our lives—at all.

"Sloane." Just a hint of Alpha bark in his tone to make me look at him, but the rest of my Alpha was still gentle. "There you are."

"I should have known, right? Like I should have seen that he would act this way? I have to have done something to make him think this. Otherwise it doesn't make sense."

His eyes were hard. "I don't think that's true. Not that I've met the man, but if he thought he had you free and clear without resistance, he had no reason to show you anything else because he had what he wanted." Squeezing my thighs, he pulled me a little closer. "Not that anyone should ever think they have you or own you without your permission. How did you meet?"

My body started to curl in on itself, and Gabriel didn't let it happen. He pulled my legs down from where they were crossed and put them around his waist. My arms found his shoulders on their own.

I swallowed. "After a show last season. Some of us went to a bar. I don't usually, but Dion convinced me. Craig was there, and he said he'd been at the show. Said he loved the way I danced and..." My cheeks flushed. I remembered calling Petra, more than a little tipsy, to ask whether I should let him fuck me. "I let him take me home. We kept seeing each other for a while. The glamor wore off, but he was *someone*." Someone instead of no one. And recently, I'd been so tired of being by myself that it was easier to go back to a person I knew didn't really like me than be alone.

Guilt built up in my chest, and I looked down.

"Do you need anything else for the night?" Gabriel asked.

"No."

"Good." Without shifting our positions he lifted me and carried me out of his office and up the stairs. Into his bedroom. The same warm, sandy colors and blonde woods. But comfortable.

"You have a fireplace?"

"Would you like a fire?"

Pretty much all Omegas loved warmth and closeness. Because I was cold so much, I craved heat like oxygen. "Yes, please."

He set me on the bed and built a fire with practiced ease. There was kindling next to it and ashes already in the hearth, so it wasn't the first time he'd built one. Soon it was burning merrily, and he came back to me, tugging Roman's hoodie up and off. I didn't stop him from stripping me completely and him doing the same before he buried us beneath the comforter, my back to his chest.

Gabriel's purr relaxed me, a kiss brushing the back of my neck. "Now that I have you comfortable..."

He couldn't see that I rolled my eyes or smiled. "I knew this was a trap."

"Do you think we're upset with you because of him? That we would judge you?" Gabriel didn't take my teasing bait.

"No." I didn't think *they* were upset with me. It was clear they weren't. That didn't change how I felt about it. I felt sick to my stomach and filled with shame that I'd ever let someone like that so close to me.

I turned over, needing more of him against me than my back.

In a moment we were both beneath the blankets, enclosed in the dark, warm, close space, nothing but the sound of our breath and the crackle of the fire. Gabriel's scent was all vanilla right now, soft and comforting.

"I hate that look on your face, little one."

Tears welled, and I tucked my face into his neck, seeking, allowing the combination of fear and shame to overcome me where it was safe to let it happen. I felt so foolish, and so guilty, even if those things didn't and shouldn't belong to me.

Gabriel didn't tell me to be quiet, and he didn't push me to speak further. He simply held me, purring and touching me wherever he could without releasing me.

Suddenly it was about more than Craig. I hadn't *really* cried about any of it. Even when Asher confronted me in the shoe room, the tears had been brief and brushed aside. This was ugly and raw, releasing all the things I'd shoved down through the rehearsals and my hormones still balancing after the heat.

And I could let it all go. Because I was safe.

By the time all the tears were done and my breath was hiccuping softly, I couldn't keep my eyes open anymore. And still, Gabriel held me close, purr steady, the sound never stopping, even as I slept.

CHAPTER TWENTY-SIX

JACE

I knocked my knuckles softly on Gabriel's door frame. His head moved, the only indication he'd heard me. Sloane was asleep now, but not before I'd heard her crying. Agonizing sounds that made my chest hurt.

Slowly, I moved to where he could see me. "Is she okay?"

Gabriel lifted one shoulder, but the same pain I felt was in his eyes. Sloane clung to him like he was an anchor, and I understood why he didn't want to speak. Not to disturb her.

"Let us know if you need something, okay?"

He nodded once.

I went back downstairs, taking the actual stairs instead of the elevator because I needed to burn off some of the energy inside me. Ash hit the button on the dishwasher as I entered, and Roman was finishing wiping down the countertops.

"What do you know about this fucker?" I asked, bracing myself on the island.

Ash looked at me in surprise. "Sloane's ex?"

"I don't think we should call him that, but yes. Tell me more about him, because Sloane just passed out after fucking *crying* in Gabriel's arms, and I'm about to track him down and rip his head off."

The energy in the room suddenly matched mine.

"I don't know much, but," Ash told us about Craig showing up the morning after he spent the night with Sloane. "He was an ass," he finished. "But honestly, I didn't get the vibes I saw in all the texts. I saw the edges of it, but he didn't seem unhinged in person. The fact that I *didn't* get those immediate vibes is what scares me more. Because he's a good actor."

"Do you think he's violent?"

I saw the look on Asher's face before he checked it, and it told me more than he could tell me in words. "I don't know. I desperately want to say he's all talk, but I can't say for sure. His entitlement makes me think he could be pushed into something. And the texts don't make me feel better. I imagine he's banking on Sloane feeling guilty enough to bend to his wishes."

We all knew that wouldn't happen. Barely any time with our Omega, and I knew enough about her to know she didn't bow unless she wanted to.

Roman stood with his arms crossed over his chest and a glare that would likely kill the Alpha we were talking about.

"Should we have a talk with him?"

"Honestly?" Ash mirrored my pose on the island. "While I'm sure that would be satisfying for all of us, I don't think so. We need to smother the fire, not add fuel."

It made sense, even if it wasn't what I wanted to hear. We were going to move Sloane in here and make sure Craig couldn't find her and had no access. I hoped that would be definitive enough for him to move on.

Blowing out a breath, I hung my head. "Yeah, I get you."

"But don't think I'd rather choose the first option."

"Same," Roman said.

A few days ago all of us would have taken the other option without another thought. But now our Omega was the priority. Her safety, security, and happiness were more important than our instincts for revenge or anger.

"She cried?" Roman asked.

I nodded. "Badly. Could be the build-up of everything, though, and not just this."

"Should have taken her back to the nest."

"I think she's good now," I told him. "Gabe has the fire going and she's basically nesting with him as a pillow."

Roman reluctantly agreed.

Looking between the two of them, I launched the idea that had come to me once the heat broke earlier today. "What do you guys think about turning the extra room on Sloane's floor into a studio for her? It wouldn't be too difficult." Then I laughed. "I guess you could use it too, Ash."

"I think that's a great idea. Do we make it a surprise?"

"Not sure how we'd be able to," Roman pointed out, looking decidedly more relaxed. "If she's already living up there."

Thinking about it, I loved the idea of being able to surprise her if we could pull it off. "Let's talk to Gabe when we can. I think we can make it happen."

Ash pushed up from leaning on his elbows. "If we can, I think it would be great. But I think I'm going to go for a ride real quick."

I raised an eyebrow. "Will that ride take you past Sloane's apartment?"

"It might."

"What happened to smothering the flame?"

Ash sighed. "Yeah, I know. I'm not going to stop or anything. But if he's just standing outside the building and waiting, that tells us something."

"And if you see him?"

"I keep driving."

"You better," I told him. "Because if he's getting beat down, I want a piece."

His grin turned feral. "You'll be the first to know." Grabbing his leather jacket and helmet, he went straight for the front door.

Roman sighed and looked at me. "Do you think it will get better?"

"What?"

"Being away from her. All I want to do is barge into Gabe's room and snuggle her."

It made me smile, because I felt it too. Not being in Sloane's presence made me feel a physical *absence* I'd never noticed before we met. It had always been there, like a phantom limb, but her being here brought it to the forefront. In a good way. Because I was now tied to her even before we were bonded.

"While Gabe probably wouldn't mind, and neither would Sloane, I'd leave her for now. She's exhausted. But yes, I think it will get better."

"Thanks."

He turned and went out the back door toward his own studio. For everyone else in the world, Roman could seem abrupt. Not to us. It was who he was, and none of us cared.

I grabbed a bottle of water from the fridge before jogging up the stairs to my room. There was research I needed to do. Who the fuck did we hire to build us a dance studio?

CHAPTER TWENTY-SEVEN

SLOANE

I felt stuffy when I woke.

Crying your eyes out before you slept would do that to you.

Gabriel still held me. He was behind me now, but his skin was on mine, and that made everything better. Then the amount I'd cried hit me again, and I went stiff. I'd basically used Gabriel as a tissue.

His voice was soft and sleepy. "You just woke up, little one. Are you overthinking already?"

"No," I lied.

One hand drifted lower on my body, over my hip and between my legs. "Would an orgasm help?"

"I think orgasms always help things, *but*..."

"But?"

"But I would rather not be turned on right before we go meet my grandmother. When we get back?"

He purred, circling a finger around my clit. "When we get home," he said.

"I'm sorry about last night."

"Why?"

"Cause I cried all over you?"

A slow kiss warmed my shoulder. "Little one, you don't have to apologize for feeling what you feel. I just want to make sure you're okay."

"I don't know," I said. "I mean, yes. Because I'm here with you. But I still feel stupid and naïve for not seeing what he was. Is."

Stroking a hand over my hair, my Alpha gently guided me to lie on my back. "I suppose me speaking reason to you won't do much."

"No," I smiled. "Probably not."

"Fair enough. However, I want to make sure you know that none of us are judging you for this. You're not responsible for someone pretending to be someone they're not, and we all had lives before each other. We're just concerned about keeping you safe. That's all."

"Thank you."

He smiled down at me, purr growing stronger as he kissed the tip of my nose. "I'm your Alpha. You're my Omega. I don't give a shit if we're not bonded... yet." He winked. "You're everything, Sloane."

I whined and closed my eyes. "You're going to make me cry again."

"We can't have that."

He kissed me instead. Long and slow, Gabriel sliding his hands beneath my body to deepen the kiss as much as possible. Deep enough I was considering changing my mind about an orgasm before he pulled back. "I heard the doorbell earlier. I think your clothes are here."

"I love being surrounded by your scents, but it will be nice to wear clothes that fit."

"You're welcome to any of my clothes any time."

"Thank you."

Gabriel smirked at me. "Now get that gorgeous ass out of my bed before I can't help myself."

I laughed, but obeyed, grabbing Roman's clothes and my phone. It felt a bit weird to be walking through the house naked, but there wasn't anyone here who wasn't allowed to see me.

Like I suspected, the bags from Nest, Inc. were already in my bedroom upstairs. Frothy bags with tissue paper and fun colors. The purple dress I bought was what I wanted. To pair with black leggings and boots for warmth. It wasn't even deep fall yet, but fall was my favorite season, and I couldn't wait to be able to dress in absolutely nothing but sweaters.

A luxurious hot shower later, I felt remarkably more human. Lighter, too, after I cried everything out. Amazing how tears could do that. They never felt good while you were in the middle of them. But purging pain and sorrow never did.

The makeup I had them send wasn't much, but it was

enough. I let my mind wander as I touched up my face. I was here. In a house with *my* Alphas.

We're not bonded... yet.

Petra, Eva, and Esme all bonded quickly once they met their packs. I think Eva had taken the longest, and it was only because of her true celebrity status and the public's interest in her relationships that she'd waited for her bonding ceremony to be public.

The others hadn't wanted a bonding ceremony. Esme because while her sister lived in the limelight, she hated it. Petra because it needed to happen quickly to protect her. Not only from the people who were trying to harm her, but to prevent her stepmother from forcing her into a bond she didn't want.

Where did I fall?

Definitely not in the camp of wanting what Eva had. People knew who I was, but I didn't need the entire world to see me bond. But having a ceremony? The dress and them seeing me appear? Yeah. I wanted that. The same piece of me that craved being chosen wanted that choice to be shouted to the world. If I happened to look fucking fantastic at the same time, so be it.

Granted, a public bonding ceremony meant prolonging the absolute *fuckfest* that came afterwards. But all of us already knew we could handle waiting, and I wasn't going to argue that the week we spent barely hanging on hadn't made my heat *exquisite*.

I left my hair down. Something I did often since I lived half my life with my hair in a ballet bun. Bending over in the elevator, I fluffed my hair until the bell chimed, which left me completely unprepared to stand up and see Roman in dark jeans and a white button-down with the sleeves rolled up.

Holy hell.

The door started to close on me because I was just staring at him, and he smirked when I had to force it back open. "Morning."

My hands had minds of their own, and I couldn't stop myself from grabbing those forearms and making sure they were firmly around me. "I didn't think I'd find something I like as much as you naked, but I'm proven wrong."

"Really?" One eyebrow quirked.

"Never underestimate the power of forearm porn, Alpha."

He rumbled his approval, his hair curtaining around us as he kissed me hello. We both tasted like minty toothpaste, and I didn't care that he was ruining my lipstick. I had it in my bag. Lipstick could be fixed as many times as it needed. Kisses, however, could only happen right then.

"You cried?" He asked against my lips.

It made me smile. "It's been known to happen. Won't be the last time."

"It will if I have anything to say about it."

God, these men. My stomach tumbled into butterflies.

"You look beautiful, firefly."

I let him tuck me into an embrace. "Thank you."

Footsteps entered the kitchen. "Ready to be a backpack?"

Pulling back, I stared at Ash where he stood in the entrance of the kitchen, looking just as good as Roman did. But the shirt he wore was tighter—showing off his physique without screaming about it.

Well, not screaming at everyone else. It was *very much* screaming at me. And it was saying 'climb me like a tree, Grandma can wait.' He was looking at me the same way, gaze traveling down the dress and all the way back up. It slid over my skin like sunshine, warming wherever he looked.

Gabriel hit him lightly on the back of the head with an eye roll. "We're taking the car."

"Bikes are more fun, and you know it."

"Maybe," I said. "But I'd rather not peel you off the pavement before we see Grandma."

Ash shook his head, smiling the whole time. "Your grandmother loves me."

That, at least, was true. Grandma grilled me when I dropped out, asking me if Ash had anything to do with it. I told her no.

"Let's go, baby girl." Jace pushed past the two of them and grabbed my hand, pulling me out the back door. "Before they can argue about who's going to drive."

"I already have the keys," Gabriel called. "Tough luck."

The backyard was nice. Long and narrow between the two

fences that separated us from the neighbors, lush grass covered the space, a walkway down the center. Near the house there was a patio with comfy chairs around a fire pit. I would be using that now that it was getting colder.

A two-story carriage house rose in front of us. I'd seen it from the windows. Roman's studio. Jace didn't stop as we passed through, but I wanted to. Big blocks of stone and unfamiliar tools. The scent of dust and lingering traces of my Alpha. I twisted my head, trying to take it all in before we were out the other side and entering a smaller garage.

"Roman," I called. "I need you to show me the studio."

"I will," he said, sliding in on the other side of me in the back seat.

I sat squished between my two Alphas in the best kind of sandwich. Leaning my head on Jace's shoulder, his hand rested gently on the inside of my knee, tracing patterns up my thigh on the leggings.

"Where are we going, little one?"

Rattling off the address, Gabriel turned and looked at me in shock. "Really?"

"Yup."

"Damn, baby girl." Jace laughed. "That neighborhood? Your grandma's house is going to put ours to shame."

A shrug was all the answer I had for that. I could pretend I didn't come from wealth, but there was no point. I did, and I tried not to let it affect who I was as a person.

"Your parents?" Roman asked.

I winced. "They're alive. They just... didn't want to be parents. Which is fine. I don't want to be one either." None of them sounded shocked or horrified by that revelation. "My mom and dad are both Betas, and they were pretty young when they had me. No pack, just each other."

Jace laced our fingers together. "Where are they?"

"Who knows?" I shrugged. "They travel. My mother's inheritance and my father's job help with that. He works on digital infrastructures for big companies or something like that. I don't really know. But they never stay in one place. Last time I heard from them they were somewhere below the equator on an island."

"I'm sorry," Roman said.

"I'm not." I shook my head. "They've never been my parents. Not really. Even when I was young, the most I got from them were birthday cards. It doesn't bother me."

I'd had plenty of time to process the feelings of being abandoned and the angst of not having parents the way others did. There was probably something deeper to the reason I struggled so much with loneliness and the need for affection, but I'd moved past the *need* to understand the deeper meaning of why they hadn't wanted me. Some things simply weren't that complicated.

Apart from that, parents weren't always a picnic. All I had to do was look at my friend's lives to see that. I got lucky with Grandma.

Speaking of Grandma, we were turning down the drive that led to her house. If you could call it that. This section of Slate City was practically unrecognizable between the rolling green lawns and giant estates. You would think you were deep in the country if you didn't know better.

The mansion I grew up in appeared on the left, a tangle of classic architecture with more modern additions. It was a little over the top for my taste, but it was undeniably beautiful.

Asher cleared his throat. "Okay, sweetheart, you win."

"What did I win?"

"Meeting your grandmother at school is very different from meeting her on her turf in a house like *that*."

My smirk was victorious. "What's my prize?"

"A lifetime supply of orgasms?"

I narrowed my eyes. "That better have already been part of the deal."

All my Alphas laughed, and Jace kissed my cheek. "Can't argue with that, baby girl."

"I'll think of something," Ash promised.

Briefly, I looked at each of them. I needed to dig into each of my Alphas. Now that we had the time, I wanted to know everything about them. Including their family. I already knew about Asher's family, and it wasn't something he wanted to talk about. Some of his tattoos covered up scars he'd received as a child. For obvious reasons, I hadn't met his family and probably wouldn't. He'd gotten out as soon as he could and never looked back.

The others, though.

"Am I going to meet everyone's family? Besides Ash, I mean."

"I'm sure my family is going to love you," Jace whispered. "They're in Concordia, but we'll figure it out."

"I only have a brother," Gabriel said. "Good terms, but he's much older than I am, so we don't talk much. I'm sure you'll meet him at some point."

Roman didn't return my gaze when I looked at him, instead sliding his hand into mine and interlocking our fingers. It was enough to tell me he didn't want to talk about it. At least for now.

I squeezed his hand and he squeezed back.

"Anything we should know before we go in?" Gabriel asked as he parked in the gravel drive.

"That you're walking into a zoo?" I muttered.

Roman choked back a laugh.

"A zoo?"

I loved my grandmother, and nothing she did surprised me anymore. As for everyone else? No telling what we were about to walk in on.

The door opened before I could even knock, my grandmother's housekeeper greeting us. Gorgeous orchestral music floated out of the house at an ear splitting volume.

"Hi, Sloane."

Pulling Marnie in for a hug, I sighed. "Hi."

The woman, who'd been working for my grandmother almost as long as I'd been alive, laughed. "She's expecting you."

"What is she doing?"

"Right now? Aerial silks."

Someone behind me coughed. Suspiciously.

I pinched the bridge of my nose for a second. "Okay. Marnie, can you take my Alphas to the greenhouse?"

"Of course."

"We're going with you," Roman said.

"You will be, but I need to see her first," I said, adding under my breath. "To make sure she's actually decent for company."

None of them protested further, Gabriel leaning in and kissing my hair on the way by. As soon as they were out of sight, I took a deep breath.

Here we go.

CHAPTER TWENTY-EIGHT

SLOANE

Sophia Glass did not give a fuck what a single person thought of her.

Which was why she now had an aerial silk setup in her grand salon. She claimed Pavilion got the idea from her, and refused to back down when I told her someone designing a circus club probably wasn't paying attention to her living room.

The bright red silk she now hung from dangled all the way to the floor. My grandmother bent backwards, the silk wrapped around her hips so she couldn't fall. Her eyes were closed, and she looked so peaceful she could be napping.

She'd been a dancer too, and our name opened doors in that world. But I'd made sure to make a name for myself and only myself. There was no point in being a Principal dancer if you hadn't earned it.

"Grandma?"

The music was too loud, and she didn't respond. The remote to the stereo rested on the arm of her chair. I flipped it off, and she groaned. "Marnie, how many times have I told you not to break my flow? You owe me another batch of cookies."

"If Marnie makes cookies I want some to take home with me."

She opened her eyes, staring at me upside down. "There you are. Fine, I'll let Marnie off the hook this time."

"No, keep her on," I teased. "I want the cookies."

Grandma unfolded herself and eased down the silks until her feet touched the floor. She wore a vibrant green bodysuit, her blonde hair—so similar to mine—up in a messy knot. Picking up a floral robe, she wrapped it around herself before wrapping us both up in a hug. "You've been gone for too long. Some people would say you're avoiding me. But we both know better, right?"

"Right."

I hadn't been avoiding her. Just busy. But it had been a few months since I'd seen her.

Waving a hand to a pair of cushy armchairs, she sat, and I sat with her. Marnie came in with tea on a cart and a folded newspaper. There were a couple of paperback books on the tray as well. "I told you on the phone to bring your Alphas. And yet I don't see them."

"They're in the greenhouse. I wanted to make sure I saw you first."

Her eyes sparkled. "Wanted to make sure I'm presentable enough for company?"

"Something like that." I laughed.

"I don't know. I think hanging in the air upside down is a hell of a first impression. If they can't handle that, they can't handle you." My cheeks flushed, and it was her turn to laugh. "I guess they're handling you just fine."

"Oh my *god*."

Picking up the paper and the books, she set them on the small table between us. "You'd think I'd raised you without knowing what sex is, the way you're blushing. We both know better. How was your heat? I need details."

"Grandma."

A single motion of a single eyebrow was all she gave me as she picked up her tea and stirred it.

"It was very good," I said. "They fucked my brains out for a solid four days. Happy?"

"Very." She took a sip and winked. "Heats are important."

"I'm aware," I said dryly.

"Good. Now, am I actually going to meet these handsome men? Or are you going to force me to embarrass you some more?"

Looking over at Marnie, I nodded. She disappeared, and I made myself a cup of tea while we waited, and Grandma flipped through the arts section of the Slate City Chronicle.

The door opened, and Marnie led them in. Gabriel first, then Roman, Jace, and Ash last.

Grandma rolled up the newspaper in her hand and smacked me on the arm. Hard. "*Ow*. What was that for?"

"You lied to me. You told me it had nothing to do with him."

"I know. It's a long story. One probably better rehashed at a different time?"

She glared at me, but I knew that look. It was one I'd seen practically every day of my childhood. The *you're lucky I love you*, look. I blew her a kiss.

"Very well. But I expect to hear it."

"You will."

"Grandma Glass," Ash said, stepping forward. "Nice to see you again."

"Did you break Sloane's heart?" If there was one thing Sophia Glass was, it was direct.

Ash, for once, wasn't teasing. His face was entirely serious. He sank to one knee in front of her. "Not intentionally, and never again." And then, like the charming Alpha he was, he took her outstretched hand and kissed the back of it before winking. "I'm a very happy man."

"You fucking better be," she said with a laugh. "Who are the rest of you?"

Each of my Alphas introduced themselves as I sat, slowly burning alive. Nerves and embarrassment were going to consume me. Ash picked me up and sat with me, so I was halfway across his lap.

Grandma smiled in approval.

"See?" He murmured. "That wasn't so bad."

"You weren't here while she asked me for details about the heat."

He laughed quietly into my neck. "Sorry."

I leaned back into him, the closeness relaxing.

"Sloane here thought it would scar you too much to see an old woman like me climbing silks."

"I did not say that," a laugh cracked through me. She was in rare form today, and she didn't look nearly as old as she was.

She took a sip of tea. "You were thinking it. Now, tell me what you do. I already know this one," nodding toward Ash before pointing at Jace. "You first."

One by one they spoke to her, answering questions about who they were and what they did. Even Roman, though his

207

answers were shorter. It didn't seem to bother her though, and the more he spoke, the more comfortable he became. Every time he looked at me butterflies broke out in my stomach. He was doing this for me, even if it wasn't fully comfortable.

Pure instinct drove me from Asher's lap and into Roman's. He was stiff, not relaxing until I moved his hands around my waist and held them there. One deep breath in, and another. His body eased under mine, and we listened to Gabriel as he spoke. But Grandma still had her eyes on the two of us.

When Gabriel finished, Grandma looked around at my Alphas. "Well, I think it's a little late for me to give my blessing to you, but you have it. Take care of Sloane. She deserves it."

"We will." Jace. His words sounded like a vow.

She lifted a hand to bring Marnie over before dropping her hands on her lap. Marnie handed Gabe what looked like a business card. "When you're ready to take the next step, you let me know."

Gabe nodded once and repeated the words. "We will."

"Now, my synchronized swimming instructor will be here any moment."

I blinked at her. "Who are you synchronized swimming with?"

"The instructor."

"But—"

Grandma waved a hand. "Please. I can synchronize with myself. You think I would let anyone else have the spotlight even in my own pool?"

Everyone laughed.

"We'll meet you at the car," Gabe said, standing.

Roman set me on my feet, and they left us briefly alone.

Grandma held out arms, and I walked into them. "You like them?" I asked.

"I do," she said. "And I'm not simply saying that because they're your matches."

"Not a long time to get an impression."

She laughed. "I'm an old lady, Sloane. Maybe not as old as some, but old enough. When you're my age, you don't need a long time to take the measure of someone. They're good men, and they're good for you. Even the quiet one."

I smiled, and we pulled apart. "Do you really have a synchronized swim class? Or are you just trying to kick me out so I can have sex I'd rather you not know about?"

"Wouldn't you like to know?" She tapped me on the nose. "Call me when you know your schedule for the next run, and we'll figure out a time to have lunch."

"Okay."

She swept away dramatically—in a direction that was not toward the pool—and left me standing alone in the room.

I closed my eyes and shook my head, smiling. She was who she was, and I loved her for it. Even if she was trying to get me laid. On that note, I didn't hesitate to get back to my Alphas.

CHAPTER TWENTY-NINE

SLOANE

"So that whole time, you watched all of us fall in love and you were alone? God, I'm just going to kill you," Eva said, lounging in one of Petra's giant bean bags.

Petra laughed. "You can't kill her *now*. She's finally getting dicked down appropriately. That wouldn't be fun."

Eva narrowed her eyes. "Fine. But only because of the dick."

"Generous of you," I said, scratching behind Stormy's ears as she bumped my shoulder with her head. "At least Stormy isn't mad at me."

"I'm not mad at you." Eva let her head flop backward. "I just can't believe it."

"Bitch, get in line," Petra said. "But it's all fine now."

We were having a girls' day while my Alphas took care of my apartment. When everything was out they would come pick me up so I could say goodbye to the place like I'd asked. In the meantime there was food and a couple of drinks.

By the time we walked back into the house after being at Grandma's yesterday, none of us had been able to wait. Being in the car with all four of them was a dangerous—and sexy—combination.

Gabriel had been about to lay me out on the kitchen island. Only Jace insisting none of us wanted to clean it made us hold on while the elevator took us upwards.

You win, Grandma.

But I'd spent most of this time catching my best friends up. Esme and I weren't as close, only having officially met a month ago. We invited her, but she couldn't make it. Something about her and her pack and a photoshoot? She hadn't given many details.

"And I'm sorry," Petra said. "I wish I'd never told you to fuck Craig."

I smiled at her. "That's nice of you, but we both know I was going to do it anyway."

"Between the three of us, I think we have enough Alpha energy to take him down. Hell, I'm sure Esme's pack will help. I don't think Cole has killed anyone in a while, right?" Eva teased.

Petra went pale and winced.

"Too soon?"

"A little, yeah."

"Sorry, Bee," Eva whispered.

Stormy went over to Petra and collapsed in her lap. The cat was almost supernaturally sensitive to people's moods. Especially Petra's.

"It's okay. I'm getting better. Haven't had any nightmares in a few days, and I finally rescheduled my interview with the orchestra."

"That's great," I said. "And you came to my show, so you're getting out of the house."

She pinned me with a stare. "Can we talk about that, by the way? Because holy *fuck* you were so good, Lo."

"Thank you. I'll be honest, I don't remember most of it."

"It's a damn good thing they recorded it," Eva pointed at me. "Because I need to see you dancing through a fucking heat."

I shook my head and tipped back the last of the white wine in my glass. We hadn't drunk enough to make any of us more than tipsy, and even then it had been long enough for me to be pretty much sober. Pulling out my phone, I checked the time. No texts from my Alphas. There were some from Craig, but I ignored them.

"Oh my god, look at her," Eva said. "You're literally pouting."

"I am not."

"Do you have any texts from them?"

"No."

"See? Pouting. You checked your phone and your whole face dropped."

I said nothing, and Eva caught it. "What?"

"Nothing."

She pounced, moving faster than I thought possible given

how deep she was in the bean bag. My phone was in her hand, and since it was already unlocked...

"Don't worry, I'm not going dumpster diving for your weird sex texts."

"I don't have any weird sex texts, Eva," I said, slowly stretching my legs out and doing a split, enjoying the gentle pull in my hamstrings. Even though rehearsals didn't start back for another week, I needed to get back to class. My body was feeling the lack of training already. Tomorrow I'd make Ash go with me.

"Lo, this is way worse than you said it was."

Petra held her hand out for the phone. "Let me see."

I shrugged. "Yeah. It's bad. But what can I do about it? We're already moving me out of my apartment and doing our best to *not* see him. The only other thing I could do is block his number, and I don't want to do that. Because if he goes further down this path, I want a warning.

"It's not like I can hide. I'm not giving up my career because I made a mistake, fucked the wrong guy, and he somehow has it in his head that I belong to him."

"We should tell Harrison," Petra said.

"What's he going to do?"

"I don't know, but he could do something."

I looked at her. "I don't need a bodyguard, Bee. And I'm not saying that because I'm stubborn. I'm saying that because I already have four of them, and they get to keep me safe *and* give me orgasms, so it really wouldn't be fair to anyone else."

We all collapsed into giggles, and she tossed my phone at me. "There. You don't have to be sad anymore."

Glancing down at the screen, there was a text from Gabriel saying they were almost here. "Stormy," I whispered. "Want to race me downstairs?"

Her ears perked up, and when I moved quickly, she jumped up, hunching down and ready to pounce for whatever game I was playing.

Sprinting, a playful snarl came out of her as she came after me, giving into the fun of running and passing me on the stairs without stopping. I was never going to beat a literal leopard down the stairs, clouded or not.

"Woah, girl." I heard Emery's voice before I rounded the last corner. Stormy was on her back legs, paws on his chest while he stroked her ears. "Hey, Sloane."

"My pack is almost here."

"Harrison just got the call. He's bringing them up."

"Thanks."

The elevator in their foyer opened. Petra took Stormy's place with Emery before looking at me. "You know there's an elevator, right?"

"Why would I need one when I can race this girl?"

Soft male laughter reached me a second before Harrison came in, followed by all my Alphas. Tension snapped between us as all of their focus fell directly on me. It had only been a few hours, and I *missed* them. Holy fuck.

Stormy focused on the newcomers, going to check them out in the way only a cat could do. She sniffed them one by one, before stopping in front of Roman. Her entire body went still, and she watched him intently—he looked right back at her.

Like she'd found what she needed, she went forward and shoved her head against his legs, leaning her whole weight on him as she rubbed all over his jeans and twisted in a figure eight through his knees.

"I think she likes you."

"I like her," he said.

Emery introduced himself, all the guys doing the kind of male greetings they did, while I hugged Petra and Eva. "Thank you. I needed some girl time."

"This much testosterone will do that," Eva said. "We need to make a schedule for the four of us now that we all have packs."

"I'd like that."

"Yes," Petra agreed. "Let's do that. But first... Harrison, Lo needs Atwood Security's help."

I glared at her, getting a grin in return.

"And why does she need it?"

Petra stared at me long enough that I wilted. Gabriel came over and stole me away. "Show him."

Taking out my phone, I unlocked it, pulled up Craig's texts, and handed the phone to Harrison. He scrolled, looking at me and Gabriel briefly before back at the phone. "I see."

I winced, fighting the urge to hide. Having made the mistake and having people know about it were two different things. Gabe kissed my temple. "Stop it."

"What?"

"You know what." A soft whine came out of me and he kissed me again. "You're all right, little one."

Harrison fixed his eyes on me. "Are you all right with me forwarding his number and these messages to myself?"

"Yeah. What are you going to do?"

"Nothing yet. But I'd like to look into him a little."

Jace stepped forward. "We appreciate that."

"Unfortunately it's more common than I'd like," Harrison said. "Some are worse than others. We'll see if he's one that has bite to go with the bark."

Finally, he handed my phone back to me.

"Let us know," Gabriel said. "Cost isn't an issue."

"I don't charge for things like this," he said with a smile. "It'll take a few days."

"Thank you."

Stormy was still loving on Roman, with him now on the floor petting her. I couldn't help but smile. She didn't need words to communicate with him.

Asher tugged me out of Gabe's arms. "Ready to go say bye to the apartment?"

"Yeah." I waved to the girls. "I'll text you."

"You better," Eva said, winking.

Stormy didn't want to let Roman go, but released him when Petra called her back. "When's the stuff getting there?"

"Tomorrow. We'll stop by the apartment before heading home."

"Did you have fun, baby girl?"

I stretched up on my toes in the elevator and draped my arms around Jace's neck. "Yes. And no, I didn't drink enough to make me drunk."

"I wasn't going to ask that." He smirked and brushed his lips over mine. "But that's good to know. Do you need to eat?"

215

"No, I'm good."

"Do you need to be eaten then?"

My eyes went wide, and he smirked. "Ninety percent of problems can be fixed by one or the other, baby girl."

"I'll remember that," I murmured. Then I looked over. "Ash, we need to go to class tomorrow."

Roman cleared his throat. "I thought you weren't rehearsing?"

"No," I shook my head. "No rehearsals. Just class. Can't go for two weeks without taking class or even normal rehearsals will be painful."

"Yeah, we can go," Ash said. "Should probably get back to it myself."

Gabriel nodded. "Okay, but no more. Not until rehearsals start or your pickup rehearsals for *Giselle* in a few weeks."

"No arguments from me."

The drive to my apartment didn't take long. It felt strange that this was the last time I would be here. I needed to get the keys back to the management company. "Did you find the dead bodies I hid?"

"No, but we found your collection of toys."

"You already knew about those."

"True," Ash said. "But now they'll be at home where *we* can use them."

Perfume floated through the car. I couldn't think about them using toys on me if we wanted to make it home. "I need to stop taking car rides with the four of you."

"Or you could take more... rides," Jace whispered.

I flushed hot before he kissed me, barely letting me breathe before Gabriel parked the car. "Okay, maybe I'll take more."

"Thought so."

I knocked on Noreen's door first, and she answered right away. "I thought that might be you. Your guys have been here all day."

"It is me. I wanted to say goodbye, but you can always call me if you need something, okay?"

She patted my arm. "Oh, you know me, dear. I'll be fine."

Noreen was older, and true to her word, she always seemed

happy and fine. But that didn't mean I couldn't worry. "Still, if you need me, I'll be here right away."

"I appreciate that. Now don't waste more time with an old lady like me. Not when you're going home with *that*."

I laughed and hugged her briefly before I crossed the hall. The apartment seemed so much bigger empty. But it felt good to stand here, look around, and feel absolutely no sadness.

There were good times in this apartment, and a lot of loneliness. I worried I'd walk in and feel like I was missing something by leaving, but I didn't.

Wandering to the bedroom, I leaned against the door frame and just looked. The scent of fresh-baked cookies enveloped me. "You okay, blue?"

"Yeah, I am. I thought I might feel... I don't know. Nostalgic? Guess it just proves how little I had that I don't feel much about leaving."

"You had things," he whispered, pressing his body gently into mine. "You had your grandmother, and you had your friends. Your job. I'm glad you'll be with us because it's where you're *supposed* to be, sweetheart. But you still had a life. Don't regret it."

I leaned back into him, not wanting to say anything further. Would I always regret not telling him? Probably. The rest he was right about. I'd lived life and tried to do it well. It was enough.

They'd really cleared out everything. It looked like it had been cleaned, too. Better than when I'd moved in. One last look in all the rooms, and I was ready. "Should I just... leave the key?"

"Yes," Gabriel said. "We spoke to the management company. You can leave it on the counter."

The key they'd borrowed already sat there, and I added mine. I closed the door for the last time. No turning back now.

Roman touched my shoulder. "You okay?"

"Yes." And it was true. "Let's go home."

Jace grinned. "I like the sound of that."

The early evening air was mild. A tinge of cold heralding the weather would change soon. But right now it was nice. It would be a perfect night for that fire pit.

"*Sloane.*"

My whole body froze. Asher's growl tore the air, and suddenly I was surrounded by a wall of Alpha on every side.

I peeked around Asher's arm, in the space between him and Roman, and saw Craig. He looked rough. Unkempt, tired like he hadn't slept, beard out of control, eyes feral.

"What do you want, Craig?"

"I want you to talk to me, and I want answers."

"I think I've been pretty clear. What more is there to say?" I pressed my forehead into Asher's spine, inhaling the scent of leather from his jacket.

"You actually going to *talk* to me? Or are you going to hide behind your pretty boys?"

Growls rose low, but I reached out and touched them. We needed to keep calm, despite it being the last thing I wanted. Craig was a question mark, and we didn't know what he would do if we pushed him too far. I tried to step out of the circle, and Roman stopped me. "No."

"I'm going to stand right in front of you," I said quietly. "Where you can still touch me. But he'll never stop if he can't see me."

"He's not going to stop anyway," Ash said.

Roman's fingers curled into the loop on the back of my jeans as I stepped in front of him. The others spread out. How Craig was still fucking standing there while they were throwing every bit of Alpha dominance toward him was beyond me.

"Okay," I said. "Whatever you want to say, go ahead."

Craig snorted. "Whatever I want to say? *You're* the one who has shit to say, Sloane. One day I have a girlfriend, and the next I'm ghosted, and you're in bed with another man. I've been gracious with you, considering. It's time for you to stop this."

I stared at him. "We were friends with benefits, Craig. Six weeks of sex a year ago, and three dates in the last month do not constitute a relationship."

"You are *mine*." He took a step toward me, and Roman's fingers tightened. All my Alphas tensed, but we didn't move. "I told you when you called me I wasn't doing casual again. What the fuck do you think that means?"

Shaking my head, I tried to understand. "You never said that, Craig."

"Yes, I did."

Closing my eyes, I threw my mind back to the conversation. It hadn't been a long one. Go figure I would have called him instead of just texting so we could have actual proof.

"Fine," Craig said. "But it's going to be less casual this time. Be at—" He'd named the restaurant where we went a couple weeks ago and told me when to be there. We had dinner, went back to his place, and I left. That was it.

"You... said less casual. Which is why we went on those dates." The concert clearly didn't count. "I just..."

Panic and confusion combined into nausea. This didn't make any sense, and it wasn't going to. I needed to let my instinct to rely on logic go. He was inventing responses from me that I'd never given. But how could he get anything from my *silence*?

"I'm sorry, Craig." The apology burned on my tongue. "I'm sorry you misunderstood what was between us. I'm not sorry for leaving after you disrespected me." I held out a hand to cut him off before he could protest. "And no, you having arranged a surprise does not make that disrespect better."

"You fucking *bitch*."

I snapped. "What the fuck is wrong with you? You understand that even if my pack wasn't in the picture, your behavior would have made things end, right? This is ridiculous. I've tried to be gentle, and I've tried to be understanding. I haven't even *said* anything to you since you showed up, uninvited, at my door and you think we've had full conversations. I'm done. Leave me the fuck alone."

Craig growled. "You *agreed*, Sloane."

"For fuck's sake." Rage shook me to my core. "When?"

"When I *told you*." He was drawing attention now. Not a lot of people walked around in this neighborhood, but his volume and mine drew the few heads there were. "I told you that if I put energy into this, that you were mine." He held out his hands wide. "So far I'm the only one holding up my side of the bargain."

Tears of frustration burned in my eyes. "What are you talking about? You said that. I never agreed to it. The only thing I said was that I would give you money for the concert ticket. I never agreed."

"You never told me no, Sloane."

Roman growled, low and deep. A sound that meant death, and right now I wasn't fucking opposed. "Seriously? I can't believe I even have to explain this. Not saying 'no' is not the same as saying yes. So allow me to correct your absurd assumption. *No*. I do not want you to 'give me another chance.' I don't want you to put effort in. I don't want to fuck you. I don't want to talk to you. I don't want to see you ever again. Is that fucking clear enough for you?"

He stared at me in stunned silence.

"Even if you somehow had a claim to me, which you *do not*, and someone made me go home with you right this second, why would you want that? Why would you want someone who doesn't want you? There are tons of other women in the world." Not that I would wish Craig on them with the power of a thousand suns.

The belt loop wasn't enough for Roman anymore. He slid his hands around my stomach at the same time Jace took my hand. I got the feeling they both needed to touch me in order to hold themselves back. As it was, they didn't want me standing here, talking to him.

I didn't want to be here either.

"If you had owned up to the fact that you were an ass, Craig, we could have moved on and left things between us on good terms. But we were never going to be together. I never viewed you that way, and hopefully, *hopefully*, you'll learn something from this, but I doubt it."

The way he looked at me and then at each of my Alphas gave me chills. Pure, black hatred. He drew himself up to his full height and his face went blank. No emotion, no clue to what he was feeling. It almost seemed like he didn't care.

It didn't fool me.

"It's okay, Sloane. I understand, and I forgive you." Unlike before, his words were soft and calm and a thousand times more terrifying than the opposite. "You're a little lost, and that's fine.

Entranced by some dick. You're not the first Omega it's happened to." He shrugged. "I'll give you time to get it out of your system. But that's the last chance you get. I let you go the first time. And I put everything on the line for you the second time. You can deny it all you want, but you *are* mine. Eventually you'll see that, but I understand if I have to wait. That's fine. I can be patient. It doesn't change anything." His smile made me want to vomit. "You know how to push my buttons, darling. But I forgive you. Later, you'll need to know that I did."

I rolled my eyes. "Okay. If you want to act like a cartoon villain, whatever. You sound ridiculous. Don't text me. Don't call me. Don't ever contact me again. Got it?"

He smirked. "Got it."

"Take me home," I said to my pack.

They didn't hesitate, sweeping me into the car and pulling away from the curb in seconds. Now that we were away, I melted, folding into Roman's side and letting him hold me.

"Don't ever call me darling," I said.

"Never," Ash vowed.

In the front, Jace looked over at Gabriel. "Did you record all of that?"

My Alpha met my eyes in the mirror. "Every word."

At least there was some good news.

CHAPTER THIRTY

GABRIEL

I watched Sloane in the back of the car, my knuckles white on the steering wheel. It took all of my self-control to keep my mouth shut and my fists to myself back there, and I was fraying. Hanging by a thread.

As soon as we got home, I was sending the recording to Harrison. Though we'd only met earlier today, I knew who he was by reputation. His family was one of the wealthiest in the country, and his security company was the best.

In the mirror, I saw the same look on Sloane's face as I had last night. One that told me she was questioning herself. However clear it was to the rest of us that Craig was out of his mind, Sloane had been the one to go to him. Because of that, she felt guilty.

We would put an end to that.

My Omega would not suffer guilt or shame because an asshole decided he didn't like being rejected.

I pulled into the garage and nearly forgot what we'd arranged in the house. Sloane might not be up for it now, but it also might be a good distraction.

We entered the kitchen, and I heard our guests out in the front room. Before I could say anything, Sloane did. "I'm sorry about that."

My control was already too far gone. I turned and pulled her against my body, her back pressed to my chest, my hand at her throat, my lips at her ear. "What did I tell you about apologizing for things that aren't your fault?"

"But—"

"*No.*" I stroked my thumb over the point of her pulse, inhaling every delicious breath of her sweetness. Right now there was a touch of sour laced through the blueberries, but she wasn't afraid.

The way her scent turned while she was in front of Craig?

223

That was fear. Sour that bordered on rotten. What I smelled now was merely the slightest apprehension or anxiety. No fear.

"I know, little one. I know you feel like you brought this on yourself somehow. But it's not true, and I—" I cut myself off. "*We* will not tolerate it. You have every right to be angry, and you have every right to be scared. But guilt? Shame? Over an asshole who's trying to make you feel like *nothing*? Never."

She shuddered in my arms, surrendering. The others had surrounded us, so she had someone on each side. Safety. Warmth. Comfort.

"This is not my fault," I whispered in her ear. "Say it."

"This is not my fault."

"Good girl. Do you believe it?"

"Yes," her voice shook with unshed tears. "I believe and I know it, but I don't feel it."

I released my purr, savoring her curves pressing against me as her body soothed. "I'll tell you the truth, little one. The only reason we're not in your nest right now with you over my knee is because we have company." Slowly, I kissed her neck. "They're here for you, our own little surprise. Are you up for it?"

"I don't know."

"We'll go and see, okay? But later, I think we all need some time in your nest."

At that, she nodded. I turned her around in my arms, and she hid her face in my shirt. I ran my fingers through her hair. "Will you look at me?"

She did, slowly, and I carefully examined her face. "We're still new at this. I need you to tell me if this is okay. My Alpha instinct wants this. To give you structure and make you feel safe. But I don't have a *right* to it. And we are not like him. We will never take what's not offered."

Panic slid over her face. "I know you're not. I don't think that. Please don't—"

I kissed her softly, and Roman stepped up closer behind her, offering more touch. "I'm saying it because I want you to hear it, little one, not because you think we're the same. But I still need you to tell me if this is okay."

"Yes," she breathed, letting her head drop once more. "I never

224

thought I would before you, but yes. I get... caught in my head. It's nice to have you pull me back."

"Then I always will." I held her close and let her breathe, meeting the others' eyes. All I saw there was love. I hadn't said it yet, and I wouldn't now. Not in the wake of something like this. But I felt it. Hell, I'd felt it the moment I realized what she was to me. How could I not?

And every second I spent with her made me fall for her more. Even this. Because I needed to care for her and lead her just as much as she needed me to do those things.

"Say it again."

Sloane took a small breath. "This is not my fault."

"Good girl," I told her again, running my palm down her spine. "Thank you. Let's go see who's here, okay?"

"Okay."

Before we did, the others held her. And every one of us that touched her, I watched her get lighter.

Taking her hand, I led her into the formal living room, where both Addison and Claire waited. The room now smelled like bubblegum because of the Beta flitting around the space looking at all the decorations.

"Sloane!" She pounced, stealing my Omega from me and wrapping her in a hug. "*Congratulations*. I was going to schedule lunch, but when Jace called me again, this was even better."

Sloane smiled, but it was hesitant. She looked at Claire and then at me. "It's great to see you guys, and I hope this doesn't sound rude, but what are you doing here?"

"I thought they might keep it to themselves," Addison said with a laugh. "I'm here to help design your bedroom before your things arrive."

"Really?"

"Really," I said.

Her face crumpled and she threw herself at me, arms curling around my neck. Claire and Addison looked at us in concern, but I held out one hand. She was okay. "Thank you."

"I don't want you holding back this time," I said. "Whatever you want. And I have spies."

My Omega laughed. The sound was pure ecstasy. I wanted it injected straight into my veins. "Fine. I *guess* I'll go wild."

"Make sure you do."

She brushed tears off her face and turned to her friends. "I guess I'll show you guys around?"

"Sounds good to me." Addison grabbed her tablet and Claire gave Sloane a hug.

"You okay?"

"Not really, but I'll explain."

She looked at us, and Roman was the one who spoke. "Go ahead, firefly."

All of us waited until they disappeared into the kitchen and we heard the elevator doors close to speak. "Anyone else feel like they need to go to the gym and run a marathon?"

"If by marathon you mean 'find and kill a fucker,' then yes," Jace said, rage coloring his tone.

I pulled out my phone and immediately emailed the recording of Craig to Harrison. He'd given us his card when he met us in the lobby of Starling Tower. "Yes, that is what I mean. But that's not an option, sadly."

Jace turned to Ash. "You never said. Was he there when you drove by last night?"

"No. It was clear, but that doesn't mean he wasn't there. Nothing all day and he happens to show up the minute she's there? He was watching."

I grit my teeth. "We should assume he knows where we live."

Roman growled. "If he tries to hurt her here, I *will* kill him."

"Let's try to avoid that. Not because I have any love for him, but I think we'd all rather you not be in jail," I said.

"We need a restraining order," Jace said.

I tacked on a reply to the email, asking Harrison if he could take care of that, asking what we needed for it, and if the recording and text messages would be enough. "Yes."

Realistically, a restraining order wouldn't do much. But it gave us rights we might not otherwise have.

"Ash, when you take Sloane to class, take your bike around back and park it inside the back entrance. Put it in the garage while here." The last thing we needed was his bike messed with.

I'd rather her be in the car, but if we were thinking about the worst-case scenario, a motorcycle had the ability to maneuver that a car didn't. Of course that came with a whole host of other risks, but it felt like everything was a risk right now.

He cleared his throat. "Yeah, I can do that."

Roman shifted on his feet, the only sign he was struggling. He didn't fidget. "Where does this end?"

"What do you mean?"

"I mean that Sloane can't be harassed by this asshole forever, and neither can we. It's no way to live. Based on what he said, it doesn't seem like he's just going to go away, so where does it end?"

Silence fell over us, none of us knowing the answer. Finally, I swallowed. "Let's see what Harrison has to say. For the next few days, while Sloane doesn't have rehearsals, let's do what we had planned. Court her, show her exactly how much we want her, and we'll keep her safe while we do it. We can't do anything until we know more."

"Let's get her a new phone," Jace said. "New number. That way we can have her phone and he can keep texting it, but she doesn't have to see it."

Ash crossed his arms. "Good idea."

"I was planning on taking her to the aquarium anyway," he said. "While I'm making those arrangements, I'll grab one."

"Aquarium?"

Jace smirked. "Just a hunch."

I needed to do something else with my energy while Sloane was upstairs planning. I didn't actually want to run a marathon. Might as well go to my office and channel some of the anger into getting control of the situation at the company. Then, I would take care of my Omega.

"One more thing," Roman said. "I have an idea, but I want to make sure you're all on board."

Ideas for Sloane were my new favorite pastime, and we needed the distraction. "I'm listening."

CHAPTER THIRTY-ONE

SLOANE

*M*y room was a big blank canvas, and Addison had about a million and one ideas. She'd peeked in and seen the space when she was here working on my nest. "I nearly salivated and begged Roman to let me design this too, but with the time crunch, thought it was better to wait."

"That's the only reason?" Claire asked. She sat next to me, leaning against the wall, watching her Beta with a fond smile.

Addison made a face that told me they'd had this conversation before. "Yeah, yeah. No pressuring people for jobs."

I leaned my head on Claire's shoulder, most of my energy gone. Between the wine and Craig? I was ready to curl up in my nest and sleep. But having the perfect bedroom was a nice idea. They had the cliff notes, so they knew why I was low energy.

"Other than your little interaction, how are things going?"

"Good." My smile couldn't be stopped. "Better than I thought it could be."

"And you were worried," she teased.

"I have other things to worry about now." A sobering thought. "I know you're off, but the other cohorts?"

Claire snorted. "Happy to report that Ian is, in fact, still an ass."

"Perfect."

"Don't worry, everyone is ready to handle him once *Swan Lake* starts."

Addison sat down cross-legged in front of me now that she was done measuring the room. "Okay. So, how did I do on the nest?"

"It's beautiful," I told her. "Truly. I love it."

"Would you want something similar in here? Or something different?"

I thought about it. "Adjacent."

Her fingers flew on the tablet. "Okay, adjacent in what direction?"

"If that's the sunset, then in here I'd love it to be dusk."

"Ooooh, love that. So like darker blues and purples and stuff?"

Pulling my knees up to my chest, I rested my chin on them. "Yeah. Maybe the last touches of the deep reds."

"God, this is going to be gorgeous. Now, tell me, do you want the space to be dark and cozy? I promise it won't be stuffy or feel like you're in a cave during the middle of the day."

"That's fine."

"Any special requests? Like a hanging bed or anything?"

A laugh bubbled out of me. "A hanging bed?"

"We have them. They're very popular. Kind of like sleeping in the middle of a marshmallow, but like... pack-sized."

"That's okay." The mental image of getting railed while it moved made me laugh. Even if it was sturdy—which I was sure it was—Roman might be hesitant because of his height. "I wouldn't say no to a normal sized swing though."

"Noted."

She asked me more detailed questions about colors and finishes, and if there was anything furniture wise from my apartment I was attached to. There wasn't.

"If I do anything you hate, we'll fix it."

I gave her a look. "Addie, you created my perfect nest from Ash's vague recollection of my doodles. I can't imagine you doing something I *hate*."

"Still."

"Still, I appreciate you doing it at all."

She grinned. "Are you kidding? This is my dream job. Anyway, unless you have anything else I can think of, that's all I need. We'll be back in the morning, and everything will be done by dinner."

Slowly, I shook my head. "It never ceases to amaze me how quickly you can do this."

"Practice and preparation," she said. "We pay our people well, so they don't fuck around. Get in, get it done, get out."

Claire leaned over and whispered. "You don't want to see her when her team is running behind. Not even Gabriel would mess with her." She smiled sweetly at Addie, who glared back.

"I know where you sleep," Addison said.

"I would hope so. Unless you *don't* want me between your legs tonight."

"*Claire.*"

I smothered a giggle with my hand. "Addison, you literally design people's sex dens. I think it's okay if your friends know you have sex."

She sighed, dramatically flipping the cover over her tablet screen. "Fine. She's lucky she's pretty."

"I say the same thing almost every day," Claire whispered to me.

Addison was trying very hard not to smile. "You're in so much trouble."

"My favorite." Claire helped me to my feet and gave me a hug. "Call me if you need me. Otherwise, I'll see you in class?"

"I'll be there." They were on the way out of the room when the thought struck me. "Addison?"

She turned. "When you guys are moving stuff in... just be careful? I don't know if Craig—"

"Don't worry," she said. "I know everyone I work with personally. I'll bring some of our security as well, just to keep an eye on things."

"Thank you."

Her smile told me Claire was right. I didn't want to mess with her. "No one fucks with my friends on my watch."

They made their way to the elevator, and I made my way to the shower. I needed a long one. And I let myself soak in the warmth for a long time, pampering everything I could.

I rubbed some shimmery oil into my skin when I finished, using some of the stuff I had delivered, and finally put on a night-gown. Not unlike the one I teased Ash with in my apartment. But this one was an icy blue.

Then I went to my nest. The guys knew where I was, and they would find me eventually. It really was beautiful, the actual light of sunset streaming through the one small window.

The metallic gold blanket laid on the edge of the nest, and

that was what I grabbed. The nest had been cleaned, and I wasn't sure when that happened, but it made me smile. They took care of things without me even noticing, and I loved it.

It was nice not to have to think about *everything* all the time.

Curling up in the corner, I snuggled down into the blanket and let myself breathe. No one really knew why we needed this— the warmth and the darkness and all the soft things, but we did. There was no denying how safe nesting made me feel. Like the world couldn't touch me in here, and it was exactly what I needed.

A soft knock came from behind me.

I turned over to find Gabriel leaning in the doorway, hands in his pockets. The others were nowhere to be found.

Smiling, I just looked at him and enjoyed the view. He did the same. "I thought we all needed nest time?"

"They'll be here in a bit."

Untangling myself from the blanket, I went to him, instincts driving me. Until I had to look up to meet his eyes. "Is this where you spank me?"

I was teasing, but I didn't know for sure. If he wanted to, I would let him. Something told me we both needed it. Or would, at some point.

Gabriel's mouth smiled, but his eyes were serious. He reached out, fingers curling around the back of my neck. "I'd rather not tonight, little one."

"Why not?"

He smirked. "Is my Omega eager for that?"

"I... don't know."

With that hand on my neck, he tugged me into his body, his forehead on mine. Then, like something collapsed in him, he gathered me up in his arms, my feet lifting off the floor as he held me. "I can't bear it right now," he whispered. "Causing you any kind of pain."

The admission struck me in the chest. The urge to apologize rose, and I shoved it right down where it belonged. Instead, I held him right back.

Gabriel kicked his shoes off and carried me into the nest, sweeping me down into the cushions. His scent was richer tonight. Not as sweet. The darker notes of tobacco lingered at the top. My Alpha had a darker edge to him, and I wanted that.

Was tonight the night for it?

"There will be times when I spank you," he said. Not a request or tease. Simply a statement of fact, along with a hint of a smile. "And I'm sure you will deserve it. But tonight, little one, I just want to make you feel good."

He kissed me. At once gentle and unyielding. My Alpha of delicious contradictions. There was something so hot about him still fully dressed and me in this scrap of silk, the heat of his hands sinking through it to my skin.

"I'm not apologizing," I said when we broke apart. "I just hate that he was there. I hate that he was anywhere near you. I hate every decision I made that led to me letting him in again. It's so fucking *frustrating*."

Gabriel made a rough sound in the back of his throat, his teeth coming down on my shoulder. Not biting—not breaking the skin—but making me freeze, an Omega beneath her Alpha. He licked over the place his teeth grazed. "One favor for me, little one."

I whined, wanting more. "Yes."

"Don't bring him in here with us. Just like the heat. Keep everyone else out. There's no one here but you and your pack, okay?"

That would be hard. It was all I could think about. But he was right, and hadn't I thought the same thing? That this was a safe place? "I'll try."

"Good girl."

My breath went short, my body reacting and heating up with his approval. "You can't say that every time."

"Why not?"

"Because."

He smiled, lowering his mouth to where the top of my nightgown met my skin. "That's not a real answer. Because if you squirm like that every time I say it, I'm going to say it a lot."

One of his hands gathered the fabric of the nightgown slowly, bunching it up so more and more of me was revealed. Until all of it was shoved up above my breasts, exposing what he was looking for. "Mmm." He kissed the skin directly between them before lightly teasing one nipple with his tongue. "The frenzy of the heat was amazing, but I find myself wanting to explore you slowly."

"Not too slowly," I begged, the word slipping into a moan when his whole mouth consumed me.

Gabriel's tongue swirled around my nipple, drawing it to near painful hardness. "I don't know," he said. "I think slow can be kind of nice."

Grabbing his hair, I pulled him back to me. "Is this actually what you want and need, or is this what you think *I* need?"

"What if I tell you it's exactly what I want?"

"Then *good*. But I don't think it is."

A wicked smirk crossed his face, and he bent to tease my other nipple. "Why not?"

"Because the only time you haven't held back with me is during the heat, and even then it was when you needed to get me out of my head." My breath caught, words trying to evaporate under the attention of his mouth. "Do you think I don't notice?"

He didn't respond, instead dragging his mouth up my skin and beneath my jaw until his lips pressed against mine without kissing me. "Are you telling me you don't like gentle softness?"

I studied his eyes, that soft warmth of the green in them. Tiny flecks of a bluer shade. "You're deflecting," I told him. "Am I your Omega?"

The growl in his chest rumbled through both of us. "Fuck yes, you are."

"Then you're my Alpha." Just like he asked me if he could guide me, I had a job too. My job was to push him so he didn't get lost in that protection. Alpha and Omega. Push and pull. Each of my Alphas would need something different, and this was what he needed. "And I can handle you. Letting yourself be who you are isn't going to cause me pain, Gabriel. You don't have to spank me, and I'm not going to pretend I don't love it when you tease me so much I feel like I'm drowning. I love gentle softness. But that's not what you feel right now."

"No?" It wasn't a full denial. He was waiting to see what I would say.

"No. Because the Gabriel that held me downstairs and told me it wasn't my fault? That Gabriel was holding on by a thread. You know it and I know it. You're all holding on by tatters because of that dick biscuit, and I don't need you to temper the feeling." He smiled at the term but didn't interrupt me. "You're angry? So the fuck am I. He claims I'm his, and I'm not. Show me that I'm *yours*."

Fire burned in his gaze. A shift. Everything he'd buried coming to the surface. I felt the power of it, and my perfume exploded around us. All I wanted was him. Who he really was.

Grabbing both sides of his face, I pulled him down to me. "Do what you wanted. Make me feel good. But do it the way you really want to and don't be afraid to show me who you are. And later, when we're both happy and sleepy and cuddly you can spend all the time you like exploring me. Lay me out in front of your fireplace and torture me with gentle softness if you want to."

One hand smoothed the hair back from my face, that power still in his eyes. "Are you sure, little one? I didn't lie. I can't bear punishing you tonight, and I'm happy to make this all soft as the velvet you're laying on."

"But I'm not wrong?" I pressed.

"You're not wrong, little one."

"Then please." A whine slipped out. "Please."

He kissed me softly one more time, grabbing my hands and stretching them over my head. "There's never a time when we can't stop."

I laughed, a giggle I couldn't suppress because I couldn't ever imagine wanting to stop. "Okay."

Gabe's eyes went hard, and then his mouth *slammed* down on mine before he growled in my ear. "Careful, little one. I won't punish you tonight, but I'll still be counting."

"You say that like it's a deterrent."

Another growl that morphed into a purr. He got rid of my nightgown and transferred both wrists to one hand so he could gently grip my throat. "Bratty Omega. Don't move your hands from this fucking spot," he pressed my wrists harder into the cushions. "Don't come without permission from your Alpha. And don't ever, *ever* doubt that you're *mine*."

The feral word sent delightful shivers through me, tightening everything. My nipples were so hard they could have torn through his shirt, and the way he laid on me, between my legs, I didn't doubt there would be a wet spot on that same shirt when he pulled away.

A gentle squeeze on my throat. "What do you say?"

"Yes, Alpha."

"Good girl."

"*Fuck.*"

Gabriel chuckled darkly, releasing me and moving back down my body with intent and purpose. This wasn't gentle teasing. This was all him. I kept my hands where they were, lacing my fingers together so there was less temptation.

Sitting back on his knees, Gabriel looked at me, completely laid out for him. He opened his shirt one button at a time, and there *was* a wet spot soaking through it. My cheeks turned pink, and I struggled to keep still.

He dragged his fingers through my slick and licked it off. "Don't move."

Standing, he went to the edge of the nest and removed his watch. His shirt. Pants. Everything. So he was gloriously naked. I never knew I needed to see a man take off his watch so he could get ready to fuck you, but *damn*.

Gabriel spread my thighs wider when he returned. "I'm going to eat you until I'm satisfied, Sloane. Be prepared."

I was not prepared.

He gripped my inner thighs hard enough that he might leave bruises, and I wanted to see the marks of his fingerprints there. Pushed me open, nearly to the limits of my flexibility, and started slowly.

Everything in me thought he would dive in face first. But he didn't. He kissed the tip of my clit, barely touching it. I groaned. It was already swollen with need, sensitive and wanting, and I felt that brush of lips *everywhere*.

A deeper kiss, and a deeper one, every time he touched me growing bigger until he was devouring me, sucking hard and soft, sucking while he teased me with his tongue, sucking until I thought I was going to break open because it felt so fucking good.

He found the motion that made me gasp, repeating it over and over without stopping. *Yes, yes, yes*—

My whole body shuddered with pleasure, the orgasm more of a rolling rush than an explosion. Like a wave in the ocean you couldn't stop from pushing you back to shore.

"That's five spanks right on this needy little clit for not asking first."

"I—"

He looked up at me with one cocked eyebrow. It wasn't the fact that he was going to spank me. It was... "There?"

Placing one finger on it lightly, he tapped, sending little jumping spasms through me. "Right here." Closing his eyes, he licked over it. "So ask. I don't care if it's my tongue, my fingers, or my cock in your cunt. Tonight you will ask."

Not waiting for me to confirm, he closed his mouth over me and dropped lower, slowly fucking me with that infernal tongue. Savoring me. "You taste so fucking good, little one. My sweet girl." A long lick from my entrance to my clit. "At my mercy."

Two fingers slid inside me where his tongue had been, curling and finding the spot inside that instantly made me moan, and that made my clit about three times more sensitive. If that were even possible.

Gabriel sealed his mouth over my clit, creating suction in time with his fingers, and this time I saw the orgasm coming. Fast. "Can I please come?"

He stopped, releasing his mouth from me and stilling his fingers. "Not yet." I whined, shuddering under the kiss Gabriel placed on my inner thigh. It turned into a bite. "A tiny lesson for not asking."

Three fingers this time, the orgasm nearly picking up where it left off, hurtling toward me with undeniable force. The sharpness of it made me ache. I didn't think I could stop it even if I wanted to. "Please?"

"Yes. Soak my face, little one. I want more."

I groaned, pleasure snaking through me. It curled around me, sinking into every crack and crevice before draining away. My hands gripped the cushions in an attempt to keep myself still.

When I came down from it, Gabriel reached for my hands, pulling them beneath my legs where they were trapped, and I froze. I'd moved them.

Gabe's eyes twinkled with the knowledge we shared. More to add to the count. It didn't scare me. He'd have to do more than threaten me with a good time, and knew it.

But he didn't speak, simply continuing to eat his fill. Slow and fast, teasing me and then fucking me so hard and so long without taking a breath I thought he might drown in me. Two more orgasms—both asked for—later, I shook.

"Gabriel," I managed. "I—"

He rose up and took me in a single thrust.

My back arched off the cushions, and he kept me there, lifting under my back to hold me nearly suspended as he fucked me. My head was on the cushions and nothing else. I had no leverage. No way to move or control anything, and I fucking *loved* it.

Nothing about this was gentle. Every stroke was Gabriel bottoming out inside me, our bodies slapping together, the raw sound making everything so much *more.* Filling me. Fucking me. Erasing any thought of anyone else but him and my pack.

My pack. My *Alpha.*

The thought of them took me to the edge.

"Gabriel," I gasped his name. "I can't—I can't stop. Please."

"Whose are you?" He growled.

My voice wouldn't work. Every bit of focus went to fighting the pleasure lighting me up like a neon sign, and trying to fight it somehow made it better. Not even a flicker of him slowing down.

His own voice was rough enough to tell me he was on the edge. "Tell me and I'll let you come."

"Yours," I managed. "I'm yours."

Gabriel slammed home, knot swelling. "*Mine.*"

I came. Pure white light. It might have been my voice I heard, or his, ragged with pleasure. We went over the edge together, falling and landing softly with him knotted inside me. Kissing me hard.

"Mine," he purred, rocking his hips so his knot pressed in different places for him *and* me. Gabriel's teeth scraped over my neck, and I imagined him biting down. Bonding me. We weren't ready for it. I knew that in the same way I knew I was his. But fuck, I wanted it.

"Am I going to have to push you that hard every time?" I asked, laughing.

He placed his hand on my throat again, using his thumb to turn my face to the side and give him greater access to that place he was teasing. "Not enough for you, bratty little Omega? Guess I'll have to do better. Grab you while you walk through the house and bend you over the nearest surface. Hold your hands behind your back and fuck you till all you can say is my name. Is that what you want?"

My pussy reacted to the words, squeezing down on him so hard he moaned. "I'll take that as a yes."

"Yes," I breathed. "I want all of you. Whatever and however it is."

"What if I do that, and one of the others takes your mouth? You liked getting fucked onto Roman's cock."

"I—"

"Even better," he continued. "I'll knot you and have you sit in my lap with nowhere to go while he fucks your throat and we practice you taking all of him."

He was going to make me come just imagining all of it. "I honestly don't think I can. I mean, don't get me wrong, that makes me... *God,* that's so hot. But he's huge."

"And you're ours, little Omega. Made for us. I want to see your nose pressed to his skin and watch him use his hand on your throat to make himself come."

My eyes rolled back in my head. "What are you doing to me?"

"You wanted me, sweet girl. You've got me. There's more where that came from. I want to teach you how to play video games while my cock is inside you. I want you on your knees sucking me off while I work. I want to fuck these gorgeous tits of yours using your own slick, cum in your mouth and watch you swallow it. I want to taste myself on your tongue. I want to rip your tights, come in that perfect cunt of yours and send you onstage to dance with me dripping down your thighs. Should I keep going?"

I stared at him, my mind swirling with all the possibilities and still not able to keep up. "Holy shit."

Gabriel's eyes lit up, and my favorite smirk appeared. "And with all of that, I want to make love to you so slowly it takes hours. I want *everything* with you, Sloane."

"Give me everything." I wrapped my arms around his neck and kissed him. Neither of us stopped until we heard a throat clearing.

Jace, stripped to the waist and smiling. "Am I interrupting?"

"Never."

Inside me, Gabriel's knot eased. He shifted us so he laid behind me and Jace took a place in front of me. "You look well fucked, baby girl."

"Yeah." I was.

"You want more?"

Could I take more? Going from nothing but my vibrators to multiple orgasms every time was a hell of a thing. God bless being an Omega. Still, was I done?

No.

"I might want more," then I laughed, drunk on pleasure. "Seems a little greedy."

"No such thing when it comes to you and our cocks, baby girl."

"Amen," Ash said from the door. Roman followed him in, both of them shedding their clothes.

Reaching around me, Gabriel held my throat like he had earlier in the kitchen. "Our Omega is a bit of a brat tonight. Wanted everything I could give her and more. Wants us to prove she's ours."

"Really?" Jace let his eyes drag over me, from my eyes down my body and all the way back up. "I can think of a few ways to do that. What about the rest of you?"

Ash crossed his arms. "Only about a million."

"A million seems like a bit much, even for you." I gave him a look. "But you're welcome to try."

He grinned. "You are sassy tonight."

"Well," Jace said, pulling back. "There's only one way to start proving you're ours."

"What's that?"

"Show me what's mine," he gestured to the space in front of him, "and present."

I rolled over, baring myself to all of them, fresh wetness and arousal making me dizzy. Their eyes felt hot on my skin, and at the same time, I'd never felt more powerful. I *was* theirs.

A hand pressed to my lower back. "You want us to fuck this pretty pink cunt, baby girl? All you have to do is ask."

A shimmering burst of happiness went through me, and I arched, presenting further. "Take what's yours."

They did.

Thoroughly.

CHAPTER THIRTY-TWO

SLOANE

*J*ace was in the kitchen when I came down, eating what looked like some kind of cinnamon roll. The scent of the pastry along with his scent of butterscotch wafting around the kitchen made my mouth water.

"Have you seen Ash? We need to go or we'll be late."

He nodded toward the back door. "He's bringing the bike around front."

"Okay."

"Hey," he reached out and caught me by the arm, kissing me good morning. The taste of cinnamon and sugar was still on his lips. "Have a good class, baby girl."

"Thank you."

"You have anywhere to be later?"

I shook my head. "No, why?"

"They'll be working on your room, so I thought I'd take you somewhere."

"Where?"

He kissed me one more time, slowly. "It's a surprise." Chuckling at my pout, he handed me a to-go cup with one of his smoothies.

I made a face. "I love your smoothies, but you're not going to make me eat breakfast before every class now, are you?"

"*Make* you? No. But I'd like it if you did."

"Ah, a guilt trip. I see your games, Alpha."

Jace smirked. "I see we didn't fuck all the sass out of you last night."

"Never."

Tilting my chin up, I got lost in hazel eyes for a moment, and he grinned. "Well, in case you forgot, as your Alpha *and* your physio, it's literally my job to keep you healthy. So take the smoothie, and we'll fight it out later. Or fuck it out."

"You're just saying that cause you'll win."

"Maybe."

The sound of Asher's bike came from out front, and I waved. "Gotta go."

"Bye, baby girl."

I came out of the house to Ash stepping off his bike. He smiled as he grabbed my helmet. "Morning."

"Morning."

Asher's arms came around me, and he kissed me. The way he kissed me when we were in the nest last night. Tilting my head, tangling our tongues, stealing my breath. Slow and heated, his hands slid down my spine.

A car honked, and I broke away. Ash wasn't remotely embarrassed, eyes glimmering with amusement and heat. "What was that for?"

"I was without you long enough." He winked and helped me slide on the helmet. "I'm going to kiss you every chance I get."

"Can't say I mind."

"Good." He stowed my things and lifted me up and over the bike. "I need to get you a leather jacket, backpack."

I tucked my hands into the pockets of his in order to hold on and shield my hands from the morning chill. "I don't know that I'm on the bike enough for that."

"You might be," his voice came through the helmet speaker. "What if I want to take you on a long drive out of the city?"

Fair point. There were places we'd talked about visiting when we were in school and never did. Near Lakewood, there were huge fields of flowers. The terrain was mostly wetlands, and they grew flowers to sell. There were ways to get in, but we hadn't had time. There were some he always said reminded him of my eyes.

"Do you remember the flowers?"

We paused at a red light and he placed his hand over mine. "Yeah, sweetheart, I do."

Tilting my head so I didn't smack his helmet with mine, I leaned my head against him. The vibration of the bike and the faint traces of his scent that made their way to me through both the helmet and leather lulled me into perfect contentment.

It felt... wild. Not even two weeks ago, everything was different, and now I was here. With a pack.

"Do you know where Jace is taking me?"

"Yup."

"Wanna give me a hint?"

Instead of pulling up to the curb of the plaza like he usually did, Ash pulled around the back of the theater, opening the door with a code on the lock. It was the same door they'd ushered me out of when I was going into heat. "Why are we parking here?"

Ash shut off the bike and took off both his helmet and mine. His face was carefully guarded when he looked at me. "Gabe asked me to. Because we don't know if Craig would do something like sabotage it."

I swallowed. "Oh."

"Blue, look at me." Somehow I'd looked away and I hadn't even realized it. "It's just a precaution. Like hell am I risking your life."

"Is that the real reason you want to get me a leather jacket?"

"No," he handed me my smoothie. "I want to get you one because I do want to take you places, and you would look sexy as fuck in one. And no, I'm not telling you shit about where Jace is taking you." He laughed, lifting the mood again.

"Come on. Please?"

Ash grabbed my hand and wove our fingers together. "Absolutely not."

I wrinkled my nose. "You're no fun."

"I just value my life."

Class was sparser today, and Madame Hubert didn't seem to care. If anything, I saw understanding in her eyes when she saw me. It felt good to get back to it, even if my body protested a bit. Served me right for going this long without even a warm-up, regardless of the hellish rehearsal week.

When class was over, this week's cohort with Chloe as Giselle went to their pickup rehearsals. Madame Hubert and the accompanist went with them, and we were alone in the class studio.

I snorted and grabbed my phone, laying out on the floor. "That was fast."

"Everyone's eager to get *Giselle* over with."

"No kidding." Asher stood above me, looking down and

245

tilting his head. I looked at him from where I was texting Petra. "What?"

His only expression was mischief. "Have you seen those videos online?"

"You're going to have to be more specific than that," I laughed.

"The ones where they do this." He dropped to his knees by my legs, inserting them beneath my knees and flipping me over in a second. I landed on my stomach, and he was on top of me, body lined up perfectly. He whispered in my ear. "Ringing a bell?"

I was no longer capable of speech, but I nodded. Those videos of male strippers doing the move on stages all over the world and gone viral. But holy *fuck*, nothing would ever compare to how that felt.

"Remember what I said to you during your heat? What I used to think about?"

Ash was so wrapped around me, he brushed his lips over my cheek. "Someday we're going to do all of those things."

"And get fired for indecency at work."

"The good thing about having the Executive Director as a member of your pack. Not using it to get ahead, but what's the fun if there's *no* benefits?"

Rolling beneath him, I smoothed my hands up the tight material of his shirt. "You might be right, but I think I need some more convincing."

"Done."

A throat cleared at the door. Ash looked up and his entire expression changed. Hardened. He backed off and pulled me off the floor immediately, spinning me so he was the one closest to the exit.

I looked around him and saw Ian staring. "Last time I checked, the class studio wasn't a pay by the hour motel."

"Good thing, too." Ash kept his voice light. "The floor would be terribly uncomfortable, and there's no turndown service."

Ian came further into the room, and I busied myself with getting out of my pointe shoes and gathering my things. Ash still stood between me and him. I wasn't afraid of Ian. Not in the way

I was afraid of Craig. But he clearly had some kind of beef with me.

Well, it wasn't just me. From what I'd seen, he didn't seem to like anyone at the company very much. Which made me wonder why he'd come here at all? If he hated Slate City Ballet, there were plenty of other companies that could better suit his attitude.

"If you're not in rehearsal, don't linger in the studios."

"And if we are rehearsing?"

"Fucking isn't rehearsing."

Asher went entirely still. "Clearly we weren't doing that. And if you ever even think, insinuate, or speak anything so fucking inappropriate about Sloane again, you'll regret it."

Ian's eyes went flinty. "Is that a threat, West?"

"Yes."

"Ash," I said quietly. He wasn't going to lose his job over something like this. Sure, Gabriel *was* the Executive Director, but even he could be put into a position he couldn't get out of.

Looking between the two of us, Ian smiled. It was a look I wanted to slap off his face. "Careful, West. You're good, but no one is irreplaceable."

"Seems like you're content to make threats of your own."

"If I have to."

Ash turned and saw me ready to go, stalked over to the barre and grabbed his own things before holding out his hand to me. I took it without question, letting him pull me past Ian and back down to the bike. It was clear Ash was wound tight as a new set of shoe elastics, so I didn't say anything. But he was still gentle with me as he put on my helmet and got me on board.

We went home in silence, and when we pulled up, the street was congested with a moving truck and also one from Nest Inc. True to Addison's word, there was a man standing outside the door, watching. Our neighbors must hate us right now.

I got off the bike, and Ash caught me by the arm. "I need to go ride for a while."

"Are you okay?"

His hair was mussed from the helmet, and he took my hand carefully. "I will be."

"Ash—"

247

"He reminds me of my father, blue. That cocky, smug attitude like he can do anything he wants and is untouchable. And the fact that it was directed at you makes me want to do something... inadvisable."

I squeezed his hand. Ian bringing up those kinds of memories hadn't occurred to me. "He's just an ass, and I'm okay."

"I know. I just need to ride for a bit and let it out."

"Okay. Don't be too long."

He smirked. "You're going to be busy anyway."

"Tell me *something*."

"Nope." He smiled, and the fact that he could was a good sign. Leaning over, he kissed me quickly. "But have fun."

I watched him rev the bike and speed away, ignoring the warming in my chest. Something about watching Asher on his bike had always done things to me I couldn't explain. Especially when he was doing it because of *me*.

The guard at the door didn't stop me, and I found Roman in the lobby, observing. He smiled, but said nothing. I just hugged him, enjoying that feeling, closing my eyes and imagining being surrounded by trees and mist and Roman. That could be fun.

"Ash?" He asked.

"He needed to take a ride. Am I allowed to take a shower before Jace takes me wherever you guys won't tell me?"

"No, no, no. You're not allowed up there," Addison called from somewhere. She came from the direction of the kitchen, hair in a bun that was sticking up everywhere. "No peeking."

Jace followed her, his eyes on mine. "You can use my shower, baby girl."

I still remembered what he said the night he massaged me. That he would take me to his shower if he had any less self-control. "Are you joining me?"

"I'll get you some clothes from upstairs so you don't have to peek."

"You're killing me," I muttered, still not letting go of Roman. "I don't like surprises."

A rumbling purr. "Do you not like surprises? Or have you not had anyone you trust surprise you?"

There was a snarky retort on my tongue, and I held it back.

248

Grandma never really surprised me. She was loud and vocal about everything she did, and it was wonderful. The only surprises I'd really had were... bad ones. "That's an uncomfy thought," I murmured.

"Sorry," he said, purring. "Hope you'll like them more with us."

"Me too."

"Addison," I called, gently pulling away. "Make sure Jace grabs something cute."

My Alpha put his hands over his chest. "You wound me, baby girl. You don't think I can choose clothes for you?"

"Can you?"

"Honestly? No idea." He tugged me away from Roman and took me upstairs.

"I got you a new phone. I'll give it to you before we leave. It's so you can have a working phone while we still have access to the old one and Craig's texts. This way you don't have to block him, or do anything that might piss him off."

That made sense. "I have stuff on it I want, though."

"We'll make you a copy of it."

"Thank you."

I hadn't been in his room yet, and like the others, it felt like him. Neat and organized, but comfortable too. Slate blue walls and oyster tones. There was a nice computer setup and some bookshelves, but it didn't bear the stamp of his hobbies or time spent the way Roman and Gabe's rooms did.

It made me realize how much more about them I needed to learn. "What do you do for fun?"

"Besides working out and spoiling my Omega?"

"Yeah."

He shrugged. "I read a lot. And I'm working on learning some code."

"Really?"

Chuckling, he showed me to the bathroom. "Is it that surprising?"

"No," I told him honestly. "I just don't know many people who do it."

"I like figuring out the bugs and details. Plus, I can use it to help my actual job. Like make an app for appointments and consultations to make it easier for people at the company to get the help they need without always having to be in the physio room."

That would be good. Sometimes you didn't realize something hurt until you got home, and by that time you didn't want to go back to the theater because you weren't sure if it would make things worse. I wouldn't have that problem anymore while living with Jace. "People will love that."

"I hope so."

The bathroom was... "Okay, I see why you wanted to bring me in here that night." It continued the color scheme, but was structured in a way that most bathrooms weren't. A giant tiled shower that was just... open. Tiled, with what looked like a hundred shower heads pointing in every direction. It was like the bathroom in the gym times a hundred. "How much work did you guys have done on this place before you moved here?"

"A fair amount."

I looped my arms around his neck. "You're going to leave me alone in the shower again, aren't you?"

"Mhmm, but don't worry, baby girl. I plan on having you in here. And by having, I mean pinning you against the tile and seeing how many times I can make your voice echo."

"You can't say that and then take me somewhere we're not allowed to have sex."

"When did I say that?"

He slipped out of the bathroom with a wink and left me staring after him.

Maybe I would learn to like surprises after all.

CHAPTER THIRTY-THREE

SLOANE

*J*ace had me put on a blindfold. A literal, actual blindfold. So I couldn't see where he was taking me.

My legs bounced the whole way until he reached over and squeezed my thigh. Then they were shaking for a whole different reason, with his fingers so close to my pussy.

But his hand on my skin calmed me.

"You really *don't* like surprises, do you?"

"I mean..." I swallowed. "It's not like I think you're going to take me anywhere I don't like. It just makes me nervous."

The car slowed and stopped. "We're here, so you can see soon. Hang on."

Helping me out of the car, he placed me where he wanted me and stood behind me. "Ready?"

"Yes, please."

I blinked against the light and stared up at the building in front of me. Somewhere I hadn't been since I was a kid, but *loved*.

Slate City Aquarium.

My mouth dropped open in a gasp. "How did you know?"

Jace wrapped his arms around me and purred. "When we were helping pack your things, there was a picture stuck to your bedroom mirror. Little Sloane in front of all those jellyfish. A little digging told me it was here."

I knew the picture he was talking about. Taken on a day when I'd been sad because I hadn't gotten the part I wanted in my dance school's show, and grandma took me there to cheer me up. I'd been back since, but it had still been years.

"Is this okay?"

"More than okay," I whispered. "I love this place. Haven't been in forever. But..."

"But?"

I laughed. "There's no way we can have sex here."

251

His purr grew stronger. "You sure about that?"

"Of course I'm sure. I—"

While *I* hadn't been here, I still went past it regularly. There were always people around, kids with field trips and families on days off. But the surrounding sidewalk was completely empty, and the aquarium itself almost looked closed.

"Come on." He pulled me to the door, and a single employee met us there, opening the door and ushering us inside. But he didn't stay.

All he did was nod to Jace. "It's locked, so be ready to leave when you leave."

"Will do."

I turned to look at my Alpha. "Are we alone in here?"

He grinned. "Scared?"

"How the fuck did you even get them to do this?"

"I have my ways."

"Jace—"

Pulling me against his body, Jace kissed me like the world was on fire and we had moments until we burned. I lost myself in everything—the scent and taste of butterscotch and the scratch of his beard. The way his hands slid down to grab my ass and lift me up so I could reach him just a little better, my legs tangling in the long skirt of the dress Addison helped him pick. The way he made sure I was okay even as we crashed against the ticket desk in our passion.

"Damn, baby girl. Keep kissing me like that and we might not actually make it through this place."

I heaved in air, trying to catch my breath. "You kissed me first."

Jace laughed, letting me slide down to the floor. "To answer your question, it doesn't really matter how I did it. All that matters is that I saw the smile on your face in that picture, and I wanted to see it again. And that you realize there's nothing we won't do for you to see that smile. Because there's nothing worse than hearing you cry."

"When did you hear that?"

"You were in Gabriel's room. I went to see if you guys needed anything and heard. I'm sorry."

I shook my head. "That's not what I meant. I just wasn't sure." This time my smile was sadder. "I'll probably still cry sometimes. Just so you know."

"Of course you will. We all will. It happens. But we'll be there to make sure you're smiling again."

My whole body flushed from head to toe, filled with an emotion I was afraid to put a name to. It was too soon to feel that. Too fast. Wasn't it?

Petra and her guys were bonded within a month. Bonded and *happy*. Esme was the same. With scent-sympathy, everything was different. It took you to places faster than you ever imagined.

Jace gently bumped my head with his. "What's that look, baby girl?"

There was no way to explain the thoughts running through my head right now. They were too big and absolutely fucking terrifying. I needed time to sort through them first, because when I said them out loud I wanted it to be perfect. I wanted to feel confident and nothing else.

"Nothing."

"You sure?" His smile told me he knew I was lying.

"Yeah. I'll tell you later."

He kissed my nose. "Okay. Want to see some fish?"

"Yes."

Which was exactly what we did.

This place was well designed, taking you on a journey from the top of the building with light and shallow water all the way down to the bottom, where darkness reigned and the creatures got weirder and weirder. There were also some cool rooms where you could be immersed on all sides while you looked through the glass at swimming rays. Sharks. Schools of silvery fish that followed each other in crazy patterns.

But it wasn't my favorite. We both knew what it was.

The jellyfish room.

Smaller and out of the way, but beautiful. A perfect circle that rose well above my head, the tank filled with moon jellies. Pale white jellyfish that were lacy, ethereal, and picked up the colors projected through the tank. The lights shifted from rich blues to reds, purples, pinks, and finally pure white before starting the entire circle over again.

That, along with the vaguely haunting music they played in the background...

I loved it here.

For whatever reason, I'd always felt peace in this space.

A round couch mirroring the room sat in the center where you could just sit and exist in the middle of the jellies. When the place was open, there were people, but the kids usually preferred other places in the aquarium which were more exciting. The sharks, rays, and electric eels. So this room always felt like a sanctuary.

I went and sat on the couch, letting the tank take up the whole of my vision. I pulled my knees up, leaned my head back, and just soaked it all in.

For a while, it was just me, existing in the dimness, nothing but me and the jellies.

Jace slowly came around the room and sat down next to me. I sank my head onto his shoulder, humming in contentment. He turned his own head and kissed my forehead. "Happy, baby girl?"

"Yes. Thank you."

A purr answered me.

After a few minutes, Jace shifted so his arm was around my shoulders. "If I kiss you here, and it leads anywhere, will it ruin this room for you? Or should I carry you to another part of the aquarium?"

I bit back a smile, enjoying the fact that it was a given. He was going to kiss me, whether it was here or somewhere else. "Kissing you could never ruin anything, Jace."

The deep, rich sound of his laugh made me shiver. "Good to know. But if you want to keep this space as something else, I'll happily fuck you in front of the sharks."

"No." I wanted this moment with him.

Jace slipped off the couch and knelt in front of me, pushing my skirt up over my still bent knees and parting them. "I thought you were going to kiss me?"

His eyes dropped between my legs and flicked back up to mine. "I am."

Without hesitation, he licked over the lace of my underwear, the friction of the material and the heat of his tongue making me melt. "Fuck." The word was long and soft, and I felt him smile against my skin.

"That's it, baby girl. Relax, watch those jellyfish, and let me take care of you."

He slipped my underwear off my legs, dragging his mouth over my skin as he did so. Moving slow and sensual and with such tenderness and care that I wasn't sure I was still breathing.

Jace licked into me, and there was nothing in the fucking world hotter than the sound of an Alpha coming undone because of the way you tasted. His fingers dug into my skin, pulling me closer to the edge of the seat so he could press deeper.

They were all learning me so quickly. He swirled his tongue around my clit in the way that made everything tighten and my body gush a whole new wave of arousal purely for him.

He groaned again, the words murmured against my clit. "I'm so fucking lucky. I have the sweetest omega ever born."

If his tongue hadn't already turned my pussy into a fountain, his words would have. Jace's soft laugh had my hips lifting toward him for more. If I didn't already know what he felt like, I would need a vibrator with *exactly* that sensation.

"I love how much you love dirty words, baby girl. Makes me want to see how wet I can get you with those alone."

"The four of you are going to ruin every pair of underwear I have."

A long, slow thrust of his tongue inside me. Sweeping up and over my clit and back down again, drawing out pleasure from shadowy places I didn't know it could hide. "Mmm, if I'm honest, baby girl, I think the four of us would prefer if you never wore underwear at all."

"That would be…"

"Perfect," he groaned. "It would be fucking perfect. To lift up all these pretty skirts or pull down those leggings that drive me crazy and taste you whenever I want? My cock would never be soft again." He sucked my clit between his lips, teasing it. "I want blueberry syrup on my tongue every fucking day, baby girl."

I shuddered, the words and images sinking into my brain. He

was right. I did love the way they talked to me. Raw and carnal and not shy about how much they wanted everything about me.

The way Jace teased me, it wasn't driving me straight into an orgasm. It was simply... pleasure. Slow and almost lazy, the warmth of him and his mouth curling around me like my favorite blanket. Every movement of his lips had me loosening and easing. Melting into something he could mold and shape.

But I was taking a long time, and I realized it. "Your knees must be starting to hurt," I whispered.

"Hmm?"

I repeated myself and he looked up to me, the shine of me on his lips both gorgeous and obscene. He smirked, making my stomach flip with desire. "I like that you're worried about me. But if you're worried because you think I don't thoroughly enjoy having my mouth between your legs and my tongue in your cunt, I'm not doing nearly as good a job as I should be."

While I stared at him, he shifted my legs farther apart. "We have this place to ourselves for as long as we want. I'm not in a hurry. And as much as I love the taste of your cum, that's not my goal. All I want to do is make you feel good while I drown in this pussy."

My head dropped back onto the couch, pure heat running through me like he'd dunked me in gasoline and lit a match. It was luxurious to relax and not think. Only feel. Watch the colors and the shifting creatures in the water and lose myself entirely.

I didn't know how long it took. When I came, it rushed in like a breaking wave, my voice desperately echoing off the glass surrounding us, thighs shaking, every nerve spent from being overloaded with so much delicious attention.

And Jace wasn't finished with me.

He lifted me off the couch and pushed me against the glass, wrapping my legs around his waist and pushing into me. I was so sensitive from his mouth, it pushed me over the edge again, the curve of him hitting exactly where I needed.

"Look at me, baby girl."

Those hazel eyes were so close, the emotion in them so stark and vulnerable, I couldn't breathe. His dark skin reflected the rich colors projected through the tanks, painting him like a picture I wanted to hang on our walls. Gorgeous. He took my breath away.

"I know what you were thinking earlier," Jace whispered. "And I know it scares you. So I'll say it first."

We hung in the infinite moment, him buried deep inside me, surrounded by beauty.

"I love you," he said quietly. "I know it feels too fast, and it's so big it's terrifying."

I grinned. "It is big."

He fought a smile, pulling out and thrusting back in purely to make me gasp. "Naughty Omega, stealing the moment."

Jace spent long minutes making me pay for the interruption, fucking me with aching slowness, until I nearly begged for more.

"I love you," he said again. "I'm not afraid of it. You're mine, and I was meant to love you. I hope you knew without me having to say it, but I fully intend on loving you forever, Sloane Glass. No matter what." Pressing his forehead to mine, he breathed me in. "You don't have to say it, baby girl, if you're not ready. But I wasn't going to let another day go by without telling you. Because the words are on my lips every second, and you need to know that you're it for me. You're mine."

There was no way to speak. Jace unleashed everything he'd been holding on to, driving deep and fucking hard, pushing me over the edge again, and another time after that before he came, filling me with all the heat he'd been dragging out of me.

We didn't move. Didn't breathe. Suspended in the middle of all that light. I managed to move my hands. Reach up to his face and make sure he didn't look away. "I want to say it," I breathed. "It's so fast I feel like I shouldn't, but god, I feel it. I love you." My voice cracked. "Of course I do. I love you so fucking much."

Jace smiled brighter than the glowing creatures around us, and kissed me. We didn't move from that spot, and I let myself linger in the feeling of his lips on mine.

When we finally came back to ourselves, I felt like I was floating on a cloud. Jace carried me back to the couch and set me down gently, disappearing for a few minutes and coming back with supplies for us to clean up. I flushed, embarrassed at the idea. But I couldn't exactly be embarrassed when we'd shared everything we had.

Jace liked taking care of me, and my Omega loved that he did. I loved *being* taken care of. I loved him.

"Are you hungry?" He asked.

"I could eat."

He lifted me into his arms easily, carrying me back through the aquarium. It was a magical place to be by ourselves. "Let's get some food then. We still have time before you're allowed at home."

"Surprises," I sighed.

"I can't say there will be no more surprises. But they'll only be good ones, baby girl."

"Promise?"

He grinned and held me tighter. "Yeah. I promise."

CHAPTER THIRTY-FOUR

ASHER

I rode until the anger writhing under my skin cooled off, and then I turned around. This morning I'd come dangerously close to hitting Ian in the face. That smug look, like he had the upper hand, and there was nothing I could do...

It sent me back to a place of powerless rage I thought I'd long since left behind. But there were some scars that never left you, even if you tattooed over them the way I had.

My skin crawled, the feeling of being watched and having to look over my shoulder making me paranoid. I lived that way for years, and I hated it. I never wanted to feel that way again.

But the open road and the sharp cold of wind took the edge off and allowed me to breathe through it and let it go. Something had always felt right about driving a machine like this. Power only I could control, and the only way anyone could join me was if I offered it. Sloane was the only other person who'd been on my bike. Ever.

Not even Vivian, the person she thought she had to sacrifice her happiness for, had ever sat on the back of it. Because even then, it had always belonged to Sloane. I didn't want anyone else at my back.

Turning around, I headed back toward the city. Sloane's room would be done soon, and I wanted to be there when she saw it. I also needed to tell Gabriel about what Ian had said.

When Ian and I had worked together in Concordia, I hadn't been a principal. Just a soloist, and in that production of *Le Corsaire*, I didn't have a large role. We hadn't had nearly as much interaction. Was that why I hadn't noticed what an ass he was? Or was he different here?

I didn't really care. All I cared about was the fact that he seemed to have it out for us, and I had no idea why. It wasn't a joke, either. If he made another comment about Sloane, I wasn't going to be able to hold myself back.

Sliding into the garage, I left my helmet there and went straight to my room to shower. Then I went upstairs, where Addison and the crew were almost finished. She saw me standing there and smiled. "What do you think?"

"I think she's going to love it," I said honestly.

The walls of the room were a rich blue bordering on purple, the ceiling a paler lavender with subtle patterns that looked like clouds.

An absolutely *giant* four-poster bed with frothy curtains wrapped around them that looked like they would close and make her bed into a little sanctuary. A swing in the corner along with pillows and blankets, a vanity that matched the bed, and a host of other details that made it perfect.

Addison had gotten the poster of *Giselle* printed and framed, along with the review of Sloane's performance from the Slate City Chronicle. It was a glowing review of her debut as a principal, and I wasn't even sure she'd seen it yet.

Her clothes were in the walk-in closet, her cosmetics were all in the bathroom, and the entire space looked like it had been taken out of a catalogue and placed in our home. "You're great at what you do. I'll give you that."

"Thanks," she said. "I love my job."

"We're thinking about turning the room across the hall into a rehearsal studio for Sloane. Is that something you can do? Don't tell her, she doesn't know."

"Maybe. I've never designed a dance studio before. I could do some research about what it needs and get back to you?"

I nodded. "We'd love that." Jace hadn't put the final plans for it in place yet.

The crew went around putting on the last touches, and I went to see Gabriel. He glanced at me as I entered the office. "If you're here to tell me about Ian, I already know."

"How?"

"He called me and told me to 'get my pack in line and make sure they don't fuck in the studio.'"

My jaw tightened, my hands curled into fists, and I had to start breathing evenly all over again.

"Since I know if you were going to do that you'd be more careful, what happened?"

I allowed myself one breath of amusement. Gabe didn't give a shit if we *had* fucked in the studio. He cared if we got caught, and he was right. I wouldn't have been so careless. The idea of laying Sloane out on the floor of a studio was one of my fantasies, but I wasn't going to fucking share that fantasy with anyone else at the company, or risk embarrassing her.

It took me a couple minutes to tell him what happened, and Gabriel had the reaction I expected. "I'll talk to him."

"You should fire him."

He clenched his jaw. "I can't do that."

"There isn't some kind of clause that can get him out?"

"There is, but I can't do it alone. I'd need to take it to the board, and right now I can't. Not that I don't want to, and you *know* it kills me to say it, but he needs to do something worse than make a comment like that. The board will side with him about dancers getting it on at work, even if they're pack. Even if you were bonded."

Bonded.

The word hit me straight in the chest. Fuck. I wanted to be bonded to Sloane more than I wanted to keep breathing.

I pulled the feeling back and set it aside, trying not to be distracted by the idea of feeling her in so many more ways. "And all the shit he's pulled isn't enough?"

"I'm working on it, Ash."

"We're done," Addison said, appearing behind me. "We're going to clear out. But I'd love to know what she thinks."

Gabriel came over and shook her hand. "Don't worry, we'll make sure to tell you everything. Thank you, Addison. Truly."

"You're welcome. I'm going to go take the longest shower of my life."

We watched her go. I glanced over at Gabe. "Did Roman get the—"

"Yup."

I smiled. "Good."

Given the season was slowly shifting into fall, it was getting darker earlier. The sun was already setting, and I looked out the window, just to watch. Jace and Sloane would be back soon. But I didn't see them. I saw what I hoped I wouldn't. "Gabe."

At first glance, it was just a person walking down the street. But it wasn't just any person, it was Craig. Walking slowly, hands in his pockets, looking where Addison and her team were packing up and finally moving the trucks that had blocked the street. The fucker.

"I'll call Harrison," he said, lifting his phone to snap a picture.

"I'll call Jace." I was already dialing.

"Hello?"

I kept my eyes fixed on the Alpha below. "Where are you guys?"

"We're on our way back. Why?"

"Craig is outside the house."

Jace didn't let anything leak into his voice. "Got it. We're almost there."

"Everything is ready. See you soon."

Outside, Craig looked up and saw me watching. In the darkening light I saw him smile. The fucker was toying with us on purpose. I shook my head. Whatever he thought the end result was going to be? He was wrong. There was nothing that would make Sloane go back to him, and that wasn't coming from us, it was coming from her.

Craig turned and kept slowly walking down the sidewalk, eyes fixed on our front door.

Roman came down the stairs as I exited Gabriel's office. "She's almost here."

He just smiled.

A few minutes later, the sound of the back door opening faintly reached me. I watched the street from a different window. Craig wasn't in sight anymore, but it didn't mean much. I suppose it was too much to hope that he'd actually listened to Sloane, despite his promise not to.

"You don't have to carry me all the way upstairs, Jace," Sloane laughed. When she came into view her cheeks were pink, her eyes sparkling, and holy shit, my Omega was fucking gorgeous. I only ever wanted to see her like this, and I wasn't going to ruin the moment with Craig. It could come a little later.

"You're right, I don't have to," he said, bringing her to me. "We can all take turns."

Jace locked eyes with me before setting her in my arms, and I tried to show him I was grateful. Between Ian and Craig, I needed to hold her, and he saw it.

Sloane looked up at me as I took her in my arms. "Hi."

"Hey, sweetheart."

"Are you okay?"

I smiled and told her the only truth I could. "I am while I'm holding you."

She reached up and touched my face. "It's okay if you're not, Ash. You forget I know everything."

"You're too fucking good for me," I whispered, carrying her up another flight of stairs. And another. Roman waited for us at the top. I set her on her feet, reluctant to take my hands off her, but unable to wait for her to see her room and everything else. "You want to see your room?"

"I want to make sure my Alpha is okay first."

The way she said *my Alpha* had my heart pounding, and I couldn't keep my lips to myself. She moaned into my mouth, the scent of her perfume whirling between us almost too quickly. Our girl was already turned on. Probably more than that. *Well done, Jace.*

"I'm good. And I'll be even better once you see your room."

She narrowed her eyes like she didn't believe me, but I also saw the eagerness and curiosity there. I squeezed her hips. "Go."

Sloane only hesitated for a fraction of a second before she darted past Roman and into her room. I heard her gasp. The four of us followed her, Jace and Gabriel trailing behind where they'd followed us up the stairs.

I loved watching her take in all the little details with wide eyes. Jace stepped up next to me and spoke low. "She says she doesn't like surprises. I think we'll get her to see differently."

"The aquarium?"

His smirk told me everything I needed to know.

Gabriel went into the room first. "Do you like it, little one?"

"That's an understatement. I'm never leaving. You'll have to replace me at the company because I'm never going outside again. Only staying in here." She curled up in the round swing, rocking back and forth.

"Noted," Gabriel said.

"There is another surprise," I said, nodding to the box she hadn't noticed on the bed. "Roman's idea."

She glanced at the box. "What is it?"

"Go see." It was the first thing Roman had said since she got back.

The box was a bit of an odd shape, almost like a little house, and I wondered if she would figure out what it was before she opened it. It didn't look like it.

She took the top and opened it. "What—"

Sloane's face went slack before she turned to look at all of us. "Really?"

Roman nodded. "Yes."

There was a look of awe and emotion on her face as she reached into the box and pulled out an orange kitten. He was small, gangly, and excited. He was already scrambling up onto her shoulder and rubbing his face on hers. Sloane picked him up and held him to her chest. "What made you do this?"

Roman looked at her. He was hard to read sometimes, but I saw how happy he was that *she* loved the kitten. Also a little flustered with the attention on him. "I saw you with Stormy."

She laughed. "I think Stormy likes you more than she likes me. Does he have a name?"

Roman slowly crossed to her, drawing his finger over the little cat's head where he cuddled in her arms. "The adoption place gave him one, but you can change it if you want."

"What is it?"

"Mango."

Sloane looked down, her smile so wide it must have hurt. "Mango. That's perfect. He's perfect."

Roman kept scratching behind his ears. "You like him?"

The way Sloane looked up at him, her face told him she did, and also that he was out of his mind that she would think anything else. "I love him."

None of us thought she was *only* talking about Mango.

"He's got food and water downstairs, and a nice, fancy robot litter box in the storage closet. He already knows how to use it too." Roman laughed. "He'll probably have to learn his way around this place since he's so small. But we'll move things around if we have to."

Now that Roman was comfortable with her reaction, his words came easier.

"The room?" Gabriel asked.

"Addison was worried she would do something I didn't like," Sloane said. "I said that was impossible, and she was right. This is more than I ever thought..."

Her eyes snagged on the review I'd seen earlier. The photos in it were stunning. Us together in act one, the moment her character died and I couldn't stop myself from kissing her. And her alone in act two, the photograph catching her in a perfectly executed arabesque.

Walking over, she read it.

Tears glossed her eyes, and she went to sit on the bed, curling herself around Mango and not moving. A single tear slipped down her face and into the violet comforter. Roman was the one to walk around the bed and lie down next to her. "What's wrong, firefly?"

"Nothing's wrong," she said. "I'm overwhelmed with how great everything is."

The waver in her voice told me the words she wasn't speaking. Years of knowing her before gave me a little insight, and that was how Sloane sounded when she felt like she didn't deserve something. It was how she'd sounded when she got her first lead at conservatory. When she'd won *Young Dancer of the Year*. Even when she got perfect marks in our normal academic classes, blowing everyone else out of the water.

I hoped that when she got the news she would be a principal she had celebrated and felt like she deserved it.

Gabriel's phone chimed in his pocket. He glanced at it and sat on the edge of the bed, touching Sloane's ankle. Mango wiggled out of her grasp and started exploring her bed. Roman put an arm over her and dragged his fingers over the comforter for him to chase.

"That was Harrison. He hasn't finished digging yet, but we now have a restraining order in place. Today was the last nail in that coffin."

"Today?" she asked. "What the fuck did Craig do today?"

"He was here," I said. "Outside. Just walking down the street. No more than that."

Anger flashed hot in Sloane's eyes before she pulled it back. Scooping up Mango, she turned on her back and lifted him into the air. His little arms flailed, but when she put him on her chest, he was sniffing and nuzzling in seconds. Roman picked a good one.

"We don't care about him, do we, Mango?" She whispered with a smile. "We're not leaving this perfect bedroom."

His little meow made us all laugh.

The lightness in the room and the feeling of resonance between all of us together, it lifted the last of the weight from my shoulders. Stealing Mango from Sloane, I handed him to Roman and kissed her until she giggled. Then I kept going until she melted beneath me.

Where I always wanted her to be.

CHAPTER THIRTY-FIVE

SLOANE

The next two days were nothing but sweet luxury. Ash and I went to class and avoided any further incidents with Ian. When we got home and showered, I spent the days playing with Mango,—the most adorable, perfect kitten in existence—sleeping, getting absolutely ruined with pleasure by every one of my Alphas, and finding my feet living in a new place.

Gabriel kept his promise, bending me over surfaces whenever he could, tasting me and taking me, counting up the spankings I owed him later. I didn't know how many there were, but a little thrill went through me whenever he pulled me close and whispered in my ear that I'd earned one more.

I may or may not have been extra sassy to him just to add to my count.

Last night they'd finally built me a fire on the patio, bundling me up in a blanket like a burrito while I sat in Roman's lap. I was so comfortable, I barely realized I was asleep until I felt him carrying me all the way up to my room, tucking us both into my new, *huge* bed.

Consciousness came to me now, and everything felt *good*. Lying on my stomach, curled around a pillow, snuggled perfectly. It felt like I was waking up already swimming in golden honey. Because Roman was once again between my legs, licking my clit like his life—or mine—depended on my orgasm.

I whined softly, not awake enough to move or speak, but thoroughly enjoying every bit of sensation.

Roman hummed, pulling away and making that whine just a little more desperate. But he wasn't finished with me, just moving. His mouth brushed over the curve of my ass and up my spine to the edge of the oversized t-shirt I had on.

Even if his mouth hadn't just been on me, I would be wet just from the feeling of him touching me. Roman's hands were so large, they nearly spanned the width of my body. And the feeling of them smoothing up my skin, curling around my ribs... the intense weight of him pushing me down into the bed... I whined sleepily again. Needy and wanting.

His voice was a rough whisper. "Didn't mean to wake you, firefly. You can go back to sleep. I just need to be inside you." Roman's knees gently shifted mine wider apart, and he lowered his body onto mine. He was a warm blanket, enveloping me. A warm blanket with a hard cock currently pushing deep into my pussy and stealing every sleepy breath I still had.

He had to go slowly because he was so big. I didn't think there would ever be a time when he didn't stretch me open, with how giant he was compared to my petite frame. Every time he took me was a delicious ache that put me on the edge of so much more than I had words for. Almost like dancing on pointe. It hurt, but it was so fucking worth it.

When every inch was buried in me, he stopped. Brushed my hair off my face, and kissed my temple. Nothing else. The weight of him and the warmth. The safety of knowing nothing could touch me while Roman surrounded me. The subtle pleasure of being filled...

I sank down under the surface again.

His movement woke me.

There was no way to tell how long it had been, but it wasn't just a few minutes. I'd been *fully* asleep again, consciousness dragged up from the depths of dreams when he pushed into me. My body was used to him now, cock sliding all the way in so easily, I almost startled.

How long had he been inside me?

Not knowing sent a little thrill through me, followed by a flush of embarrassment that did absolutely nothing to cool off my arousal.

On my stomach as I was, nothing touched my clit but the sheets beneath me, and Roman's body had me pinned so I couldn't move as he slowly thrust in and out. It wasn't a rhythm meant to drive me over the edge. It was a little too jagged, a little too slow, and a little too gentle to get me off.

Which made me hot all over again. Roman wasn't fucking me for me, he was fucking me for *him*. Because I told him he could, and that made my pussy *sing* with a need that wasn't being met. And I was still too drowsy to even move my fingers to tell him I needed more.

Roman's low moan had me squeezing down on his cock involuntarily, and he shuddered, fucking me harder. Still not enough for me. Not quite hitting the right places. Not even that delicious drag of his piercing. Not quite, not quite, not *quite...*

"Your face is very red for someone sleeping, firefly."

I moved, but didn't get very far. It felt strange to be so drowsy, but that had been common the last few days. I felt so safe with them after years of being alone that I was catching up on what felt like years of missing sleep. So instead, I curled more firmly into the pillows, earning me a rumbling laugh I felt absolutely everywhere.

The rhythm of his movement changed, harder thrusting into me, slower glides on the way out, his piercing hitting me gloriously. Roman grunted softly every time he buried his cock in me, taking exactly what he needed. "Fuck, Sloane," the words were hot against my neck. "Sleepy firefly. Gonna fill you up with so much it'll drip around my knot."

"Roman." A strangled, muffled moan into the pillow.

"Don't open your eyes," he told me, moving harder and faster. "Just relax."

Somehow, I did, letting my body go soft and pliant as he let loose, finally fucking me like I was fully conscious, the delicious ache of taking all of him rising up.

His hands found my lower back, pinning me to the bed while he rutted me. Rough groans scraped over my skin like he was dragging his teeth over it. I wanted to feel them on me, biting down, bonding me. Fusing us together forever.

Roman pulled me onto his cock at the same time as he rammed into me—deeper than he'd ever been, knot swelling so large it only made the ache sharper. Made my clit more sensitive. Made me want to *beg* him to get me off. Wave after wave of heat filled me, cum seeping around his knot to wet my thighs, just like he promised. It all added to the sensation of being too fucking full.

I couldn't get enough.

"Gonna open your eyes for me now, firefly?" He asked as he released the last of his cum so deep I wasn't sure I would ever get it out. Thank fuck for super-powered birth control. His swimmers weren't going anywhere I didn't want them to, even if being full of him made me desperate for his knot to loosen so he could fill me up again.

Dragging my eyes open, I turned my head to the side on the pillow and glanced up at him. After that? I could probably go to sleep again.

He smiled. "Good morning."

"Morning."

Rocking his hips into me, I groaned. "That feels too good."

"*Too* good? Or just good enough." He did it again, knot pressed up against all the sensitive places inside me.

"It feels incredible. Not enough to get me there."

"Wasn't trying to," he admitted. "I can if you want me to."

I wrinkled my nose. "Why wouldn't I want you to?"

One big hand slid under me, spreading between my breasts and gently pulling me against his chest as he shifted to the side. He groaned as his cock shifted in me. "Denial isn't my game, firefly. But it might be yours."

My breath went tight in my chest. "What?"

Kissing along my neck, he ended up right beneath my ear. "You loved Gabriel telling you when to come during the heat. You don't mind me using you and your perfect cunt to get myself off without you." There was no way he didn't feel the way my heart was racing like a hummingbird beneath his palm. "So you tell me if you want me to make you come, or if you want me to tell the rest of our pack that I fucked you and left you wanting, so they can help make it last."

Without warning, my body jerked, arching, reacting to the immediate charge of excitement and longing. Like he'd plugged me directly into a lust battery, and now every circuit was fucking glowing.

"That's a pretty clear answer," he murmured.

"I don't know why," I said when I managed to speak.

His purr rose, softening everything and taking away the vicious sting of arousal. "Do you need to?"

I thought about it. Until I met them, I didn't want anything to do with pet names or spankings or any of the things my entire soul craved with them. Why should this be any different? "I guess not."

"Denial isn't my game," he said again. "Not in the same way, at least. I don't want you to hold on until I tell you yes. I want to make you scream, or I want to give you nothing. Get you riled up and send you off, knowing you'll have to wait or beg one of your other Alphas to take care of it."

"You're a little evil," I said, breathing in the richness of our scents together. He was talking so much more easily right now. Comfortable alone with me. I laid my hand over his on my chest. "Any other kinks I should know about?"

Instead of answering, he drew his tongue over the space his mouth had just been. "Guess you'll have to find out."

That's it. I was going to spontaneously combust. End of story. Here lies Sloane Glass. She burned to death because her Alphas turned her on too much.

"Where's Mango?" I asked.

"Put him outside before I started eating you. Didn't think kitten claws and fucking were a good mix."

I laughed, and Roman's knot began to shrink, allowing us to slip apart. He growled in my ear, feeling the rush of his cum. "Think I can fuck you without you waking up at all, firefly?"

"With the coke bottle you manage to carry around in your pants?" I snorted. "Not likely."

"Doesn't mean I won't try," he told me. "And don't worry. I like hearing you moan too much to leave you unsatisfied every time. Especially when that satisfaction is on my tongue."

Turning over, I slid up the bed so we could be face to face. "You're talkative today."

"Your pussy loosens my lips." He smirked. "But I'll be quiet later, if you say yes."

"To what?"

Roman dragged my bare leg over his hips, pressing us together even though he wasn't taking me. "I want to sculpt you."

My eyebrows shot into my hairline. "Really?"

"You can't be surprised."

"I mean, a little. I didn't see many women in your portfolio."

His eyes lowered, his fingers tracing a circle around my nipple. "You looked me up?"

"You're saying you didn't look me up?" The tiny twitch of his mouth told me otherwise. "Yeah, I did. Your sculptures are incredible, Roman."

The way he managed to create flowing shapes out of hard stone was nothing short of a miracle. Many of his creations were somewhat abstract, with a few lifelike figures in the mix, but there weren't many humans, and not many women. His style didn't seem like realism, so I wasn't surprised. "Did you start with art because of your words?"

Roman nodded. "Drawing was easier sometimes. Still is, if I get to that point. But I wanted more than something flat. It came naturally, and once I'd felt it, I knew I didn't want to do anything else."

The feeling was exactly the same one I'd had when I'd first experienced ballet. Grandma took me to see The Nutcracker, and it blew my five-year-old mind. When I couldn't stop talking about it, she took me to more. Showed me videos of her dancing. I ended up creating costumes and twirling around the house.

That was when she put me in my first dance classes and I never looked back.

"I would love to be sculpted by you," I whispered. "But how would you do that? I'm not sure I can pose that long."

His laugh rang out, and he rolled me beneath him, crushing me under his weight in the best way possible. "I'll take pictures, firefly. Work from those."

"What do you have in mind?"

With a mischievous smile, he got off the bed and opened the door, letting in a wild Mango, who sprinted across the room and leapt onto the bed like he was being chased by a lion. "Go to class, and when you come back, I'll show you."

CHAPTER THIRTY-SIX

SLOANE

*M*ango was not a parrot kitten. I tried to get him to ride around on my shoulder, but he was too excited about exploring everything, and the fourth time I had to snatch him out of mid-air in order to keep him from launching to his death, I just let him be.

As it was, I was nervous about him being loose in Roman's workshop. But my Alpha promised he'd be fine.

The carriage house where it was located had that dusty feel you saw studios have in movies. But instead of regular dust or sawdust, it was stone dust. Pale, white, and so fucking soft when I ran my fingers through the piles of it built up on some of his carving surfaces. It hung in the air, catching the light and creating something hazy and beautiful.

A flat slab of stone sat balanced on some sawhorses in the middle of the upstairs space. There was a pillow on one end, and I eyed it as I passed to where Roman sat, shirtless, in jeans, at a huge worktable.

Papers were spread in front of him. Sketches of ideas, and I immediately saw he was working on the idea he had of me. Like a Grecian goddess, lounging on her side, mostly naked.

"What do you think?"

My cheeks turned pink. "I think it will be beautiful."

"Before you say yes, you need to know one more thing."

"What's that?"

Roman pulled out a different image, one I recognized. It was a building downtown. The Crown Spire. A skyscraper that held about a million offices, but also one of the biggest banks in the country. The inside lobby was known for its historical decoration on the ceiling, and plenty of tourists went there just to look up. "This sculpture is a commission. Several sculptors are contributing pieces for the lobby."

"Like an installation?"

"Permanent," he said.

I saw his eyes drop to my mouth at my intake of breath. In all the sketches, the woman was naked. Draped under fabric that left little to the imagination.

"I—"

One hand wrapped around the back of my neck. "I'm not going to let anyone see what's ours," he whispered in a growl. "That belongs to us. No one else." Then he smiled. "But I will absolutely sculpt you *completely* naked, just for us, some other time. If you'll let me."

Something in me eased, and suddenly I was curious about how he wanted me for this. "Show me."

Roman stood, stepping around me and around where Mango was chasing a scrap of balled up paper on the floor. Fabric covered a table in the corner. I hadn't even noticed. Every style and weight. It made sense, given how many of his sculptures contained fabric-like elements.

He sorted through the fabric, and I looked down at the sketches. If he wanted, Roman could sell these, and galleries would buy them. Even the simple ones breathed life naturally. They showed just how much he took in visually, because he'd had to. The subtle details that others might not notice.

I stripped my shirt over my head, undressing entirely before he even turned around. The idea of him sculpting me naked was... hot. I just wasn't quite brave enough to have that statue be available for everyone to see forever.

Mango leapt onto Roman's jeans, and he cursed, making me giggle. After prying the orange mountain climber off the fabric, he dragged the long, heavy piece of gray velvet across the floor for Mango to chase. Which he did, gleefully.

God, I loved this cat. And as much as I did, I thought Roman might love him more.

It took him a second to notice me standing there naked, and when he did, he took it all in, eyes traveling from my feet all the way up my body and back down. Which made me wish I'd let him make me come earlier, because now the air was charged with heat and perfume, and I knew I wasn't going to get any relief with his eyes on me like this.

"This might be harder than I thought."

I smirked. "Sculpting? Or your cock?"

"Both. Definitely both." The bulge in those damned pants confirmed it.

Nodding to the slab in the center, Roman ran a hand through his hair. "Hop up. I'll pose you."

His own hair now hung around his face, and I realized he pulled the elastic out of it. Stepping up behind me, he gently combed my hair back, twisting the sides of it and arranging it. "You know how to do hair?"

"I have long hair, don't I?"

Smiling, I leaned into his touch. His fingers on my scalp had tingles and goosebumps running over my skin. My nipples hardening in response. I loved the feeling of it. "Yeah, I just didn't think about you knowing how to do mine."

Slowly, Roman moved me. Propped up on my elbow over the pillow, lying on my side, legs bent a little, my arm lying along my body like I was seducing someone. In a way, I guess I was.

The velvet flowed over my body perfectly, covering everything that mattered. My stomach and back showed, the fabric tangling in my legs, but honestly, it revealed no more than a bathing suit or a daring dress. And the way Roman touched me—gently, reverently—I trusted him completely.

He crouched down in front of me. "I'll take some pictures and sketch you a little. Try not to move."

"Okay."

We locked eyes, and what I saw there... it surged and flowed between us like an electric current. Roman leaned in and pressed his lips to my forehead. "You're fucking beautiful, firefly."

"You're not so bad yourself." His body was fully on display, and I didn't hide the way I was looking.

Before both of us got carried away, he turned back to his table and grabbed a digital camera that sat there, taking pictures from every angle imaginable, and some I hadn't.

Then he grabbed his pad and sat on the stool, starting to draw me. Knowing how he drew, and seeing how his gaze snagged on every revealed part of me...

"If you ever sculpt me naked—"

275

"I will."

"If you ever do," I repeated, "there's no way you're not fucking me at the end of every session."

A smirk stole over his face. "You won't have to pose live the whole time, firefly."

"I will if it means you look at me like that."

My only warning was a meow. Mango jumped up onto the slab in front of me. Without thinking, I smiled and reached for him, petting him, rolling him to his back and scratching his belly.

The camera clicked again. I looked up at Roman taking more pictures. "I moved."

He didn't say anything, just took more pictures of me and Mango, even when the little furball curled up in the velvet draped over my chest, falling asleep instantly in that way kittens did.

"Good thing you got pictures before," I murmured.

"Maybe I'll put him in it too."

Footsteps sounded on the stairs, Asher's head appearing over the break in the second floor. "How's it going?"

Roman nodded and went back to sketching, Ash joining him to lean against the workbench. "Any chance you'll make two identical statues?"

"He said he'll make a different one for you guys."

"I won't argue with that." Ash crossed his arms, looking at me. "Holding up?"

He knew exactly what happened this morning, and he knew nothing had been done about it. Even riding with him to and from class, he'd done nothing to tease me or help me. The traitor.

My phone chimed in my pants where I'd left them on the floor.

"Want me to check that?"

"Sure."

Ash retrieved the phone and looked at it. "Adina?" He asked.

Oh, shit. In all the chaos, I hadn't even thought about Pavilion since that night I left Craig at the concert. I'd missed at least three of the nights I normally danced there. Since I wasn't on the regular payroll, they wouldn't be mad at me. But Adina and the others would be concerned.

"Who's Adina?"

I pressed my lips together. "Sometimes I dance at this club called Pavilion. The company doesn't like it. She's one of the other dancers. I've missed some nights since all this started. They probably think I'm dead."

Asher's eyes flared with interest. "What kind of dancing?"

"It's a circus themed club. There's all kinds. Aerialists, which my grandmother did *not* inspire. The rest, you'd just have to see."

"You're supposed to go tonight?"

I counted the days in my head and stretched my hand out for the phone. "Yeah. I'll cancel."

"Don't do that. If you wanna dance, we'll go with you."

My eyes flicked to Roman. All he did was smile. He would go. They all would. The idea of dancing with all of them... *for* all of them? When Ash handed me the phone, I didn't tell Adina I was canceling. Instead, I told her I'd be there.

Then I texted Petra.

CHAPTER THIRTY-SEVEN

SLOANE

*P*avilion was packed.

Walking in the front of the club was different for me, but we were on the list, and I wanted my pack to have the full experience of entering.

Lights pulsed along with the music, Adina was already in the air, and fog poured from the cannons to make everything feel hazy under the draped ceiling of the faux big top. Bodies writhed on the dance floor, the vague floral scent of cancellers in the air. It did nothing to stop my Alphas' scents from wrapping around me as we moved through the club toward the VIP alcove I reserved for them.

Right where they could see me dance on one of the veiled pedestals. Adina had worked her magic, making sure that one was saved for me. They hadn't even seen what I was wearing beneath my coat, other than the sparkly tights and the dark high heels that were likely to break my ankles.

I pulled aside the curtains in front of the alcove and tied them back, turning to where Gabriel stood behind me. "You're sure you don't mind me dancing here?"

"Little one, as long as you're safe, you could dance anywhere and I wouldn't mind. If you wanted to dance on top of the dumpsters in the alley, I'd watch you."

"What about SCB?"

"What about it?" Leaning down, he gripped my hips and reversed our places so he was closer to the table. "Ballet is not the only kind of dance, nor is it the only respectable one. As long as you can do both comfortably, I think I'm going to enjoy the show."

They'd left their coats at the door, and the sight of Gabriel in a black button-down, sleeves rolled to the elbows was a welcome one. He sat, spreading his arms along the back of the booth and stared at me like he was daring me to show him exactly what kind of show he was going to enjoy.

Roman sat, and then Ash. Jace took the last seat on the other side, a hand snaking around my waist. "You finally going to show us what you're hiding under there, baby girl?"

My lips curled into a smile. "Maybe."

They were quite possibly going to kill me when they saw it, and it would be worth every extra spanking I earned by wearing it out of the house. That, or they were going to love it so much they took me straight home to the nest.

I untied the coat and handed it to him, revealing the smallest pair of black dance shorts I owned. They were more ass than short, combined with the sparkly tights made my legs look fucking incredible.

Those paired with a bra that was sparkly in its own right. The bra was nearly the color of my skin so it looked like I wore nothing but glitter. I'd made sure to cover what was bare with body glitter too. I looked like a constellation.

It was a contradiction, wanting to wear this for them in public and yet not wanting the statue of me to be more revealing. But here, with them, I felt safe. And it was just for them. Before the rest of my friends got here and it turned into a party. I wanted their eyes on me, and they were.

None of them spoke. Even if they had, I wouldn't have been able to hear them over the music. But their attention lit me up hotter than a spotlight. Meeting each one of their gazes, I tossed my coat to Jace and stepped back until I reached the veiled platform, disappearing into the fabric and becoming nothing more than a sparkling silhouette.

The music changed to something just a little slower, and I grabbed the fabric, dragging it around myself, leaning into the moment. It felt incredible. The last time I was here, I was trying to lose myself in the music because I'd been so sad about having no one. This time I sank into the music purely so I could perform for *my* Alphas.

Every single one of them knew I hadn't gotten off this morning, because Roman told them I hadn't. Energy zinged between us, even through the fabric. Fuck, their eyes felt like fingers dragging down my skin. I was so wired I thought I might be able to come just like this. Without them so much as laying a finger on me.

Song after song passed, and I didn't stop, melding with the music and just *moving*. This was why I really danced here. It wasn't about perfection and choreography. It was raw and messy and only about what you felt in the moment.

It wasn't an act.

Just you.

Sweat covered my skin, the glitter damp and my hair sticking when Ash appeared, pushing into the fabric with me. One hand pressed my hips into his, the other gripping my hair just enough to bring our lips together. But he didn't kiss me. Between our bodies, his cock was harder than the railing of the balcony behind us.

"Sure you're meant to be a ballerina, blue? You might have missed your calling with contemporary."

"Does that mean you like it?"

He groaned. "If you even have to ask..."

Our mouths collided, no holding back. Exactly like our first kiss in that hallway below the theater, neither of us could take it slow. My body was about to combust. The dressing room would be empty right now. I needed to drag him down there and—

A ripple went through the club, and a couple of screams. Happy and shocked ones. Ash and I broke apart and looked. Through the filmy fabric, I saw an army of people coming toward us. Including Eva and her team of bodyguards. Which was why the entire club was watching.

"Saved by the bell, sweetheart."

"Who said anything about wanting to be saved?"

I took one step to go see everyone, and Ash pulled me back, a hand around my throat. "You haven't spent a night in my bed yet, sweetheart. I want you riding my face and I want to ride yours. With my cock all the way down that sweet throat. Roman may have started this, but I'm going to fucking finish it."

My moan was lost in the sound of the music.

Ash leaned in and licked my throat, tasting sweat and glitter on my skin before groaning. "Go see your friends before I put you on your knees and see how you feel about being watched."

My knees were jelly stepping off the platform. I barely had a chance to recover before Eva was on me, sweeping me into a hug, Petra and Esme not far behind her. "This was an incredible idea," she shouted.

"You can thank Asher," I said. "He thought it might be fun."

Esme laughed. "I haven't been here since the picture. Nice to be back." Ben, the Alpha who featured in the scandalous picture with her, smirked before pulling her back into his arms. They'd gotten a little carried away, and the paparazzi took advantage of it.

According to Eva, the pack had a copy of the image framed somewhere in their mansion. And more, the photoshoot she'd skipped our girl's night for was an extension of that photo. But with all of her Alphas.

"Yeah." Petra cleared her throat. "I haven't been here in a while either."

I shared a secret smile with her. The last time she was here, I called Cole to come get her because she needed him more than she needed me. And they absolutely had sex in the closet. I'd watched them go in, and when they came out, Petra's hair looked like she'd gone through a wind tunnel, along with being flushed brighter than a sunburn.

Behind the four of us, our packs mingled together, mine being introduced to the ones they didn't know. I saw Gabriel and Harrison talking quietly, and my stomach tumbled. We had a restraining order, but was there anything else?

From the dance floor, people looked up at the VIP area with curiosity. They knew *someone* was here, even if they didn't know who. I wasn't worried about paparazzi. If Eva was here, she had security outside. No scandalous photos for any of us tonight.

Dion and his Alphas crashed up the stairs a second later, with him bursting into our midst. "The party is truly here. You're welcome." He hugged me. "It's about time we partied. It's been too long. Thank you for the excuse to grind on my Alphas' dicks."

I laughed, hugging him back. "Anytime. Though I didn't think you'd need an excuse to do that."

"Nah, but sometimes it's fun. It's been a while since they've been in rut, and some of them could use it. If I'm lucky they'll knot me so hard I go into heat. Then I can make Ian pissed at *me*."

Covering my mouth, I snorted with laughter. "I've got your back if that happens."

"I know you do. Now I need a drink."

Claire and Addison couldn't make it tonight, and we would miss them. Next time, I would make sure they were here. Whatever the next time turned out to be.

Petra pushed through the others and threw her arms around my neck. "Thank you."

"What for?"

"For inviting me."

I pulled back to look at her. "Of course I would."

"Yeah. I just..." She shook her head. "It's one of the first times I've actually left the penthouse other than your show. I was scared, but knowing everyone would be here made me feel better. So thank you."

Hugging my friend, we stood there for a second. She'd been through so much, and deserved every bit of happiness she had. *Earned* it.

And... so had I.

It wasn't easy for me to admit that I did. But after sacrificing my own happiness for so long, I deserved some too, and these four Alphas with me were exactly who I wanted to find happiness with. Emotion swelled in my chest, and I hugged Petra tighter.

"Okay," Eva said, prying us apart. "I sense that we need some drinks and some dancing for whatever's going on here."

"I would love a drink," I said. Through the crowd of Alphas, I saw Roman still sitting in our alcove. "I'll be right back."

I slid into the booth next to him, straddling his lap so I was pressed between him and the table. His hands came around me instantly. "Are you okay?" I asked in his ear.

Roman squeezed my ribs, but he said nothing. I hadn't thought about what he might feel in an environment like this. Just the five of us was fine. But now there were nearly twenty more people in our immediate vicinity, and he didn't know them

283

well. Plus, it was loud. Speaking was already difficult without the addition of having to project over noise and the anxiety of new people. None of them would judge him, but he had no way to know that.

"I'm sorry," I said. "I should have thought about how hard this would be for you."

"I-I—" He cleared his throat and pressed his face into my neck, breathing deeply. Beneath the music I felt the hum of him vocalizing slowly before words formed. "I'll be okay, f-firefly."

"Are you sure?"

"Yes," he breathed out slowly.

His hair was pulled back into a low bun, and I drew my fingers up the back of his neck so I could sink them into the silky strands. "All these Alphas are good guys. They would never make fun of you, and they won't care if you're quiet. And I don't care if I have to sit in your lap all night."

Where Roman's lips touched my neck, they curved into a smile. His big hands slid up my back, holding me to him, and somehow enveloping me in this small space. "Love you, firefly."

I gasped, heart pounding. Our mouths found each other in the colorful darkness. Roman's words might falter, but his kiss didn't. This was all Alpha. All Roman, entirely focused on me. "Go," he said roughly. "Dance. Have fun."

"You can't possibly expect me to go dance when you just told me you love me."

Another kiss. "You didn't know?"

Clinging to him, I held on, wrapping around him as much as I could. "I love you," I said. "I love you, I love you." There was no way I couldn't, and there was no hesitation. I loved all of them. It didn't matter how fast it was, or how terrifying. I loved my Alphas, and there was only one more I needed to tell.

"Have fun," he whispered.

"Will *you* dance with me?"

"Not good."

A giggle escaped me. "I don't care if you're good. I just want you with me. At least for a little while. If you feel okay." I bit his ear gently, causing him to growl and harden underneath me. "Dancing doesn't need talking."

Roman finally nodded. "For a bit."

I couldn't stop the smile on my face, pulling him out of the booth with me. Jace was speaking with one of Esme's Alphas, and one of Petra's. He grinned when he saw the two of us, and winked.

Ash joined on my other side, the two of them accompanying me down to the crowded dance floor. The smoke caught all the shifting colors, painting the three of us in light. Roman spun me so he was behind me, and Ash pulled my arms around his neck, and we danced.

Them touching me reminded me how little I was wearing, and how much I wanted them to make me come over and over again. Roman knew. He remembered. This time he bit *my* ear. "Desperate, firefly?"

"Yes."

"Good."

Roman turned me to face him, and Ash slid a hand down my stomach to the edge of my shorts. "I brought a present for you."

"Oh?"

His hand disappeared and reappeared with something in his fingers before he glided his hand beneath my shorts and tights. "*Ash.*"

"Just keep dancing, sweetheart." All the way down between my legs, he touched me. The hard little thing in his fingers rested against my clit, and a second later, vibrations came to life.

I'd known the second he put it there, but it was still a shock to the system. Ash had already told me he liked toys, but this wasn't one of mine. '*But the toys always work with you and never against you. Team players and all that.*'

It wasn't quite enough to get me there, but it could be if I danced long enough. Or maybe he wanted it that way, knowing it would drive me crazy before he took me home, pinned me to his bed and fucked me.

Everything came to life. It felt like everyone *knew* pleasure spiked between my thighs. Could see the way I shook between my Alphas. Watched as they stroked and teased, pretending to dance when all they really did was drive me mad.

Inside my shorts, slick soaked my tights.

"You're evil," I moaned to Asher. "Evil."

"I'm not. Evil will be when I lock us in the nest on a day off and use every toy you have on you before I push you over the edge and then don't let you stop."

Roman turned me back into Asher's arms and whispered in my ear. "Break."

Asher took my weight, moving us together. "When we were in school," I said, barely loud enough for us to hear. "And I would fall asleep in your room. You would tuck me into your bed."

"I remember."

"How did I never know?"

He unleashed a growl that vibrated all the way through my toes. "I have no idea. Every time it happened, I thought you were going to wake up and feel how fucking badly I wanted you. Sometimes I hoped you would, and sometimes I prayed you wouldn't."

Something deep drove me to push him. I wanted the part of him that had wanted me all this time. He hadn't truly snapped yet. Shown me the depth he'd buried for so long. I *loved* the soft side of him that held me when my feet ached and tattooed my doodles on his ribs. But I wanted the delicious feral side of him just as badly.

I wanted all of him.

"Did you wish you could pin me to the bed and fuck me?"

"Blue," he said in warning.

"Alpha."

He moved suddenly, and the vibrations against my clit got stronger. He spun my back against his chest, locking our bodies together so our hips could move with the rhythm of the music.

We were surrounded by dancers who weren't paying attention to us, both strangers and not.

Beside me, Petra appeared, dancing with Emery and Cole. Esme was with her Beta Rylan, and Eva danced with Tyler. The rest of our packs were upstairs overlooking the dance floor and talking. I loved that we were all here and together. But I loved the way Asher's hand stole back inside my shorts even more.

Under the shorts, over my tights, using his fingers to press the

286

tiny vibrator more firmly against my clit. "Ash," I gasped. "I can't."

"Do you trust me?"

"Yes." Of course I did. But coming in front of people?

His purr added to everything. "Dance, sweetheart. No one's watching us."

"I don't know if I can... in front of people."

Ash laughed, one hand returning to my throat the way he'd held me upstairs. "Don't forget how well I know you, Sloane. You wanted to see how far I'd go, so I'm going to take you all the way. Let go and give it to me."

"And when we get home?"

"I'll pin you to the bed exactly the way I wanted to."

His middle finger pushed the vibrator more firmly against my clit, and I closed my eyes, letting him move us in the dance, giving myself over. It wasn't immediate. So much was in my head, I still wasn't sure I could get there in the middle of a crowd of people.

But those fingers around my throat tightened a fraction. "Trust me, Sloane."

Trust him the way I hadn't when I ran. The way I hadn't when I thought he'd be disappointed to be matched with me. Trust him like I would be able to for the rest of our lives.

I came.

Pleasure rushed in out of nowhere, jerking my body against his and moaning into the hand that had slipped up to cover my mouth. A fizzy, bubbling, intoxicating burst of pleasure that flashed brighter than the club lights behind my eyes before the vibrations disappeared and we were just dancing again.

Thank fuck for scent cancellers. It didn't do shit for me scenting my Alphas, because I was so attuned to them, and they to me. But it would knock back the scent of my orgasm for everyone else.

I looked up at the balcony to find both Jace and Gabriel's eyes on me, like they knew exactly what was happening.

"You need a drink, sweetheart?"

I never got one before because I'd ended up in Roman's lap. "Maybe not a bad idea."

"Want to come with me, or keep dancing?"

Turning, I looked him up and down, teasing him with my eyes. "I think I like you waiting on me."

He smiled, kissing me hard. "Don't think I won't tell Gabriel about you being sassy."

I placed my hand on my chest, gasping in mock horror as we swayed. "Why, Asher West, I never took you for a tattle tale."

"I'll happily tattle if it gives me a chance to turn your tail red. Maybe we'll take turns."

It was like he hadn't just made me come, the way my whole body lit up with arousal.

"Be right back."

I danced by myself, in the center of my friends, basking in the feeling of happiness and calm, until a presence appeared behind me, hands on my hips. Taller. Roman was back.

"Sloane." I saw Petra's shocked face a second before the pleasant but not overwhelming scent of coconuts and limes wrapped around me. Spinning, it wasn't my Alpha with his hands on me. It was Craig.

CHAPTER THIRTY-EIGHT

ROMAN

I couldn't get to her fast enough.

I'd gone to the bar to get a drink, and when Asher joined me there, I turned to look for our Omega. She danced like there was no one else in the club but her, with her friends and their packs around her.

Someone pushed through the crowd, and my entire body went stiff. Across the room, Alphas from the VIP area—Jace, Gabriel, and some of the others, flooded down the stairs. But Sloane was halfway between the two of us, and Craig was already too close. How the hell was he here?

"Ash," I ground out, already moving, pushing through the dancers. Behind me, I heard him swear. The people didn't know why I was shoving through them, but I needed to get to her. They weren't moving out of the way quickly enough.

He reached out and touched her. She smiled, relaxing into his touch because she didn't know it wasn't one of us. Petra saw. She called out. I was almost there. Almost there.

Sloane turned. The terror on her face tinted the world red. She lunged away, and he caught her by the arm, pulling her back. I shouldered my way through the last of the crowd, and didn't hesitate. My hand came down on his arm and I punched him in the jaw before I'd made the conscious decision to do so.

Shoving Sloane behind me, people screamed as Craig fell back, recovering before he hit the ground. I followed him, getting in one more hit, my knuckles splitting against his jaw. And then Ash was there, grabbing him by the collar and putting his face into Craig's. "If you *ever* touch my Omega again, I will *kill you*. Do you understand? I will. Kill. You."

Ash came from abuse. He learned to defend himself the only way he could and had every ounce of rage and skill to follow through on the threat.

"Get the fuck off me. You're the dead one. Keep thinking

she's yours. You'll see. Try me, pretty boy." Craig shoved him and Ash didn't move, staring him in the face. Their heights were equal.

Gabriel, Jace, and the others reached us a second later. Harrison and Cole stepped up behind him. "If I'm not mistaken, you've been informed that this woman has a restraining order against you." It was a good thing he was here, because none of us could be so calm.

Jack—one of Eva's Alphas—held a hand up in the air, and her security swarmed from the door, meeting us as the crowd backed up, forming a circle to watch what was happening.

There weren't any words in my head. Nothing but pure instinct. I backed up, making sure Craig couldn't see any part of my firefly.

She was in the center of her girls, Omega rage nearly matching that of the Alphas, and even the Betas around us. Jace stood with me, shoulder to shoulder, Gabriel with Harrison, holding Craig back from lunging at Ash. "You want to kill me? Go ahead," he taunted. "You'll never be able to touch me, and restraining orders don't mean shit. You're still mine, Sloane."

"Go the *fuck away*, Craig," she shouted. "Just leave us alone. You lost whatever... game you're playing. Leave me alone."

The club was near silent now, security having cut the music so things could be taken care of. "You owe me, Sloane. You owe me." He shouted the words as security dragged him out of the club. "Don't forget it. *I'll get what I'm owed*."

Everyone watched him get dragged away, Craig staring down Ash like he was throwing poison from his eyes. The smile on that Alpha's face spoke of nothing but unhinged anger and revenge.

"Call the police," Harrison instructed security. "I'll speak to them, along with the Alphas involved. Make sure they know he's in violation of a restraining order."

That was one good thing. In situations where there was a crime against an Omega, they weren't required to speak to the police in the immediate aftermath. It could come later when they were calmer, and both they and their Alphas knew they were safe.

As soon as he was outside the music started again, but people didn't immediately start dancing. Sloane pushed her way to me, and I lifted her off the ground. Everything in me needed to touch her. If he'd done more than what he had, I would be out of my fucking mind. As it was, anger seethed beneath my skin. "I thought he was you. I thought he was you." She spoke into my neck.

Ash stood guard like a lion, pacing back and forth and watching the door like he expected Craig to burst in again at any second.

"Can he press charges against Roman?" Gabriel asked. "For hitting him?"

"He can try," Harrison said. "But considering you already have the restraining order, and he was touching your Omega without consent, I doubt it will stand. Still, we should probably head it off at the pass with a report."

"And I should look at Roman's hand," Jace said.

My hand was fine. There was no way for me to say that at the moment, but it was. Even if it wasn't, feeling the hits and watching him fly backwards was the most satisfying thing I'd felt in a long time.

Worth the ache in my knuckles and blood on my skin.

Jace put his hands on Sloane's shoulders, smoothing them over her glittery skin. "Are you okay, baby girl?"

"Physically? Yes. Otherwise? I'm fucking pissed. And sad."

The packs had drawn into their groups with their Omegas at the center, except for Harrison standing with us. Eva's security formed a bubble around all of us, and one of them whispered in Harrison's ear. He glanced around. "Let's go back to the VIP area," he said. "Regroup. The manager has offered us a space that's more private."

Following security, I carried Sloane up the stairs, her fingers bunched in my shirt, and when I set her down, Ash was on the other side of her so she sat wedged between the two of us. She didn't complain. Jace knelt in front of her, hands gliding up the tops of her thighs. He was making sure she was all right as subtly as he could while offering her touch.

Gabriel and Harrison stood close, blocking out everything else.

This was further back in the club, through a hallway to a

large room that looked like it could be used for private parties. It was still decorated like the rest of the club, but there were poles and a stage, lights, and what looked like a karaoke machine along with the lush curtains and couches. It was empty, and most importantly, it was much quieter, though the bass of the club still thumped through the walls.

Everyone filed in, and though I wanted Sloane to be with her friends, I couldn't quite let her go. The other girls' packs seemed the same. A large, redheaded Alpha held Esme on his lap, and Petra was wrapped up in the arms of a blonde man.

"Did I put all my friends in danger?" Sloane asked, looking at Harrison. She sounded miserable. I hated that. But there were still no real words in my brain. I couldn't tell her otherwise, so I took her hand, wove our fingers together, and squeezed.

My firefly squeezed back.

"No," Harrison told her. "First, you didn't put anyone in danger, because whatever Mr. Sullivan's intentions were, you're not to blame for them. Second, as much as I hate to say it, he's entirely focused on you. There aren't any reports in his history that back up this kind of harassment as a pattern. Not that we've found."

"So it's just me?" Sloane shook her head. "Perfect."

"I didn't say that either."

Gabriel crossed his arms, eyes hard. I recognized the posture. It was one that said he was holding himself in check despite simmering beneath the surface. Sloane may not have noticed, but Gabriel took that posture a lot in the first week we knew her, while she was in pain. "Harrison said he'd found some things, but we haven't discussed them yet." The briefest of smiles. "We didn't want to interrupt your time here."

"Too late."

Jace squeezed our girl's thighs and began to purr. Ash took his cue from him, and the low combination of sound and vibration helped her relax so she wasn't strung so tightly it felt like she might break in two.

"How much do you know about Craig Sullivan?" Harrison asked, pulling up a chair and speaking low and even. Loud enough for us to hear, but not loud enough that Sloane felt she was the center of an interrogation.

She sighed. "Probably not as much as I should. I know the basics. Early dating kind of stuff. Job, family basics, favorite color. Oh, and apparently he's a possessive psychopath, so there's that."

Jace laughed once. "There she is."

"Well," Harrison said. "What we found isn't probably something you'll know. He's in a lot of debt."

Gabriel's eyebrows rose in surprise. "How much?"

"A metric shit ton," Cole, Harrison's business partner, said from nearby, where he stood between us and Petra. "The kind of debt you don't acquire without fucking up on a massive scale, and the kind you don't come back from without serious luck, help, or government intervention."

"You're right," Sloane said. "I didn't know that. But what does that have to do with me?"

Harrison spread his hands and shrugged. "I don't know yet, and possibly nothing. But where that kind of debt lives, foolish actions often follow. We're still looking. This obviously isn't going to be something he *wants* found."

Looking down at the ground, Sloane paused. "I wonder if it has something to do with the concert?"

The four of us shifted, attention focusing even more on her. Gabriel stepped closer. "What do you mean, little one?"

"He had a surprise for me, right? That's what he said. That he was going to have me meet the composer. And later in the texts he said I humiliated him by leaving. He never told me what he had planned until those texts. But it's not just him saying I'm his or whatever the hell. It's more. He's pissed about *that night*. That he 'put himself on the line.' And he just said he'll get what he's owed. And I don't think he just means me or sex. I don't know..."

Cole nodded. "It's a start. Thank you."

"Sorry," Sloane whispered, looking at her friends. "Not exactly the evening I had planned."

"No," Dion said, standing and smiling. "But eventually, once Craig is done, we'll look back on tonight and laugh."

"Roman," Harrison said to me. "Will you and Gabriel stay to speak to the police and file a report?"

"If they stay, I stay." Sloane stood up. "I can give a statement."

"No. We don't know how long it will take for the police to speak to us, and we don't know if they're going to arrest him. I'll try, but there's no guarantee. And as long as he's here, I don't want you anywhere near him." Gabriel took her by the shoulders and kissed her forehead. "Hundreds of miles away would be my preference, but home will do for now."

"Gabe—"

"This isn't a discussion, Sloane. Ash and Jace will take you home."

Her lower lip trembled, the only true sign she wasn't doing okay. "I don't want us to be separated."

Pulling her into his arms, he whispered something in her ear that had her nodding as he stroked a hand over her hair.

"It won't take long," Harrison promised. "Not that you need this, but I agree with your Alpha. It's better you're not in the same place Mr. Sullivan is right now."

"And considering several hundred people just heard me say I'd kill him if he touched her again, I probably shouldn't be here either," Ash said. He meant it to lighten the mood, and it didn't.

Gabriel kissed Sloane softly. "Go say goodbye."

She did, hugging her friends.

"Harrison, I'd like guards around our house for the time being, since I assume they're not going to hold him long."

The other Alpha was already on his phone. "They'll be there by the time Sloane gets home."

"Thank you," Jace said.

Ash looked at the three of us. "It's not fair for me to ask this—"

Jace cut him off with an outstretched hand. "Yes, it is. I'm not going to be able to think straight unless I'm watching out the fucking windows, and she needs to be distracted. Do what you need to do, Ash. It won't be the last time one of us needs her."

Since Gabe and I wouldn't even be there, I agreed. Firefly

needed to be guided out of her head, and Ash was the person to do it tonight.

We waited until she'd said goodbye to all her friends and moved as one out of the club. We surrounded her on every side, security getting us out to our car. I wrapped her up and breathed her in, managing the first words since it all happened. They still stuck in my throat and burned. "See you soon, f-firefly."

We watched her pull away, my hands curling into fists at the loss. Gabe's hand came down on my shoulder. "Let's get this the fuck over with."

CHAPTER THIRTY-NINE

SLOANE

*T*his was *wrong wrong wrong.*

I shouldn't be driving away from any of my Alphas. They all needed to be here with me. Even though Gabriel had whispered in my ear that he would find me as soon as he came home, I still didn't feel good. I whined, panic clawing up my throat. "Turn around," I begged. "Please turn around."

"No, baby girl." Jace's voice was gentle but firm. "They'll be home soon. Promise."

"It's not right. It's not *right.*"

Ash turned and pushed me down onto my back across the rear seat, his teeth at my throat. "Nothing's changed, sweetheart. That asshole isn't going to ruin your night. Jace is going to make sure we're safe, and I'm going to pin you to the bed with my cock, just like I promised. And by the time you remember your own name again, all your Alphas will be home with you."

Every thought in my head turned to sparkling dust.

Sometimes I hated the way the sound of an Alpha's command could make me stop in my tracks. Not this time. This time I welcomed it and took it as a refuge. It shut up all the thoughts about how I should have known better, endangering my friends by putting them in the path of someone like Craig, and the fear that it would never end and I'd be looking over my shoulder for that maniacal grin for the rest of my life.

"That's it," Ash said, moving my legs apart to thrust between them though we were both still fully clothed. The little toy was still nestled in my panties, and it blazed to life, made even more powerful by the way his body thrust against mine.

Feral need rocked through me, driven by instinct and my Omega need for my Alphas to show me I was safe and protected. I wanted them. So much *more* than them. They were my Alphas, and I wasn't sure I wanted to wait anymore. Ceremony be damned. Why had we waited this long to begin with?

"Bite me," I told him. "Bond with me."

Ash only paused a second before he kissed me, pressing me down into the seat, rocking his hips into me, fucking me without fucking me. Driving me to the edge and making me absolutely desperate.

"You want that?" He asked.

"Yes."

Another kiss. "Because of him?"

"Because you're *mine*." If I could growl, I would have. "Why do we need to wait? I don't need the dress or anything. You can just bite me."

Ash kissed my neck, right beneath my jaw. Was that where he would do it? "We don't need to wait, but we're going to bond you together, sweetheart. All at once. Claim you. Make you ours. Whenever we're all together and you're ready."

I was ready right the fuck now, but he was right. It needed to be all of them together.

"And I think you want the ceremony," he said with a grin.

The sound of the garage door opening startled me. Jace stopped the car and hauled the door open, pulling me out from beneath Ash. "I'll bond with you any time and any place, baby girl. Whether that's with you in a pretty dress or just up in your nest. We'll talk about it when we're all together, okay?"

"Yeah."

Chuckling, he pulled me closer. "And if we're going to do that, I need to make a call."

Butterscotch overwhelmed me. And cookies. I inhaled, letting the scent of him overwhelm me. I hoped it never got less intense. For the rest of our lives I wanted to be able to close my eyes and drift, carried away by scent alone.

His hand came up between my legs, holding the vibrator in place again. It had slipped. Not vibrating right now, but I was still sensitive. He smirked. "You danced through a heat. Think you could do an entire show with one of these right on your pretty little clit?"

"No."

"Hmm," he released me. "That wasn't very convincing. Something we'll have to think about."

"Unless you want me breaking an ankle because I'm falling off my pointe shoes, it'll still be a no."

"Then maybe a performance just for us."

That—

I bit my lip. That could be fun.

"I've got to make some calls, and I'll be watching."

Before I could even ask him if he was sure, Ash had me off my feet and into the house. He pressed me into the back of the elevator like he had for my heat, but this time it wasn't the nest we went to. It was his bedroom.

We paused in the doorway momentarily, Ash letting me slide down his body and look. He pressed close behind me, lips dropping to my shoulder. Soft and easy.

"Ash," I whispered.

"Yeah?"

I turned to him, stripping his shirt over his head and looking at all his tattoos. Stark branches of a tree across one shoulder. A lion that turned into dissolving shadows on the other. Dark pools of ink draining into veins on the inside of his wrist. His mother's initials over his heart. My doodle on his ribs.

Placing my fingers right over that tattoo, I looked up at him. "Do you remember the night I found you in the studio?"

"I'll never forget it."

It was our second year at school, and I hadn't seen him all day. Until I got a call from Asher's friend, Will. They grew up together and were still friends. He couldn't get through to him, and he thought I was the only one who could.

I went to the dance building and found Ash in the dark, dancing, music so loud you almost couldn't hear anything. So loud he didn't hear me, and I startled him. He had me up against the mirror in a second before he realized it was me.

He'd nearly collapsed, showing me the side of him he never showed anyone else. I held him while he cried. Later I found out his mother had died, and he took on all the guilt of it, because he'd left her there even though he didn't have a choice.

All that darkness in him, he ignored it and pushed it down. But it was darkness that had been *earned*. It wasn't darkness that lived in his soul. Merely the echo of dark things. And that? I wanted it too.

When he grabbed Craig, I knew where the anger came from. I loved every second he protected me.

"I'll tell you as many times as you need me to," I said. "But I know you. I know everything, and I don't need you to hide it."

"I don't want to hurt you, blue. I'm not that man. I swear it. I'll never be like him."

Gripping his face, I pulled him down to me. "No, you won't. Not once have you ever done any of that shit. And don't get me wrong, I love the fuck out of the part of you that pampers me and is gentle with me. I love it when you're sweeter than your scent. But that's not *all* of you."

He stared at me, vulnerability showing in his eyes.

"I want all of you. Like hell am I going to live a life with you pushing down every instinct you have because you're afraid of being something you *are not*. All those things you said to me in the heat? At Pavilion? I want them. Not just the words. You pulled me out of my own head, now let me do the same. Stop thinking and fuck me the way you want to."

One more look in my eyes, and he did. With a growl, Ash tilted my face up and kissed me hard enough to bruise. His fingers dragged over my skin, finding the clasp on the sparkly bra and tossing it aside as he backed me up to his bed.

I giggled when he pushed me back on it, memories of flopping on his dorm bed appearing in my mind. "These shorts are a crime." He popped open the button and nearly tore them down my legs, the starry tights joining them, the little vibrator, and my shoes on the floor in a pile of sparkles.

"I'm going to glitter bomb your bed." My skin was still covered in it.

"You could glitter bomb my entire life, and I wouldn't care. Now get up there." He pointed to the head of the bed.

I collapsed on the pillows, watching greedily as he shed the rest of his clothes. Lean and built from years of dancing, I never got quite enough time to simply stare at these men. I needed them to line up in the nest, naked, and just look at them for a while.

Ash crawled up my body like a predator, eyes fixed only on me. His knees settled on either side of my chest, looking down at me. I loved the weight of him, the way I saw new ridges of his body in the warm light, how his eyes took me in with love and dark lust that had me squirming. His cock, hot and hard on my chest, right between my breasts.

Smirking, I pushed them together around his shaft, satisfied when he closed his eyes and groaned. His hips moved on their own, like he couldn't help it.

"Is this something you want?"

"Yes, and I'll use your own slick to fuck them," he growled, pulling my hands away and bringing them to his thighs. "Now open your mouth."

I did.

With one hand Ash grabbed the headboard, and with the other he fed me his cock. Closing my eyes, I moaned around it, sucking down the taste. Like biting into a hot cookie fresh from the oven. I wouldn't bite into this one, but the taste of him already had my body rising into pleasure, recognizing the scent and taste of *my* Alpha.

Ash hesitated for one final moment, looking down at me with every ounce of power he had, and he let himself go.

CHAPTER FORTY

ASHER

I drove myself all the way down Sloane's throat, and I nearly came right then. She'd sucked my cock during her heat, but it wasn't like this. God, the number of times I'd imagined myself balls deep in her throat didn't compare to her spread out beneath me with those gorgeous blue eyes meeting mine before fluttering closed like she was in heaven.

She wanted all of me? I would give her absolutely all of me. "All the way down, sweetheart. Every single inch."

Her eyes flew open, hands tightening where they wrapped around my thighs. She shook her head a little, telling me she couldn't.

One half of my mouth tipped into a smile. We both knew that wasn't true, and I was going to see her lips stretched around the base of my cock.

Reaching down, I slipped my hand around her throat, squeezing gently. "Better try. I'm not letting you breathe until you take all of me."

Sloane's eyes widened, and then narrowed on mine. Not with anger, but with both intrigue and determination. She gripped my ass, hauled me closer, and relaxed. I slipped the rest of the way into her mouth, my hips pressed all the way to her face. Beneath my palm, I felt my cock in her throat. "*Fuck*, Sloane."

I pulled back, letting her breathe just like I promised.

Not looking away, my Omega licked her lips. My hand squeezed on pure instinct. "Good girl."

She moaned, arching beneath me. "It's not fair. You all know what that does to me."

"I'll never play fair with you," I told her. "Not ever."

"Good." Her eyes were fire.

I didn't give her a warning, slipping between her lips again and fucking her throat the way she dared me. Riding her face. Holding onto the headboard as I took her. God, I wanted to knot her mouth. Have her just like this and watch those gorgeous lips stretch. Talk to her while she couldn't respond, gagged on my cock.

The beginnings of pleasure gathered at the base of my spine, and I pulled back, letting her gasp for breath. Backing off the bed, I took her with me, pulling her to the edge and lining myself up with her mouth again, pushing deep.

God damn.

This position hugged my cock like her throat was a mold made for it. I drew the heel of my palm over her neck, feeling the added pressure on me. Incredible.

Sloane swallowed, her throat strangling my shaft, and I wasn't going to last like this. Yanking myself out, I looked down at her. "Take a big breath. You're going to need it."

I didn't let her speak, driving home between her lips and spreading her thighs. Her pussy was a soaked mess. Some of it was from all my teasing with the vibrator, but not all of it. Some of it was fresh.

"Is this all for me, sweetheart?" I rocked my hips into her mouth, fucking her even as I drew a finger around her clit. "I think you like having my cock in your throat."

A whine reached me—desperate and aroused. God, she was perfect for me. She got wetter while I watched. I had to taste her. Blueberry syrup exploded on my tongue. I dragged through the slick, using my tongue the way I was going to use my cock later. Deep inside her perfect cunt, making her shake.

I'd been so out of my mind I hadn't thought to stop in her room and grab more toys. A mistake on my part.

"Breathe," I told her.

She did, eyes wide and dazed, but she was smiling. "You good, sweetheart?"

"Yeah."

That was all the time she got. I drove home, gripping the sides of her face and taking her mouth like I'd always wanted to.

"I forgot your toys," I ground out. "But I won't next time. Next time, I'll make sure I have that big vibrator. The one I *know* you have. I'll keep you just like this, impaled on my cock, and make you come over and over with me in your throat."

Sloane's hand crept down between her legs, playing with herself. *Good*. I wanted her to come, and I wanted her to do it while I controlled her breath. While I used her.

I loved every part of her body, but there was something about her mouth. Her sassy words turned me on just as much as them being stolen away because she was full of *me*.

"I'll make you come so much that I won't be able to fuck your throat without you needing to come," I growled, pushing harder. She would need to breathe soon. That dark part of me she craved told me I could push her further.

And I did.

The sound of her inhale like she'd just come up from the depths of the ocean made my cock twitch. My Omega would rather taste me than have air. "Fuck." I fisted my cock, driving myself that much closer to orgasm as I spoke. "I want to make you come so much like this that you learn to come the second I take your mouth. Until just the thought of me being balls deep in your throat makes you this wet."

Sloane's fingers moved faster, her voice hoarse. "Ash."

"Take another breath, sweetheart. You don't get another one."

Not until I came.

She breathed in.

I took her like a savage.

Pinned her wrists to the bed and consumed her cunt while I buried myself in her throat so deep I never wanted to come out. I didn't hold myself back, letting the pleasure build while I savored every flavor of her pussy and every shiver of her body.

Her orgasm washed over my tongue, sharp and sweet, soaking my face. "Good girl," I murmured against her clit. "Good fucking girl." The way she shook made me crave her more. Every lap of my tongue over her clit caused her to writhe. I wanted to keep going and *ruin* her.

Sloane swallowed.

Light exploded behind my eyes, a blaze of pleasure clawing through me so fast my shouts echoed off the walls. I barely managed to pull back in time to come across her tongue and keep my knot out of her mouth.

She didn't let me go, sealing her mouth around me and drinking me down. Swirling her tongue around the head of my cock to make sure she didn't miss a single drop. "You're better than ice cream," she managed when she released me, fully soft and spent. The makeup she wore to the club was wrecked. Running down her face from her eyes watering. I loved that I was the one who wrecked it.

"Don't give me ideas, sweetheart."

"What kind of ideas?"

Lifting her, I turned her around so her legs were off the bed. Just because my knot was already swollen didn't mean I wasn't going to fuck my Omega. "Ideas about you, my cock, and a bowl of ice cream."

I watched her swallow. "I don't hate that idea."

"No?"

Easing inside her, my knot pressed against her entrance. She shook her head. "No."

Grinning, I leaned closer. "Am I dark enough for you yet, Sloane?"

She gripped my shoulders. "What happens if I say no?"

It was still a wonder at all that she wanted those parts of me. The kinky, slightly fucked up side I hid from most people. There was plenty I hadn't explored because I didn't know how deep it went. But for the first time, I felt like I could explore it with someone.

Images played through my mind. Sloane tied to this bed while I used my mouth on her until she begged. Painting her with that ice cream we just talked about. Taking her back to Pavilion and fucking her inside those filmy curtains, knowing that anyone might look over and watch. Like the rest of our pack.

"I don't know," I told her. "But we'll find out together."

"Then no," she whispered. "You're not nearly dark enough for me, Ash."

"I should wait," I told her. "Until this has gone down a bit. But..."

Sloane's cry of pleasure was music to my fucking ears. I pushed my fully swollen knot inside her pussy, settling where we both wanted it, and kept going. My knot ached and felt so fucking good. My breath went ragged. "I want to be knotted in you forever."

Dropping over her, I circled her throat with my hand once more. She loved this. The way her breath hitched and eyes closed. Her pussy squeezed me, on the verge of coming again.

"You like me holding you down," I breathed in her ear.

All she did was lift her hands, crossing her wrists above her head, her eyes opening to lock on mine. Desire, love, need, and pure trust.

I covered her wrists with my other hand, pressing her into the bed with both, and fucked my Omega. She melted underneath me. Surrendering. Coming. Accepting every part of me and offering it all in return.

The orgasm hurt.

My knot was deliciously painful inside her, the ache of going over again almost too much. Almost.

I closed my eyes and rode out the storm, letting my forehead press against hers. My lips met hers without ever opening my eyes.

Sloane tugged at her captive wrists, and I didn't move my hand. I smiled at her. "I don't want to let you go yet, sweetheart."

A shudder ran through her body—a good one. Sloane bit her lower lip. "Okay."

My purr rose softly, easy as breathing. "Thank you."

She snorted. "Why are you thanking me? You just made me come so hard I thought I was going to pass out."

"Oh?" One eyebrow rose. "I wonder what it would take for you to go all the way."

Finally, I moved us back up to the top of the bed, our bodies still locked together. "You know why I'm thanking you, blue."

"Yeah." Her fingers traced one of my tattoos. "But you don't need to. I want it. All of it. I know there's more."

"There is."

"You going to show me?"

"Without a doubt. But we have a lifetime for it."

Her cheeks tinged pink, her eyes dropping to my chest. "It seems so strange to say that. I know it's true, but it's like... before you got here, I thought I was just going to keep doing life by myself. Now I have *plans*. I love it. Just hard to wrap my head around it."

In the car she'd asked me to bond her. "I don't just remember your nest doodles, by the way."

"What do you mean?"

"I remember you making those pages for a bonding cere-mony. Pretty dresses. Purple lilies. Candles. Lights strung over a dance floor."

Her lips popped apart, and it was impossible not to kiss her. The softness of her mouth. Traces of her flavor mixed with mine... God, I would never get tired of it. I could live on it.

"I don't need that," she said, voice soft. "I just need the four of you."

"You don't need it," I admitted. "But it's something you wanted. And if you still do? We'll make it happen, Sloane. There's nothing you could ask for that we'd tell you no."

Rolling her eyes, she snuggled closer. "That is absolutely not true."

"Well, close to nothing."

Her breath fanned over my skin, and she kept drawing those little shapes along my ribs. "I do want that," she finally said quietly. "But I want you more. And if I'm choosing between a ceremony and bonding with the four of you, then I'm choosing you."

Gathering her close, I smiled into her hair. "That's the thing, sweetheart. Why would you ever have to choose?"

CHAPTER FORTY-ONE

SLOANE

$\mathcal{M}$y body curled around something. Something warm that smelled sweet. And purred. Hair scratched my chest, and I realized Jace had wrapped his arms around my ribs, and I was nearly folded over him, his ear pressed to my heart.

Ash still laid near me, his head near mine, holding one of my hands, and warmth lined my back.

Roman sat across the room, near the windows, a sketchpad in his hand and earbuds in, sketching us. His knuckles were wrapped in a bandage. He saw me looking and smiled before looking down at the paper again.

Gabe kept his promise, though clearly I hadn't woken up.

I squeezed Asher's hand, and he stirred, his eyes finding mine. "Hey."

"Hey." Pressing a little where our heads touched, I kept my voice quiet. "You don't mind them in your bed?"

Smiling, he shrugged. "Not really. We've never had those kinds of worries. It just works."

It did just work.

Now that it was the morning, I had a question for him. "Would you really kill him?"

"Craig?"

"Yeah."

Ash pulled my hand to his heart and slipped the other behind my neck. "There's actually two answers. Considering I just found you again, I really don't want to go to jail. So *will* I kill him? I'm going to try my very best not to. *Would* I kill him? Yes."

That statement shouldn't warm my heart or make it pound in my chest like I was going down the best rollercoaster in the world. "Because he touched me?"

"Because you're *mine*." He reflected my words from the car last night back at me. "And because he didn't just touch you. He touched you after you told him not to. He threatened you. He scared you." Ash's fingers tightened on my neck. "I saw enough fear on your face when I thought I was the one who put it there. No more."

I tilted my chin just enough, and Ash gave me what I wanted, kissing me as deeply as he could without us crushing Jace. "I don't want you to go to jail. But watching you do that was really hot."

"Yeah?" He smirked. "Good to know."

"Mmm," Jace turned his face so it was buried in between my breasts. "This is the only way to wake up." He reached up and gripped my hair at the base, exactly like he had when he gave me that massage. I desperately needed another one. I moaned, and he kept pulling gently until I was limp and relaxed.

A hand squeezed my hip, and lips kissed my naked back. "You okay after last night, little one?"

"When did you guys get back?"

"Not too late. Took about an hour for everything to get settled."

I tried not to let the nerves show on my face. "Did they arrest him?"

"No, they didn't."

My body wilted. I couldn't help it. There would have been some comfort in knowing that he'd been held, even if it was overnight. Gabriel turned me over, Jace's kisses now peppering along my spine. "There are guards outside the house," he said. "They'll be there until this is resolved one way or another."

Relief spread through me. "Thank you."

He smiled. "No protesting or telling me no?"

"No. It makes me feel better."

"Maybe I should take one away from your spanking count for being a good girl."

Behind me, Ash laughed softly. "I don't think she actually wants that."

My face flamed red, but it was only a reflex. I couldn't be embarrassed with them. Not about anything. And lying in the middle of my Alphas *was* the perfect way to wake up.

Slowly, I dragged myself onto Gabriel's chest. High up

enough to speak into his ear. This needed to be him and me. "Thank you for keeping me safe, Alpha."

The fierceness of his purr matched the way his arms came around me, crushing us together. "You're welcome, little one."

"I realized last night you're the only one I haven't told, and I don't want to wait anymore."

"What's that?"

My breath shook. "I love you."

Fisting his hand in my hair, he brought my mouth to his, his response written in every movement of lips and tongue. He kept me close, pressing his cheek to mine. "Saying that scares you a bit, doesn't it?"

"Yeah."

"Thank you for saying it. I love you so much it hurts to breathe when you're not in the same room with me. The thought of you hurt makes me want to burn this city to the fucking ground. I'm not going to let anybody touch you, okay, little one?" There was no space between us. Only the two of us in this moment. "I love you."

A meow interrupted my thoughts, Mango coming into the room. I swore his little face looked relieved to find us all in one place. "Hi there."

He leapt for the bed and nearly missed. Ash caught him and lifted him the rest of the way. "You're going to be jumping on top of the fridge in no time."

"Don't encourage him."

"He's an orange cat," Ash deadpanned. "He only has one brain cell and he doesn't need any encouragement to do random shit."

I reached over and pulled Mango over next to me. "Don't listen to him, Mango. You definitely have more than one brain cell."

He flopped on the bed and curled into a circle upside down, stretching like he was trying to prove me wrong. I didn't resist leaning in and kissing the fluffy, exposed belly. He purred too. Little tiny orange Alpha.

"Roman," Ash said. I looked over in time to see him tap his ears, telling him to take out his earbuds.

Gabriel sat us up together before shifting me to sit against the headboard, and Roman joined us on the bed. I squirmed under the covers again, sinking down until I was covered nearly to my neck. Mango crawled onto my chest and curled up in a classic cat loaf.

"Cold, baby girl?" Jace took his place again, lying over my legs.

"Not anymore."

"Good. Remember what we said we'd talk about?"

"No." I cuddled down even more, content to go back to sleep surrounded by all of them.

Gabriel stood off the bed. His glasses were on, and he still had his pants on from last night without the shirt. I enjoyed watching him walk over to Asher's bookshelf. It looked like he was examining the books there, but I didn't think he was. "Jace called me last night after you guys got home. Let me know what you said in the car."

Bonding.

"I was scared," I said. "Overwhelmed. We don't have to rush it if you're not ready. It's fast, and—"

Jace pushed up on his arms and kissed me quickly. "Take a breath and listen, baby girl."

Gabe put his hands in his pockets before he looked back at me. "After everything was finished, Roman and I made a stop on the way home."

"Where?"

"First," he came and sat on the edge of the bed. "We love you. And I wouldn't mind biting you right this very second."

Ash leaned in and kissed my shoulder. "We're forever. No changing our minds."

Managing to tug one of my hands out from underneath the comforter, Jace kissed my palm. "This hasn't been a traditional courting. And we'll wait as long as you want to. But we want you to know where we stand."

Roman said nothing, instead passing me the sketchbook he'd been working on. The drawing was us the way we'd woken up. I curled around Jace, Gabriel behind me, Ash diagonally with his head next to mine. My hand draped over Jace, relaxed in sleep.

And on my drawn hand was a ring.

I looked up and met Roman's eyes in shock. All he did was smile.

There was a box in Gabriel's hand that hadn't been there a second ago. Ring glimmering in the morning light. A dark blue stone that sparkled like there were stars inside it, shaped like a diamond. A gold band with smaller, clear stones on either side.

It was fucking beautiful, and I knew the ring. I'd seen it nearly every day growing up when I snuck into my grandmother's room. She kept it on the vanity in that same little blue box. It belonged to her mother. My great-grandmother.

I looked up at the four of them, words sticking in my throat. My mouth opened and closed, not knowing what to ask first because I had a million questions.

Jace took the box and set it on my legs. I scooted back up to sitting, setting Mango aside, staring down at it, still speechless. "What do you say, baby girl? Will you be ours forever?"

Tears flooded my eyes, and I nodded, still unable to speak. He picked the ring up and slid it onto my finger. When I was little it was always too big. Now it fit perfectly.

Then I laughed once. "I mean, I kind of thought I already was."

They laughed with me, Roman coming around the bed to kneel beside it and kiss the hand with the ring before kissing my forehead. My jaw. My lips. Anywhere he could reach. "Always were," he said.

Clinging to him, I breathed him in, the knowledge settling me. I didn't need a ring to know I belonged with them and to them, but I loved the physical sign of it.

"How did you get this?" I finally asked. "I've always loved this ring."

"Well, when Jace called me, we still had some time to kill while everything was still being settled with the police. So I took a risk and called your grandmother, thinking I'd leave a message. But she answered." Gabriel chuckled. "It sounded like she was having a party."

I rolled my eyes. "Yeah, that's Grandma."

"As soon as I said hello she knew what I wanted and told me

to get my ass to her house to get the ring, and she'd do whatever else we needed."

"That was the stop you made," I said, the whole thing clicking together.

"Yes," Roman confirmed.

Looking down at the ring, I smiled. "I didn't realize she knew."

"She did," Gabriel said. "And she told me to tell you 'it's about fucking time.' Her words, not mine."

I laughed, letting my head fall back against the headboard. "Of course she would say that."

"Now, we have a different question," Ash said.

"All right, but I have a limit of three life-altering questions per day," I said.

Jace laughed. "That seems fair."

"We still have two days until rehearsals start again and our lives go back to being busy," Ash said. "Remember when I said you wouldn't have to choose?"

I stared at him, an inkling of what he meant whirling around in my mind. But like hell was I going to be the one to say it.

Ash grinned like he could see the wheels of my brain turning. "Want to have a bonding ceremony tomorrow?"

My mouth dropped open. "Really?"

"Another thing your grandmother said. She'll happily let us use anywhere on the property."

Going back to rehearsals, being *bonded* to them. Feeling everything they felt and knowing we were permanent. Wanting it and asking for it was one thing, the reality of it being tomorrow was another.

Joy bubbled up from somewhere deep. "Yeah."

"Yeah?" Roman asked.

"Yes." I pulled the covers up over my head, all the emotions too much. "I want that. But there's no way we can do that tomorrow."

A weight dropped on my stomach on top of the blanket, and when I peeked out, my hair wild and rumpled, my phone lay there. Jace raised an eyebrow and grinned. "It's a good thing we know someone who's very, *very* good at getting things done quickly."

I only paused for a second before snatching the phone and dialing. Mango jumped and batted at the phone like it was a toy, and Roman intervened, distracting the kitten with his fingers dragging over my blanket-covered legs instead.

She answered on the second ring. "This is Addison."

"Addison, it's Sloane."

"Hey! I hope you're liking your bedroom."

"I am *loving* my bedroom," I said. "But I'm actually calling about something else."

Through the phone her environment got quieter, like she'd shut a door behind her. "Oh?"

All my Alphas purred, and I had a hard time containing my smile. "What are you doing for the next two days?"

CHAPTER FORTY-TWO

SLOANE

*M*y heart was in my throat as I looked in the mirror. The dress was perfect—a silvery white with hints of iridescent blues, purples, and oranges that shone whenever the fabric moved. And it never stopped moving because of the way it draped. Off one shoulder, it looked like it hung off the other one too, the bodice somehow making it stay upright before the dress clung to my body and dripped down to the floor. A filmy train flowed from the back, spreading out behind me, lighter than air when I walked.

"You look fucking stunning," Eva said. "Iris is a miracle worker."

"Yes, she is."

The minute I told Addison what the plan was, everyone rallied. Eva jumped in to help, calling her favorite designer—who she happened to have on speed dial—and suddenly I was being whisked away from my Alphas and to Bergman's with security in tow.

My grandmother was beside herself with happiness, helping Addison with ideas to make everything even more over the top.

And all I could think about was them.

Petra placed her hands on my shoulders behind me. "I want to hug the shit out of you right now, but I don't want to wrinkle the dress."

"After the pictures you can hug the shit out of me," I giggled.

Esme reached forward and adjusted one of the curls hanging down around my face. "I'm really happy for you, Sloane."

"You don't regret not having one?"

She snorted. "God, no. But remind someone to take a picture of me here to slip to the paparazzi. They'll finally have a picture of me at a bonding ceremony where I don't look miserable."

"No paparazzi," Eva said. "I'll kick their asses. Plus, Sloane is lucky enough to not have them on her tail."

Petra rolled her eyes. "But they're on your tail, Eva."

"We were careful. And Grandma Glass has a fence that's approximately a million feet tall."

I reached out to the table nearby and picked up the necklace I'd chosen. "That's definitely not an exaggeration."

"Never. I would never blow things out of proportion."

I held the chains back, and Petra hooked the necklace. The little charm fell in the hollow of my throat, and emotion rose. It was a small thing—and one I'd honestly forgotten about until Petra reminded me—but it felt important.

Ash gave me the necklace for my birthday one year. A teardrop crystal that was simple and lovely. '*Blue*' was inscribed on the back of it. I shoved the thought of it out of my mind when I ran, but it stayed in my jewelry box. Now it was my 'something old.'

I usually didn't put much stock in traditions like those, but today? I wanted every cliche moment and little memory. My ring was blue, the dress was new. I didn't have anything borrowed, but considering how quickly this came together, you could say I borrowed my grandmother's entire house.

"Oh my goodness, you are a vision." My grandmother swept into the room. Her dress was wild, a bright red that looked like flames. There was a subtle pattern in there that might have been an animal print, but I didn't question it. She pulled it off.

"We'll give you guys a second," Petra said, and my friends excused themselves so I was alone with Grandma.

She squeezes my shoulders. "Are you nervous?"

"Yes," I admitted.

"Good."

Nervous laughter slipped out. "Good?"

Leaning her chin on my shoulder, her eyes sparkled. "Nerves are good. It means you've thought about every side of a decision. You know how big it is, and you're choosing to do it regardless. If you weren't nervous, I'd be surprised.

"Now," she said, "are you happy?"

I nodded. "Yeah."

"They're good for you. And nothing came up in the background checks."

"Grandma," I gasped.

"What?" She gave me a look. "You didn't really think I was just going to let some pack have you without making sure they deserved you, did you?"

Honestly, I had no idea. "I love you, Grandma."

"I love you too, dear. I wish your parents were here to see it."

"That would have been quite the trip," I said. "I'm sure they'll enjoy the pictures."

A glimmer of hurt showed in her eyes. Grandma had always taken my mother's indifference to motherhood harder than I did. What I didn't tell her was that it would be strange if they were here. Everyone I truly cared about in my life was here.

It was more than enough for me.

Grandma cleared her throat and pulled away momentarily. "I'm giving this to you at a later date. But today, it will be borrowed."

She lifted a bracelet I'd never seen, but it matched my ring. A golden chain spangled with smaller versions of the sparkling blue stone. She clasped it on my wrist opposite the ring. "It suits you."

"I didn't know this existed."

"I can't give away all my secrets yet, dear." Reaching up, she pressed a hand to my cheek. "I've still got some life left to live. When I'm ready to go, I'll make sure all the secrets are yours."

I hugged her, not caring about the wrinkles in my dress or any touch ups to my makeup. "I love you," I told her. "And I couldn't do this without you." The fact that she approved soothed any lingering nerves I had about us moving too fast. Grandma would never do anything to hurt me, even if it meant telling me I was out of my mind.

"You could," she said quietly. "But I'm glad you're not."

Then she stepped back and looked at me, quickly fixing any smudges my misting eyes had made. "Though I didn't have time to buy you the kind of gift I want to."

"Grandma, you're literally hosting the ceremony. You don't need to get me a gift."

"That's never stopped me before."

A soft knock at the door. Petra leaned her head inside. "It's time."

"Yes, it is." Grandma squeezed my hands before leaving the room. I looked at myself one more time. There was nothing out of place, and if someone had told me a month ago that I'd be here, looking so fucking happy, I never would have believed them.

"You ready?" Petra asked.

"Yes."

It was true. I was ready.

She handed me my bouquet, which was a mixture of purple flowers that matched the girls' dresses, the hint of color in mine, and all the other decorations I'd gotten a glimpse of.

Addison had let herself loose, taking the colors she already knew I loved and creating a wonderland. I didn't know how she managed to do it, but when I saw her, she was beaming like I'd given her the greatest gift in the world.

Almost everyone was here. The girls and their packs, Dion and his, Claire, other friends from the company, and some friends of the guys. Asher's friend Will couldn't make it today but would visit soon, and Jace's family couldn't make the trip on short notice. Someone would be streaming it for them.

Petra guided me downstairs and to the back of the house. I hadn't seen outside yet—they wouldn't let me. Grandma's estate was huge, but I was told they created a space for the ceremony that would double as a dance floor later.

After we came back from the room the five of us would escape to as soon as the ceremony was over. Because we would need a minute—or an hour—to give in to pure instinct.

Another good reason this dress exposed so much of my chest and shoulders. So my Alphas had room to bite.

Music flowed through the air, and I gasped, looking at Petra. She just smiled. It was Alexander Serrat's music. The concert I was meant to go to. No matter what happened that night, his music was still my favorite.

"Was this your idea?"

"A suggestion."

"Thank you."

She smiled and leaned in close. "I've always got your back, Sloane. Even when you're shoving me into closets."

"I remember that turning out pretty well for you."

320

"It did. And this aisle? It's your closet."

Esme went first, walking down the aisle, and then Eva. Petra right before me. Then it was my turn, the music swelling naturally, and I stepped around the corner...

My breath stopped entirely.

Over the large marble veranda, they'd created a lattice that suspended flowers, crystals, and lights which were starting to glow as the sky darkened and the sun began to set. Candles hovered at the edges with more flowers, all the seats draped in fabric that matched the theme. Everyone had turned to look at me, my throat going dry with an entirely different kind of spotlight.

But more than anything, my eyes were on them.

Matching dark suits, with each Alpha in a different color vest and tie. All of them looking at me with forever in their eyes.

The weight of their gazes on me brought tears to my eyes, but I didn't want to cry. I didn't want to miss a second of this. And for a moment, I almost wished we were alone in the middle of all this beauty.

I began to walk. Down the steps from the house and towards them. Every step made me calmer and more sure. My body still shook, but it was anticipation and joy. They were with me, and I was with them. Always.

Our ceremony would be simple and quiet. Some who weren't scent-sympathetic and chose to marry instead of bond, like my parents, had more complicated ceremonies with vows and speeches.

Even some, like Eva's very public ceremony, had elements of that. The five of us didn't want it or need it.

Bonding needed no vows. It was a vow in itself. Unbreakable and irreversible, what could you say that would ever live up to that kind of trust? So we chose for our ceremony to be beautiful, and have all our witnesses. But the words my Alphas spoke to me before we bonded would be for us alone.

I stepped up across from them, briefly glancing down at my grandmother in the first row. She smiled, telling me everything I needed to know. This was right, and there was no going back.

Reaching out, they all grabbed my hand before Gabriel

stepped forward and gently took my face in his. "I've been trying to think of what to say, and everything I think of just doesn't seem big enough or real enough."

"I know the feeling," I whispered.

"So I'll tell you this. That morning in the studio, I was nervous. I know transitions are difficult, and I was worried what everyone would think about me and Jace and Ash working there as a pack. And then..." He took a small, hitching breath. "It didn't matter anymore. Because the entire universe turned my head and pointed at you. It said *there she is, she's yours.*"

"Gabriel."

He kissed me, softly and slowly. "I love you, little one. Can I make you mine?"

"Yes." The word was barely a breath.

Gabe tilted my head, pressing his mouth to that little space beneath my ear where my neck met my jaw. He bit me, the pain making me gasp before it disappeared entirely, replaced by the feeling of Gabriel in my chest. My steadfast Alpha whose power ran so deep it made me shake. Every breath of that power now lived in me, along with the feeling of love so desperate I could only look at him.

"Now you know how much there is I can't say," he whispered.

Somewhere I heard applause, but my entire world was him. The urge to strip myself naked and pounce on him was so strong, I was already questioning our choice to do this in public.

Amusement and desire gathered in his eyes, and he ran a thumb over his bite, making me shudder. "Soon."

He stepped aside. It was only because I wanted all of them so fucking much that I could let it happen. Jace stood in front of me now, not hesitating to spin me so he held me in his arms, my back pressed to his chest. Gabe took my bouquet. Jace pressed a kiss to my bare shoulder. "Hey, baby girl."

"Hi."

It was like we were entirely alone, minus the feeling of Gabriel through our new bond. It nearly burst with pride, joy, and the feeling of rightness.

"I know we don't need vows," he said. "But I have one. I will always take care of you, baby girl. I don't care if we're in a fight or we're exhausted. Doesn't matter if I'm sick or busy, if you need me, I will be there. Even if it's only making sure you eat breakfast, or that your feet are iced."

I smiled, leaning back into him.

"You're mine, and I love you."

"Love you."

"I'm going to bite you here." His hand released me to touch my shoulder blade. "So when you're on my massage table I get to see my mark. And make good use of it."

He leaned down and broke my skin, our bond snapping into place with a warm sweetness that felt like him. The comfort of the way he cared and the brightness of his smile. That same gravity and perfection. Resonance. I pressed a hand to my chest.

When he moved away, I turned and found Roman staring down at me. Roman in a suit was something I needed more often in my life. He was stunning—powerful—and reaching for me.

"You don't have to say anything," I whispered. "I love you."

Pulling me closer, he kissed my forehead. "Firefly, you make everything easier."

"How?"

"When they told me about you, I was anxious. And then I saw you. Scented you. And I knew I would never have to be nervous with you."

I pressed my face to his chest, fighting back all the overwhelming emotions.

"I know I never have to speak for you to hear me. I love you." He picked up my arm where it was draped on his shoulder, turning his head to bite the underside of my forearm. Where he could reach it and touch it, but it wouldn't be constant.

The depth in the bond that sprang to life...

Roman was still water on the surface with an ocean beneath. He felt so much and so intensely, it leveled me. To him I really was a firefly—beautiful, the light in his darkness, and precious. "Roman..."

His soft smile, along with the bond, told me everything he couldn't.

Only Ash remained, and as he stepped closer, his eyes fell to my neck. He froze for a moment. "Blue."

"It felt right."

"God, I love you," he gathered me in his arms and held me. "I'm so fucking grateful I found you, Sloane. The first time *and* the second time."

Neither of us were the people we had been back then, and it was a good thing. I had regrets, but I could live with those because of what we had now. It made sense for him to be last and complete this circle.

Asher's lips quirked into a smile, but his eyes were serious. "No more running, sweetheart."

"Never again," I promised.

He leaned in and bit where my neck met my shoulder, his bond exploding into existence like a star. It wasn't only him, but the combination of all of us. Like a piece of a puzzle you couldn't even know was missing until you found it. How was I meant to know there had been empty places in my soul before they filled them?

Applause from our friends and family erupted again. They'd clapped every time, and I hadn't heard it. I did now as Ash kissed me, dipping me back and putting on a show.

But something else was brewing, because if I didn't have their hands on me and their cocks inside me soon, I would burn alive. I smiled out at our friends, seeing more than one teary eye before the others stepped up with me, and we retreated inside.

They had me up the stairs to my old wing of the house in less than five minutes, sealing us inside the room that had been prepared so we could seal this bond we just forged.

Me and my Alphas.

CHAPTER FORTY-THREE

SLOANE

*W*e barely made it through the door before Jace's mouth found mine. My mind and heart were a riot of unfamiliar feelings and overwhelming desire. All of them wanted me so much it was terrifying and exhilarating, and I didn't know how I was just going to *exist* feeling them like this.

Petra, Eva, and Esme did this every day?

It was a miracle they weren't constantly locked at home, tearing each other's clothes off.

Well, then again...

"I know you have to put this dress back on, baby girl, so help me get it off. If I don't have you naked—"

"Yes," I breathed, turning around so he could access the nearly hidden zipper beneath the train at my shoulder.

When we were done, I'd have the girls touch up my makeup and help me back into the dress. Right now? I needed them. The way I felt their attention focus on me as the dress slipped down my body...

Fuck.

"I'm never going to get used to this," I told them. "It's so much."

"It is," Ash said. "We can feel each other now too. A little at least, through you."

Jace undid the clasps on the bustier I wore beneath the gown. "I, for one, am thoroughly going to enjoy teasing you with it. Winding you up from afar so you can't wait to pounce when you get home."

"God," I moaned. "How are we going to live normal life?"

"Very carefully," Roman chuckled.

They shed their suits while I stepped out of my shoes, now in nothing but jewelry. In the same way I felt their appreciation, they felt mine, desire and arousal spinning back and forth between, building on the echoes.

Gabriel stood in front of me. "I know we can't get as lost in here as we might like," he said. "With everyone downstairs. I want you to enjoy your party."

"And I want to enjoy *you*."

"You're going to," he said, turning me to kiss his bite. It shook me to my core, pleasure blooming beneath my skin and racing south. "But since we don't have as much time until we go home, we had a thought."

"*We?*"

"We, firefly."

Ash took one hand, lifting it to his chest where I could feel his heart pound, even as Gabriel kept teasing me. "We had some time to talk while you were getting everything ready."

"Think you can take all of us at once, little one?"

The world went still. "All of you?"

"All of us," Jace confirmed.

"How?"

Gabe pulled me to the bed—huge and decadent, with four posts and a canopy—and fell onto it with me on top of him. "All we need to know is if you want to try. If you do, we'll take care of the rest of it."

"Take care of *you*." Jace spoke the words against his healing bite. I grew wet between my legs, just the feeling of him touching there and the echoes of whatever naughty things he thought sending me into a frenzy that almost felt like heat.

I nodded, feeling dazed and wanted nothing more than for them to take care of me and give me the pleasure which flowed through our connections. All of them. I just needed their hands and mouths on me. More. "Yes."

"Come here, sweet girl," Gabriel said, guiding me down onto his cock. I shuddered, able to feel exactly how good it felt to *him*. So sharp and delicious it was going to make me come fast. Him too. Everything would be so much *more*.

I couldn't wait.

Jace gripped my hips, letting Gabriel thrust up into me a few times before he slowed. I didn't need a warm up right now. Feeling them in my chest was enough. I could bask in the glow of their love forever and be happy.

Fitting himself to my ass, Jace eased in, filling me up to bursting. *Yes*. Not the first time I'd had them like this, nor would it be the last. But all of them? How?

Roman was suddenly there, kneeling and hard, cock in his hand. I vividly remembered Gabriel telling me I could take more. And maybe I could. Looking up at my big Alpha, I wanted today to be the day I did that. Even if I couldn't, I felt how much he treasured me. There wouldn't be disappointment.

I groaned when my tongue touched his skin. He was addicting, the feeling of him sliding into my mouth sending echoes through our bond. Through *all* the bonds. None of us would last long like this.

"Take him all, little one. I know you can." Gabriel reached up and took control, guiding me down Roman's shaft, helping me take him. The other night with Ash...

I relaxed, opening everything, and Roman sank into my throat with a muttered curse. "Firefly."

"*Good girl*," Gabe said. "Fuck, Sloane. Keep him there. And if you have to breathe, you take him right back down. We're almost there."

Where would Ash go? My thoughts were light and cloudy, like I was floating on a sea of silver mist, simply enjoying every sensation. Filled up in every place they could take me. Jace drew his hands up my stomach and toyed with my breasts. Kissed my neck. They fucked me together, even Roman, driving into me in sync so I was delirious. Drunk on them.

Roman drew out of my mouth so I had a chance to breathe, but I didn't want to breathe. I wanted to taste him on my tongue and in my throat. My mouth watered at the idea of more, and he could feel it. He gave me more.

My lips were locked around the base of him when Jace and Gabe slowed down, Jace shifting closer to my back, wrapping around me entirely.

And I felt it.

Ash, pressing into my pussy, despite the fact that Gabriel was already buried deep inside it. That wasn't possible... was it?

Fingers found my clit, circling and teasing, adding more pleasure to everything, and I found myself relaxing against Jace's purr. It felt so good. The world was lined with shimmering starlight.

The last, glorious beams of sunset painted everything through the windows, and I orgasmed. Sheer delirium and bliss, body shaking, unable to take a proper breath. Ash kept pushing in, and my body let him in.

I thought I knew what it meant to be full.

I was fucking wrong.

Jace took over working my clit as they moved in sync, all four of them fucking me together, strokes lining up and falling into separate rhythms. My brain pulled itself in a thousand different directions, thoughts evaporating into nothing in the face of *this*.

My hands were held, fingers woven together. Gabriel.

"You're doing so good, baby girl," Jace whispered, voice ragged. He was on the edge of his own pleasure. They all were, and I could *feel* it. If my mouth wasn't jammed full of Roman, I would have smiled.

I hummed around him, sinking into pleasure and trust, and came again.

Every movement they made sent me into overdrive. The combination of new bonds and Omega biology equaled fucking perfection.

Roman came first, pulling back to spill cum across my tongue. I drank him down greedily, almost wishing he would have knotted my mouth so I had the excuse to keep tasting him. He leaned down and kissed my temple, lining our faces up to see me. I was still being fucked. Viciously. Ruthlessly. Perfectly.

"Beautiful, firefly."

A tornado of an orgasm rolled through me. Jace bit down where his bite was, not breaking the skin again. It was like a vibrator laced with lightning. My voice was so loud they might have heard it down at the party. But Roman was smiling as he watched, and Jace dragged kisses over my shoulder as he eased away, leaving me impaled on two cocks.

Both of them in my pussy.

I couldn't breathe, collapsing down onto Gabriel's chest. Ash came with me, pressing me between the two of them. "I—I—"

"Yes you can, sweetheart," Ash whispered. He was deeper

inside me now that Jace was gone. The friction of the two of them together, the stretch...

It might kill me.

Ash brought his hand up to circle my throat, palm pressing the chain of his necklace into my skin. "One more," he said. "Give us one more. Come all over the two of us, fucking your cunt at the same time. Knowing that you can take that now. And we'll do it again. Filling you up with our cocks until you scream. But we'll take our time, because we have all the time in the world."

That was all it took.

This time I didn't scream.

It felt like plunging into the depths of a perfumed sea of all their scents. Bathing in warmth and the purest form of desire. I was their craving and their obsession. They loved giving and feeling my pleasure as much as I loved receiving it. Every moment spent under the surface cementing the bond we forged at the altar.

They came together, groaning before we ended up in a spent, sweaty, messy heap of limbs and love. I laughed, barely able to wrap my head around it. "Fuck me."

"Pretty sure we just did," Jace said, reaching over to swat my ass.

"Very much so." I swallowed, trying to catch my breath. "Holy shit. How are we supposed to go back downstairs with everyone knowing we just did that?"

"Proudly," Roman rumbled.

Gabriel agreed. "I'll gladly tell them exactly how well our Omega took our cocks, little one. Nothing to be ashamed of."

"I'm not. Just not used to the idea of my grandmother knowing I've been thoroughly *railed*."

Ash smiled against my ear. "Sweetheart, your grandmother was rooting for it and you know it."

Another laugh overtook me. That was so fucking true.

Jace rolled over me, pinning me to the bed. "We'll grab your friends and wait for you down at the party. I'm assuming you don't want to make a grand entrance."

"God, no." My face burned. Knowing my friends, they were

already going to make a big deal out of it. We didn't need to solidify it by walking in and announcing we'd just fucked. That would be apparent.

He grinned and kissed me. "All right, baby girl. But don't take too long. There's only so long I'll be able to keep my hands off you."

Through our new bond, I felt the way his attention turned entirely toward me with both awe and desire. He was mine, and I was his.

"We really did it," I whispered.

"Yes, we did, little one."

They all touched me somewhere on my body, the combination of all of them combining in me in a pleasant hum. "Okay. I want to stay in here, but I also want to dance with you. So send the girls up."

Because we had all the time in the world now.

"I want to dance with you too," Ash whispered.

"You get to dance with me every day."

He smirked, letting me get away with it before he dressed. I loved watching them put on suits. Granted, I loved watching them take them off too.

Now fully dressed, Roman came and knelt in front of me where I sat on the edge of the bed. I'd pulled a sheet from the rumpled bed around my chest, but hadn't done anything to dress yet.

Roman picked up one foot, and I cringed. I took care of my feet, but they were still ballerina feet. They were a little fucked even if I managed to have enough toenails left to paint.

But he didn't flinch or even notice, lifting my leg to brush a kiss over my ankle and higher up my skin. "What are you doing?" I breathed.

From him, I felt the stunning depth of his emotions, and it took me a second to place the feeling there. It felt like...

Like I was a goddess and he was on his knees for me. I wasn't sure I liked the idea of him on his knees, but I *loved* the way he looked at me. When he reached my thigh, he stood, leaning in to kiss my cheek. "Save me a dance."

"Okay," I squeaked out.

They left, not before shooting me looks that could burn down this entire estate. I was meant to get up and start getting put back together, but I couldn't. All I did was sit with the sheet wrapped around me, listening to the bonds in my chest. Their happiness and joy that mirrored my own.

I did it.

A knock came on the door. "Come in."

Petra came in first and froze, Esme stopping up short behind her.

"What are you guys waiting—" Eva stepped into the room, gaze traveling from my head and my fucked up hair, down to my bare feet. She looked at the others and smothered a laugh before looking back at me. "We have so much work to do."

CHAPTER FORTY-FOUR

GABRIEL

The party was in full swing when we stepped out of the mansion again, and Addison's design shone in full glory. It looked like someone had created a false starry sky, spangled with flowers and gems that threw rainbows across the space. It was perfect for Sloane.

I felt her laughter in my chest. She was with her friends, getting ready now that we'd released ourselves on her like wild animals. I quite liked the way she looked rumpled and disheveled, because I liked everyone else knowing she was mine. But my little one was also more private, so I wanted her to look perfect.

Across the room, Jace waved to his family on the tablet we'd streamed the ceremony on. We needed to get them down here for a visit soon. I'd told my brother about the ceremony and gotten congratulations in return, but I didn't expect to see him.

We were Asher's family now, and Roman?

It had taken him more than a year to tell us the truth about his family. Abuse, but not in the overt and violent method Ash had been exposed to. His was neglect. Because of his difficulties speaking and reading, and the resulting anxiety and silence, his parents thought he had a mental impairment instead of a disability. They took care of him, but in a sparce and barely there way.

He didn't speak to them anymore, either.

"Gabriel."

I turned to find Petra's Alphas approaching me, Harrison at the front. He held out a hand, and I shook it. "Thank you for coming."

The shorter blonde Alpha chuckled. Blake. "Pretty sure Petra would have come with or without us, and none of us are quite ready to have that kind of separation."

I knew enough about what had happened to their Omega that I couldn't blame them. If Sloane had been taken, I didn't know that I'd even be able to let her out of my bed, let alone leave to go places like rehearsal. If Craig—

Quickly, I shut the thought down. The only thing he did was bring me thoughts of anger, and while it was justified, I wasn't going to bring that to Sloane tonight. She could feel us now.

"Thank you for the other night," I told them. "If you hadn't been there it might have been a murder charge."

Cole's cold anger showed on his face. "I wouldn't blame you there."

"I know this isn't exactly the place, but have you found anything else?"

Harrison glanced around, seeing who was close by before speaking. "I might have, yes. Are you familiar at all with Hourglass Investments?"

"No. Can't say that I am." What investments I had were managed by my brother. He was the one to talk to about that. My financial skills came in the operations side, not the *making it* side.

"Well—"

"Gabriel."

I turned and blinked. My brother walked toward me like I'd conjured him out of my thoughts. "Robert," I said, embracing him when he stepped in. "What are you doing here?"

"I happened to be in Slate City. Figured I should come say hello when my little brother bonds."

"Your brother?" Emery, Petra's fourth Alpha asked. "You guys don't look much alike."

Robert clapped me on the shoulder. "No, we wouldn't. I've got twenty years on him. Two different moms in the same pack, but this one," he jerked his thumb at me, "was an accident."

"He never lets me forget it either," I said dryly.

I made introductions before I turned to him. "You're exactly who I wanted to talk to, by the way. Harrison was just going to tell me some things about Hourglass Investments. Have you heard of them?"

My brother choked on the champagne he'd just snagged from one of the waiters circulating. "Is that a joke?"

"No."

"I swear to fuck, Gabriel, if you move any of your invest-ments to that company—"

Holding my hands up, I laughed. "I'm not. Cross my heart. But that gives me an answer about whether you've heard of it."

Staring at me for a second, he relaxed once he realized I wasn't going to ruin myself financially. "I have definitely heard of it. What's left of it, anyway."

"What's left of it?" I glanced at Harrison. "What about it?"

Harrison smirked in satisfaction. "Craig Sullivan is the CEO of Hourglass Investments. Or, like your brother said, what's left of it. Seems like they've had trouble for years. Likely due to... unwise decisions."

Robert groaned into his glass of champagne. "Sullivan couldn't make a good choice if it were presented to him on the platinum platter he *wishes* he could afford. He's a laughingstock in the industry, and no one will touch him with a ten-foot pole."

"About a year ago they had an influx of cash," Cole said. "Looked like they might recover, but didn't. Lost everything, predictably. He couldn't maintain it. Everything fell apart a couple of weeks ago, and he filed to dissolve the corporation."

I looked between the two of them. "A couple of *weeks*?"

"Thought that might interest you."

Since that first day at the company when Ash and I encoun-tered Sloane, it had been three weeks. Two weeks ago would have been after Craig found Ash at her apartment, and before we saw him outside, when he looked positively wrecked.

Robert watched me carefully. "I missed something."

My mouth firmed into a line. "Sullivan is Sloane's ex. Or he likes to think he is. The amount of time they were together is so minimal she never considered them together, but he's having... a hard time letting go."

Cole growled. "And by 'a hard time,' he means stalking her and accosting her in public."

"Shit." Robert shook his head. "I mean, he's a fool, but I never heard any rumors like that. He barely seemed like the kind of guy to have a girlfriend at all."

Harrison cleared his throat. "For this next bit, Gabe, we need to speak somewhere more private."

I touched Robert's arm. "I'll be back. I want to introduce you to Sloane."

"Absolutely."

A pleasant surprise. Curiosity bloomed near my heart where Sloane's bond now held residence. I loved feeling her there. The unconscious anxiety I had when she wasn't near me was eased by feeling her safety and her happiness.

"Why the secrecy?" I asked when we reached the corner of the veranda.

"Because the rest of the information I have for you was not obtained through legal means, and I want to limit that knowledge. Nor do I want to give the impression to people I don't know that we carelessly give out confidential information. No offense to your brother."

"None taken." It was a good call to limit liability. "Is this going to make me want to kill him?"

"No more than you already do, but I think it will provide some closure, both for your pack and for Sloane."

"Should I get them?"

"Might as well."

Through our now echoing bond, I called them to me. They came quickly, Jace grinning like a fool. "I like this. We don't even have to text. Harrison," he greeted the Alpha.

Once they were all there, I spoke. "He has something about Craig. Figured it was better to hear it all at once."

We all looked at him, determination and focus echoing through the four of us.

Harrison briefly recapped what he told me about Craig's company before continuing. "The injection of money he got last year was from a man named Vidal Maher. Overseas investor, he's got more money than god and has it in a bunch of places. I'm not sure what convinced him to take a chance on Sullivan's company, but he did."

Ash shrugged. "Clearly it didn't pan out."

"No. But he was still trying to make it work, and I think it was because of Sloane."

I bristled. "What?"

A look of grim satisfaction covered Harrison's face. "When

Sloane mentioned the concert, I had my... less than legal resources go digging. Vidal Maher is one of the founding members of that concert hall. He's a patron of the arts, but mostly music. Generally, he keeps a low profile, so I wouldn't have expected you to know of him."

That last bit was to me, and no, I hadn't.

"He also happens to be a big fan of the composer who performed that night."

Things started coming together in my head, suspicion growing. "The surprise?"

"Yes. Sloane was right. Emails confirm he'd arranged with Maher to have her meet Serrat, the composer."

Jace frowned. "If he lost all of Maher's money, why would he be inclined to agree?"

With one hand, Harrison gestured around us. Suddenly, the truth slammed into me. "Sloane's grandmother?"

"Indeed. Craig lied. He told Maher that he had the full and complete *imminent* investment in the company by Sophia Glass. It was the reason he gave to convince Maher to keep investing, blaming the losses on bad luck and the market, not his own decisions. Maher wanted proof, and Craig saw the opportunity."

Roman looked like he was about to go hunt Craig down, and I couldn't blame him.

"But Sloane wouldn't have been that proof," Ash said. "Even if she'd gone with him to the meeting, that doesn't prove anything."

"With the way he sold it, that wouldn't have mattered. Craig Sullivan is an excellent liar. He had Maher convinced that Sloane and he were well on their way to either bonding or marriage, and because of that, Sophia trusted him implicitly. Showing up with Sloane on his arm would have been enough, and I don't doubt he would have forged whatever documents he needed. And further, I'm sure he would have come after the Glass fortune later."

"So that's what he meant at Pavilion." I looked at the others. "He told Sloane he'd get what he was owed."

"It's my theory that he approached her last year with this intention all along." Harrison crossed his arms. "Then got lucky with Maher. When Sloane reached out this time, it was the perfect opportunity."

Then not only had Sloane wounded his pride, she unintentionally humiliated him *and* deprived him of what would have been a sizable investment. He blamed her for losing everything. No wonder he was coming after her. In his mind, she was the only thing he had left.

Not anymore.

Bonding with us would put the nail in that coffin for good, but I had a feeling he wouldn't care.

"You're right," I said. "That does bring some closure. But it doesn't solve the problem."

"I have a feeling that will resolve on its own. The man is desperate and makes increasingly bad decisions. While I can't prove anything illegal in a way that will stand up in court, it's only a matter of time."

I wasn't so sure about that, but it wasn't a problem to deal with today. Reaching out, I shook his hand again. "Well, thank you. And until it is resolved, we'll keep the security."

He smirked. "I'll keep sending the invoices."

"If Petra finds out you're charging them, she's going to lose her shit." Cole spoke from behind me. He'd approached quietly, and Harrison clearly didn't mind him being in the audience.

I laughed. "If she does, I'll pay it without an invoice."

Everything else faded away because my Omega was here. At the glass doors to the house, flanked by her friends, somehow she looked even more beautiful than when she'd walked down the aisle to us the first time.

Harrison released my hand with a laugh. "Go get your girl."

We already were, crossing the space to her, though everyone had already noticed and cheered for Sloane as she entered. She smiled, her embarrassment filtering through. When she was on stage dancing she *loved* being the center of attention. Here, on a more personal level, she struggled.

Roman reached her first, sweeping her into a kiss that had the crowd cheering again. She was surrounded before I got there, friends from the company speaking to her, Dion, Claire, Addison, and others I recognized but didn't know.

"Congratulations." Mark came up to stand beside me.

"Glad you could make it."

"Wouldn't miss it." He lowered his voice. "Are you going to call Angela?"

Slate City Ballet's public relations and marketing director. "I hadn't planned on it. Why?"

"Announce this," he said. "Show it off and make it a thing to be celebrated and not hidden. I get the impression that's needed right now."

We hadn't had a chance to fully debrief about what happened while he took over during Sloane's heat, but it looked like we needed to. He wasn't wrong. "I'll call her."

"Good. Now I won't bother you anymore tonight."

I laughed. "You're not a bother."

"But you'd still rather be with your Omega."

Couldn't argue with that. And my little one owed me a dance. But I watched her for a while. Let her dance with the others and drink probably too many glasses of champagne.

The evening got slower, Omegas and their packs dancing, and I couldn't hold myself back anymore. I needed to have Sloane in my arms.

CHAPTER FORTY-FIVE

SLOANE

I didn't remember ever being this happy. The initial embarrassment of walking back into the party was nothing compared to the *love* showered all over me. Dion, Claire, and all the other principal dancers pulled me onto the dance floor for wild, sloppy line dancing that would make Madame Hubert assign us about a hundred technique drills.

The champagne was delicious, and every time I looked up, I got lost in the incredible sky Addison created—flowers, stars, diamonds, and lights. It was beautiful. Was I a little tipsy and just wanted to keep staring at everything that was pretty? Maybe. But that didn't mean she hadn't knocked it out of the park.

A photographer I hadn't even noticed during the ceremony snapped pictures, and I couldn't wait to see them.

Finally, when my Alphas decided they'd had enough of sharing, Jace pulled me into his arms on the dance floor, slowing everything down. "How you doing, baby girl?"

"I'm good," I said. "Perfect. Maybe a little drunk."

"I think we can handle that." His purr vibrated against me, unable to be heard through the chatter and the music. "I can't wait to start doing life with you, Sloane."

"Me too."

I laid my head on his chest until there was a tap on my shoulder, and Jace spun me into Asher's arms. He held my hand with another arm around my waist, a more traditional pose.

The deep contentment in his bond was echoed in my own.

I felt all of it. The darkness he felt he had to hide, and the regret of not knowing I was his. How he'd held himself back, hoping to make up for it, and how until the other night he'd worried he might frighten me away again.

"I was never scared of you, Ash. I know I already told you, but I'll say it again. It never crossed my mind. And I don't want you holding anything back from me."

Ash brushed his lips across mine, asking wordlessly for more, and I gave it to him. Words weren't needed right now, because we could both feel it. It didn't matter the time we'd lost, because we were always meant to be here in each other's arms.

When he broke the kiss, he pressed his cheek to mine, still moving us slowly around the dance floor. "I'll still spend our lives making it up to you, blue. Because I know what it's like to be without you, and I'll never take it for granted. I promise."

In the echoing connection between us, it felt like a vow.

Ash bent to press his forehead against mine, and we stayed that way, eyes closed, and I loved the feeling of just existing with him, nothing else between us.

"I need to buy you more jewelry," he finally said softly. "Because I love seeing that necklace on you."

I smirked up at him. "Need to remind everyone I'm yours?"

"Something like that."

"I should get you guys some rings. If I'm showing I'm taken, I want it for you, too."

He kissed my forehead and pulled me closer. "I'll wear anything you buy me, sweetheart. I would shout that I'm yours from the rooftops if I thought anyone would listen."

"May I?" Roman appeared next to us, and I smiled as I spun to him, Ash's fingers lingering for just a moment.

Even in high heels, Roman was so much taller I had to crane my neck to see his face. I decided I didn't care much about decorum at my own bonding and jumped up. Roman caught me easily, holding me as my knees perched on his hips. Now we were face to face, and I wrapped my arms around his neck. "Much better."

He squeezed my ass, and I laughed. "I do like this," he said.

We just held each other, with me listening to the flickers of emotions he had. Love and contentment, happiness, some darkness and anger too that didn't seem to match the rest. "What's wrong?"

"Nothing, firefly."

"Can't get away with that anymore," I whispered. "Not now that I can feel you."

Roman tilted his head, acknowledging my statement.

"Nothing you need to worry about tonight," he finally said. "I'd rather think about how you promised to let me sculpt you naked."

"I will. But where would we put a statue like that?"

He thought about it. "I'll sculpt it small enough to be moved around. We can keep it wherever you like in the house."

When I blushed, he smiled. "Why are you embarrassed, firefly? It's only for us."

"I know. It's still strange to me."

"Why?"

I reached up and brushed a stray hair back that was escaping from where it was gathered in a low bun. "I've been alone for a long time," I told him. "I'm still getting used to anyone even wanting me, let alone wanting a statue of my naked body."

"Who wouldn't want you?"

Gratefulness washed through me for the bond we now had, because I didn't have to speak for him to feel my pleasure at the thought, and I didn't have to explain anything else.

Lifting my arm away from him, he pressed his mouth to his bite. Need raced through me like he'd set fire to a fuse lining every limb. "Fuck me, that's something else I'll have to get used to."

"Another way to wake you up."

"Yes, please."

We'd neared the edge of the dance floor, and when a waiter passed within reach, I snagged another glass of champagne and drank it. Considering I hadn't eaten anything more than finger food, it was probably a bad idea, but I did it anyway.

"You want some?"

Roman shook his head. "Not tonight. You're my drink."

I giggled, the drink building on the ones already in my system as Roman set me down and took away the glass. "Where are you going?"

"Nowhere," he said, turning me. Gabriel stood there with his hand out. "May I have this dance?"

"Yes."

Gabe spun me under his arm before pulling me to his chest. "Hello, little one."

"Hi."

"Was it everything you imagined?"

There weren't words to answer him, so I let him feel them instead. I hadn't had any true expectations for something like this, because I'd given up on it. So being with them, in a place so beautiful, in a dress pulled from my dreams?

I was happier than I ever imagined I could be. Even with everything else outside of this that seemed like it was teetering, this was *perfect*.

Twirling me to the center of the dance floor, he grinned. "I'm glad."

"Will you let me get you a ring?"

"If you want me to, little one. But I might already have rings in the works for the rest of us."

"Really?"

"Mhmm." Gabe's hum transformed into a rumbling purr. "They're taking a bit longer than the time we had for this."

"Makes sense."

His scent wrapped around me, gorgeous, sensual vanilla and the deeper, richer scent of the tobacco. "I need your suits," I said.

"Our suits?"

The champagne was hitting a little harder now. "Yeah. All of them. Need them in the nest."

Gabriel froze before he smiled. "Okay, little one. You can have my suit."

"Good."

"If you're thinking about your nest, are you all right? Do you want to leave?"

I was tired and wanted to curl up with my Alphas, but it was also so *pretty*. "Not yet. Soon."

"Then I want you to meet someone."

Gabe didn't stop me from snagging another glass of champagne, but he did lean down to whisper. "That's the last one."

"Why?"

Fingers curled around my waist, stroking heat through the thin silk of my dress. "Because I don't want you to have a headache in the morning that ruins all of this."

"Fair." I took a sip.

"Sloane, this is my brother Robert."

I blinked up at a man who looked nothing like Gabriel. Clearly older than him, but when he smiled at me, I saw the similarities, few as they were. "Oh, it's nice to meet you. I didn't know you'd be here."

"Neither did I." He shook my hand briefly. "But I'm glad to see my brother finally settling down. Not sure he deserves you." The smile on his face told me he was joking.

I burrowed beneath Gabriel's arm further. "He does."

"And I'll keep it that way."

The photographer approached us. "Can I get some photos of the five of you?"

"Of course!" I forgot all about that. And I wanted to *remember* this. She arranged us how she wanted near where the ceremony had taken place, and I lost myself in them touching me. Them kissing me as she took pictures. My entire mind was buried in the strength of their bonds, and by the time she declared us finished, I was finished too.

Everything was gorgeous like I was in a fairy wonderland, but I wanted to be home with them. "I'm ready," I told them.

"All right, little one," Gabriel said. "I think they'll want to send us off."

They did. The party followed us through the grand salon out to the car, where Ash swept me off my feet and carried through a tunnel of sparklers Addison provided. Tears filled my eyes. I needed to send her the biggest gift ever for doing all of this.

All our friends cheered for us, but I was focused on them. I pressed my face into Asher's shirt, inhaling warm baked cookies. "You smell so good."

"Right back at you, sweetheart."

"I need your suits."

We slid into the car, and Gabe looked around from the driver's seat. "You'll get them, little one, as soon as we get home."

"Okay."

My head swirled pleasantly, absorbing the heady combination of Alpha in the car. They were mine. They were *mine*.

It pulsed in my mind like a heartbeat.

Mine. Mine. Mine.

I didn't even notice the drive until Ash was carrying me inside and into the nest. *Yes*. The soft, warm lights and the softness of the cushions were perfect. Roman pulled off my shoes, and Jace was within reach, so I tugged on his jacket. "Off."

"You want this?"

"I want all of it," I said, struggling to my feet. "Help me." Their suits I wanted in the nest. My dress I wanted to keep safe.

Gabriel unzipped me and helped me out of the dress. I didn't bother to peel away the bodice and panties, grabbing Jace's suit jacket and diving straight in. I placed it along the edge, tucked in between some cushions and blankets. But his vest didn't go there. It went on the other side. Asher's jacket was next, and it went on the inside corner.

I couldn't describe how I knew, but I did, and they kept passing me pieces of their clothing until they were naked and there was nothing left. Looking around, my chest settled. This would do. For now.

"You finished, baby girl?"

"Yes." I settled in the center, happy.

"May we come in?"

I nodded and curled up on my side. Now that the nest was good, I was even more tired. But happy too. Jace stretched out behind me, peppering kisses over my arms and shoulders before becoming the big soon. The rest of them were with us. I felt it. Heard their purrs. Listened to their contentment.

"Love you," I murmured, words slurring a little with tipsy exhaustion, and I was asleep before they said it back.

CHAPTER FORTY-SIX

JACE

*T*he water in my bathroom still ran, Sloane humming as she took her time. I smiled to myself, having made good on my promise to take her in my shower, and grateful we opted for the water heater which never ran out when we updated this house. It meant I could savor my Omega as long as I wanted.

Sitting down at my desk in a towel, I opened some emails while I waited for Sloane. We were headed to the theater today for some preliminary things before rehearsals fully started again.

One of the emails was the press release of our bonding.

Slate City Ballet congratulates the Lys Pack and Sloane Glass on their bonding.

I smiled when I saw our pack name, and I doubted there would be a time when I didn't. The four of us met on a small production, shortly after Ash and Roman graduated. Roman was on the scenic team, brought in by Ash, and Gabriel was trying his hand as an executive director. We all learned pretty quickly that obscure ballets from over a century ago weren't the way to the heart of an audience.

But we knew instantly we were pack, and we took the name Lys from the ballet *Le Lys*. Or *Lilies*. A beautiful little show that brought us together, and that was about it. I looked back at the release.

SCB is overjoyed to announce the bonding of principal dancer Sloane Glass with the Lys Pack, which includes SCB's new executive director, Gabriel Black, principal dancer Asher West, physiotherapist Jace McKenna, and renowned sculptor Roman Hughes. The scent-sympathetic pack encountered each other at the beginning of the season and never looked back. On behalf of the Slate City Ballet, congratulations to all of you, and good luck!

Several pictures from the ceremony were posted. The moment Gabriel bit Sloane, her face dreamy with happiness. She and I on the dance floor, wrapped up in each other. One of the photos of the five of us together, and Asher carrying her through the tunnel of sparklers. It was a good release, and all of our emails and messages were full of congratulations from friends and people we barely knew.

I even got a lukewarm congratulations email from Ian, which was confirmed by the others saying they got it as well. Fun.

The last couple of days had been lovely and lazy, most of it spent in the nest with our girl, with breaks to play with Mango and to surface for food. But reality was coming back in, and I didn't mind it. Reality meant we were settling into a life with each other, and that made me happier than I could verbalize.

Ash knocked on the door, his phone held up. "You decent enough to say hello to Will?"

"Sure."

He walked over to the desk and held the phone in front of me. Will grinned and waved, "Hey, Jace."

"How are you doing?"

"I'm good. Hoping to see all of you in person."

"Really?"

Ash nodded. "He wants to come down for a couple of days. I just want to make sure Sloane is okay with it."

Sloane knew Will too, from their school days, so I doubted she'd mind.

Will and Ash grew up together, with similar environments. One of their teachers put them in the dance classes she taught purely to keep them away from home longer and out of trouble. It stuck.

I didn't think she imagined her act of kindness resulting in two professional ballet dancers, but it was proof that a simple decision could echo a thousand times.

"It'll be good to see you," I said. "Are you going to go to class while you're here?"

"Might as well," he said. "I want to see what Ash has been telling me about Ian. Cause it's hard for me to believe."

I made a face, and they both laughed. "Yeah," Ash said. "Will worked with Ian a few years ago at the Jupiter Ballet."

It was a traveling company, well known for their over the top productions. "You like him?" I tried to keep the question as neutral as I could, but given what I'd seen, especially during the week of rehearsals with Sloane, Ian would have to do a lot of work to change my opinion.

Will shrugged. "I mean, he was really generous with us. He came on late, and we had to rush the production—"

"Sounds familiar," I muttered.

"But we couldn't get it together the way you guys did. We ended up asking for him to push it back, and he did. Despite the company losing money on tickets and marketing. He pushed it back and gave us the attention we needed to make the show great. Still shorter than normal, but we did it. He was there for a few years, and I had no complaints."

I glanced at Ash, and he shook his head. He couldn't believe it either. "I will say that when I worked with him he wasn't like this, but I figured it was because I wasn't a principal and didn't interact with him as much."

The water in the bathroom shut off, and Sloane came out, a towel wrapped under her shoulders, damp hair dripping water on her skin. Her scent was that much sweeter fresh from the shower —and being freshly fucked. I couldn't get enough of her.

"Okay," Ash said, moving the phone so Will could see none of her. "You're not looking over there."

"Who's that?"

"Will."

She smiled and slipped beneath Asher's arms to look in the camera before he could stop her. "Hey, Will."

He laughed. "Hey, Sloane. Good to see you, but maybe duck out of frame before Asher murders me through the phone because you're in a towel."

She blinked, looking at Ash's expression in the camera. He was tense, and holding himself back. Ducking back out of frame, she grabbed his hand. "Don't go too Alpha on me."

Ash relaxed and gripped her hand more firmly. "As I recall, you like it when I go *very* Alpha on you."

"And you saying that isn't worse than Will seeing my shoulders?" She looked pointedly at Ash.

From the phone I heard a choking sound that was Will covering a laugh. "He's making sure I know you're his. Don't worry. I know."

Covering the camera, Ash kissed her quickly. "Love you."

"I know," she smirked. "I love you too."

"Anyway. Will wants to come down for a couple days."

Sloane started to dress—well away from Asher's phone—and looked back. "That would be fun. When will you get here?"

"Well, that's the thing," Will said. "I think I can be there tonight."

"But?"

"But," Ash said. "He thought it might be fun if I rode out there to meet him and ride back together."

Now Sloane had on a leotard and a sweater, so she ducked back into the camera frame. "You're coming on your bike?"

"Yes, ma'am."

"What do you think?" Ash slung his arm around her shoulders, holding her to his chest.

She smiled, and I loved feeling the happiness both of them had right now. Would still be awhile before I was used to it. "Why are you asking me?"

"Because I'll be gone for the whole day," Ash said. "And it's still your honeymoon time."

Sloane turned to him. "You don't have to ask permission to see your friends, Ash. *Our* friends. It'll be good to see you again, Will."

"You too," he said. "Ash has been very cagey with the story. I look forward to hearing it in person."

"See?" Sloane said, looking up at Ash. "You don't need permission to go somewhere."

"Just making sure you won't miss my cock too badly," he whispered.

"Oh my god, you're so much worse than I am. Yeah, get the hell out of here if Gabe said you can skip today."

"Hear that, Will? I'm on my way."

A chuckle. "See you when you get here, loser."

Ash ended the call before they said anything else, sweeping Sloane in for a deeper kiss. "Sorry, sorry."

"You better be," she grumbled while still smiling. "But really, go. The sooner you go, the sooner you can be back."

He kissed her one more time. "Have fun today."

"We'll try," I called after him.

"Gonna go take care of Mango," Sloane touched my shoulder. "I'll meet you downstairs."

We still had some time. "There's a smoothie in the fridge for you."

"Thank you."

I smiled to myself as she left the room. Her thanking me didn't mean she would drink it. I'd have to make sure. But at the moment, I was still stuck on what Will said about Ian. The disparity between his behavior here and elsewhere seemed strange. So I did what anyone could do: I looked him up.

He'd worked with plenty of companies, sometimes for residencies, sometimes for a few years. It wasn't uncommon. Some creative directors didn't like to stay anywhere long term so they could work with more people. Or maybe there was a different reason. Maybe he didn't stay because he couldn't.

I made a note to look into it further, because it was a mystery that didn't make sense. But we didn't have time for me to fully dive in. Later, when we got home, I would. There were some people I could call who'd worked with him before.

Dressing quickly, I went downstairs and looked in the refrigerator, seeing the smoothie exactly where I left it. Sloane sat at the kitchen table putting on her shoes. She glared at me when I set it down on the table. "I'm okay."

"You will be."

"Jace."

"Drink at least half of it, baby girl. We've been fucking you so much I've barely been able to feed you."

She sighed. "Fine." But as Gabriel came down and grabbed the keys to the car, I saw her smile.

CHAPTER FORTY-SEVEN

SLOANE

Everyone knew.

I'd invited the whole company to the ceremony, knowing many of them wouldn't be able to make it on such short notice. But now even the people who I hadn't invited knew. Jerry congratulated me on my way in with Jace. Gabriel took the car around the back of the theater.

Madame Hubert was already in the studio for company class, and she caught my hand. "I'm sorry I could not come to your party, but you looked beautiful, dear."

"Thank you, Madame."

She leaned in to speak lower. "I hope to see that happiness on your face more often now."

"What do you mean?"

"I've trained many dancers, and the best always have something that drives their movement. Yours has always been sadness. You hide it well, but I hope it will be happiness from now on." She patted my shoulder. "You've never been better than when you have been happy these past few weeks."

"Thank you."

Tapping her cane against my thigh, she gave me a look. "That doesn't mean I will go easy on you."

"Wouldn't dream of it, Madame."

Everyone wanted to see the ring, and those who hadn't made it or hadn't had a chance to see me at the party wanted to say hello. Class started a bit late, with a twinkle in Madame Hubert's eyes. She pushed us extra hard for the delay, but it was worth it.

Afterwards, Ian stepped into the room. "Welcome back. I'm eager to start rehearsals after our... break."

There were looks around the room at the bitterness in his tone. "I commend you for handling the compressed schedule so well, and I look forward to the last few weekends of *Giselle*."

353

Asher, myself, Dion, and Claire would be performing again in two weeks. The final weekend of the show. I didn't look forward to those pickup rehearsals, but at least we could leave that show behind. It was a ballet I loved, but now I couldn't look at it the same way.

"Here are the cohorts for *Swan Lake*. We'll start with the large group scenes to get things rolling, so we'll need everyone initially, and then we'll narrow as we go on."

Reading off his phone, he read off the cohorts. Everyone clapped when I was read as the Swan Queen, and Ash was my Prince Siegfried. The look on Ian's face told me he did it more to avoid Asher's wrath than anything else, but I wasn't going to complain.

This time Claire was also the Swan Queen, so she was in a different cohort. Dion was Prince Siegfried to our friend Skylar.

"There's a list on the bulletin board for who the costume shop needs to see. Dismissed."

He left without fanfare, and Dion made a face. "Bye."

"Dion," I managed, but I barely managed to suppress my laughter.

"I don't give a shit, Sloane. The man is an asshole, and I'm not a fan. I'll work with him because I don't have a choice, and be civil in rehearsal, but respect is earned, and he's already lost all of mine."

"Fair enough." It was the same for me, but I needed to keep myself a little more neutral. At least publicly. Being a part of Pack Lys now meant I needed to be conscious of it.

My name was on the list for a fitting, but Dion's wasn't. "I'll see you later, babe. The guys are taking me out for dinner and I need time to prepare."

"Prepare?" I laughed. "How?"

"It takes time for all this beauty," he said. "That, and making sure I'm ready to be absolutely railed. They've been busy, it's been too long, and I need my ass knotted like... yesterday."

Male Omegas had a knot that female Alphas could lock to. But like every Omega, we were stretchy. Dion had no problems taking his Alphas exactly where he wanted them, knots and all.

"Have fun."

"You too, Lolo."

The costume fitting was just a check on the measurements they already had for me. Since this was a full production and not a re-up like Giselle, there would be new costumes to match whatever vision Ian was bringing to the project. I was curious about it, regardless of how I felt about him.

Anna, one of the admin assistants, stuck her head into the costume shop. "Sloane, Mr. Black wants to see you in his office when you're done."

"Thank you."

The seamstress, Beatrice, chuckled. "If that's what you call it now."

"God," I shook my head. "Even if we don't do anything, you guys are going to think about it every time I go to his office, aren't you?"

"Absolutely, yes." She spoke with a mouthful of pins. "So you might as well lean into it."

"I'm still a professional, Beatrice," I laughed.

"Be a professional, girl. But his office isn't a studio, and if he weren't so thoroughly taken, I wager to say plenty of the people in this building would jump through fire for a chance to be unprofessional with him."

The immediate flash of jealousy was treated with interest by my Alphas in the building. Ash and Roman felt farther away. Still there, but a touch muted. But Gabriel's attention sharpened. Deepened.

Still, the jealousy quickly faded. I had nothing to worry about in that department, and Beatrice wasn't wrong. Gabriel was hot as fuck, and even the business casual clothes he wore couldn't hide it.

"I'll keep it in mind," I finally told her as she took out the pins.

"Good. Now go have fun."

I rolled my eyes, but as soon as I was out of sight, I practically sprinted up to Gabe's office. He sat at his desk, looking up in amusement when I shut the door behind me and leaned against it. "Are you hiding from the law?"

"No, I'm hiding from the rest of the company."

"Are they waiting outside?"

I laughed. "Anna told me you wanted to see me while I was in the costume shop. Everyone will know I'm here soon, and yes, they absolutely are going to think we're having sex, even if we don't."

Gabriel smirked, sitting back in his chair. "Well, we wouldn't want to disappoint them."

I gasped. "Is that why you wanted me up here?"

"I always want you, little one. It wasn't the reason I called you, but we'll see how it goes."

"Why did you call?"

"Besides wanting to see my Omega?" He tapped the desk in front of him. Dropping my bag on the floor, I went, perching there. Something about his posture told me it wasn't about wanting to see me. He looked... tight. In my chest he felt like it too.

"Yeah, besides that."

Gabe sighed, sliding his chair in so he could wrap his arms around me and press his face into my stomach.

"I need to talk to you about Craig."

I stiffened—couldn't help it. "Please don't tell me he did something else."

"Nothing new. It's about what he's already done. Harrison found out quite a bit."

With his arms firmly around me, he outlined the truth of Craig's desire for me. How they theorized it was why he approached me in the first place. I felt sick.

"So," Gabe said, "when you left, it was one blow too many. And the hits kept coming. You wounded his ego, he lost what he hoped was the salvation of his career, had to shut down his business, and then showed up at your apartment and found Ash.

"In his head, you're the only thing he has left. And maybe, if he still has you, he can fix things."

It certainly explained the behavior, and it was a relief to know, but it didn't make me feel better. If anything, it made me feel worse about the whole thing. Not one piece of it had been genuine, and even now, he thought of me as something to be claimed and owned rather than cherished and loved.

356

I swallowed down the nausea. "Clearly... he had to have thought all those things he said before. I know he snapped, but you don't snap into brand new thoughts. All that stuff was already in there."

"You're right," Gabriel said. "This is who he is."

It hurt more than I thought to know someone you once trusted never even saw you as a person.

"I still don't understand how I didn't see it. Was I that desperately lonely? And I walked right back to him, opening up the door for all of it."

"Sloane," my name was a command on Gabriel's lips, along with the strength of him now through our bond. "Look at me."

Tilting my head downward, I met his gaze.

"Not your fault, remember?"

Of course I remembered. But I wasn't blameless. You could say it wasn't my fault forever, but I was responsible for some pieces. If I'd just gone to the fucking concert, maybe I could have let him down gently. And then...

I sighed. And then he would have tried to keep me regardless to get Grandma's money. He would have done this either way. Even last year, if he hadn't gotten what he needed, he would have turned into this monster. Only last year, they wouldn't have been there to help me.

Guilt spiraled through me. This had been bad, but it could have been so much worse because I let my own loneliness and needs get the better of me.

"I think my Omega needs a distraction," Gabriel murmured. "Both a distraction and a reminder."

"A reminder?"

He stood between my legs, forcing me to look up at him. "You still want me to pull you out of your own head, little one? If not, tell me now. Otherwise, I'm going to lock the door and make good on a promise that's been too long in coming."

Closing my eyes, I took a breath and listened. Gabriel's emotions didn't push me one way or the other. He was carefully waiting for me to choose. But I also felt the significance of the choice.

This wasn't about Gabriel spanking me, whether it was a real punishment or a playful one. It was about trust. Even now, bonded, mated, it wasn't my first thought to rely on anyone else. Years of building up those walls made it hard to let them go.

Something in me rebelled at the idea of reliance on anyone. Especially like this. Giving him power and control and letting him command something of me. But I did it gladly in the bedroom, and before, those moments in the kitchen where he overrode my guilt and my panic, it felt right.

More than that, what I knew of my friends' relationships with their packs told me I was not alone in needing the safety of the dominance Alphas could provide. It was who we were, and fighting it only hurt us more.

Finally, no matter what, I knew that none of my men would ever take more than I wanted to give. Which, in turn, made me want to give them everything.

Gabe smiled before I answered, feeling my resolve, and in him, I felt relief. That he could help me—that I trusted him to do this.

I would always trust him.

I was still working on trusting myself.

"Yes, please."

He stepped away quickly and flipped the lock on the door. The sudden flood of power from our bond, the strengthening of his scent, and the hand on the back of my neck when he returned had me squirming and dampening the fabric of my tights.

"Should I bend you over the desk? Or take you over my knee?" He wasn't asking me, but I gave him an unspoken answer.

The low laugh skittered over my skin, and suddenly my nipples were visible through my leotard. Gabriel grabbed a chair from the other side of his desk—one that didn't have any arms—and sat down.

"Come here."

I slipped off the desk and obeyed, standing in front of him. My hair stood on end as he focused on me. Those green eyes filled with all the power I craved when I begged him to let go the first time. He wasn't holding back.

"Take your clothes off."

A small smile crossed my lips, and I sank into his lap instead, feeling how hard he was and grinding down on him. Already, my mind was clearing, feeling better. Because the game was me and him, and he had permission to put me in my place. Underneath him. Exactly where I wanted to be. "Make me."

Gabriel gripped my hair, tilting my head back. "Found your sass, did you?"

"Maybe."

A kiss against my throat. "You've racked up quite a debt, little one, and I'm content to make this last. Sure you want to push?"

My only answer was to rock my hips against his cock again, earning me a low growl. "Take your fucking clothes off, or they're getting ripped. You choose."

I didn't have to. Need streaked through me so hot and bright he didn't need the words before he released my hair, reached down, and tore the fabric of my leotard open like it was nothing.

The tights followed.

I was bare to him, already panting.

Leotards weren't thin or weak with what we put them through. And he made it feel like paper. I whined, my Omega reacting to her Alpha. Gabe's fingers touched me through the rip, stroking around my clit. I shuddered, leaning into it, and he pulled away.

"I'm going to make you feel good, little one. But it won't at first. Because I need you to remember what this is for."

"What's it for?"

"To remind you that other people's actions aren't your fault, and you're not allowed to apologize for them. To remember your own value and stop questioning it." He smirked. "A little for your sass and bratty tendencies too, but mostly the first ones."

"So if I keep being bratty you'll do this again?"

"I haven't started yet and you already want to add more?" He grabbed my hair again, pulling my face close to his. "You're brilliant. Kind. Beautiful. Talented. Like hell am I going to let you forget it. I'll spank it into you every day if I need to, and fucking enjoy it."

The temperature in the room had to have risen ten degrees,

because I was sweating and very sure I would enjoy it too. My mind didn't want to face what he was saying, because it was easier not to. But he didn't let me look away—not from him and not from myself.

"Can I trust you to understand the lesson? Or do I need you to speak it every time I redden your perfect ass?"

"*Fuck*." I rocked my hips again, and he held me still so I couldn't get the friction I desperately needed. "I got it."

"You sure?"

"*Yes,*" I said. "Promise."

"Mmm." He dragged his mouth up to his bite mark and kissed me there, setting what was little left of me ablaze. "Know that if it's not true, we'll have to do this all over again with you saying it every time. It will be much slower and probably hurt more."

That shouldn't have made me want it, but it did.

Gabe lifted me off his lap, turning me to lie over his knees. Cool air shifted over my skin as he ripped my tights further, exposing my ass completely. It tickled the wetness between my thighs too, but Gabriel ignored my arousal.

One stroke of his hands across my skin, savoring it. I shuddered, arching into the touch. "I think my Omega *is* eager for this," he said. "Even if it's discipline."

"Yes, Alpha."

"Would you like me to tell you how many?"

I clenched my thighs, and it wasn't even close to enough. Did I want to know? Waiting for it to be over? I shook my head before I spoke. "No."

What I needed was to sink into it and know that it was over when he decided, no matter the debt I'd racked up. I needed to trust him and take what he gave me.

"All right." Another stroke of his hand. "I love you, little one. Remember that."

The first hit of his hand stung, morphing into a burning pain that eased into heat. It wasn't too bad, and I thought it would be easy.

What a mistake.

Gabriel spanked me, every fall of his hand adding more pain

and more heat. One hand on my back held me in place when I tried to jerk away, but as much as it hurt, I needed it. We both did. The pure satisfaction pouring through Gabriel's bond was enough to turn the heat into something else entirely.

But every slap reached down inside me and grabbed a little of the pain and guilt, pulling it to the surface. My eyes burned along with my ass, emotions rising that I couldn't fully control.

"It's okay, Sloane," Gabe said. "I've got you."

The words allowed me to give in and sob. Just like I had in his bed that night. How many times would I have to purge this for it to stay gone? It was like a poison that crept back into my mind. Subtle. Sneaky. Insidious. I didn't want the feelings I had about it. I wanted them *gone*.

So I cried, making an absolute fucking mess out of myself.

I had no idea how many times he spanked me. It felt both eternal and faster than light when he finally stopped, smoothing his hand over my burning skin. Slowly, he turned me upright, carrying me back to perch on the edge of his desk. The feeling of it made me hiss.

"You'll feel it for a few days. Hopefully it will help make the lesson stick."

"Yeah."

Gabe got some tissues and cleaned my face, kissing my forehead through my sniffles. "Feel better?"

"Yes," I admitted. I felt lighter and clearer. *Way* more solid.

"Good. But before I make you feel even better, we're not done."

A whine escaped. "We're not?"

"Nope. Because you owe me five on your clit."

Shit. I'd forgotten about that entirely. Despite my emotional outburst, I was so fucking turned on, I was pretty sure Gabriel breathing on my clit would send me over. But spanking it?

"Spread your legs, little one."

I obeyed, not looking away from him. He dragged a knuckle through my slick slowly. "You can always stop, Sloane."

"I know."

Gabe raised his eyebrows, and I felt the question, and no. I didn't want to stop.

Pushing my thighs wider with one hand, he focused on my clit. "Close your eyes."

For whatever reason, it was the hardest command he'd given. I bit my lip and obeyed, the anticipation of this making it so much better and so much worse.

The sound of his fingers stinging my clit reached me before the pain bloomed like a delicious fire. My eyes flew open, and I reached for him. "Keep your eyes closed."

"Gabe—"

"*Now.*"

They fell closed with the next drop of his hand, my moan getting caught in my throat. I dropped my head to his shoulder. "Gabe."

Number three hurt. His fingers lingered there, teasing me through the pain and transforming it into need. Riding the line between the two sensations.

Number four had me throwing my head back, and number five came immediately after, blowing pleasure through my brain. Gabriel kissed me just in time to capture the scream that left my lips from the nearly violent orgasm.

"Good girl, little one. You did so fucking good."

Gabriel dropped to his knees and covered me with his mouth, soothing my clit with his tongue and drawing the pleasure out. It was so swollen and hot, I could come again. He would make me come again, I was sure.

Standing, he pulled me off the desk and flipped me around. I barely heard the sound of his belt before he pushed inside me in one thrust. "Guess I'm bending you over the desk too."

My words were gone. Only moans. The rest of my Alphas were fucking jealous of the pleasure at the same time they loved feeling me come.

Each time he drove in, his hips brushed the bruised heat of my ass, giving me just enough of that pain to drive me wild. This wasn't going to last long. This was hard and fast and dirty, and in that moment I decided I didn't care if the whole company thought we were fucking every time I came in here, as long as he fucked me like this.

The second orgasm swept over me in a smooth wave. I was no

longer Sloane, I was just a melty Omega, fucked by her Alpha the way she was meant to be.

On Gabriel's desk, his phone chirped. "Mr. Black?"

He didn't miss a beat, thrusting into me so hard my hips were trapped against the desk. "Yes?"

"Mr. Montmay is on the line. He has a question about this week's board meeting."

"Can he wait?"

"He was... very insistent."

Gabriel sighed, the only sign he was the least bit bothered. "Fine, put him through."

The line went momentarily dead. "Gabri—" His hand slapped over my mouth.

His voice was only Alpha growl. "*Quiet,* my filthy little fuck-toy. Don't make a sound."

"Gabriel?" A masculine voice came over the line, and Gabe fucked me *harder.* Like just hearing another man's voice made him feral enough to claim me.

"Hello, Gavin. My secretary said it was urgent. What can I do for you?"

I was on the verge of another orgasm, and if that happened there was no way I could keep quiet. This was a big one, driven by Gabriel's cock hitting me deep, hard, and with the exact same rhythm until my body said *fuck yes.*

"I wondered if you could send me the projection for this year's earnings compared to the last few seasons. There are some expenses that concern me and I want to be prepared for the meeting this week."

"Of course," Gabriel said, calm and easy. "I'm about to step into a meeting, but I'll send them as soon as I'm finished."

"Oh, my apologies. And thank you. I'll see you at the meeting."

"You will."

One stab of Gabe's finger ended the call before he pinned me down, driving into me, rutting so deeply I came, gushing over his cock and yelling into his hand. "*Fuck,*" his voice echoed off the windows.

He came a second later, pulling back just far enough to keep his knot out of me. Which I understood. Fucking in here was one thing. Being knotted was another. Still, his orgasm felt endless, cum overflowing.

His forehead rested against the back of my neck. "Good job, little one. You were so quiet they didn't know I was filling this pretty cunt up with my cock. Did you like knowing they could catch you?"

"Yes." I loved it.

Easing back, he released me, his cum spilling out of me. "You made quite a mess of my cock."

"Did I?" Pushing up, I turned to face him.

"Make sure you clean up your mess."

How in the goddamn world did a few simple words turn me into a flushed, panting mess? I didn't know. But they did. I sank to my knees and opened my mouth, savoring the flavor of Gabriel's vanilla on my tongue. The tobacco lurked beneath, rich and sweet, mixed with my own blueberries. Even not fully hard, he filled my mouth, nearly pressing his knot in. I could tell he wanted to.

When he was clean, I pulled away and licked my lips.

Gabe cupped my face, tilting my chin up. "God, I love you."

"I love you," I told him. There was no doubt. Both of us felt perfect and settled. Harmonized.

He chuckled. "I should have asked if you had any extra clothes before I ripped yours."

"I do." My bag was on the floor where I left it. Good thing I had some shorts. They covered the ripped and stained tights and leotard and would last until I got home.

"I wish I could leave right now," Gabriel said. "I didn't lie. I am supposed to have a meeting in a few minutes."

"With who?"

A knock on the door.

Gabe nodded. I flipped the lock and opened the door, coming face to face with Ian. His gaze flew off me and over to Gabriel before he *inhaled*.

The office smelled like the two of us and sex. We were both perfectly dressed, but there was no way he didn't know. Something in me wanted to smile, but I held it back.

"Am I interrupting?" He finally asked, disdain in his eyes.

"Not at all. Come in, Ian." He gestured to the remaining chair across from him. Then my Alpha looked at me and winked. "I'll see you at home, little one."

I went to find Jace, feeling like I walked on clouds.

CHAPTER FORTY-EIGHT

SLOANE

I was the coziest Omega in existence.

Showered and relaxed from the crying and orgasms, I was dressed comfortably—I fucking loved big sweaters in the fall—curled up in my hanging swing with Mango in my lap, just dozing. The little kitten purred even with his eyes closed. He was so fucking cute I couldn't stand it.

"I bet you just jumped on Roman when he came to pick you out, huh?" Lifting Mango up to my chest, I settled the little furball there, snuggling down.

"He did jump on me," Roman said, peeking in the door. "Jumped on me and wouldn't leave me alone. Guess he knew he'd love it here."

"Hi."

Roman sat down in front of my swing, catching it gently so he controlled the rocking. His bond felt steady and content. Peaceful. "Hey, firefly."

"Where have you been?"

"Sculpting."

"The one of me?"

He nodded.

"How is it?"

"Not far along yet. It still looks like a lumpy bit of rock. But it's going okay. Gabriel just got home, by the way."

My Alpha did feel closer, and I felt his happiness at the sudden attention.

I reached out my hand and caught Roman's. "Good."

"Sleepy?"

"Not really, but I am very comfortable."

"Looks like he is too."

"Yeah."

Outside, it was getting dark. Glancing at the clock, I realized

367

it was past the time I expected Ash to be back with Will. Nothing felt wrong. Ash still just felt distant.

Picking Mango up, I handed him—limp, sleepy body and all —over to Roman as I climbed out of the swing and grabbed my phone from where I'd left it.

I called Ash, waiting for the ring. His voice sounded resonant through the helmet. "Hi, sweetheart. Everything okay?"

"Just checking in. I thought you'd be back by now. Where are you?"

"We did something in Concordia, and it took a little longer than we thought. But we're getting there. Just about to come over that big hill outside the city."

There weren't real mountains anywhere near Slate City, but there were hills big enough to feel that way. The one Ash talked about was one that drew hundreds of families every winter as a favorite sledding spot.

You crested the hill, and the whole city was laid out in front of you like a glittering paradise. If you caught it at the last rays of sunset, like Ash was right now, the view was breathtaking.

"Okay. Just wanted to make sure. I miss you."

"I haven't been gone very long."

Leaning against my bed, I looked at Roman and smiled. "Does that mean I can't miss you?"

"No," Ash said with a laugh. "I miss you too."

"Good."

A pause, and I heard the faint sound of wind and engines on the road. "All right, I'll see you soon, swee—*shit. I—*"

Screeching and crashing echoed in my ear before the line went dead. "Ash? *ASH?*"

Pain and fear flared in the piece of myself that only belonged to him. Horror dropped over my gaze like a film.

"Firefly?"

"Something's wrong," I managed to get out, running out of the room and down the stairs, not even bothering with the elevator. My voice was at the top of my lungs, that pain and fear echoing through me like acid. "We need to go. We need to go *now*."

"Little one? What's going—"

I crashed into Gabriel in the kitchen, pushing past him to get to my shoes. "I was talking to Ash and I think he crashed. He was on the big hill outside the city. Can't you feel it? He hurts, he *hurts*. We need to go right the fuck now."

There was no other hesitation except for Roman picking me up on the way out the door. Jace joined us, tense silence raining as we piled into the car and broke every traffic law in existence.

Panic and pain clawed at my insides and I couldn't breathe. It was like inhaling razor blades that cut me open on the way down.

I didn't even realize I was crying until Jace took my face in his hands and brushed them away with his thumbs. He pressed our foreheads together. "It's going to be okay, Sloane."

But none of them knew that, and none of them felt like they believed it. Jace's bond was as bleak as all of ours, laced with bitter fear. The scents in the car were hard. Burnt butterscotch, scorched forest, and tobacco that smelled more like ash than the sweetness I was used to.

Ash didn't feel in pain anymore. It didn't feel like anything but dread. Was that what this felt like if—

My mind shut down even the possibility of *thinking* it.

"Please," I said, curling in on myself. "*Please.*"

"Almost there," Gabriel said tightly.

Every minute felt like a century until one low word. "Firefly."

I forced myself to look and see the flashing lights. Red and blue. So fucking vibrant in the dark they scarred my eyes. Please, please, please—

Gabriel pulled over on the side of the road next to the low stone wall that ran alongside it, just behind the ambulance and cop cars and nothing in the fucking world was stopping me. I shoved out of the car and ran.

"*Ash.*"

I stopped short, the world crashing down on me. A body lay on the side of the road, a sheet covering it. My own body went cold. "No."

This couldn't be happening. This couldn't be *real*. This couldn't—

Grief speared through me, shredding every piece of my soul, just as arms came around me from behind and turned me.

Pointing me straight to where Ash sat against the wall, still in his helmet, still in the clothes I'd seen him in this morning. Alive.

I sprinted, crashing to my knees beside him. Now that we were here, I knew why he felt like dread and nothingness. Because if he was alive, then that meant Will wasn't.

"Ash." I managed his name before it turned into a sob. His visor was open, but all he did was stare straight ahead. No words. No movement other than to pull me tight when I hugged him. So hard I couldn't breathe, and I didn't care. If it meant he was here, I would never fucking breathe again.

Every gulp of air was ragged with pain. With his, with mine, with all of us and what almost happened and what *did* happen.

I pulled Asher's helmet off, noting the scrapes on it. One glance told me his bike was on the ground. He'd fallen and skidded.

Holding his face in my hands, I made him look at me. And there was nothing there. Just a terrifying blankness. "I'm sorry," I whispered, my face and chest crumpling again. "I'm so sorry."

How did you do this? Tell someone you were so fucking sorry for what happened while at the same time being selfishly grateful it wasn't them. Through the depths of that blankness in our bond, I found the pain, buried so deep it felt like a dark echo. Waiting for its moment.

"I thought I lost you," I told him.

Ash didn't speak when I buried my face in his neck, but he held me. Clung to me just as desperately. It was the only sign my Alpha was still in there.

Gravel crunched, and a hand touched my shoulder. "Little one, we need to get Ash checked out."

I knew I needed to, but I couldn't let him go. My Omega wasn't ready, scared that releasing him would mean losing him all over again and I couldn't do that, even if it was only the feeling of it. I wasn't leaving him. Ever. No.

Gentle hands lifted under my arms, pulling me away. "Come on, baby girl."

"*No*," I struggled against it, but Jace held me fast, pinning me to his body.

"Sloane, listen to me, baby. It's me. It's Jace." His voice

sounded like I felt. Blasted and empty. "Ash is alive. He's alive, baby girl. The paramedics are going to check him and take him to the hospital. I'm not taking you away from him."

A sob broke out of me, all that pain and fear cracking through. Another warm body pressed against mine. Roman. Offering his strength and presence. When I looked up at him, there were tears in his eyes, too.

"If—" I swallowed. "If—"

"Don't even think about it," Jace said. "I can't either. But it didn't happen. He's safe. He's here. You're okay and he's okay. We're all okay."

"No we're not."

"No," he finally said, leaning his head against mine. "We're not."

One ambulance was gone and another arrived. Will's body must have gone with the first one. Thinking about him brought on a whole new wave of pain and tears. Will was a good person and was such a good friend to Ash...

And to me.

I should have kept in contact with him more. Should have been a better friend with so many people after I left.

Ash climbed into the ambulance, and Gabriel watched as they closed the doors. "Wait," I called. "Wait, he can't go. *Please*."

Gabriel was with us in seconds. "We're going to follow him, little one. We're going right where he is. I just have to give the details about where to take Asher's bike, but they're going to take you to the car."

"We can't leave him." My thoughts weren't rational, and I couldn't stop them. "If we can't see him, then—"

"I know," Gabe said, crushing me to him. "I know. I'm sorry, little one. We're going to be right behind him. I promise." The break in his voice wasn't imagined.

Roman scooped me up again, laying me across the back seat so my head could rest in his lap. I turned into him, letting him stroke my hair as we drove. Nothing felt right. Everything felt wrong. I needed closeness and darkness and warmth. I needed my Alpha. The world was too big and too dangerous, and I couldn't handle it. I couldn't feel that again.

You could never go back from understanding this kind of fear.

Roman purred the whole drive, and Jace occasionally reached back to touch me. But our bonds told me the truth. They were in just as much pain as I was. The reality of it was too close and too harsh.

And this would happen.

Not today, and not like this, but it would happen. Eventually. Not for a very long time, I hoped. But all of us would suffer pain unlike anything else when it did. My only relief was that it wasn't *now*.

I walked into the hospital on my own two feet, but they still touched me to keep me steady. A doctor stood outside the room where they'd put Ash, talking to a man. "You'll have to get it later, detective," the doctor said. "He's not speaking."

Gabriel stepped around us. "Can I help you, detective? We're his pack."

The cop looked us over, noting my tears and the general gray pall we all had. "We're not sure what happened, and I'd like to talk to your packmate to see what he remembers and if he can help us find who it was. They didn't stick around." He didn't have to clarify how he felt about that.

"Here," Gabe said, pulling out his wallet and giving his card to the detective. "If you'll put your number on the back of that, we'll call you as soon as he's ready to talk to you."

The man nodded and scribbled his number down. "The sooner the better," he added quietly. "Whether whoever hit the other driver was drunk or asleep at the wheel, we don't want them driving around."

"Of course."

Ash sat on the end of the hospital bed, still staring into the middle distance, seemingly unresponsive. He obeyed the doctors when they told him to move, but nothing more. I wanted to touch him, but being near him was enough. For now.

I sat in the chair by the door, knees pulled up to my chest, watching him and trying not to give in to the instinct to wrap myself around him like armor so I could protect him and never let him go.

The doctor stepped outside, and the others went with him. I stayed where I was, but could hear.

"He got lucky," the doctor told them. "Mild concussion, but that's common with accidents like these, even with a helmet. Some abrasions where he hit the ground. He'll be sore for a while, but all things considered?"

That question hung in the air. Stabbed me in the gut. All things considered, Ash was alive and healthy.

And Will was dead.

"Can we take him home?" Jace asked.

"Yes. We'll get started on that paperwork. Keep an eye on him for the concussion, and if anything changes or he has any strange symptoms, bring him back."

The paperwork didn't take long.

Ash stood off the hospital bed stiffly. Clearly in pain, though he was okay. I felt it. The flashes of discomfort he felt like he deserved. Because he was the one still here.

Roman kept me on his lap because I needed the contact, but no one spoke. What could we say? The one person who needed to speak was Ash, and he wasn't ready.

When we got back, he said one word—"Shower."—before disappearing. I went to follow and Gabriel held me back. "Give him some time, little one. Let him breathe."

He pulled me into his arms and purred, trying to comfort me as best he could and keep me from hovering, but we both knew there was only so long I could last.

CHAPTER FORTY-NINE

SLOANE

I lasted all of twenty minutes before I squirmed out of Gabriel's arms, unable to keep still any longer. But I went to my room, telling myself I wanted to change before I went to check on Ash. Forcing myself into slow motion, I put on sweatpants and a camisole. Because if Ash let me comfort him, I wasn't leaving his side, even to change my clothes.

I was about to go find him when my door floated open. He stood there, looking lost, but also looking *at* me for the first time since it happened. His bond was still shockingly blank.

One step into the room, and then another.

"Ash?"

He wordlessly crowded me against the wall. The sweatpants he wore hung low on his hips, the rest of his bare skin still warm and damp from the shower.

Still, not a word.

Asher's lips brushed mine, only the briefest touch before he kissed me deeper than he ever had. And in that kiss was all the words he was missing. All the pain and all the grief. It came roaring to the surface in the bond between us, making us both shake.

A few seconds later, his hands caught up with us, wrapping around my whole body. Enveloping me. He lifted me, carrying me to the bed and laying me out. Following me down, still kissing me.

Everything in me wanted to ask questions. Was he all right? What happened? Was there anything else I could do?

But Ash didn't need my questions. Right now, Ash needed me to hold space for his pain. To be a place he didn't have to speak those things. He needed me, and I would give him every piece of myself.

It wasn't about sex or pleasure. It was about me being his Omega. A craving that went beyond mind, body, and reason. We barely noticed shoving our clothes off because it didn't matter. What mattered was that we kept touching each other. Contact every second.

When he entered me, he hissed like he was in pain. I wrapped my legs around his hips and held him. Arms curled around his head. Our faces so close we shared breath.

Wordless. Desperate. Raw.

The most basic form of connection.

Pleasure wasn't the point, but we found it anyway, shuddering and gasping, coming to stillness knotted together.

Ash breathed into my neck, not moving until he could pull away from me. He tried, and I didn't let him. "Ash."

His eyes flickered to mine, glassy with emotion.

"It's okay," I told him. "It's okay."

He knew I didn't mean what had happened. But for him to feel what he was feeling and let it out. He was safe with me.

One ragged sob broke through, and he dropped his face to my neck again, gathering me in his arms as he rolled us together, and cried.

I felt every bit of it through our bond, and it didn't frighten me. Somehow I managed to keep my eyes dry and simply hold my Alpha, feeling the beat of his heart. Right now I wished Omegas could purr so I could make him feel the way they did me. Cherished. Precious. Safe.

This was the broken boy I found in a dark studio all those years ago, shattered and grieving. Will was the one who *told me* to go find him that night, and now he was gone.

How close had they been in the five years we'd been separated? I had no idea. All I knew was that Will had been Asher's closest friend other than his pack. Other than me. And he just watched him die.

Ash gave me everything.

And when it finally subsided, he didn't move, still holding me.

"I'm so sorry, Ash."

One hand slipped into my hair, and he was kissing me again. "I love you, blue. I love you." His voice broke. "I just need to hold you, okay?"

376

I fought tears. "I was so scared. When we got there, I—" A single, choked breath. "I thought it was you."

All his guilt came crashing down between us, along with his own relief, which came with more guilt. "I know," he said. "I'm sorry. I couldn't move or think about anything, even to call you back and tell you I was fine."

The thought which had been lurking beneath the surface rose. "Was it because of me? Did I distract you?"

"No." His lips brushed my forehead. The way we wrapped around each other there was barely room, and still, he found that tiny space to kiss and comfort me. "No, it wasn't you, sweetheart."

"Can you tell me what happened?"

Asher's body shook, but he finally sighed. "Yes. But with the others. I already know I'm going to have to tell the police, and I don't know how many times I'll be able to say it."

Reaching into my chest, I pulled the others to us. Ash reluctantly pulled back enough to retrieve his sweatpants, and I put my clothes back on before he pulled me back to him, sitting me between his legs where he rested against the headboard. Still holding me.

Jace entered the room cautiously, a sleepy Mango draped over his arm. "You wanted us?"

"Yes."

He disappeared again, briefly, and Ash tucked his arms around me. Not before I saw something. I grabbed his left hand and lifted it, seeing a new tattoo there. A thin, black band around his fourth finger. Simple and stark, but I knew what it was.

"You tattooed a ring?"

"That was where we went," he said, turning his hand over. "We got tattoos. His took a little longer than mine." On the underside of his finger, along the thin black band, was my name in tiny, curling letters.

Fierce possessiveness electrified me. I loved seeing this on him, and knowing the world would look at it and see he was mine. "Thank you," I whispered. "I love it."

Knowing Ash, it would be easy for him to fall into the guilt and let it build. Think that him going and riding with Will had

377

been the reason it happened. Or that if they hadn't gotten tattoos everything would have been okay. But we had no way of knowing that, and I wasn't going to let him sink into it and regret a beautiful gift like this.

Ash curled himself around me, his mouth brushing his bite. The motion shivered through me. It wasn't meant to arouse me, though I couldn't help the longing the touch created. It was him clinging to what bound us together.

The others came in, Jace setting Mango on the bed. He woke up long enough to move over next to Ash and me, curling up against his leg like he knew we both needed it.

Gabriel stood near the door. He was stiff, eyes burning as he watched the two of us. Beneath everything, in his bond, was barely contained rage. At whoever had driven away after killing someone. And pain for all of it.

I grabbed Asher's hands and pulled them more tightly around me. "Okay."

"There's honestly..." he took a breath. "Not much to tell. The ride there was easy. We went, got tattoos, and started the drive. Everything was fine. Then you called, blue. It happened so fast.

"Headlights out of nowhere, coming straight at the two of us. I didn't have time to think. I just moved. Dumped the bike in the process and just went flying until I stopped. Will, he—" His hands tightened on my waist and I felt him swallow. "He hadn't been able to get out of the way in time. The car was there on the side of the road, his bike still stuck on the grill. And I didn't have to move to know it was already too late. He'd gone flying."

"Ash," I whispered.

"I went," he said. "I tried. Didn't even get my helmet off. He was already dead. By the time I looked up, the car was gone. I don't even know who called the police."

We were all silent for a moment.

Jace spoke quietly. "I know this is shit consolation, but he didn't suffer. If the car was going full speed, it would have been instant."

"Yeah."

It was shit consolation, but it was a small comfort.

"Will didn't have a pack, right?" Gabe asked.

"No," Ash shook his head. "But he has a partner. Jeremy. *Fuck*, he might not even know. I need to call him."

"The hospital may have done it already. Give me his number, I'll do it," Gabriel said.

"It's... okay. I need to. He was with me. It needs to come from me."

Slowly, I turned around to face him, still maintaining all the contact I could. "Are you sure?"

"Yeah. I should do it now."

"You need me with you?"

Ash moved Mango aside onto a pillow before doing the same with me. "No. I need to do this by myself. But I'll be back. I would..." I hated the hesitance in his voice. It didn't belong there. "I'd still like to hold you."

"I'll be waiting."

We watched him slip out of my room, and I laid down on the bed beside Mango. Burying my face in his fluffy belly.

"Are you okay, baby girl?"

"Better now. I'm just worried about him."

Roman leaned over the bed and held me briefly. "We'll give Ash space, but if you need us, we're all here."

"Thank you."

They left quietly, and I kept snuggling with Mango until Ash came back and shut the lights off. We curled up together under the blankets, as close as two people could be. And until we fell asleep, we savored the sound of the other breathing.

Alive.

CHAPTER FIFTY

SLOANE

*M*y texts were swarming in the morning. I'm not sure how the girls found out, but they had, and everyone wanted to make sure Ash was okay.

No one more than me.

He still curled around me from behind, and I dropped my phone before turning over in his arms. He was awake—I could feel it—but he didn't move.

"How do you feel?"

"Physically or mentally?"

I traced my finger over my symbol on his ribs. "Both."

"Physically, it feels like I got run over. Which I guess I kind of did. Nothing that's really damaged but, I've felt better."

"You're not coming to rehearsals for a few days, right?"

He nodded before rolling over me, pinning me to the bed. It reminded me of the first night he spent in my apartment, when I was the one in pain.

"No, I don't think so. Not just for the bruises, but because mentally I... can't face everyone."

"Are you okay with the company knowing?"

A shrug of his shoulders. "They're going to, one way or another. If they know right away maybe they'll be less horrified when they see me."

They wouldn't. No matter what, Ash's first day back at rehearsal wouldn't be easy. "Okay. I'm sorry I have to go."

"Don't be. You're the Swan Queen." He smiled faintly. "You have to be there for your subjects."

I pulled him down to kiss me. "How can I help you? Tell me, please."

"Just be you, sweetheart. I don't need anything else."

A whine slipped out of me. "Are you sure?"

"Yeah. It's going to take time. But I've been here before. I know I'll get through it."

Pulling him again, he let me pillow his head on my chest, breathing me in. "I love you."

"You're everything, blue."

We laid there until I had to leave. I didn't want to, but Ash got up with me and promised he wouldn't spend the whole time in bed. Still, it was hard to go to the car with Gabriel and Jace.

Class passed in a daze. Petra, Eva, and Esme had known, probably because of Harrison if Gabriel called him. Or because the security he'd hired had reported us tearing out of the garage like a bat out of hell.

But none of the company knew yet, and I didn't know how to make that announcement. Maybe Gabriel would, or maybe the news would filter out slowly. Ash was correct. Everyone would know eventually.

Claire put her arm around my shoulders on the way to the studio. "You okay?"

"Not really?"

"What's wrong?"

"I'm fine," I said. "I'll tell you later, okay?"

She looked at me, assessing, before releasing me. "Whenever you want."

"Thank you."

We were in the big studio today, with almost the entire company, to work on blocking out the crowd scenes like Ian had scheduled. "Think we'll have to do the *fouettés* today?" She asked.

"I hope not, but knowing Ian? Probably."

Swan Lake was a notoriously hard ballet for the role of the Swan Queen Odette. Especially during the period when you were playing the character's opposite. The Black Swan, Odile. The choreography famously had a sequence of thirty-two *fouettés*— whipping turns that were fast, difficult, and on pointe.

"Dion, can you do me a favor?" I asked quietly.

He bent over in a stretch. "Sure, Lolo. What's up?"

"Ash can't be here today. If he has us dance individual cohorts, can you step in?"

"Is he okay?"

"He needs a couple days." Not an answer to the question, but correct nonetheless.

"Sure," he said. "I can do that."

"Thank you."

Rehearsal went fine for the first block. We had lunch and came back, Ian walking us through the choreo for an hour—including the *fouettés,* which we all marked without doing them—making sure all four cohorts had a handle on it.

The Corps didn't really need to be here for this. They were basically standing on the sideline while the principals learned it. It wasn't the first time it happened, but generally they weren't forced into it until closer to the production.

I should have known better than to expect anything normal from Ian.

Listening to my bonds, everyone seemed alright. Normal ranges of emotions, even from Ash, though I still felt the sadness and pain.

"Let's test your memory and technique," Ian called, gesturing his assistant to the side. "No worries if you haven't got it yet. I just want to see where we're at in terms of fast retention. And I would like *full* choreo, please."

"Fucking hell," I grumbled under my breath. Of course he would have us go full out on one of the hardest moves in all of ballet the first day of rehearsal.

"Glass, you're up."

Schooling my face before I turned around, I moved to the center of the space, and Dion came with me, filling in for Ash. Ian looked between the two of us.

"Where's your Alpha, Glass?"

"He couldn't make it today. Dion agreed to fill in." I went back to my bag to grab a sip of water before we started.

"Why not? You fuck him so hard he couldn't walk straight? Or do you only do that when you're alone here in the studios?"

Gasps sounded around the studio, and the air went taut and silent. I turned back to him. "What did you just say to me?"

"I think you heard me. Would you like me to repeat it? Or should I tell everyone how I found the two of you? What I scented when I went to Gabriel's office yesterday?"

It wasn't anger I felt right now, the emotion going far beyond that. "Feel fucking free. You didn't catch Ash and me doing anything but lying on the floor. Fully clothed. Really scandalous. As for Gabriel's office? It's an enclosed room. I'm an Omega. Welcome to ventilation one-oh-one."

Some people laughed, but he sneered and looked like he was about to say something else, so I kept going.

"And as for where he is? He was in a motorcycle accident last night, and his best friend was killed. So maybe it's not out of the question that he takes a couple of days to recover. I was going to let him tell everyone, since it's none of your *fucking business*, but here we are."

The company reacted exactly the way I knew they would. With shock and horror. Claire and Dion looked at me with sudden understanding, and the room came alive with chatter and whispers.

Ian at least had the grace to look a little shocked. It didn't last long. His eyes grew cold. "Better dance then, so you can get back to him."

I shook my head and went to the center of the floor. Dion tried to ask me something, and I didn't answer. Now wasn't the time. When this was over, I'd be pestered with questions, and gladly. I'd take the questions for Ash so he didn't have to.

First, I had to show this asshole he couldn't break me.

The pianist began, and I danced. With Dion and without. Was it perfect? No. Did I really care? Also no. It would be perfect eventually.

The *fouettés* arrived, and I went into them with as much energy as I could. I had planned—and still did plan—to train specifically for this sequence. *Fuck* it hurt. Thirty-two whip turns on one leg, on pointe? Without building up to it? Jace would be massaging me tonight.

I lost it on the twentieth *fouetté*, stumbling out of it. Dion moved to help me get ready to move on, but Ian held up his hand to stop the music. "Back it up to the beginning of the sequence, please."

Gritting my teeth, I started again, bracing through the pain. I made it, but barely, my leg like jelly when I came out of the final turn, still stumbling a little.

"No. Again. You traveled far too much."

"We can switch out and let her take a breather," Skylar called, coming over to me.

He pinned her with a stare. "No, you're fine. We're going to wait until Sloane Glass, the ballerina who danced through her heat, gets it right."

Dion went for the door, and Ian pointed at him. "Where are you going?"

"I'm going—"

"*Don't you fucking move,*" Ian snarled. "Any of you. You go tattling to management and I will end your contracts."

"What is wrong with you?" I turned to see the voice. Jacob. The corps member who made sure I was okay with Ash, and a general sweetheart. "Is there a reason you're such a dick to all of us? The whole company? Sloane in particular, but also Dion, Claire, Skylar, Isabelle, Chloe, Ash? Pretty much all the principals. Don't think we haven't noticed."

Ian glared at him. "What's your name?"

"Can't end my contract if you don't even know my fucking name, can you?" Jacob smirked. "You're an ass to everyone, but at least the corps have it easier because you ignore us."

I held out a hand to him. "It's okay."

"No, it's not," Brette said. "It very much is *not*."

"Stop talking," Ian said. "This company is due for some new talent. So by all means, keep going."

Looking around at everyone, I held my ground. "Don't do anything that will cost you your jobs. I can handle it."

"Of course you can. Why wouldn't you? Sloane Glass can do anything she wants, right? Even the impossible?"

I stared at him, my mind unable to find where the hostility was truly coming from. "Is this about the meeting? How long are you going to make me pay for being late to a meeting I didn't even know you would be present for? It was five minutes."

"It's more than that."

Crossing the distance, I stood in front of him. "Then explain it to me." I lowered my voice. "You know we were all excited for you to come here? The amazing Ian Chambers. We all heard such amazing, glowing things about you and your vision. I'm not sure what we did to deserve this side of you, but I'm sad I never got to see the other one."

"Give me respect, and I'll give it to you."

Straightening, I kept my cool, resisting the urge to tell him that respect was earned, and he hadn't, just like Dion said. "I'm not afraid of you. Whatever this is that you need to get out of your system, I can take it. So let's get it over with."

"I don't take arrogance well, Miss Glass. Whatever you present will be served right back to you."

A clatter drew all the eyes in the corner, Claire falling halfway down the barre, nearly to the floor. "Sorry. Tripped on a bag."

In the corner of my eye, I caught movement. Dion leaving the room. I didn't say anything. Instead, I locked eyes with Ian. I wouldn't pretend to understand, but I wouldn't let him affect me. Whatever the hell was in his head? It had nothing to do with me, and it would bite him in the ass as soon as Dion got where he was going. "Where would you like to begin?"

"The top of the sequence. No traveling this time, and your arms are sloppy. Just like *Giselle*."

Pushing the pain in my foot and leg to the side, I boxed it off in my mind. Ian had already put all of us through hell, and I'd already danced through worse. Nothing in the world would compare to the pain and fear of last night. Ian Chambers and his grudge couldn't touch me.

The piano started, and I began.

CHAPTER FIFTY-ONE

GABRIEL

I rubbed my temples and tried to focus on the numbers in front of me. The same numbers I'd been asked for while balls deep inside Sloane. The board meeting was tomorrow, and Montmay wasn't wrong. The year-over-year numbers didn't look right. But for the life of me, I couldn't figure out *where* they went off track.

Not to mention, I didn't want to be here.

Every instinct told me to be with my pack, making sure they were okay. Between Asher's grief and the determination verging on rage Sloane had in rehearsal? None of us were really coping well.

Someone knocked on the door. "Yeah?"

Jace ducked his head in the door. "You have a second?"

"Anything to stop trying to figure out these numbers."

He didn't sit down. "Yesterday, Ash came to my room before he left to ask Sloane if she was okay with it, and Will was on the phone."

I wasn't sure where he was going with it, so I didn't say anything yet.

"He'd worked with Ian before, and he had a much more positive impression of him than we do. But he said something that made me curious, so today, I've been digging."

"Curious how?"

Jace's face was grim. "He said they had an early production and couldn't manage it the way we did. And that Ian was incredibly generous in pushing it back, despite ticket sales, marketing, whatever."

I frowned. "I mean, that is strange, but we're not the first company to have a change in schedule."

"No," he said mildly. "We're not. That's not the weird part. The weird part is that *every* company Ian has joined in the last decade has had the same. A show that was trying to be pushed forward, and didn't make it."

My mind stuttered to a halt. "What?"

"Yeah."

Closing my eyes, I dropped my face into my hands. "That doesn't make any sense. Why would he do that?"

"Here." He put his phone on the desk and hit the unmute button. "Trent, you're on with Gabriel and I. Gabe, Trent is a physio at Letara Ballet. We worked together before I knew you."

"Nice to meet you," I told the man on the phone.

"Thanks." The voice on the phone said. "Jace said you're dealing with Ian Chambers."

"Yes. You have thoughts?"

He laughed. "Fucking hate that guy."

"I'd love to know why."

"Cause he pushes dancers too hard and doesn't care about the damage it might do. But there's nothing anyone can say because those same dancers worship the ground he walks on."

Jace looked at me, his expression telling me he'd already been down this thought path. "Not here," I told Trent. "Why do they like him?"

"Because he went easy on them when they 'couldn't handle it.'" It was easy to hear the quotes around the words. "Ian is so understanding and willing to shift things. Seemed like I was the only one who thought he was trying to be the solution for a problem he created."

"He created it?" The words were out of my mouth before I could stop them.

Trent sighed. "I don't have proof. But yeah, I think so. There was no reason for the schedule change in the first place. Seemed random, but I don't have a good feeling about it. Every time I've brought it up it's been brushed off, and I can't just go digging in the company's records."

My thoughts raced. "Thank you, Trent. It's been very helpful."

"Let me know if you need more. I'm not the only one who feels this way. There are a lot of support staff at a lot of companies who suspect the same."

"Thanks," Jace said. "I'll talk to you later."

He ended the call, and I stared at him. Things I hadn't considered were coalescing. "Tell me you did more digging on it?"

"I did." Jace was pleased with himself, and if he had figured this all out? He deserved to be. "You know I can be charming when I need to be."

"You mean all the time?"

He chuckled. "I called around and asked the admin assistants what all the delays were from. I told them I was doing research on the influence of rehearsal schedules on dancers and unexpected changes. Which isn't a lie."

I shook my head. With the way his mind worked, Jace should have been a lawyer. But he loved his field too much for it. "And they opened up?"

"Like desert flowers in a rainstorm. The delays were all due to theater repairs that had been inexplicably scheduled over the weekend of the performance. Always something that 'really needed to happen' and was extensive enough to take up time."

I looked down at the numbers in front of me and their dates. I punched the button on my phone. "Anna?"

"Yes, Mr. Black?"

"Can you pull me the full budgetary breakdown from both this year and last year? I want it itemized, no matter how small."

"Of course. I'll email it now."

Jace leaned his elbows on his knees. "You've got an idea?"

"I need confirmation, though I still don't understand why Ian would bother to do it. I don't see the motivation."

Grabbing my cell, I called Mark Thurman. He answered on the third ring. "One of these days I'm just going to say no, Gabe."

"No favors this time, just a question. One that might help solve some of our... problems."

"Shoot."

My email pinged with the documents from Anna, and I opened the spreadsheets. "When was Ian given access to SCB's accounts and authority to use them?"

"Six months ago. His contract was signed, and he needed some expenditures for things. It was easier, rather than him go through five layers of approval for things we were already going to agree to. I gave him a budget, he didn't exceed it. Why?"

"I'll let you know. Thank you."

He was quiet for a second. "Please do."

The stage repair that had fucked over the schedule was complete now, and it was beautiful, thanks to the substitute contractors I brought in. The work was good and it was a good investment. But the date of the original repair? Too coincidental.

"Anna," I called, not wanting to talk through the phone about it.

She pushed open the door. "Yeah?"

"Were you the one who scheduled the original stage repair?"

"No," she shook her head. "I don't know who did. Mr. Chambers informed me about it when he came in the first time for all those meetings. Seemed pretty pissed about it."

"Okay, thanks."

The stage floor wasn't the only strange expense. There was enough here to account for the discrepancies we were seeing, but because they happened in between the official seasons, they hadn't made it onto the spreadsheets. Accounted for, but in the dates we didn't usually look at.

"So he did it," Jace said. "And he's done it before. Over and over."

"But *why*? And why is he so focused on Sloane?"

He pointed at me. "I thought about that. And I think it's exactly what Trent said. Reputation."

"How does pushing people to their breaking point help his reputation?"

Jace stood, pacing back and forth. "But that's the thing. He didn't push them to breaking anywhere else. He pushed them until they begged him to push the show back, and he did. He was *gracious* and *generous*. As soon as they pushed him to give them a break, it sounds like he turned into a completely different person."

"And we didn't do that," I said, the truth dawning. "I wouldn't let him push the show back because of the tickets and the marketing. No one came to beg for it. They just buckled down and did it."

"Not only did the whole company do it, they did it *well*. Sloane was fucking glorious and she danced through her heat to do it. It wasn't a failure. The whole company, and Sloane, overcame all the obstacles he threw at them. The show opened brilliantly, and it's still going well. Instead of viewing him as a savior, they don't *owe him shit*."

"Fuck me." I sat back in my chair. He manipulated things so wherever he went, he looked like a hero. The creative director who truly cared and gave people a break when it was too much—at the expense of the company. He made them think he cared about them no matter the cost, without anyone knowing he'd put them in that position in the first place.

No wonder he was pissed. And his anger at Sloane in particular, made sense. She was the one he was focused on, because he'd tried to put her down. She'd offended him by being late to their meeting, so he placed her in the first cohort on purpose to give her the hardest task. And instead of failing, she thrived.

"Is there anything you can do?" Jace asked.

"The board meeting is tomorrow, so I'll get everything together and try. Now that there's something tangible, it might work. Anything you can give me from your digging, I need it."

"It's already in your inbox."

The door burst open, revealing a heaving, breathless Dion and Anna trying to stop him from barging in.

All my instincts went on high alert. "Dion?"

"Studio. Now. Ian is making an example out of Sloane."

Oh *fuck* no.

I was out of the chair and moving before he finished speaking.

CHAPTER FIFTY-TWO

SLOANE

"*A*gain."

I grit my teeth and started the sequence over for the ninth time. My leg ached, shin giving off sparkles of sharp pain, toes feeling bruised. I was dizzy.

Don't get me wrong, I was a damn good spotter, but even the best would be a little buzzed after two-hundred and fifty *fouettés*.

Everyone in the studio watched, tension simmering as Ian made me dance. No one wanted this, but no one wanted to lose their jobs, and like hell would I let anyone sacrifice themselves for me. The only reason I let Dion go was because he would do it anyway.

The studio door *slammed* open, hitting the wall with a *bang*. Gabriel strode in, followed by Jace and Dion. The distraction nearly made me fall, but Jace pulled me out of the turn, keeping me steady and taking my weight. "I've got you, baby girl."

The strength I'd kept up for the rest of them faded, and I leaned into him with a whimper.

Gabriel placed himself between me and Ian. The rage pouring off him was more than just through our bond. It filled the room to bursting.

Ian rolled his eyes. "Of course you come fucking running to save *your Omega*. No hard work for your precious pack, huh? West skipping rehearsal, and now this."

The growl ripping out of Gabriel's chest had the Betas and Omegas cowering. "Yes. Of course I came to protect my Omega. Because that's my fucking job as her Alpha. But if you think I wouldn't come in here to protect any member of this company you were making an example of, you don't know me very well, Ian."

"Making an exam— oh, for fuck's sake. Is that what he told you?"

Claire snarled. "Why don't you ask Sloane how many times in a row, without rest, he just made her do Odile's *fouettés*?"

Jace looked down at me. "How many?"

"That was the ninth," I whispered.

He swore, sweeping me off my feet and putting me on the floor. "Brette, go to my office and get two ice packs from the freezer. Quickly, please."

She ran off, and Jace quickly started undoing the ribbons on my shoes while Gabriel stared Ian down.

"I will give it to you, Ian," Gabe finally said, his stance easing a little when he looked back at me and found me safe with Jace. "It was a good plan. And if you hadn't let your anger and resentment get the best of you, it probably still would have worked. Maybe you could have kept going forever."

Ian rolled his eyes. "I don't know what you're talking about."

"No, because you've hidden your tracks well. Made an excellent reputation for yourself. By fixing problems you created to make you look like the good guy and a hero." Gabriel looked around the room, gaze finally landing on me. "Ian was the one who scheduled the floor repair, forcing our hand in the schedule. Because he was given authority early out of convenience. Since it fell between the seasons and in transition, it was easy to miss in all the chaos and crossover."

My jaw dropped. "What?"

Whispers raced around the room, and Ian looked pale. Frightened. That was all I needed to know that Gabriel was telling the truth.

"And he's done it before. At each company. And each company begged him to push the rehearsals back and give them more time, and like the *magnanimous* leader he was, he said yes. 'Generous,' I think, was the word some people used. But Slate City Ballet came together and pushed through. Not only, but pushed through spectacularly."

Gabriel smiled at everyone but Ian. "I'm sorry for what you went through to put up the show, but I'm incredibly proud that you were able to do it under the worst of circumstances. *Created* circumstances."

That was why he hated us. We hadn't bent to his manipulation, and he was trying to break us down. Because once we broke and surrendered, he'd treat us the way we should have been treated all along, subtly reinforcing that giving him what he wanted was the way to receive kindness and respect.

Gabe was right. If he'd let it roll off and treated us well regardless, we might have chalked it up to the stress of a bad situation, and he could have kept going forever.

But I—and all the rest of us putting our heads down and overcoming what he threw at us—got under his skin.

Brette came back with the ice packs, and Jace removed my right foot from my shoe. He'd waited for the ice. My toes were bleeding. Not unexpected, given I hadn't built up proper stamina —yet—for that sequence. But it still hurt.

His low growl had me reaching out to him. "I'm all right."

"The fuck you are."

In my chest, I felt Roman and Ash paying attention to all of us. Because we all radiated anger that was difficult to ignore.

"This is nothing but speculation," Ian said with a shrug, carefully watching me. "I know all of you are pissed about *Giselle*, but shit happens. We got through it. End of story."

"It will be the end of your story," Gabriel said. "The board is meeting tomorrow, and I will have you removed as creative director."

Ian scoffed. "With what proof? Some complaints and hearsay? This is ridiculous. I signed a contract."

"With an ironclad removal clause if the board finds you negligent. Or because you've violated your morality clause. We don't police people's lives much, Chambers, but I don't think the board will be happy to find out that you've endangered the health and wellness of every dancer in this company because you were attempting to build up your reputation. That's both negligent *and* shitty. You're done."

"With *what proof*?"

"Come to the meeting, you'll find out."

He turned, grabbing his notebook like he would leave. "Yeah. Sure. Show up just for you to make up lies about me? No thanks. The board will side with me. As for the rest of you assholes, I'll see you tomorrow."

"You curated your reputation with the dancers. Maybe even the admin," Jace said, standing away from me now that he had ice placed on my foot. "But not the support staff. We've seen the damage you could have done and *did* do. There's plenty willing to speak to it."

Ian looked at me. "What, did she say she was hurt during those rehearsals? Because I call bullshit. Can't dance through a fucking *heat* when you're injured."

He moved toward me, like he would prove I wasn't hurt, and Gabriel snarled. "You take another step towards her and I can't promise what I'll do, Ian. But I will tell you that my pack was endangered last night, so my instincts are off the charts. As Sloane's Alpha and the exec of this company, I'm telling you to back the *fuck off*."

All Ian did was smirk. Like he'd won. "You can't do shit to me, Gabriel. If you touch me, you'll never get the board on your side."

Stepping to the side, Jace blocked Ian from getting to me in a different direction. "You really want to test that theory?"

"No." His face twisted into a smirk. "I'd love to see you try to get me fired after attacking me unprovoked. But a subpar dancer who can't even keep her legs closed for an afternoon isn't worth it."

Gabriel moved so fast I barely saw it, fist smashing into Ian's jaw with a sickening thud that sent him flying back into the mirror hard enough that it cracked. He was on him in a second, punching him again. Again and again.

Jace took his damn time stepping forward to touch Gabriel on the shoulder, and Gabe shook him off, pushing away from Ian and shaking out his hand. "I'm done."

What Ian said was on purpose, provoking Gabriel, and it worked. But fuck, seeing his face bloodied was so fucking satisfying, even if the maniac was grinning. "Good luck getting rid of me now."

"Yeah," Dion snorted. "Don't think that'll be a problem. You verbally attacked the man's Omega after he told you to back off. If it had been my Alphas, your intestines would be on the floor, so consider yourself lucky."

Ian looked around, searching for any kind of support in the room, and found none. His gaze finally landed on me. "You started this. Have anything to say?"

I lifted my middle finger to him, the rest of the company finally collapsing into laughter.

Rage filled his eyes like poison. "None of you will ever work at another company again." The door banged on the wall again as he left.

"No," Claire said, "I'm pretty sure that's just you, Ian."

More laughter.

"I'm sorry," Gabriel said. "That was—"

"Can we clap?" Jacob asked. "I feel like we should clap."

They did. Everyone did. Even me. Gabriel's face flushed red, and it wasn't with anger. I'd never seen him flustered like this before. He didn't like being the center of attention. Not in this way. But he gave everyone a grim smile. The Ian problem wasn't solved, but it would be.

"Thank you, Mr. Black." I didn't know who said it, but the sentiment was echoed through the studio.

"He threatened their contracts," I said. "Something else you can tell them."

Gabriel came over and lifted me off the floor, Jace catching the ice packs before they fell. "I will be telling them that, and much more. I don't care what I have to do. He's gone."

We were out of the studio before I could say goodbye, but Jace had my things, and everyone was chatting. Clearly the day was over. Good riddance. I wanted to be home with my pack for the rest of it.

"We'll need a new creative director."

"We'll find someone."

"Could be you," I teased.

Gabriel laughed, and it broke the tension inside him. He stopped walking to kiss me. "No, it absolutely could not be me."

"Just saying."

"We'll find someone, little one. First, I need to get you home, safe, where Jace can give you the massage you deserve, and I can start making some calls. I have no doubt Ian will be making some of his own."

I looked over his shoulder at Jace. "A massage?"

He winked. "With hair pulling, happy ending, and everything." I flushed, and he laughed. "I'm in the mood for some blueberry pancakes."

"Not a bad idea," Gabe said. "We should order a shit ton of pancakes."

I nearly groaned. "Don't say things like that if you don't mean them."

"Oh, I do. And when we're done with the real pancakes, maybe we'll just eat you."

Leaning my head on his shoulder, I savored the pride and possessiveness coming across our bonds and smiled. "Promises, promises."

CHAPTER FIFTY-THREE

SLOANE

*T*he police station smelled bad.

Only years and years of grime and poorly cleaned messes could make something smell like this. If I worked here, my priority would be getting a crew here to clean it with a nuclear bomb.

I leaned on Roman's shoulder, curled up in an uncomfortable chair while we waited. Jace sat on my other side. Ash was in a room with the detectives, giving them his statement. I wanted to be with him and soothe the ache that was our bond, but they wanted to speak to him alone. It felt like it had been too long.

The doors to the station opened, and Gabe walked in. He looked exhausted. Wearing his glasses, which was a sure sign of a long day. The board meeting had gone far longer than anyone anticipated. Ian had some supporters, and he'd gone in prepared for a fight.

He smiled, satisfaction rippling off him. "It's done."

"Thank *fuck*." I tilted my head back and stared at the ceiling. "Seriously."

Gabriel crouched down in front of me, running his hands up my legs. "There are already some names on the table for a replacement. In the meantime, we may have to delay. But in the end, the whole board agrees that it's better to have a delayed and *good* season than a rushed and shitty one."

"How hard was it?"

He smirked. "Not as hard as Ian hoped. Most of the meeting was us making plans for the future. Once I showed them everything, even the ones who'd initially supported him changed their mind, thank you Jace for all of that."

In the corner of my eye I saw Jace nod in acknowledgement.

"I think Ian's still staring at the wall in shock. Or *a* wall. Somewhere. We kicked him out pretty quickly. Black eye and all."

"Does it make me a bad person if I love that mental image?" I asked.

"If you are, then so am I. Had to keep myself from smiling every time I saw the bruising."

Another stab of sadness from Ash had me curling into Roman. He tucked his arm around me, keeping me close. "It's been too long, right? The story he told us didn't take nearly this long."

Roman's fingers traced patterns on my arm. "Probably have more questions than we did, firefly."

Last night we ordered pancakes. And eggs. All the breakfast foods. By the time Jace finished my massage and I was a boneless mess, it was all ready. And delicious. It felt normal even if we were all a little somber.

Ash appeared from the direction he'd disappeared from, hands in the pockets of his hoodie. He looked gray and tired, but his bond felt relieved. That it was over and he didn't have to recount the story over again.

The detective from the hospital followed him out, jogging to catch up. "Mr. West."

Ash, almost to us, turned back. The detective included all of us with a nod. "That was the call I was waiting for."

Sudden hope burned in my chest, like the sun clearing away clouds. All of it came from Ash. "An arrest?"

"Yes." The detective laughed humorlessly. "Guy didn't even fight it. Fucking admitted to it. Not that he would have had to. The entire front end of his car is smashed. It's got paint from the bike all over it. He could have fought the charge, but it's pretty clear."

"What's the plan?" Jace asked.

"He's been arrested. He'll be charged. Likely first degree murder. Or second. They're almost here, so we'll see what else he tells me when he's brought in. But that will be up to the judge and the prosecutor."

I blinked. "First degree murder?"

Knowledge of laws and crimes weren't my forte, but that was a pretty easy one. First degree murder was when it was planned out. Intentional. My body went cold. "It wasn't an accident?"

The air around us went tense, and the detective winced, like he realized how casually he said it. "My apologies. Yes. I don't have all the information yet, but that's what he said. He didn't mean to hit your friend, Mr. West. He was aiming for you."

Like the whole world slowed down, I realized. Yelled, angry words echoed in my mind from the night at Pavilion.

Get the fuck off me. You're the dead one. Keep thinking she's yours. You'll see. Try me, pretty boy.

The doors to the station slid open, and two uniformed officers came in, Craig handcuffed between them. He saw me and smiled. The smug, satisfied smile of a person who had no regrets and no remorse.

My world tilted and turned red.

The scream coming out of me wasn't human.

I didn't remember how I got across the room, only that Craig was in front of me, and then underneath me as I tackled him, scratched his face. I would kill him.

I would kill him.

He tried to kill Ash over fucking *nothing*. Because of *his* mistakes. He used me and hurt me and tried to murder my family. I would kill him.

My hands hurt. Blood poured from his nose where I hit it. Good. Let him fucking *bleed*.

Hands grabbed me and pulled me off, but I fought my way back to Craig on the floor, kicking him hard enough to fracture his ribs. I hoped they would puncture a fucking lung.

More hands dragging me down to the floor, pinning me down. A hot, heavy, hard body on mine. "*Firefly*." The word caressed my ear. "Stop."

"Let me kill him," I screamed. "I'm going to fucking *destroy him*."

"Let her up," a voice said. The weight came off me, and I sprang—straight into Ash. He grabbed my face with both hands and looked at me. "Sloane. Sweetheart. Look at me."

"*No*."

"*LOOK AT ME*."

My mind went quiet. I looked at him. I felt the terror and the pain in the bond between us. For me. Because of me. Anger lived there too. Omega rage still slithered under my skin, *begging* to be free. To protect *my* Alphas, no matter the cost.

But Ash held me fast, his Alpha making my Omega back down, even as I felt how badly he wanted to set me loose. A whine slipped out, and he relaxed, pulling me to him. I sobbed into his hoodie, unable to let go.

"No, no, no." It was the only word I could fully say. The only thing I could think.

Ash pressed his mouth to my ear. "I want to kill him too," he whispered. "You know I do. You *know* I do, but I can't let you do it."

"Why?" My voice cracked.

"Because I love you more than I hate him. I'm not going to let you ruin your life because of him. Will wouldn't want that, and this asshole is going to jail forever."

I broke further. "I'm sorry."

"Don't." He sounded broken too. "Don't apologize, sweetheart. God, I love you. Your Omega rage is a thing of fucking beauty, but we had to stop you."

Omega rage. Right. No wonder it felt so powerful. And good fucking thing too. In the same way no one would blame Gabriel for punching Ian in the face, no one would charge me for assaulting Craig in Omega rage. Especially not with our history and the restraining order we had. It was the one saving grace about it.

As long as I didn't kill him.

"I'm going to turn you around now. He's still here, but I'm not letting you go."

"Good."

Craig's eyes were wild and on me. Scratches marred his face, his lip was bloodied, and his face was dark from the blood of his broken nose, but he looked fine and far too *alive* for my taste. He spat blood on the floor. "I want to press charges."

The detective looked between him and me. "You know I can't do that, Sullivan. We can't charge someone for instinct. If you need extra medical care from your... injuries, we'll bill the Lys pack for them."

Rage contorted Craig's features. "You fucking bitch. You cost me *everything*."

My own anger flared, only Asher's hands on me keeping me in control. "Yeah? And what about me? You came to me knowing who I was and wanting everything from me. I know all about your fucking plan, Craig. You brought this on yourself. All of it. And then you *killed someone*."

I wouldn't say all the things I wanted. Not out loud. Omega rage didn't have me now. But I hoped he would rot. Or maybe he'd follow the man who tried to kill Petra into whatever afterlife we had. Either way, he deserved whatever hole he would be buried in.

"I just want to know why," I finally said, my whole body shaking with the need to hurt him again. "You knew it was never going to change. Why would you do this?"

"Because you looked so fucking happy in those pictures. *Bonded*." He spat again. "I wanted you to feel just a fraction of the pain and anger I've felt because of you. And that pretty boy had it coming."

Asher tensed, and I felt my other Alphas close ranks around us, making sure he didn't try to kill Craig himself.

"Get him out of here," the detective said, and they took Craig away.

I thought about watching him until he disappeared, because he kept fighting to look back at us. But it was too good for him. I curled into Ash, burying my face again and turning my back on Craig, making sure he knew it was the last time I'd ever look at him.

I never wanted to think about him again either, but I knew that couldn't be true.

"Baby girl?" Jace came around on my other side and crouched. "Let me see your hands, please."

I gave them. They were bloodied. Not mine. And they hurt more than I'd realized. "No breaks, thankfully. You got some good hits in there."

"Yeah." I looked at Roman, horror dawning. He had a red mark on his face. "Did I hurt you?"

"No."

"Your face…"

Ash let him lift me up. "Caught a quick elbow. I'll be fine in the morning."

"Sorry."

He stroked his fingers down my cheek. "You were beautiful, firefly."

Not a normal compliment when you tried to beat someone to death, but I'd take it.

"Do you need anything from us, detective?" Gabriel asked.

The man looked between the five of us. "No. You can go. We have your number if we need you."

Exhaustion rolled over me. I barely remembered walking to the car, all that instinctual anger draining me to the point of sleep. I wanted to talk to them. Apologize, but I couldn't keep my eyes open.

I jerked awake when Roman laid me down in the nest. "You're fine, firefly. We're all here with you."

"Need to talk."

"We can talk in the morning, little one." Gabriel rested near my feet with Jace, and Ash pulled me in to him, sandwiching me between his body and Roman's.

In spite of everything, all the sadness and pain, knowing Ian was gone and Craig was in jail, I felt… better.

CHAPTER FIFTY-FOUR

ASHER

I shouldn't be here.

It was the thought that kept circling around in my brain. Through the entire wake and memorial service, and now at the reception. I shouldn't be here. I was the reason Will was dead.

Sloane kept close by my side, weaving our fingers together and showing me without words she was here for me no matter what. It helped more than I could ever tell her.

We had a quiet couple of days with rehearsals suspended. Watching movies together as a pack, sleeping in the nest, letting wounds heal and our instincts settle.

My Omega had her own struggles. Guilt because of Craig. In her head, it felt like she was responsible for Will's death as well. The reality was, neither of us were, and we were back to the start, both of us feeling guilty for something that ultimately wasn't our fault.

But we knew it, and each time we felt the other sinking, we tried to pull the other back. The rest of our pack was good at it as well. Jace made sure we were fed, whether it was ordering pizza from Sloane's favorite place or making pasta like the first night she came home.

Roman was *there*. A presence that didn't change and didn't question. Sometimes all that was needed was not being alone.

Gabriel, still tangled in the mess of Ian's firing, was absent the most, though he made sure to always be with us in the nest. He pulled Sloane aside when he felt her spiraling. And the two of us had talked. A long conversation out by the fire pit while Sloane and Roman were occupied.

It felt good to let everything out. I would never hide anything from Sloane, but she didn't need to be the sole bearer of all my grief. That's what packs were for—why we were all together in the first place. Something deep and visceral knew we all needed each other, strengths and weaknesses included.

We were waiting to speak to Jeremy, Will's partner, and then we would make the long drive back home. I didn't know if I could stay much longer than that. The line in front of us moved, and finally we were face to face.

I didn't know him well, but we were familiar enough after so many years of Will and I being friends. They'd only been together a few years.

"Ash," he pulled me into a hug. "Thank you so much for coming."

"Thank you for allowing it," I said.

"What do you—" He released me and sighed. "You and Will are so much alike, you know that?"

It made me smile before the hurt slammed in.

"If the situation were reversed, he would say the same thing to your pack and your lovely Omega here."

Sloane held out her hand, and Jeremy shook it. "Will was a great guy," she said softly. "I wish I'd known him better."

Jeremy stopped. "I actually have something for you, Ash. Come with me." He glanced at the line behind us. "Just a second, everyone."

I followed him away from the crowd and to one of the rooms everyone was keeping their things. He dug around in his coat and finally pulled out something I would know anywhere.

A keychain. Horrendously tacky miniature fuzzy dice. I'd bought the keychain for him as a joke when he got his bike. And though it was a joke, he kept them attached to the bike itself. For years.

"I think he'd want you to have these," he said.

My breath shook. "Thank you."

Jeremy looked at me. "I know it hasn't been long, but have you ridden since it happened?"

I shook my head. Even if I wanted to, my bike was a mess. I wasn't sure it was fully drivable, and the idea of getting back on the bike right now made me sick to my stomach.

"Promise me you will." Surprised, I looked up at him, and he smiled sadly. "I know bikes are dangerous, but the two of you have been riding for years. I know you're careful. This was different. This was an attack."

Guilt threatened to swallow me, and I pushed it back. "Yeah."

"Believe me, I'm going to make that asshole pay," Jeremy said. "Beyond the charges, I have another case already filed. He's never going to leave prison if I have anything to say about it. But, regardless, don't let this steal something you love away from you. Will wouldn't want it, and neither do I."

Gritting my teeth, I looked down at the tiny fuzzy dice in my hand. Grief opened like a maw in my chest. How was I supposed to get back on the road like it was nothing? Will had always been with me, and now—

"I'm so sorry, Jeremy."

For the first time, I saw the real pain on his face and not the mask he was keeping up for everyone out at the reception. "Thank you." His voice cracked. "I'm sorry too."

He hugged me again, and I hugged him back just as fiercely. "If you need anything, please call me. Even if it's just to talk about him."

"I will. Promise."

What else was there to say? There wasn't anything you could do to fill the void left by a person who took up so much space. All that was left was a charred hole until you started to heal it. Gently. And even once it wasn't a blackened scar anymore, it would never be the same.

"He really loved you, you know," I told him. "The tattoo—"

"I saw it," he whispered, turning away. "Too late, but I saw it."

The tattoo I got on my finger for Sloane... Will had gotten one over his heart for Jeremy. Larger and more complex than what I'd gotten, it had delayed our trip. I thought that if we hadn't gone there maybe we could have avoided all of it.

Now I knew it didn't matter. No matter what time, something would have happened, because it wasn't an accident.

Jeremy dropped his head into his hands, and I heard the stifled sound of a sob.

"Call me anytime, Jeremy. I'll give you some space."

He nodded, and I slipped out the door, emotion gathering hot behind my eyes. The others waited for me in the main room, and they all noted the dice in my hand. "We can go," I said thickly. "Jeremy needs a minute."

"Are you okay?" Sloane asked.

Taking her hand again, I let her pull me through the room and around the people who knew who I was or other friends from school neither of us could bear to speak to. "No," I told her. "I'm not."

We slipped into the back of the car together, Sloane between me and Jace. She leaned her head on my shoulder and squeezed my hand. No words were needed when we could feel the others' pain and sadness. All the heaviness and regret.

But we were together, and we were going home.

I fell asleep on the drive home and woke with Sloane's head in my lap, her feet in Jace's. We were pulling into the garage. It was the sound that woke me.

Sleep, the magical healer, always made me feel better. Not that grief could be cured with sleep. It was simply easier to face when you weren't as tired.

"We're home?" Sloane asked, groggily.

"We are, baby girl. Which means you get a surprise."

Sloane groaned, and I laughed quietly. Our girl didn't love surprises, but she would learn to. We liked the look on her face too much, and there would never be bad surprises from us.

"What if I'm too sleepy for a surprise?"

"I think you'll like this one," Gabriel opened my door, and Sloane climbed out over my lap.

She looked around when we entered the kitchen, like whatever it was would jump out from behind every corner. The only thing that jumped out at her was Mango, meowing his displeasure at us being gone the whole day. And from being locked in Sloane's bedroom, but she didn't know that yet.

Roman rescued the kitten, lifting him up to perch on his shoulder, and Sloane's jaw dropped as we all crowded on the elevator. "He never lets me do that."

"Maybe he likes being higher," Roman said. "You're short, firefly."

"I'm not short. You're just a giant."

I smirked. "No, I'm pretty sure you're short."

The annoyed look on her face was adorable. I moved so she couldn't immediately see which floor had been pressed. "This was Jace's idea by the way. He's been working on it since the beginning."

She looked over, and Jace just smiled. That smile turned to confusion when the doors opened on her floor.

"Close your eyes, baby girl."

"The surprise is up here?"

"It is."

She closed her eyes, and he walked her to the door we never used. As far as she knew it was storage, and until yesterday it had been. Might as well use the time we were out of the house, and Gabriel made sure Harrison's security was present the whole time. One of the last things we needed them for.

The little studio was beautiful. Jace had done more than enough research about which floor to have installed, and I helped with that. It was painted a beautiful teal color, contrasting with the bright white of the walls. It helped the small space feel bigger and brighter than a black or gray floor would have. Addison had executed everything brilliantly.

Barres ran along two walls, mirrors along the third, and images of Sloane dancing on the last one. There were even some of the two of us. Both from *Giselle* and from school. I'd helped with that as well.

Jace maneuvered her into the doorway before taking a step back. "Okay, you can open your eyes."

In the mirror, we saw them open, and her shock at what she saw. She wandered into the room, spinning to take in the whole thing. The pictures and even the little cubbies hidden in the corner for charging our phones and keeping extra pairs of shoes.

"You made me a studio?"

"Of course we did," Jace said.

I walked forward and wrapped my arms around her from behind, meeting her eyes in the mirror. "And the best part is we can be as naughty as we want in here and there's no one who will get us in trouble. Only join in if they want to."

She smiled, but her eyes still bounced around the room greedily. "It's beautiful. Everything—" her voice hitched. "You all make everything so *perfect*."

Tears sounded through her words, but it wasn't sadness we felt. It was so much more than that. How much we'd gone through this past month, and us coming out on the other side, no matter how painful.

Releasing her, I peeled off the suit jacket I wore to the funeral and handed it to her. She'd released our other suits from the nest a couple days after our bonding. "I think your nest might need some replacements."

She took one look at the jacket in my hand, eyes sparking with desire and instinct that erased the heaviness there. In turn, I felt lighter. My Omega always made me better.

Always.

Sloane snatched the jacket out of my hand and sprinted for the nest, a giggle trailing behind her. By the time we followed, she was already undressed, tucking the jacket in the space only she knew was correct.

We all undressed to give her more of what she needed, and my whole soul settled. No matter what we were going through, this, us together, would always be right, and always be home.

I smiled, watching my precious Omega build her nest.

CHAPTER FIFTY-FIVE

SLOANE

"*I* hate that it's already getting too cold for this," I said, burrowing deeper under the blankets draped over me. A cold snap had flowed over Slate City, sending us firmly into fall and further. These kinds of temperatures were straight up winter. I hoped it would be a little more mild. I wanted a few more weeks of cute sweaters and leggings before I had to be constantly bundled up in scarves and coats.

The fire burned merrily in the pit, and the heat was nice, but it wasn't enough.

"We need another inside fireplace," Gabriel said.

"You already have one."

He smirked, taking a sip of the drink he held. "I do. And as much as I love every member of this pack, I'd prefer for my bedroom not to become the central hangout of the house. I thought we might turn my office into something more comfortable than the formal rooms downstairs."

"Wait," my jaw dropped open. "But you love your office."

Gabe tilted his head. "I *like* my office. But I don't need an office that takes up half a floor, little one. I can still have my desk in a corner. Hell, I'll make myself a gaming nook that has an extra beanbag for you."

I liked the sound of that. "I still might want to koala on you."

Last night I'd climbed into his lap while he played a few rounds of a shooting game, and he purred while his arms moved around me and he played. It was nice.

"You can koala me anytime, little one."

"Anytime?"

He laughed. "If I'm not on a work call, yes."

"I can't koala you during a work call, but you can fuck me during one? Seems fair."

Jace choked on his drink. "What?"

I sipped my hot chocolate and kept my face neutral. That little detail must have slipped past them. "You'll have to ask Gabriel about that."

The other three Alphas looked to him, and he shrugged. "The man wouldn't wait, and I wasn't going to stop. Sloane was a good girl and stayed very quiet."

A shiver ran down my spine, reliving that particular memory.

Roman looked at Gabe from across the fire. "The package came, by the way. I left it in your office on the desk."

He immediately set his drink on the ground and went into the house. I looked after him. "What package?"

My big, silent Alpha said nothing, a smile on his face.

"Is this another surprise? You have to give me, like... at least two weeks in between them."

Ash laughed. "It's a surprise, and it isn't. You already know about it, but may have forgotten."

Watching him through the flames, I picked his bond out of the hum in my chest. He was doing a little better. Sadness still tinged the edges, grief underlying everything, but he was dealing with it. It wouldn't be an overnight thing, nor did I expect it to be.

He had an appointment for another tattoo—with Esme's Alphas at their tattoo studio—to get a memorial piece, and I knew it would help.

Gabe came out of the house with a wooden box that looked like a cigar case. But it wasn't. Gold lettering spun across the front of it.

Vernier

I did a double take. Vernier, the jewelry smith, was world renowned and exclusive. I needed to learn to stop being surprised about them having connections like this, because every time I didn't think something could be achieved, they did it and made it look easy.

Suddenly, it clicked. "Those are the rings?"

Gabe grinned. "They are."

I pushed my blankets to the side in spite of the temperature and sat up. My Omega needed to be closer to them. All of me did.

"First," Gabriel said, setting the box on his chair and opening it, "There's one for you."

"But I already have one."

"This is in case you don't want to wear your great grand-mother's ring all the time," he said. "Either if you want to protect it, or you want something simpler for any reason. You don't ever have to wear it, little one, or you can wear both, but I still want you to have it."

He held his hand out for mine, and I gave it to him. Gently, he slid off my current ring, placing a thin silver band on my finger. It glimmered in the firelight. Not quite shining, but that was because there was a pattern on it. When I looked closer, I saw a hint of what looked like... petals? "What is it?"

"Lilies," Roman said. "Like our name."

A smile stole over my face. They told me the history of the pack name that was now mine. It was perfect. Subtle enough to just look decorative, but that extra layer of meaning made me feel so loved.

Pulling it off, I looked closer, spying something on the inside. *Forever yours.*

The date of our bonding was etched beside it.

I looked up at them, meeting each of their eyes. "Do yours say anything?"

Jace stood and crossed to the box, carefully picking up a ring before sinking to one knee in front of me, holding it out. "This is mine, baby girl."

Warm gold, a thicker band than mine. The same subtle pattern on the outside, and on the inside...

Forever mine.

Along with the same date.

"Do I get to put them on you?"

"I wouldn't have it any other way."

Grabbing his hand, I pulled him closer, putting the ring on his finger. It fit perfectly, and looked *good*. Possession dropped through me, along with desire. They were *mine*, and I loved seeing the evidence.

I kept staring at it, and Jace chuckled. "What's going through your head?"

413

"I'm thinking looking at a ring shouldn't be making me feel these kinds of things."

"I'm glad it does," Jace said. "Because I love it just as much. I want everyone to know you're fucking mine, and I'm only yours."

He kissed me, and I could have kissed him forever. But I had more rings, and I wanted them all on.

I went to the box, and it was easy to see who had picked what. Roman's ring was larger, a cool, darker metal, with the same engravings. This time I approached him. "I should kneel, firefly."

"Don't do that. I don't need you on your knees. All the time, at least." I winked, and his grin spread so wide, his happiness struck so deep, I had to smile back at him.

The awe I felt when the ring slid on wasn't a feeling I deserved, but I savored it regardless, knowing I would never take the kind of love they gave me for granted.

"Going to enjoy waking you up with this ring, firefly."

"And how are you going to do that?"

He smirked. "While it's on my finger. Inside you."

I flushed with heat. Being woken up by him any way he chose was fine with me, and he knew it.

"Blue."

Turning, Ash knelt in front of me. My heart stuttered, the sight taking me off guard. Never in my wildest dreams had I ever imagined Asher West on one knee in front of me with a ring in his hand, and I would never forget it.

His ring was a pale silver closer to mine.

Like he'd read my mind, he stopped me before I took the ring from him. "I imagined this so many times, Sloane. How I'd do it and what I'd say. The look on your face right now is more than I ever imagined."

Emotion stole my voice, but I found it just enough to whisper, "I love you," before I slid his ring home. Right over the tattoo. His ring that could never come off.

Gabriel handed me his ring—a warmer tone, nearly rose gold —and kissed me before I found his finger, not letting me breathe until it was firmly in place. He put my other ring back on, my new one thin enough for them both to fit. I decided at that moment I was never taking either of them off. Not unless I had to.

"I'm going to fuck all of you with nothing but those rings on," I said, breaking the moment and all of us falling into laughter.

"Only if it's the same for you, firefly."

"It's fucking freezing out here," I said. "Take me inside, warm me up, and I'll be shedding my clothes in no time."

Roman picked me up and carried me into the house, the others scrambling to put out the fire, gather cups, blankets, and everything else we'd left. I managed to spot a very sleepy Mango passed out on top of the refrigerator, exactly where Ash said he would be, and smiled to myself.

At the entrance to the nest, Roman put me down, only long enough for us both to shed our clothes down to our rings before he spread me out on the velvet. He kissed me while we waited for the rest of our pack.

The idea came to me without warning, and I blurted it out. "Will you draw me a firefly?"

His eyebrows rose in shock. "If you want me to. Why?"

"Ash is getting a tattoo. I thought I might get one too."

Roman's eyes went wide. Then he was kissing me so hard and so deep my mind went utterly blank. "Yes," he murmured between kisses. "Yes."

"Starting without us?" Jace asked, stripping.

"Not quite," I managed a full breath, but butterflies still flew around in my stomach. Everything felt new and bright and different, even though this was who we were and what we'd have forever.

They all stepped into the nest with me, and I sat up, tears blurring my eyes. "I love you. So much. I never want to miss a chance to say it, and it... it feels important."

Gabriel's hand came behind my neck and he kissed me, one of them after the other until I was breathless and dizzy from all of them at once, their murmured words whispering across my skin and painting me with love in more ways than one. We sank down together into pleasure and purrs until we were spent. Tangled together.

Happy.

It took me a while, but this was where I belonged, and I was never running away from it again.

———

SLOANE

TWO MONTHS LATER

I stepped into the rosin box, coating the tips of my pointe shoes, when I felt heat behind me. The rich scent of chocolate chip cookies curling around me, the bond of my Alpha telling me he was not thinking at all about the show we were about to put on.

"Last time you and I were like this, you were going into heat," he whispered into my neck.

"As fun as that was," I said with a laugh, "I'm glad I'm not going into heat now."

The orchestra was warming up, and on the other side of the curtain the crowd could be heard entering the house. Not every production of *Swan Lake* started with the prologue, but ours did. Which meant I would be the first on stage to be cursed by Rothbart, the villain, and have an absolutely insane quick change into the costume of the Swan Queen.

"Me too, but only because you'll actually get the recognition you deserve. I get to show you off."

"Like I'm a prize?"

He lifted me, turning and placing me against the wall. "No, like my beautiful Omega who I can't get enough of. Who I can't wait to take home and after this and work out all the tension we're about to build up."

Having your dance partner at home was nice. Especially when you had a studio in your house to rehearse—both the real versions and the sexier versions of the dances and roles we played. It had only been two months, and the amount of sex Ash and I had in our studio was more than I'd ever admit to anyone outside our pack.

The guys loved using the mirror, and I loved letting them.

"Unless you want to dance this entire show hard, don't tease both of us."

Ash laughed, low and soft, kissing my lips gently enough not to ruin my lipstick. "Sweetheart, I'm almost always hard or halfway there when I'm dancing with you. I'm used to it."

Part of me felt bad for it, and part of me thrilled at the idea that he was so affected by me, and hoped he always would be. He felt it, his smile taking on a feral edge. "Careful, blue."

"Never."

The overture started, and Ash slipped a hand around my throat gently, pinning me to the wall before he kissed me again. Our rings were in the dressing room we shared, waiting to be put back on after the show. With his fingers ringing my neck, his lips on mine, reminding me of those moments when he let himself completely, I couldn't help but smile.

"They're going to need me in a second."

"Just a little more."

I let out a giggle. "Later, Prince Siegfried."

Ash nudged my forehead with his. "See you on stage, Odette."

Flexing my feet, I went over to my entrance and stretched my arms quickly. My other bonds lit up with well wishes and love. I had to wipe the smile off my face for the character, but they felt me sending it right back to them.

The curtain opened, the stage lit in blues and greens of a night by a lake, and I stepped onto the stage into a wave of enthusiastic applause.

"You were so good," Eva said, scooping me into a hug as soon as I got to the reception. "Like, fuck me, I should retire. You're so good."

"Dancing and acting aren't remotely the same, Eva," I laughed. "You wouldn't want to see me on camera."

"That's bullshit and we both know it," but she was smiling.

Petra hugged me tight. "Congratulations. Did that feel better?"

"So much. And it's nice to see everyone here too instead of being smuggled out the back of the theater."

"You look beautiful," Esme said, gesturing to the dress I wore. A pretty violet, and flowing. I loved it. It made me feel graceful even when I wasn't trying to be.

The way my Alphas looked at me when I wore this color didn't hurt either. If you looked closely, the back exposed part of the lovely little sketched firefly tattooed on my ribs, beneath my shoulder. High enough that some clothes showed it, and low enough that almost all ballet costumes didn't.

My rings were back on my finger, and I preferred it that way. It felt strange not having them. Not that it mattered. My Alphas were still mine, and they were headed right for me.

Ash appeared behind me, now dressed in a dark button down and slacks that made me want to jump him even more than his ass in his costume tights.

All the rest of my Alphas were in tuxedos, and I'd already informed them that I would be nesting with their clothes. Something about seeing them in suits made me want to claim them in every way possible.

None of them minded as long as I gave the suits back.

Eventually.

"Firefly." Roman scooped me up and inhaled me. Pride and awe radiated through our connection. "So beautiful."

"You've seen me dance before," I whispered.

"It's different."

I curled my fingers into his lapels. "Thank you."

My hair hung loose around my shoulders, so when a hand slipped in it, close to the scalp, and *pulled*, I let myself fall back into Jace's chest. "Are you trying to tell me something?" I asked.

His purr roared against my back. "You were amazing, and you look absolutely edible, baby girl."

"Now, now, she gets you all the time. Give me a chance to say hello."

No need to look to know who said it. "Hi, Grandma."

She turned me to face her and put her hands on my shoulders. "You, my darling girl, were exquisite. Much better than I ever was."

"That's not true." I rolled my eyes.

"Yes, it is, and I won't hear anything to the contrary." Slipping her arm through mine, she walked me toward the tables filled with finger foods and a mountain of champagne. "When are you all coming over for dinner? I want to get to know them better and I need to speak to Roman about a sculpture for the gardens. The last time wasn't nearly enough."

"Soon, I promise. We'll have a little more time after this weekend."

"Good. Otherwise, I might become one of those crazy old ladies no one wants to visit, and that would be a tragedy."

We'd always visit, but like hell was I going to be the one to tell her she'd reached crazy status a *long* time ago. I was going to say something else, but our new creative director flagged me down and grabbed Ash.

Grandma saw them heading my way and leaned in to kiss my cheek. "Duty calls. I'll see you soon."

Genevieve Nicholls was an absolute legend in the ballet world. How Gabriel and the board convinced her to come here for us was a mystery, but I loved her.

She worked us hard, but was fair, kind, and knew everything about what had happened with Ian. She put her arm around my shoulders and squeezed. "Wonderful performance, Sloane. Truly lovely."

"Thank you."

"I'm sure you're already familiar with this, but given that you didn't get to do it on your principal debut, I thought I'd walk you through it."

I smiled. "I appreciate that."

She wasn't wrong. I did know many of the donors and board members from my time at the company, but I rarely interacted with them. Being walked through it was completely fine with me.

Ian wouldn't have done that. He wouldn't have done shit. But the last time I'd checked, there were people across the dance world telling the truth. Plenty of dancers with stories that went against his glowing reputation. If he ever worked in the entertainment industry again, I would be shocked.

The next hour was a whirlwind of speaking to people, being congratulated, and making small talk with the people who made our world go round. Many of them were excited to talk to me in the wake of Giselle, and were truly lovely. Ash was never far away, having his own conversations.

A few times we were able to talk together, when the donors were aware of the fact that we were together. But it was more efficient to split up.

By the time I'd made the full rounds in the room, I was parched and my energy was running low. A full performance and now this amount of people equaled an Omega who was fading fast.

Gabriel approached with two glasses in his hands. "Water or champagne?"

"Both." But I reached for the water first, glancing around before I took it like a shot. Fuck yes. There wasn't anything like water when you were parched.

Slipping a hand around my waist, Gabe kissed my cheek and switched out the glasses, passing the empty water to one of the waitstaff. "I have someone I want you to meet."

I whined softly, leaning my head on his shoulder. "Okay, but I only have a few more conversations in me."

"This is one you'll want to have, I think."

He maneuvered us toward the corner of the room. Roman, Ash, and Jace stood nearby. Not close enough to participate in whatever conversation we were going to have, but enough to tell me they knew about it and wanted to watch. "You Alphas and your surprises."

"If you weren't so adorably angry and then delighted, maybe we'd stop."

I made a face, causing him to laugh. But he pulled me up to a man I recognized, and one I didn't. "Robert?" I asked. "It's nice to see you. I didn't expect you here."

Gabe's brother took my hand and shook it. "I'm sure you know Gabriel can be very convincing if he wants to be. It was a lovely show."

"Thank you."

"The main reason I'm here is to introduce you, and everyone else here, to this man." The one who stood beside him. Handsome, with dark hair with silver at the temples, he looked to be around Robert's age. "This is Vidal Maher."

Searching my memory, I knew I'd heard his name before, but I was also certain I'd never seen this man in my life. Gabriel cleared his throat and murmured, "Craig," under his breath, and it all clicked.

This was the man Craig had taken advantage of, and who he promised would meet me at the concert. My face paled, and he held out a hand. "I'm so sorry that's the only knowledge you have of me, Miss Glass. That... interaction isn't why I'm here. Rather, I hoped to make up for it."

I took the outstretched hand and shook it. "Thank you. I'm sorry that my family was used to mislead you. I had no knowledge of it at the time."

"So I hear. My own sympathy for a person I believed needed help got the better of me. Believe me, I will be more careful with both my investments and decisions from now on. Not to mention there are grounds for me to sue the hell out of Sullivan for fraud."

I hid my smile, but not fast enough, and he laughed. "Don't worry, Miss Glass. You're in good company with your feelings there."

Craig was in jail, and everything pointed to him staying there. He wouldn't go to trial for a bit, but there was irrefutable evidence against him. Jeremy's civil suit. And now fraud? He was done, and I was glad. As soon as his trial was over, I would blissfully never think about him again.

"I appreciate you coming. I was told you preferred to patronize music?"

"Generally I do, but I think I can expand my interests. Especially when my musical taste and other art forms come together." He looked behind me like he was pointing someone out, and I turned to find another man standing behind me.

This one I recognized, and would *anywhere*. Alexander Serrat. The composer we'd been going to see. My jaw dropped.

Alexander laughed. "I won't lie. That's not the reception I usually get, but I don't mind it."

"I'm so sorry." I closed my mouth and reached to shake his hand. "It's an honor to meet you. I love your music."

"And I love your dancing. I wouldn't say I'm an expert in the field, but I recognize quality when I see it."

My brain short-circuited. Alexander Serrat just complimented me on my performance, and I didn't think I would ever receive a better one.

"When Mr. Maher found out about Craig's actions. *All* of them," Gabriel said. "He wanted to meet you, and he wanted to do what he could to undo the damage that was done. At least in one way. Like you not getting to meet Alexander."

I looked at Maher. "Thank you. Truly. This is... incredible. I'm still hoping to make it to one of your concerts, Mr. Serrat. I would love that."

"Consider it done," he said. "But I think you'll be sick of me before long."

"I doubt it." His music was ethereal in the best way. It made me fly and float and want to dance forever.

Mr. Maher cleared his throat. "I have to admit something to you, Miss Glass. I did come here with an ulterior motive. But not a bad one, and all your Alphas knew, so I hope I'm in the clear."

I glared up at Gabriel, then over at the rest of my pack, and they were all smiles. Because of course they were. Gabriel put his hand back around my waist. "Never a bad surprise, little one. Haven't we proved that? Trust me." He squeezed my hip.

"Dare I ask?"

Vidal slid his hands in his pockets. "Like I said, I like it when music and other things come together. In the course of my conversations with Gabriel here, he mentioned you were a fan of Alexander's music. To the point that you would love to dance a full ballet to it."

"Absolutely," I said, looking between the two men. Alexander had moved within my line of vision. "Your music... There's nothing else like it. Dancing to it would lend itself to modern ballet. I think it would be beautiful."

"I agree," Alexander said. "I'd never thought about it before, but as soon as Vidal told me, I liked the idea. And fortunately, so did she."

He gestured to where Genevieve stood nearby, speaking to one of the board members. She spotted my shocked look and came over to our group. "They told you?"

"Maybe? I'm not sure because I'm not sure I believe it's real."

Genevieve smiled. "Gabriel and I agree, and so does the board, that for Slate City Ballet to excel and grow, the classics can't be all we produce. They have their place, and I will happily produce them. But we need new work as well."

Hope filled me so deeply and intensely, I thought I might float up like a balloon. This couldn't be really happening, right?

"Because everyone loves the idea," Gabriel said. "Alexander will compose a score for a new ballet, and Genevieve will choreograph it, to be featured next season."

"That's..." I shook my head and placed a hand on my chest. "I'm sorry. I don't have coherent words right now because that's so amazing."

"Again," Alexander chuckled. "A good reaction. I look forward to seeing what comes of it."

Leaning further into Gabriel, I smiled when he kissed my hair. "Me too."

"In the meantime," Mr. Maher nodded at Gabriel. "He has my number. Anytime you want tickets for something, and I don't just mean Alexander, let me know, and I'll see what I can do."

I looked at Gabriel. "You did all this for me?"

"I should say I did it for SBC because it's the right choice, and a good business decision." The others around us laughed. "But yes, I did it for you. I'd do anything for you, little one."

The way he kissed me would set the building on fire, and I didn't care. When he finally pulled away, he looked at the small circle of our audience. "Thank you for making this happen, and for being willing to make it a surprise. But if you don't mind, I think it's time to take my Omega home."

"Of course," Mr. Maher said. "We'll be in touch."

"Two weeks," I said when I stepped into the circle of my Alphas. "No more surprises for two weeks."

Jace smirked. "It was a good one, though, right?"

There was no way to deny that. "It was a great one."

Roman subtly stroked his hand over my tattoo, just over the fabric. Other than his bite mark and between my legs, it was his favorite part of my body. He touched it all the time, and the joy he felt whenever he saw it brought *me* joy.

He rested his chin on the top of my head. "Tell me, firefly, do we need to get ready to go straight to the nest?"

My awareness of them heightened, focus narrowing on their scents. Butterscotch, cookies, tobacco, and soothing mist. The final days of rehearsals were always a little hectic, and we'd all been distracted. Not like *Giselle*, but enough.

And we hadn't had enough time in the nest.

Yes.

I nodded, already wanting to cover my nest with *them*. "Yes, please. Let's go home."

They only waited till we were out of sight before they swept me off my feet.

EPILOGUE II

SLOANE

ONE YEAR LATER

"Shouldn't these things be in the evening?" I said, yawning. "Like, when normal people are awake."

Jace laughed, helping me out of the car and straightening the flowing silver dress I wore. "Most normal people are awake right now, baby girl."

"Boring people," I muttered.

I chose to leave my jacket behind. It was still warm enough, and the coat ruined the effect of the dress. Because it was designed to match what we were going to see.

That, and photographers were everywhere. They were crawling around the building and outside, taking pictures of us, though we weren't what they were here for.

The Crown Spire was one of the tallest buildings in downtown Slate City, with the spire it was named for always sparkling above the rest of the skyline. And more importantly, today, it was the new home for Roman's commissioned statue, along with a handful of artists tasked with bringing 'Modern Classics' to life.

People already wandered among all the art, and it was easy to see how people would flock here for it. The lobby now looked like a museum. But with the classic architecture, pillars, and painted ceilings, it felt natural, like it all worked together.

A platform sat in the middle of everything with a big red ribbon. I already saw the clusters of our friends over where they could watch. Roman would be the one cutting the ribbon. He wouldn't say why or how he was chosen, but he went red just thinking about it, so I didn't force him.

He didn't say no, either.

Petra looked me up and down, smirking. "I see what you did there, Lo."

"Do you? I haven't even seen the finished product yet. Roman wouldn't let me."

"*What?*" Eva grabbed my hand. "Let's go."

No doubt some of the photographers outside were here for her.

I laughed. "He's going to take me over there in a second. I'm not ruining the reveal for him."

We both looked over to where our packs greeted each other. Over the last year they'd become friends out of necessity, since us four Omegas spent so much time together.

"Fine," she said. "But I want to see your face."

I looked at Petra again. "I can't believe you're actually here."

A month ago Petra had her first solo concert, and since then she'd been touring, giving that concert everywhere. She'd barely had time to breathe, let alone be here.

"I wouldn't miss it. Besides, I get a break for a couple weeks. After this I'm going home and *sleeping*."

A soft laugh drew our eyes, her Alpha Blake covering his mouth. She looked at him and he shrugged. "If that's what you think is happening."

"You have other plans?"

"Oh, no. You'll be sleeping. But there will probably be other things happening before you sleep."

Petra sighed, but smiled when she looked at me. "They're insatiable."

"I know the feeling."

Even now I felt their eyes on me, appreciation for the dress and the skin it revealed tingling inside my chest.

Esme stepped around Petra and hugged me. We'd gotten closer in the last year, all four of us. "You look great."

"Thank you."

She grinned. "I think Ben is going to lose his shit. He's such a nerd when it comes to art."

Bennett Gray, one of her tattoo artist Alphas, was widely known for his hyper-realistic renderings of art on skin, particularly sculpture. "Are we going to see tattoos of some of these?"

"Maybe," she said, nodding over her shoulder.

Ben was there, backwards baseball cap in tow, taking pictures of a tall sculpture that looked twisted and monstrous. Beautiful too. I needed to get closer to see the details.

"Ready to see it, firefly?" Roman leaned down, resting his chin on my shoulder, which couldn't possibly be comfortable for him.

"More than ready."

"It's over here."

He led me to the south side of the building, near a huge wall of arched windows that looked out over the river. Morning sunlight poured in through them, lighting up his sculpture.

A long, intricate bench, the female figure laying on top, relaxed. Draped in fabric that covered just enough of her, but not much. In front of her, a kitten was mid-movement, little paws open wide like he was catching the fingers she held out for him, a smile on her face.

It was me.

I hadn't been able to imagine how I would look rendered in marble, but I didn't hate it. The way the stone fabric draped over my stone body looked *real*. The curves of the statue appeared soft, and even though I *knew* it was stone, I was still surprised at the hardness when I touched it.

"Roman, this is so beautiful."

"Yeah?"

I couldn't stop looking at it. The addition of Mango and me smiling was exactly what was needed to tilt the image into the 'modern' side of the classic theme.

The statue had been done months ago, but he hadn't shown me, wanting to keep it for where it was meant to be displayed. He'd been sculpting the *other* statue of me. The one of me naked, and every time I posed for him, he followed through on his promise to fuck me thoroughly after every session.

Or he would wake me up the way I loved, choosing to deny me so that I wouldn't be able to keep from squirming while I posed before calling one of our other pack members to finish me off.

Sometimes together.

One by one, every promise they made me—sexual or otherwise—was kept.

"It's stunning," I said, slipping my arms beneath his suit jacket to hold him. "It looks *real*."

"Come here." He pulled me around the back of the statue and pointed.

I gasped. "What?" My tattoo was there too, gently etched into the skin. Barely visible unless you were looking for it, but it was there. "Roman, this is amazing."

"Glad you think so."

"I do."

He leaned down, kissing me, the sound of a camera shutter breaking us apart.

"Sorry!" The woman taking a photo smiled. "I'm the photographer for the event and I couldn't resist. I need some photos of Mr. Hughes with his piece, but I'd love to get some of the two of you, and with your pack as well."

We helped her, taking photos in various poses. I even got down on the floor in front of it, mimicking the pose, though I kept laughing.

Ash finally pulled me off the floor, dusting me off. Particularly the places where my dress exposed skin. "Are you cleaning me or helping yourself to my body?"

"Both?" He laughed at my look and kissed my nose. "I promise I'm not about to turn you on so much I have to steal you away into a broom closet."

"That sounds kind of fun, though."

He growled in my ear. "You have to pick one, sweetheart. Naughty or not."

"It's Roman's day," I whispered. "I'll let you fuck me in a closet another time."

"You and I still need to take a visit to the prop vault."

"Not until the show is over." We were in the middle of rehearsing the new show composed by Alexander Serrat, and while I didn't think Genevieve would really be that mad at us if we were caught, I wasn't jeopardizing my role in the show for anything. So far the ballet was everything I'd dreamed, and it was my favorite role I'd *ever* danced.

Gabriel raised a hand, calling us back toward the platform. I caught Roman's hand as he went up on stage, pouring every bit of pride and love through to him. He smiled.

Roman was nervous, but he didn't have to speak, so he was okay. If he wasn't, he could come to us and we would take over. There were still moments when he couldn't speak, and times when memories of his past made him go silent for days.

I'd figured out exactly how to burrow into his arms when he went to those places. We didn't have to talk, but he never pushed me away, because he knew I would simply be there with him.

The curator of the exhibit made a little speech about the collection and thanked all the contributors before handing Roman an absolutely ridiculously sized pair of scissors.

He smiled at me before cutting the ribbon, flashes going so crazy from all the photographers, he sparkled.

All of us clapped and cheered.

Roman was known in his own right as a sculptor. But the size and prestige of this installation was above anything he'd done before.

We stayed for photos, Roman posing with the other artists and benefactors, talking with fans and other people—with one of us always close by to intervene or run interference if we needed to.

But most people simply wanted to talk *at* him about his work, so he was okay. I hovered near the food table, stealing pieces of cheese and the occasional strawberry.

"Hey girl, we're going to head out." Esme found me, followed by Eva.

My friends smiled, and Eva whispered. "The guys think we don't know they've planned a surprise picnic for us at Esme's house. So we're going along with it."

"That sounds fun."

They lit up, and Esme nodded. "It will be. Especially if they bring out the Nerf guns. *After* Eva leaves."

Eva made a face. "Yeah, I'll have my guys buy their own. I love you, but I'm not interested in being anywhere near y'all when you start your games."

I just laughed. We were all used to talking about sex at this point, and there wasn't much that we didn't know about the

431

others' packs, much to our Alphas' and Betas' annoyance and amusement.

"Have fun." I hugged them both. "See you next week?"

"Have to check the new filming schedule, but I hope so!"

The shouts when they left the building confirmed my suspicion about the amount of photographers here for Eva. I was glad my fame in the ballet world didn't come with a flashing entourage. How both Eva and Petra managed it was beyond me.

Things seemed to be winding down. People still wandered around, chatting and looking at the sculptures, but the giant lobby was much emptier than it had been.

I snuck up behind Petra, who was leaning against Cole with her eyes closed. "Sleeping already?"

The dazed look in her eyes when she opened them told me yes.

"You should go sleep in a bed. Or a nest. *Just* sleep."

Cole laughed. "Don't worry, Lo. We'll make sure she's rested."

Petra just smiled. Cole's purr was soft, but I still heard it. "I'll call you when I'm not in a coma?"

"Sounds good." I blew her a kiss and followed the internal pull from Gabriel, near the doors.

He pulled me into him as soon as I was within reach, tilting my head to brush a kiss directly to his bite, threatening to make my knees melt. "Ready to go, little one?"

"I think so."

All I felt from Roman was happiness and relief. Relief that it had gone well, and relief he could breathe and relax. "How are you?" I asked, taking his hand and squeezing.

"I'm g-good, firefly."

I raised an eyebrow. He knocked his head gently against mine. "Good now."

"Well, we can go climb in the nest and relax as soon as we're home."

"Actually, depending on how you feel, there might be something else," Ash said from the driver's seat.

"Oh?"

"You'll see."

Instead of groaning and rolling my eyes, I leaned on Jace's shoulder. Another promise kept. Their surprises were always good ones. No matter what.

My chest lit up with their pleasure when I didn't protest, along with more than a little pride.

I glanced toward Asher's bike when we pulled into the garage. It sat under a sheet, much like the sculpture had been. The bike itself was fixed, but Ash hadn't been riding. Not really. The one time he'd taken the bike out, he'd come back and picked me up from my chair in the dining room and carried me straight to his room.

He didn't let me out for hours, the two of us losing ourselves in the other.

"Living room, little one."

"Let me change first."

I loved the dress, but I wasn't going to wear it all day. I wanted real comfort, and once I had it, I flopped on the couch in our cozy living room, which had been Gabriel's office. Mango found me a second later, jumping up to lie on my chest and cuddle under my chin.

"Hey, buddy." He was so big now, but no less adorable. We still found him on top of the fridge most days.

"Here you go," Jace said, putting a box in my lap and scooping Mango off me. It looked like a garment box, but no brand labels.

"I told you all I have enough lingerie. You never let me keep it on long enough anyway."

Gabriel chuckled. "It's not lingerie, little one."

Flipping open the lid, I dug through the tissue paper until my hands hit leather. Soft, thick, black leather. I pulled it out and stared at it. A leather jacket.

My gaze flicked to Ash, and he nodded once. This was the jacket he wanted to buy me all that time ago. Slowly, I turned it over, and my eyes went wide.

The giant embroidered patch on the back was custom, and I'd recognize the art anywhere. It was Roman's, a mixture and blend of so many things my eyes didn't stop dancing. A stack of blueberry pancakes covered in syrup. A pair of pointe shoes lit up by a spotlight. Mango's face hidden under what looked like my bedroom blanket. Purple lilies. The SCB logo. All set against a sunset backdrop.

"You made this for me?"

"I told you I wanted to get you one."

My heart ached. He said that back when he rode every day and wanted to take me places out of the city. Now, he barely rode.

Ash came and knelt in front of me, his hands on my knees. Slowly, he took my hands. He felt what I did. "It's been more than a year since..." he swallowed. "The accident. And I haven't been to see him."

Will. His grave in Concordia.

"I wondered if you would ride with me?" Such vulnerability shone through his eyes. It made me ache.

I slipped off the couch, meeting him on my knees and kissing him, tears coming out of nowhere. "Of course I will. Of course I will."

"Thank you. And after, I'm finally taking you to see those flowers."

Roman tapped his shoulder. "One more thing."

I looked and started laughing. A helmet, this one purple and glittering. "Is that mine?"

"It is, baby girl. If you're going to ride, we're going to make sure you look good doing it safely."

"When are we going?"

Ash still had his arms around me. "Now, if you're ready."

"I need better pants, but yes."

I sprinted for my room, changing into what I needed and grabbing the jacket from the living room. My three Alphas in there caught me. Gabriel wrapping me up. "Be safe, little one."

Beneath their love, I felt their fear. It was in me too, but we needed to move past it if we were to live with it. "I will."

He kissed me. They all kissed me. Tenderly. Lovingly. Wordless promises of what would come when Ash and I got home. I glowed with love and tears by the time I made it downstairs and out the front door.

Ash looked me up and down, grinning ear to ear. He zipped

up my jacket, lips crashing down on mine like they had that morning a year ago.

Helping me put my helmet on, he got on the bike and then helped me, pulling my hands around his waist. He was filled with grief and regret, but also determination and resolution. And love. For me, for Will, for our entire pack. For life, in spite of all the pain that came with it.

Ash revved the engine. "Ready, backpack?"

"Ready."

Finally, I was.

The End

There will be more in the Omegaverse books soon!

For a bonus scene featuring the Lys pack and a certain... sculpting project, sign up for my newsletter!

https://BookHip.com/TJTAFFA

ello beautiful readers!

Thank you so much for reading Sloane's story! This story truly took on a life of its own beyond what I ever expected, and I'm so happy you all finally get to read it!

In the meantime, I'd love to meet you! Sign up for my newsletter for updates and sneak peeks, and the occasional dessert recipe!

I also have a Facebook group where we share memes, I share snippets of works in progress, and everything in between. Come join Devyn's Deviants! I hope to see you there, and there will be more books very soon!

Devyn Sinclair

PLAYLIST

This is a playlist of some of the songs I listened to while writing *Knot For a Moment*.

You can listen to the playlist on Spotify.

*The music of Alexander Serrat is inspired by Sigur Ros

**This marks the song used during Sloane's bonding ceremony

- **2 AM** — Mellina Tey
- **Airplanes** — Adam Ulanicki
- **Alone, Pt. II** — Alan Walker, Ava Max
- **Appeasing the Chief** —Max Richter
- **Arrival of the Birds** — The Cinematic Orchestra, London Metropolitan Orchestra
- **Blóðberg** — Sigur Ros

- **Born For This** — The Score
- **butterflies** — Isabel LaRosa
- **Car's Outside** — James Arthur
- **Collateral** — Gustavo Santaolalla
- **Coma** — Taylor Acorn
- **Crying While You're Dancing** — Dayseeker
- **Deadman** — Glasslands
- **Deep Force** — Kaan Simseker
- **DON'T TALK ABOUT LOVE** — guccihighwaters
- **Drive You Insane** — Daniel Di Angelo
- **Drowning (edit)** — Anetnt, bowl.
- **Drowning (slowed + reverb)** — Vague003
- **Empty Room** — Jamie Miller
- **Everyone Who Falls In Love (Has Someone Else They're Thinking Of)** — Cian Ducrot
- **eyes don't lie** — Isabel LaRosa
- **Falling Apart** — Michael Schulte
- **Fill The Void (with Lily Rose Depp)** — The Weeknd, Lily-Rose Depp, Ramsey
- **First Step from "Interstellar": Piano Solo** — REYNAH
- **For Me** — Lo Nightly
- **Friends** — Chase Atlantic
- **glad you're settling** — Jessica Baio
- **Glow** — Time, The Valuator
- **Goddess** — Nation Haven
- **Goodnight, Travel Well** — The Killers
- **hope it kills you** — Bolshiee
- **Icy** — Kim Petras
- **i don't forgive you** — Isabel LaRosa
- **i love you** — Billie Eilish
- **I NEVER EXIATED** — Chase Atlantic
- **In Plain Sight** — August Wilhelmsson
- **Intoxicated** — Aaryan Shah
- **Intoxicated (Acoustic)** — Aaryan Shah
- **Ivy** — Time, The Valuator
- **Just Pretend (Alternative Version)** — Christina Rotondo

- **Let It Go (with Lø Spirit)** — Chandler Leighton, Lø Spirit
- **Let You Down** — Sibewest
- **LINE IN THE SAND** — KILL SCRIPT, Linney
- **Lost in Echoes** — Caskets
- **love notes** — Alexa Cirri
- **Luminary** — Joel Sunny
- ****Mór** — Sigur Ros
- **never knew a heart could break itself** — Zach Hood
- **never knew a heart could break itself - acoustic** — Zach Hood
- **No Time Left** — Hazy
- **Our Funeral** — Always Never
- **Parallel** — Dayseeker
- **rain inside** — Øneheart, Antent
- **Rain & Pain** — Christian Reindl
- **Renegade** — Aaryan Shah
- **Renegade - (Slowed + Reverb)** — Aaryan Shah
- **Re: Unwanted Tears** — Philip Daniel, Shawn Williams
- **Saega** — Trek
- **Safe Now** — Henry Jackman
- **Shallow** — Tommy Profitt, Fleurie
- **She Will** — Lil Wayne, Drake
- **Skel** — Sigur Ros
- **Some Say** — Adam Ulanicki
- **Swim** — Chase Atlantic
- **Take Me First** — Bad Omens
- **This City is a Graveyard** — Baby Storme
- **Turn On The Lights again.. (feat. Future)** — Fred again.., Swedish House Mafia, Future
- **Vengeance** — iwilldiehere
- **We Go Down Together (with Khalid)** — Dove Cameron, Khalid
- **When I Meet Death** — Time, The Valuator
- **Where the Light Goes** — Josh Kramer
- **Who I Am Without You** — BLÜ EYES

- **without you** — Isabel LaRosa
- **wonderland** — MVSSIE
- **Would You Do It Again?** — Rowan Drake
- **Your Guardian Angel** — The Red Jumpsuit Apparatus

ABOUT THE AUTHOR

Devyn Sinclair writes steamy Reverse Harem romances for your wildest fantasies. Every sexy story is packed with the right amount of steam, hot men, and delicious happy endings.

She lives in the wilds of Montana in a small red house with a crazy orange cat. When Devyn's not writing, she spends time outside in big sky country, continues her quest to find the best lemon pastry there is, and buys too many books. (Of course!)

To connect with Devyn:

ALSO BY DEVYN SINCLAIR

**For a complete list of Devyn's books, content warnings, bonuses
and extras, please visit her website.**

https://www.devynsinclair.com/

Made in the USA
Middletown, DE
02 September 2024

60314475R00269